C000260874

The Swan Pit

– DAVID BUCK –

An environmentally friendly book printed and bound in England by
www.printondemand-worldwide.com

Mixed Sources
Product group from well-managed
forests, and other controlled sources
www.fsc.org Cert no. TT-COC-002641
© 1996 Forest Stewardship Council
FSC

PEFC Certified
This product is
from sustainably
managed forests
and controlled
sources
PEFC
PEFC/16-33-415
www.pefc.org

This book is made entirely of chain-of-custody materials

www.fast-print.net/store.php

THE SWAN PIT

A catalogue record for this book is available from the British Library

ISBN 978-178456-110-9

First published 2015 by
FASTPRINT PUBLISHING
Peterborough, England.

THE SWAN PIT

Acknowledgements

I am indebted to my family, and my many friends and acquaintances, for their help and support in writing this book. Without their diligence and criticism, both encouraging and critical, the manuscript would never have progressed to publication.

I must however give special thanks to my wife for her tolerance of my incessant interest in current affairs, and for enduring the solitude whilst I laboured away in my study or absented myself to hide away in North Norfolk.

The responsibility for any mistakes, errors or omissions in this book is mine, and I apologise for them.

David Buck
2015

This book is dedicated to those from ordinary walks of life who question the role of religious faith in modern society, be they adherents, doubters or adversaries.

"All we have gained then by our unbelief
is a life of doubt diversified by faith.
For one of faith diversified by doubt: we called
the chess-board white – we call it black."

(Robert Downing)

"There lives more faith in honest doubt,
believe me, than in half the creeds."

(Alfred, Lord Tennyson)

"You can do very little with faith,
but you can do nothing without it."

(Samuel Butler)

The Author

D avid Buck is a retired Chartered Accountant, having specialised in charity finance and served as a trustee for various charities over a period of thirty years. He has a keen interest in current affairs, particularly the inter-action between religion and politics in contemporary Britain, prompting him to write his first novel, *The Swan Pit*. David is married with three adult daughters.

.

The Prologue

The Knights Templar owned land and property across Europe and The Middle East. They were renowned as men of faith. They were also warriors and crusaders. Were they guardians of Christendom's inner secrets?

They had been charged by Pope Urban II to locate and secure the burial place of Christ and thereby liberate the 'Church of God'. It was rumoured that the Templars had excavated under the Temple of Jerusalem and that the treasures they had found could debunk the doctrines of the Catholic Church. Did the excavation even include the embalmed remains of Christ? Some scholars believe the Templars took possession of the cup from which Jesus drank at the Last Supper, attributed by many to be the Holy Grail. Whatever priceless treasure had been found a significant amount of it, including hoards of silver and gold, was transported to Europe, and much of it to France, where the Templars later became established.

The Knights Templar had acted as treasury to the Kings of France, helping to finance campaigns in the Far East. In AD1307 the French King, Philip IV, who was deeply in debt to the Knights Templar movement and jealous of their wealth, issued orders to bailiffs for their arrest. He also demanded that their treasures and possessions, including all their lands and property, be confiscated and surrendered to the King.

In anticipation of imminent seizure, much of the Templar treasure was hastily loaded into the galleys of the fleet of some eighteen ships stationed at La Rochelle. The precious cargo, including the records of the Order, had been carefully clad in their customary white mantles with splayed red crosses. There was little wind and the waters were calm. In the early evening, under the cover of darkness, the fleet set sail. Its destination was not known. The impending voyage represented the end of an era. It was Friday 13th.

PART I

Chapter 1

It had lain undisturbed for centuries, buried beneath the surface; no light, and no sound, nothing – until now. Time had passed it by. The priests, the monks, the poor, the sick, and the downtrodden knew nothing of what lay hidden in their hallowed ground. Even the trapped swans swimming in the watery pit above had been unaware of what lay beneath.

Site redevelopment was under way in the grounds of the *Monastic Leisure Therapy and Recreational Centre*, in the heart of the ancient city of Norwich, in the county of Norfolk. The Centre specialised in providing short-break holidays in cottages and lodges in the grounds of what had once been a medieval monastery and hospital. Monastic Leisure Limited not only offered the usual restaurant, shop and bar facilities, but also exclusive dinners, dances and discos in the medieval banqueting halls. Its current project was to convert a late-eighteenth-century swan pit into reproduction Roman baths, with state-of-the-art steam rooms, adjoining the nearby swimming pool. In bygone days the doomed swans and their cygnets had no means of escape from the pit and, once fattened, awaited their fate on the banqueting tables of kings and queens. The ravages of time had worn away the retaining walls, which were deemed beyond repair. Because the pit was classified as a Grade II listed building, it had taken very laborious negotiations to obtain all the necessary planning consents.

Just like the poor swans, the digger driver knew nothing of what lay ahead. She had won the confidence of her male colleagues; she was enjoying her work and earning good money on a zero-hours contract. With the prospect of many days of full-time work ahead, she had just booked her summer holiday in Spain.

A sudden jolt halted the machine in its tracks.

'Christ, what the hell was that?' she shouted. It was a most prescient choice of words.

She turned off the ignition and called her fellow workmen to investigate. It looked as if the loading bucket had hit some jagged rock just below the surface of the pit. Underneath was a rusted iron handle protruding from the earth; it appeared to be an old trap door - on close inspection clearly the entrance to an underground cellar.

The site foreman summoned the Chief Executive of Monastic Leisure. Given the historical nature of the site, he knew he had no choice but to stop the construction work pending further investigation. He reluctantly called the Archaeology Department at the County Council, aware that they would have a keen interest in anything found at the old monastery and would probably delay the project.

In the early afternoon, fifty-three-year-old County Archaeologist Luke Matthews arrived on site, his thin, grey hair and weathered complexion suggesting a man of seasoned experience. He was accompanied by a young assistant trainee full of youthful exuberance. Under their supervision the workmen levered open the trap door. Beneath it was a flight of rotten wooden steps down to what looked like a cellar or some kind of dungeon. The trainee assistant gingerly manoeuvred himself down. He was greeted by a musty, but pervading, smell of rot and decay. He beckoned the others to follow. Armed with torches and flashlights they clambered down, shining them along the sides, the floor and the roof. They saw a multitude of cobwebs, illuminated like silver fairy-lights in a maze of ghostly patchwork quilts. The stream of light picked out something on the floor in the far corner of the tomb, for that was what it felt like. It was an old trunk, made of the finest oak, still secure, surrounded by chains, disintegrated rags and various artefacts scattered in the soil. The trunk was easy enough to open. Inside there was a large wooden casket containing several pieces of silver - coins, finger-rings and what looked like five large arm-rings. At the base of the casket were some pieces of parchment wrapped in remnants of cloth.

Climbing out of that dark underground pit to find a signal for his mobile, Luke Matthews summoned a colleague, archivist Professor Jane Clifford-Oxbury. She was the obvious choice – she had spent years researching the archives of the Monastery all the way back to its formation in the thirteenth century. Remarkably, they had survived the destruction of King Henry VIII and the Reformation period. Luke had been to school with Jane; they had been friends then and still were. Luke had always had a soft spot for her but then she had gone off to university, met someone else and they had drifted apart, at least so far as any matchmaking was concerned. He had often enjoyed playing practical jokes on her, hiding her lunch box at school, catching her out on 1st April, and generally finding amusement in his childish pranks. He made sure nothing was touched until her arrival.

A breathless Jane Clifford-Oxbury arrived on the scene, her thick, curly hair dishevelled in the rush to get there, but her eyes wide and alert, as she eagerly eased herself down the steps to join them. Barely noticing the stench of stale air, she put on her plastic gloves and the obligatory white coat, and knelt down at the side of the open trunk, as if in prayer. She carefully placed the coins and pieces of silver in a plastic container, ready for examination by Luke and his team of archaeologists. It looked as if someone had hidden the casket for safekeeping long before the swan pit was built above it. She excitedly, but very carefully, scrutinised the parchment. This was her domain as County Archivist. Her brain was now razor-sharp, immersed in the thrill of the find. She knew parchment was made from hide, calfskin, sheepskin, or goatskin. Sealed inside the wooden trunk and casket, she assumed for hundreds of years, the parchment was remarkably well-preserved, somehow protected from any moisture in the air outside. She deciphered the writing on the parchment to be of ancient origin, most likely French. Her journey back through time had begun all over again.

'Ouch!' she exclaimed. Despite her careful handling of the cloth, she felt several pricks from what seemed to be tiny particles of wood, like small thorns. One splinter had drawn blood.

Instructions were given that the cellar should be secured pending further investigation, and the developers were ordered to stop any further excavation work until the site had been combed for any further discoveries.

There was probably nothing unique about the artefacts but, nevertheless, they would have to be painstakingly examined. Jane left, ready to return early the following day with Luke's team of experts. Her finger was throbbing from the splinter wound and she remembered she needed to replenish her first-aid kit. On her way towards the nearest pharmacy she walked through the cathedral. Although it held no religious interest for her, she still marvelled at the beauty and splendour of its construction all those years before. She headed for the gift shop where her sister Mary worked part-time, hoping she might be there, not having seen her since Christmas. Jane never could remember which days Mary worked. There was no sign of Mary, but her eyes were drawn to a book prominently displayed ahead of her. It was about Henry Despenser, known as the 'Fighting Bishop', and a fourteenth-century nobleman. This rang a bell in her mind; she remembered that he had been associated with the old monastery. Instinctively she purchased the book. Just as she was leaving the shop her luck was in; there was Mary striding purposefully down the aisle towards her.

'Jane, how lovely to see you - long time no see. How are you? Still working too hard, lost in your world of fusty old cobwebs and grimy records?'

'Of course; in fact, as it happens, we have just unearthed some ancient artefacts in a cellar at the Monastic Leisure Centre.'

Disregarding Jane's comment, Mary continued; she clearly had something on her mind – she was normally a good listener.

'Have you got a moment? There's something I need to mention – about Paul. I haven't telephoned you about it; 'I'd prefer a discreet chat. Let me get you a quick coffee in the refectory; Evelyn will cover for me for a few minutes.'

Jane was very fond of her nephew; there was a close affinity between them. She had taken a great interest in him throughout his childhood, then the difficult teenage years, and now adulthood. Her sister, Mary, and husband Thomas, a vicar, lived in a rambling old vicarage ten miles east of Norwich.

'I do need to talk to you about Paul; he and Thomas had a falling-out before Paul's departure. Thomas is pretty upset about it, given all he had done for the boy, but Paul was determined to seek out our Oliver, in New Zealand. Thomas did not approve at all, obviously fearing Paul would find out about you-know-what.'

'What happened?'

Mary, her brown eyes moistened by emotion, recalled the conversation with her husband, recounting what he had said.

'"Heaven knows what influence Oliver will have on him. I don't trust your brother to keep the family secret. How can we after what happened? We should have discussed it with Paul, told him what happened. I am concerned, Mary; you know how we had to pick up the pieces before. What also worries me is that his friend, Hussain, is going to be over there at much the same time. They've spent a lot of time together recently. I'm afraid I really don't trust that boy. I'm not sure why; it's an instinct, I suppose."

'I replied: "I hope that's not because he is a Muslim, Thomas. Your one true God means little to him. Everyone is entitled to their particular belief – your own archbishop made that declaration only the other day. We should not, indeed must not, dissuade Paul. Oliver is hardly likely to reveal much; he can't really, without incriminating himself in the process. Paul will go anyway - it might as well be with our blessing. We will just have to keep our fingers crossed - sorry I meant, pray, that nothing comes out.'"

'Thomas took no notice of what I said and tried again to dissuade him. The result was a major spat between them. Paul told him to stuff his religion up his cassock!'

'I see. I'm sorry you've had to go through all this, Mary. I suppose I'm in trouble with Thomas for having paid Paul's air flights – I just thought it would be a great experience for him. I was pretty sure Oliver wouldn't reveal anything.'

'Don't lose any sleep over that. Come over on Thursday and stay for the weekend. You are spending too much time on your own, especially when everyone will be on their Easter break. You need to get away from your computer and those mouldy old books you bury your head in, and get some fresh air into your lungs. With Paul being away in New Zealand, Thomas and I will be delighted to spend some time with you before Thomas gets totally immersed in the round of Easter services. Peter will be staying as well. You can keep the peace between them if they get into one of their sibling spats; his new wife, Carol, will be coming as well.'

Jane had looked forward to a quiet break and some gentle research ahead of her impending trip to the United States. Her sister was very persuasive, and she had to admit it would be a relief not to have to prepare her own meals. Cooking for one had never been her idea of fun, and she knew she had got into the habit of eating too much pasta, too many chicken stir-fries and, far too often for her health, she had succumbed to ready meals and takeaways. Typical of Mary to be thinking of someone else, rarely, if ever, herself, she mused, reflecting that

Thomas, with his unpredictable and sometimes volatile nature, was a lucky man to have her as a wife. Mary had enormous strength of character, great fortitude, and a sure resilience in the face of adversity. She instinctively knew how to handle any situation. Jane was also all too well aware how fortunate she was to have Mary as a sister. She knew that, without her sister's integrity and her loyal support over the past twenty-three years, life would have been very different indeed.

'Of course, I'd be delighted to come for Easter. I've become something of a recluse recently, absorbed by my work; some would say addicted to it. A change of scene and a rest would probably be good for me, help me break free from my own little world before I go away.'

Jane had never married. She lived in a small but homely three-storey terraced house near the university. The onset of Easter did not usually mean much to her. As a non-believer, she was not planning any special celebrations over the Easter holiday. It greatly amused her that her sister had married into the clergy. If she was celebrating anything it was probably the onset of the brighter evenings now that the clocks had gone forward.

Jane was curious about the origin of the artefacts, and particularly the cloth and parchment found in and around the wooden casket. She spent all the following day examining them, alongside Luke and his colleagues. It was not an easy job in that cramped underground cellar, which had become something like a crime scene, all roped off, with people in white dungarees combing every inch. Anything found was logged and recorded then placed carefully in clear plastic covers and containers. She knew that parchment had become a substitute for papyrus in the last century BC and the first century AD, and had been commonly used through to the Middle Ages, when it was largely replaced by paper. She made arrangements with Luke for the contents of the cellar to be carefully and securely stored in airtight conditions at the university science laboratory under the supervision of Judas Swan, a forensic scientist, and a boyhood friend of Luke. Judas agreed to arrange for the testing of selected items. Some, including the parchment, were to be radiocarbon dated; others, including the cloth, were marked for DNA tests as well.

The records of the Old Monastery Hospital had provided a career-defining journey through the centuries for the archivist. She had devoted much of her time over several years researching, translating and recording the ancient writings which represented a unique insight into life in the Middle Ages, the Reformation and right up to the present day. She thought she had finished that particular assignment. She was wrong.

Chapter 2

I t had been such a relief to get away from my Norfolk home. I had felt suffocated by the unceasing presence of religion which had enveloped me ever since that fateful immersion in the font at my christening. I did feel guilty at the memory of my parting tirade. I had never sworn at my father before.

'I'm going whether you like it or not. If you won't say why Uncle Oliver disappeared to New Zealand I will find out for myself. I found his details on his business website. He's said I can stay and help out on his sheep farm, so that's it. I have my own life to lead. You've rammed your sodding religion down my throat all my life. You look after your flock - I'll tend to Oliver's.'

What I did not know was that Uncle Oliver had taken a great deal of persuading from his young Kiwi wife to let me come to stay.

'I have a new life here with you; I don't want anything to do with my family in England, the past is gone, erased, and I don't want any contact.'

'Paul is young and was not old enough to remember you when you emigrated. You should welcome him with open arms; heaven knows you could do with some help on the farm from a fit, strong young man.'

It seemed Oliver had reluctantly acceded to his wife's cajoling. I realise now he knew he had no choice – even she did not know the real reason for his hasty retreat from England.

My father had tried once more to dissuade me from going, whereupon I shouted angrily back, later regretting my final salvo. And what did my father mean by the implicit threat that, by going, I might regret it for the rest of my life, and that some things were best left in the past?

I knew I could not really blame my father; it was his livelihood, after all, but I still could not accept the Christian message of faith as my benchmark for life. I had recently graduated at the University of East Anglia with a second-class degree in Social History. The forthcoming year was a once-in-a-lifetime opportunity for me to travel, to look up my uncle, Oliver, whom I had never met but who, for some never-revealed dark secret, had been ostracized by my family. Any mention of Oliver, and my parents would clam up. There were no Christmas cards, no birthday messages - no communication at all. Even my much-loved Aunt Jane seemed reticent, giving nothing away, other than money to fund my air fares. Perhaps a change of scene, some time away, would put things into perspective. Despite expecting their opposition, particularly from my disapproving father, I was determined to go, to seek some adventure.

I planned my itinerary within the constraints of a loan from Aunt Jane. After flying into Auckland, I arranged to hire a car and drive to Paihia to visit the famous Treaty House, where the Maori chieftains had sworn allegiance to Queen Victoria, then on to Napier to see the art deco buildings. My intention was to get back by train to Auckland, where I would pick up my hire car. I expected to conclude my tour of North Island in Wellington, where I would link up with my long-term friend, Hussain Barzal. It seemed an amazing coincidence that my friend from Norwich should be attending a conference of the

Islamic Democracy Movement in Wellington at the same time.

I then planned to travel down through South Island towards Christchurch and to my uncle's farm at Rangiora. What happened after that would depend on how much I managed to earn. Whilst in New Zealand I hoped to pursue my interest in social history, investigate the Maori culture, and earn some money whilst learning the trade of a shepherd. In my naivety I thought this would give me the opportunity to break down the barriers within my family – or at least find out why it was such an emotive issue, whether my parents approved or not.

At this point a narrator takes up the story. She has met with all the participants and is able to relate the feelings, emotions and events of that dramatic period so much more objectively than I.

Chapter 3

The trauma of that day in Christchurch the previous year engulfed Laura Francis as she looked down from the aircraft window. On that fateful day, Tuesday, 22nd February 2011, Laura Francis had left work for her lunch break. It had been a calm, sunny day in Christchurch, New Zealand, and she sauntered along Gloucester Street towards one of her favourite spots by the river. Not much more than a stream at this point, the Avon meandered its way through the stunningly beautiful Botanic Gardens. The multi-coloured roses, with their exotic names, were in full bloom, but the birds had ceased their cheerful song, as if they had prior knowledge of what lay ahead.

Laura worked as a civil servant in a government department building in the city centre. She was in especially high spirits because, earlier that month, on 12th February, she had turned twenty-five. Under the terms of a settlement she was now fully entitled to a one-half share of a family trust fund. Life was good.

Without any warning the ground suddenly began to shake, the vibrations causing her to lurch from side to side, then to lose her balance. She stumbled and fell. She tried to right herself but the path ahead was gone, instead a gaping void where mother earth had been for thousands of years before. Somehow she struggled to her feet. In moments she could hear the sound of crashing masonry. Within what seemed like seconds the sky began to blacken over the nearby city centre, darkened by plumes of debris, with silhouettes of smoke illuminated by vivid orange flames leaping high above. The ground had stopped shaking, but now she could see the large fissures in what had been the path. Then she could hear the screams which would haunt her for the rest of her life.

Skirting round fallen trees and broken shrubs, the prim gardens around her now a tangled jungle, Laura ran out towards the road, but all she could see in the distance was a mangled mess of concrete and tarmac, and hordes of people, the lucky ones, heading straight for her, the route back to her office blocked. Then, high above, came the shards of light piercing the sky, flashes of bright yellow, tinged with blue, like an electrical fireworks display lighting up the night sky, more spectacular than the New Year celebrations only weeks before. Except it was early afternoon. She stood transfixed, spellbound.

She knew what was happening. Everyone in Christchurch remembered the quake which hit the city the previous September. But this time the devastation seemed much worse. She trembled, her stomach knotted with fear for the safety of her workmates, many of them friends. Had it been an hour earlier, or an hour later, would she still be alive now? The shock brought tears trickling down her face as she thought of her great-grandparents, whose lives had been destroyed by the catastrophic earthquake in the city of Napier some eighty years before.

Soon it was impossible to see anything through the thick palls of dust and the blackened smoke rising from the fires ahead of her. She covered her ears as the hysterical wail of sirens came from all directions. Then all those people, the ones who had got away, were upon her, seeking refuge in the open spaces of the gardens. She would not be going back to her office that day, or the next, or ever. The excitement of her recent inheritance was gone.

Those memories had come flooding back during the flight to Napier; her employers' offices in the city centre had been totally destroyed in a matter of minutes. Many had lost their lives. Had she not gone to the Botanic Gardens for lunch she knew she would probably not have survived.

She was a girl on a mission and this was her first visit to the city where her great-grandparents had perished in the devastating earthquake of February 1931. They had not been as lucky.

A taxi took Laura Francis from the airport to the hotel in Dickens Street. It was small, tidy and well-presented, with a friendly receptionist. A handsome young man, around six feet tall, with blond, frizzy hair, kindly, bluish-grey eyes with largish pupils, and wearing faded denim jeans, helped her carry her luggage into the lift. It was one of those old-fashioned lifts with chain-metal doors and awkward latches.

It was a good start - she recognised him immediately. She flashed her enticing blue eyes at him in gratitude, reinforced with a warm smile, one which would charm any young man; and older ones too. Paul Morgan gave her a sheepish grin and watched, mesmerised, as she disappeared skywards to the next floor.

In the morning Laura took a street map from the hotel reception. She then walked along Dalton Street, and then on to Tennyson Street, admiring the art deco buildings on all sides, with their vivid colours, a memorial to the 1931 disaster. She passed all the boutique stores, the antique shops and art galleries, interspersed inevitably with the usual coffee houses and fast-food outlets. The young man was walking in the same direction, a few yards ahead of her. He found his way to the *Hawke's Bay Museum and Art Gallery* and carefully took note of the various exhibits. Laura, not far behind, had also headed to the Museum. He spotted her.

'Hi, are you the young lady from my hotel?' he asked, knowing full well that she was.

'Oh hello, I wasn't sure if it was you,' she replied, untruthfully.

'What brings you to the Museum?' he asked innocently. On his own, thousands of miles from home, he had rather fancied the girl whom he had helped into the lift. Alone in his room that evening he had fantasised about her, hoping he would see her again.

She did not appear to have company. She told him about her great-grandparents. He motioned her to a darkened inner room, where a thirty-minute video reconstruction of the 1931 earthquake was being shown. She sat at the back behind the other tourists already seated.

Laura was much moved by the film. Returning to the main exhibition area she blinked as her eyes accustomed to the bright lights. She looked round for the young man. He was nowhere to be seen. He had been sitting behind her. She had thought, hoped, he might have been lingering outside, waiting for her. She had stupidly lost sight of him in her preoccupation with her family history. She had to find him.

She walked down past art deco buildings, turning left into Hastings Street, looking ahead, behind and down the side streets. When she reached the junction with Browning Street there was nothing of particular note for most tourists or, indeed, locals. For Laura it was a poignant moment, knowing, but not seeing. The house where her great-grandparents had lived was long gone, but she had seen the pictures. The first tear trickled down her cheek, meandering slowly at first, then no longer just one, soon many, turning to a torrent, as her imagination, fuelled by the pictures she had just seen, ran riot, trying to re-live those fateful moments so many years before. Overwhelmed by emotion she stood motionless, reluctant to leave the spot, eventually heading to the nearby Marine Parade. She stopped. She heard footsteps behind her. Was someone following her? There was no one there. It must be her imagination. Then she smelt the inviting aroma of freshly-brewed coffee wafting towards her and headed for the security of the café overlooking the beach and with a good view of the promenade. She could see nothing untoward, nor was there any sign of the young man. She could only hope he would be back at the hotel. She ordered a strong, black coffee to bolster her spirits. The smartly-dressed man with a pointed chin stepped back into the shadows.

Feeling more relaxed in the summer sunshine, she walked back along Marine Parade with its Norfolk pines, down Albion Street and back to her hotel. She found Paul Morgan had already checked out and had not left word as to where he was going. She phoned her line manager to tell him she would be cutting short her visit and returning to Christchurch. Laura was aware that she had failed. She was beset with thoughts of her great-grandparents, and had lost him. Or, more worryingly, had he deliberately shaken her off his trail?

By then Paul Morgan was on his way south. He had very reluctantly left the girl in the Museum, but she was clearly preoccupied with her family history and he had a train to catch to Auckland to pick up his hire car, and then the drive on to Wellington. There Paul was going to visit the Te Papa, The National Museum of New Zealand, a massive building with six floors of exhibition space highlighting the country's natural environment and its Maori heritage.

One of his former fellow university students, Miles Mulligan, known as "Metric Miles" by his fellow undergraduates, was now a geologist at the University of California. He had told Paul about the Museum's rubber and lead foundations, specifically designed to withstand earthquakes as it was built directly above the Wellington fault line.

It would also be an opportunity to meet up with his friend Hussain and the Museum, much of it dedicated to the Maori culture, was an ideal place to rendezvous. It was also, apparently, a suitable choice for Hussain who, whilst in Wellington, had been visiting the headquarters of the only national Islamic body in the country, The Federation of Islamic Associations of New Zealand.

Paul had discovered from an ancestry website that his uncle's wife, Kiwita, was descended from a Maori chieftain who had been an original signatory to the Waitangi Treaty on 6th February 1840 swearing allegiance to Queen Victoria, but later to become the most bitterly-contested document in New Zealand history. He hoped that Kiwita would not blame him for what seemed to be the shameful treatment of the Maori people by the British, but he hoped the visit would give him a chance to find out for himself, experience at first hand what had gone on.

His aspiration then was to become a writer. One thing was certain - he certainly would not follow the family tradition of joining the priesthood. He was especially interested in ancient civilisations: how they lived and evolved their societies, and what led in many cases, the Mayans amongst others, to their eventual decline. His friend Hussain had told him about the fate of the Knights Templar at the hands of Saladin, and the subsequent rise, fall, and then re-birth of Islam. He talked angrily about the crusades and the "Holy War" against Muslims instigated by Pope Urban II; apparently the first time the waging of war was given religious legitimacy. Paul had listened intently to his forecasts for the outcome of the so-called 'Arab Spring' and the rise of The Muslim Brotherhood.

Hussain Barzal was a mature student at the University of East Anglia. He met regularly with some fellow students, Abdul, Malik and Jarmal, who had enrolled at the University following their sixth-form college courses in Newham, East London. Their entry to the University had been secured partly because of the requirements of the selection procedures in respect of recruitment of ethnic students, with financial incentives for taking in overseas nationals, but also because of their excellent college exam results. All three were thought to have originated from professional, middle-class families in Pakistan. Having graduated the previous summer, they were now enrolled on post-graduate courses. Malik had secured a first-class honours degree in Chemistry and was determined to make use of his talent to further his career in his adopted country. Abdul and Jarmal had graduated with second-class honours in Sociology. They had all kept a low profile and were considered to be exemplary students, a credit to the University. One evening in late 2011 Malik had called his friends together. He had used a code word which they all knew meant their long wait was nearly over.

'Hussain, we need someone who is clearly English, respectable, and beyond reproach, to act as cover, and make it look as if we are an ordinary bunch of students. 'You have been in Norfolk for a long time, you must know someone. He needs to be from a good, upstanding, professional family just as we all are, preferably from the religious community, ideally Church of England, and be trusting but, crucially, gullible. Your friend, Paul, for example? We need to glean as much information as possible about the workings and procedures of the Anglican Church, obviously discreetly, without raising any suspicion.'

It was Malik who had spoken, clearly their leader, and a man they would all obey without demur. It was the first hint that their mission had a local connection.

'Malik, Paul is just the person we are looking for. He trusts everyone implicitly. I have known him for years. His father is an Anglican priest, and he is well-known in the Norwich Christian community. If we are seen with him regularly, especially around the Cathedral itself, no one will have any suspicions.'

'Brilliant, Hussain, and the perfect choice for what we have in mind.'

'And, it gets better! He will be in New Zealand at much the same time as I am attending the training conference.'

'Perfect! Our colleagues from Pakistan, who will also be over there for the conference, will be able to vet him at first hand. They will also have the opportunity to question him about western ways and cultures. We will be well out of the watchful eye of the infidel UK authorities whose gaze is focused on our homeland.'

'Be very discreet; make sure he suspects nothing. Our leader, Farim, will show great interest in him and his background, make him feel welcome. He will never realise he is our Trojan Horse.'

'Don't worry; to use an English expression I've learned, Paul will fall for it hook, line and sinker.'

Chapter 4

In mid-March Laura Francis, alerted by a call on her mobile, headed towards central Christchurch ostensibly to make a nostalgic visit to the Botanic Gardens, now re-opened after the 2011 earthquake. She was unsure how she might react to being back there in the Gardens, but this time she had to cast her emotions to one side; she had a job to do.

Paul was also heading for Christchurch, taking time off from his uncle's family sheep farm at Rangiora; just off Route One, north of Christchurch. Oliver was now established in one of New Zealand's most important export markets. Paul was somewhat cautiously welcomed by his uncle. Initially he thought him dour and insular, the result perhaps of long hours spent alone on the hillside. But maybe he was apprehensive about this renewed contact with his family from half a world away. If so, why?

Oliver was mid-fifties, the oldest of the siblings, his long, grey hair, unkempt like that of his archivist sister, falling about his ears and down to his shoulders; it was as if he needed shearing himself. His eyes were a bluish grey with large pupils, the family trademark. He had been strong and muscular, but the ravages of spending so long out on the hills in all weathers had played havoc with his knees, which were now riddled with arthritis. He had never had the time or, perhaps, Paul thought, the inclination to visit a surgeon. Paul had by now discovered he had no cousins in New Zealand. Given his youth and physique, Oliver sensed Paul would have a useful role to play on the farm, even if he lacked the skills of a shepherd.

Earlier that morning, Paul had sent a text to his mother to tell her he was going to the Botanic Gardens in Christchurch and would take pictures for her, it being a place she had always wanted to visit but knew she never could. Unknown to Paul, alerted by the text message which the authorities had intercepted, Laura had embarked on the next stage of her assignment.

The rusty, battered Jeep was more used to the bumpy tracks around the farm than the smooth open highway. The three letters, three numbers plate still tickled him – something out of the 1950s. He chuckled as he overtook an iconic Citroen 2CV. There was no reason to notice the plain black Vauxhall Vectra following behind. He turned off at the next junction and headed down Riccarton Road towards the Central Park and gardens. The main central square of Christchurch was still strangled by concrete and rubble, its beautiful cathedral in ruins, a desolate building site visible only between fencing panels and cordoned off by the Army. His mother's interest in horticulture had led him to the nearby Botanic Gardens. The Gardens were stunning, having remarkably mostly survived the 'quake of 2011. The main damage had been to ground and irrigation systems; lakes had drained as their previously impermeable foundations cracked, also breaking up the pathways. Some trees had also fallen, their roots unable to cope with the water saturation in the earth beneath. He parked in the Armagh Street car park and crossed the bridge into the Gardens, one of the finest collections of exotic and native plants to be found in New Zealand.

Laura Francis had also parked there. She headed for a temporary café near the centre of the Gardens to await further instructions. The original one was still closed, needing a detailed engineering evaluation to enable it to be strengthened to withstand future 'quakes. Some other buildings and monuments were also damaged. There were a few tourists and a rather forlorn young man being pushed in a wheelchair, but nothing untoward. She hopped on the caterpillar shuttle which toured the grounds, knowing that it was on its way to the makeshift café at the centre of the park.

In the central part of the Gardens Paul was amazed to learn of so many varieties of roses, some two hundred and fifty according to his guidebook, which in high summer would have been so vibrant in their spectacular display of reds, whites, yellows and purples. 'Mother Mary' (he always referred to his mother in this way), back home in Norwich, would have loved to have been there. The shrubs and trees were now a sea of gold, bronze and vivid red, the blazing colours of autumn, just as stunning, he felt. As he reached for his camera he glanced up from the gardens - but did not see the young blonde on the two-carriage shuttle weaving its way slowly past the rose garden. Neither did there seem to be anything notable about a fellow photographer with a raking cough and pointed chin clicking away nearby. Job done for his mother, he headed for a morning fix of caffeine. He joined the queue, deciding against the temptation of fresh cream cakes, paid, and walked off towards a spare table. Then he saw her, the girl from the hotel in Napier, sitting just two tables away. He recognised that long, blonde hair trailing down her back, hiding much of her slim but curvy frame.

Surely it was her. He recalled those beautiful, azure-blue eyes from the visit to Napier. She looked round. Their eyes met and held.

'It is you,' Paul said lamely.

'I believe so,' she responded.

'Napier,' he said, recalling their encounter at the Museum. 'Do you mind if I join you?'

She didn't mind at all. It was exactly what she had planned.

'Make yourself at home; you looked so lost,' she replied. 'Where did you disappear to? I didn't see you again at the hotel.'

'I went to fulfil a lifetime ambition, a truly significant part of my itinerary.'

'And were you fulfilled?' she replied, intrigued. 'Can I ask what or who it was you went to see?'

'Just a personal thing,' he replied dismissively, adding, 'These Gardens are a bit of a maze; I've found myself back where I started. I'm Paul, by the way.' Laura knew that full well.

'I'm Laura. You're a long way from home.'

'My English accent; it's a bit of a giveaway.'

'What brought you to Karaitiana now that we have no city to see?'

'Where?'

'It's the old name for Christchurch. It's what they call a transliteration of the word "Christian". I thought I'd see if you had done your homework on our island.'

'I've come here to see my uncle and, whilst here, study the Maori culture and their history.'

He made no mention of Hussain.

'You've got a lot to learn if you are really here to study the Maoris.'

'What do you mean by that?' he asked, unsure where she was coming from.

Laura backed off. 'Sorry, just my inquisitive nature. I don't meet Englishmen every day.'

'My mother had read about the Botanic Gardens,' he continued. 'She has a great interest in horticulture. Some of the plants and shrubs over here you wouldn't find in my home county of Norfolk. I went there to take some photographs for her.'

'That's a relief,' she replied, smiling, 'I don't usually associate young men with flowers and shrubs. Real men play rugby here. What were you doing in Napier?'

'Oh, just sightseeing, but I have played a bit of rugby for my uncle's village team as a wing three-quarter - one thing I can do is run fast.' He did not know then it was to save his life.

'Actually, I'm staying with my uncle at a farm near Rangiora, just north of here.'

Laura told him her story and of her first-hand experience of the Christchurch earthquake. Stupidly, he gave a wry smile.

'I wouldn't think it's amusing,' snapped Laura.

'It's not that,' he replied. 'I'm sorry I smiled. It's because I am particularly interested in the current series of natural disasters.'

'In what sense?'

'There are a lot of ancient prophecies which foretell dramatic events in the early part of this century.'

'Haven't they foretold the end of the world in December?' Laura asked.

'Some say that; I don't. There's much more to it than that alleged doomsday message.'

'Anyway, what brings you and that English accent to New Zealand?'

Paul related his story. He had always wanted to come to New Zealand. He had read so much about its natural beauty, its people, their chequered history, and it gave him an excuse to visit his uncle. He left out any reference to the disagreement with his father or the family feud.

'Anything else?' asked Laura.

'What do you mean?'

'Oh, anything else you yearned to see, anyone you wanted to meet? Most young people I meet have friends or contacts they've come across at university or college they want to look up,' she responded evasively, realising she might have overstepped the mark, but still hoping he might take the bait.

'As it happens I do have a friend over here, someone I was at university with. I will probably link up with him at some point.'

'So it's a "him" then, not a girlfriend,' replied Laura, trying to keep the conversation going, but feeling embarrassed that he would think she was being too forward, probing too much for a first meeting. Paul said nothing, just looked at her. It was not going well; the words weren't coming out as she intended. She decided not to pursue it any further - for now, anyway.

It was an unusually warm and sticky day for early autumn, but perfect for camera shots to please Mother Mary.

'Ice cream?' Laura asked, trying to recover her poise. It was all she could think of to prevent him leaving. It was a bit too soon to flash her legs at him. They headed towards the nearby ice-cream kiosk, purchasing two vanilla cornets adorned with chocolate sticks which, quickly melting, ruled out any attempt at conversation. They walked silently through the Gardens and over one of the many bridges crossing the Avon River. They found a park bench under a tree and took in the view. Laura trembled as she recognised exactly where they were and the memories came flooding back. She said nothing for a few moments, trying to hold back the tears which threatened to overcome her. Somehow she summoned up the determination to keep her emotions in check – she couldn't lose concentration as she had in Napier. Paul, sensing her discomfort, said nothing.

She recalled the beginning of the assignment. Her boss, Mike Tucker, had begun by telling her that the UK authorities had been watching a cell of activists at the University of East Anglia in the city of Norwich in England, a city she had never heard of. The group had been in regular contact with a young Englishman by the name of Paul Anthony Morgan, the son of a priest in the Anglican Church.

'This is where you come in. Paul Morgan fell out with his father in his teens, getting into the company of Hussain Barzal, a Muslim, who became a close friend. They both apparently rebelled against their parents and their beliefs. Although Mr Morgan seems to have later become reconciled with his parents, appearances can be deceptive. In the course of our surveillance we have recently established that Hussain Barzal has booked a flight to New Zealand. He is a mature student, with financial resources, but we have not yet established where they come from. Certainly his parents, highly respected worshippers at a London mosque, do not have significant funds, and he rarely sees them. He has never done any part-time work, so we can only surmise as to how he was able to pay for the air ticket. The family originated from Pakistan so we have to assume he has relatives over there.

'Barzal has been in contact with friends here in New Zealand, and we have also discovered that Mr Morgan has booked a flight to this country funded, we think, by his aunt, ostensibly to stay with an uncle on the outskirts of Christchurch. There is no indication that his uncle has any fundamentalist sympathies. As friends why did they not travel together? Were they trying to avoid suspicion? I want you to get to know Paul Morgan, find out what he is up to, where he goes, who he meets. He has done a lot of research into world religions, and Islam in particular. As you may know, we have a much-respected Islamic community on the Island. The headquarters of the Islamic Federation are in Wellington. We are working with our Muslim colleagues in a joint initiative with Britain to prevent infiltration by radicals. However, we have identified a cell operating in North Island with suspected contacts inside the Federation. We believe they have a training-and-indoctrination camp in a remote mountainous area of the west coast in South Island. We have information to suggest

Mr Morgan and Hussain Barzal will be in Wellington at the same time, and that meetings are planned in various parts of our beloved country. Find out all you can about this Hussain. You will spend the next three weeks learning everything you can about Islam so that you can express an interest in the subject and converse with Morgan when you meet. I know that you studied Religious History, and that may come in useful. Ask about God, given the tragedies in your own life, to get him going and see where it takes you. Here is a dossier on him. He is booked on a flight to Napier. Your seat is two rows behind on the other side of the aircraft, so you will be able to see him. He has made a reservation at a small hotel in Dickens Street, where you will also be staying. Make contact with him and from there it is up to you. Keep a full record of his movements, his conversations with you, his meetings, etc. When he returns to his uncle's farm in Christchurch we will be intercepting his mobile phone conversations and we will set up a rendezvous so you can meet him again. You will be advised when and where. You will be issued with a mini-camera, a mini-tape machine and a phone with an alarm signal for use in emergencies. This will be the highest-profile case of your career. Although you are one of our youngest operatives, you are well-experienced and highly trained. It must be obvious that you will have to get close to this Paul Morgan – you know what I mean. Your minder, Neon, will never be too far away.'

Laura knew full well what that meant. Was it just her looks, or her ability that had won her this assignment? With that thought in her mind she had left the room to take a crash course on Islam and the Koran.

'Do you believe in God or fate, or something beyond our understanding?' Laura asked eventually.

'Oh, don't get me on that subject. I hoped coming over here I could escape from all that. Why do you ask?'

'Probably as a result of my great-grandparents' experience in Napier, and mine here in Christchurch, right here, actually, this very spot, lightning striking twice and all that.'

Instinctively she picked a flower from the nearby bed and threw it into the river, as mourners had done after the earthquake memorial service a couple of months before.

For a few moments neither spoke.

'Why do you want to escape from God, and which one?' she prompted, already knowing full well the likely answer to the first question. It was the second part she wanted him to talk about.

'The God issue is all to do with my father, a priest, and his beloved faith. It dominated my childhood. All those wretched choir practices, Sunday services, they took over my life. Naturally I rebelled, railed against it all. I then got in with a bad crowd, drugs, alcohol and all that. It was my Aunt Jane who rescued me, but I still harbour a grudge at losing so much of my early years to all that claptrap.'

'And you carry all that resentment and negativity around with you, don't you?'

Laura got no answer to the second question, one intended to provoke him to talk about Hussain. She would have to try harder, but not yet.

'How did you afford to come all this way, half-way round the world?' Jane asked.

'Aunt Jane, whom I mentioned, lent me the money. She has no children and is unmarried. She is totally absorbed in her work as an archivist; she never spends much money on herself.'

'Good,' thought Laura, it tallied with what Mike Tucker had told her in her briefing.

'So, what do you do to earn your way in the world?' Paul asked.

'I work for the New Zealand Civil Service.'

'That could be deadly boring or very interesting, depending on what line of work you are in.'

'I had to sign a confidentiality agreement. We all have to, so I'm not able to indulge your curiosity. Sorry.'

'Surely you can be a bit more specific than that? It can hardly be that Top Secret,' replied Paul, fishing for more information. 'Inland Revenue, or Social Security; surely not the Secret Service?'

'Do I have to repeat it? I'm not allowed to tell you; I have no wish to lose my job,' she retorted, clearly irritated at this intrusion into her privacy. She was supposed to be quizzing him, not the other way round.

Sensing a blind alley, Paul reluctantly reverted back to her earlier question about God. He hoped the fact that his father was a clergyman would provoke some curiosity and maintain the conversation. Paul wanted to meet her again. He had come halfway across the globe to get away from God, faith and all that, and now here he was engaging in conversation about it. Nevertheless, he felt this gave them a common interest and would be worth it if he could see her again, more especially as she had gorgeous looks as well. There was something about that sweet, oval face enclosed between smooth, blonde strands of hair draped on either side, almost down to her chin. Yes, he certainly wanted to see more of her - a lot more. No doubt an attractive girl like her would have a boyfriend, and probably several admirers waiting in the wings, but he couldn't let go now and never see her again. He did not know there was no chance of that. His thoughts were interrupted as Laura spoke, her spirits apparently raised.

'Lost Englishman, perhaps I could show you something of the area? I've got some time off next week. I'll come and pick you up from your uncle's farm and we can go for a drive to the coast and you can tell me more about your beliefs - or lack of them. I'm sure with your background you can help me tackle my demons. Fancy a swim with the dolphins?'

Paul fancied nothing more, enthusiastically writing down Uncle Oliver's address- which Laura already knew. He had also always wanted to swim with dolphins and he began to picture her in black velvet swimming gear, ducking and diving, gliding smoothly, seductively, through the water towards him.

'I'd like that. It's pretty tedious talking to sheep all day.'

Chapter 5

J ane's brother-in-law, Revd Thomas Morgan, was preparing for Easter. He felt the tell-tale tremors of apprehension welling within. His joy at the forthcoming celebration of the Resurrection of Christ, as befitted his calling, was tempered by other issues. These were personal and should not have distracted or worried him, but they always did. His wife, Mary, knew the signs after twenty-five long years together; many times had she seen his periods of introspection, the prolonged silences as he confronted his demons. He would be as quiet as a church mouse - until he climbed into his pulpit. Then it would be as if the cork had burst from the bottle; he would hold forth unabated, no notes, oratory of which no one would believe him capable. Although Thomas was rarely demonstrative away from his spiritual home, he could be jovial and high-spirited in the company of his parishioners and those who knew him well – except his brother. He had a raucous laugh, hoarse and rather gruff-sounding, which belied his thin frame. Mary knew this to be a disguise, a front to hide his inner feelings. His wife could read his mind better than perhaps he could. She, and her sister Jane, were the only ones who fully understood the root causes of his doubts and insecurities.

Despite his misgivings, Thomas attempted to portray an image of unconfined joy as the celebration of Jesus' Resurrection drew nigh. To his surprise, the build-up was more successful than he anticipated and his spirits were raised. The usual round of Bible-reading, nursery-school plays and enactments portraying the Crucifixion had been especially well-supported. Even the donkey had behaved impeccably, defying the dire warnings of the health and safety lobby. The monthly Parochial Church Council, which he chaired, had also passed without the usual controversy over health and safety, the Criminal Records Bureau checks for the bell-ringers, the composition of the choir, and the style and timing of services. The exception, which particularly angered Thomas, was the primary school headmaster who, aided and abetted by his feisty assistant head, had banned any reference to the meaning of Easter as they did not approve of its religious message.

'Still no wise men there,' grumbled Thomas, repeating his Christmas gripe at the cancellation of the Nativity play, and bemoaning the secular world which he now inhabited.

Thomas was a traditionalist and not enthusiastic about the organist's insistence on setting his favourite hymns to unfamiliar tunes, which most of his congregation could only mumble awkwardly, their barely discernible sound sinking down, muffled and unheard, to the stone floor below. He knew how difficult it would be to find another organist should he complain. Thomas, the former choirboy and soloist, had sadly lost his precocious talent when his voice broke, leaving his congregations to endure the residual grating pitch, particularly unsuitable for the unaccompanied incantations of a parish priest.

By early April, just as the days lightened, his mood darkened. Mary, fully aware of what lay behind his brooding presence, tried to support and encourage him. She knew the grim message of Good Friday was not the only reason for his depression.

Mary looked forward to seeing her brother-in-law, Peter. With his love of controversy, he added a different dimension to the usual tedium, more especially with Paul away in New Zealand.

She reflected on the blazing row between father and son which had preceded his departure. Even she had been taken aback by his uncharacteristic venom, directed at her husband and his faith. Although she regarded her son as slow to chide and swift to bless, he did have a hidden fuse, a temper, that would very occasionally ignite. That was the cause of the six-inch scar on his left shoulder, the result of a knife wound in a fight as a teenager.

She realised Paul's outburst at her husband was the consequence of years of stifled anger at his suppression when growing up; all those Sunday services, acting as the dutiful choirboy, unable to play Sunday football with his friends, all manner of things had gushed forth like a volcanic eruption.

Peter, Thomas' elder brother by three years, had always enjoyed taunting his brother. This had never happened in front of their parents, who were besotted with their first-born. He was outgoing and popular, loving the rigours of debate, playing devil's advocate. Thomas thought he played that role to perfection. In one of his frequent depressions, he once remarked despairingly to Mary: 'The nature of my calling is so immeasurable, so intangible, in total contrast to Peter's profession, so firmly based in a world of logic and reason,' adding, 'I don't really know whether he is putting on an act or not.'

It did not occur to Thomas that he did exactly that when outwardly displaying his forced joviality. Both men were troubled by their Christian names, Peter especially. Firstly, he did not approve of the term 'Christian Name' at all and, secondly, he most certainly did not approve of any implied association with Saint Peter, the disciple and first Pope. One of Peter's favourite put-downs to his brother came from the *Sermon on the Mount*.

'*Be careful not to make a show of your religion before men; if you do, no reward awaits you in your Father's house in heaven.*' This would really rile Thomas. Beset as he was with doubts and anxieties, he blamed his namesake, 'Doubting Thomas', that other disciple, for his woes. Their parents' choice of names portrayed a fitting sense of irony.

Peter and his second wife, Carol, – only Thomas always called her by her proper name of 'Caroline'- arrived at the Norfolk rectory after their journey from London in the late afternoon. Jane did not make an appearance until early evening – she had been waiting, hoping to have some news from Luke before the Easter weekend began.

Thomas regarded Caroline as a socialite, with her love of fashion, glitzy dresses and expensive handbags. He wanted to say to her: '*Your beauty should reside not in outward adornment - the braiding of the hair, or jewellery, or dress - but in the inmost centre of your being.*'

Even better, it came from the *First Letter of Peter* in the *New Testament*. He relished the coincidence.

Carol had no love of the countryside, regarding it as dreary and boring compared with life in 'the city'. The late winter fall of snow was still lingering in patches; the roads were mushy, filthy and wet. A pity; that meant no chance of their cancelling, thought Thomas, as did Carol. It was one of the few times their wavelengths aligned.

Friday, 6th April was blessed with weak, misty sunshine filtering through the rectory's south-facing windows. There had been a severe hoar frost; the trees outside glistened with the sparkle of silver, the lawn white, no longer green, like a scene from a Christmas card – except it was April.

'Who's for some sea air, get an appetite for tonight's meal?' asked Thomas, just returned from the marathon Good Friday service. Peter said: 'Count me in.'

'If I must,' retorted Carol, without enthusiasm.

'And me,' piped up Mary, quickly followed by Jane. She wanted to catch up with Mary, ask about Paul. Despite the comforting presence of her family around her, she could not dismiss the strange discovery at the Old Monastery Hospital from her mind. She had an intuitive feeling that there was more to it than a collection of inconsequential relics. She could not fathom why she should feel that way; it was not in her nature as an analyst to engage in unfounded speculation. She made sure her mobile phone was fully charged, just in case of a call from Luke.

At that very moment, Luke and Judo were closeted together. *They had the test results. They must speak to Jane, urgently.*

The Morgan family had already set off for a fresh afternoon walk by the sea. In spring, or in late autumn or winter, but rarely in high summer when the area swarmed with tourists, they would walk for miles along the Norfolk beaches. Arriving at the isolated village of Horsey, just past the old mill and bird reserve, they drove down a gravelled, bumpy track hardened by the frost, challenging the suspension of Thomas' ageing estate car, parking eventually in a grassy area, separated from the ravages of the North Sea only by banks of sand dunes. Wrapped in a mix of coats, anoraks, colourful hats and scarves, hands encased in woollen gloves, their walk took them along the windswept dunes, sand blown up in their faces from the beach below. Thomas, in his worn-out old duffle coat, toggles tightly fastened -'So last century,' thought Carol - with Peter beside him, led the way, with Mary, Jane and a reluctant Carol just behind. Reading her thoughts, Mary whispered to Carol: 'My husband doesn't approve of the twenty-first century.'

'Nor, I suspect, the twentieth either,' added Carol, a cutting edge to her voice.

Jane lagged behind, her thoughts still deep inside that musty old cellar with its strange hoard of artefacts. She really could not wait until after Easter to hear from Luke.

That particular day, although cold, was relatively calm and tranquil, fleeting white clouds darting across a pale blue sky, some wispy, others in the distance more dense, turning to jet black, a potent warning. As yet, the sea showed no sign of the fury when, some sixty years before, one hundred lives were lost and property devastated along the entire Norfolk coastline, from the Wash to Great Yarmouth and beyond. It had happened many times before. Mary recalled reading about great tidal surges and storms which had drowned whole villages for ever, including Dunwich, once England's tenth largest town, whose church bells supposedly still tolled eerily beneath the waves. Despite its benign appearance that day, Mary felt it would only be a matter of time before the sea mounted another attack. Would the new flood defences hold, or would countless homes be washed away as last time?

Thomas recalled their last walk along that isolated coast, the previous Christmas. At that time of the year access to the beach was restricted, cut off by temporary fencing; not enough to hold back a marauding tide, but sufficient to discourage walkers from descending to the bloodstained sands below, littered with spawning seals and their pups.

'Nature's new-born at Christmas!' Thomas had exclaimed gleefully. Even the basking seals had looked up in amazement.

'Paul says we may not be here for many more Christmases,' Mary had responded.

Mary, intuitive as ever, noticed her husband's introspection, and interrupted Thomas' reflections on a Christmas past.

'You're thinking about Paul's idiotic ancient prophecies which he kept going on about last time we were here.'

'If you ask me he's become obsessed with them. Beware of false prophets, a bunch of Pagans, with their good for nothing notions; Ephesians, Chapter Four, if you didn't know!' Thomas proclaimed loudly, his high-pitched voice echoing across the dunes, so deafening it drowned out the sound of an incoming call on Jane's mobile.

'*For God's sake, Jane, answer your bloody phone,*' shouted an exasperated Luke Matthews from Judas Swan's laboratory in Norwich. They had to speak to her; they had some staggering news to impart. They quickly composed an email outlining their findings, unaware that its contents would trigger interest from the guardians of national security far away in Cheltenham.

'What about the *Book of Revelations*, then, brother?' Peter retorted, as Mary came into earshot, 'With all its dire warnings. And some say the Second Coming of your Jesus will be between 2018 and 2028 - a biblical generation after the founding of Israel.'

Mary quickly intervened.

'Now, now, you two, let's have none of that!'

It was too soon for the arguments which she feared would follow once Thomas and Peter were alone together, fuelled by a cask-strength bottle of Peter's favourite malt. They had never been close, their sibling rivalry always to the fore.

'Walking is so therapeutic, don't you think?' she said to Carol, lamely, unsure of how to break the silence, what to discuss. The men were by now speculating about the forthcoming rugby internationals, which she knew nothing about, and neither, she suspected, did Carol or Jane. It was obvious that Carol was becoming intensely irritated by the freshening wind and the blowing sand whipping up into her face and then permeating everything - her beautifully manicured hair, her fur coat and especially her lined leather boots, not designed for beach wear. Carol's obvious dislike of anything as crude and backward as the countryside made it unusually difficult for the women to find anything in common as a conversation topic. They followed behind the men, who were totally absorbed in their discussion of rucks and mauls, hookers and tight-head props, all entirely bizarre. It was something of a relief when Carol gave up and retreated back to the comfort of the car - and the morning play on the radio.

'Probably what she wanted to do all along; stay at the rectory, cosy by the fire with her book,' suggested Mary. She and Jane were soon into a discussion of their own, no longer concerned about rugby and its strange names. Uninhibited by Carol, they had plenty to talk about. Once again Jane's mobile rang, pleading to be answered, but to no avail; the two sisters were too deeply immersed in family matters.

'Now we're on our own, how is Paul? Have you heard any more since we spoke in the cathedral?' Jane enquired, seeking an update from their earlier conversation.

'Nothing at all. You know how it is with the young. He should be somewhere in South Island. They talk to each other incessantly on their mobiles, smartphones or whatever is the latest piece of kit, but rarely to their family.'

'Have you heard from our brother?' Jane asked tentatively.

Neither sister was in regular contact with the 'black sheep' of the family, as Oliver had become known, since he had hot-footed it to New Zealand for pastures new.

'I know how sensitive an issue it is, Jane. We don't speak or communicate any more than you do. As I told you, I wasn't entirely happy with Paul going over there, but he has the curiosity of youth and it would not help to try to stop him. Despite his calling, Thomas does find forgiveness difficult, and more especially where Oliver is concerned, so he was more than happy that he had gone to the other side of the world to start a new life rearing lambs for slaughter. Now that Paul has gone over there, it's brought it all back.'

'About the row they had; do you think they'll get over it? Unlike Paul to get that upset, he's normally such a placid boy - these days, anyway.'

Their conversation was interrupted by Jane's mobile once more. This time she heard the familiar tone. It was a poor signal, and difficult to hear with the roar of the sea and the wind getting up.

'Oh, hi Luke. Sorry, I can hardly hear you. I'm on a walk by the sea. What was that you said? Something about those forensic tests? Look, I'll call you as soon as I get a better signal, hopefully when we get back to the rectory.'

'Work calling, I suppose?' Mary enquired.

'Just that archaeological dig in Norwich I mentioned; they've got some test results for me, nothing exciting.'

Her dismissive retort was intended to mask her inner excitement, that electric feeling something unusual was unfolding. Mary knew her sister too well to be fooled, but said nothing.

Peter, just ahead, gave his withering response to Thomas' suggestion that the England rugby team would win the forthcoming world cup in New Zealand.

'No way,' responded Peter, just for the sake of a little stir, a practice, perhaps, for later.

'Sorry, can't agree with you, brother,' retorted Thomas, '£10 that England win.'

'Ah, the gambling preacher! What will the money-changers make of that in the inner sanctum of your temple?' retorted Peter, tongue in cheek and voice laced with sarcasm. 'How about a bet that Paul stays on in New Zealand for the rugby, finds work and a woman, and never returns?' The sparring had begun.

The clouds, initially distant, were now above, dark and black. A sudden clap of thunder warned them they should get back to the car. Thomas grew quiet, his inner thoughts now full of foreboding for what lay ahead, that thunderclap ringing ominously in his head. Nevertheless, with the exception of Carol, it had been good to breathe the fresh sea air and return to the rectory with glistening cheeks, burned by the breeze of the North Sea.

'I need a drink, to warm the cockles,' exclaimed Peter.

'About time too,' Carol chipped in, looking up from her book.

With the exception of Jane they settled down for a warming drink of mulled wine, sleepily watching the newly-lit fire flicker gently in the grate, its small, bluish flames rising nervously from their birth bed of kindling, peering cautiously round the first log, soon engulfing it. The flames turned yellow, lapping round the smouldering wood, spiralling high round the sides, then above, like a crab climbing up the fire-back. The display rapidly turned into a celebratory dance, reaching upwards in acclamation of Peter's snoring, the bonfire ablaze, the log devoured, asking for more.

Jane took her glass and hurried through to the study, where she phoned Luke on her mobile. He answered immediately, his tone agitated, clearly waiting for her to call, and sounding frustrated she had taken so long to respond.

'Trust you to disappear of the face of the earth just as I need to speak to you. Where have you been? Anyway, apologies for calling you over the holiday period, but I have some strange results from the tests carried out by Judas Swan at the University research laboratory, especially your piece of cloth. I've put it all into an email, so have a look and see what you think.' With that he put the phone down. Jane opened the inbox on her new smartphone.

'Hi Jane, I had a lot of work on so I went over to the lab last Sunday, 1ˢᵗ April, to see Judo; you may recall that was his childhood nickname. We arranged for the tests to get under way on your cloth and parchment. We now have the results. The fragments of wood or thorns have no special characteristics. However, there were some stains on the cloth and, crucially, we were also able to extract some matching DNA from particles of human hair and from particles of fingernail near one of the rings. Remarkably, it seems the cellar was cold enough to limit the bacterial degeneration of the DNA. Tests show the hair came from a human, not an animal; a male, but we found he possessed extraordinary and, I have to say, unique, characteristics. The crucial feature is that they are not matched by any genetic structure in any global blood-bank. What amazes me is the chromosome structure, the genomic DNA signature. It is the gDNA, as we refer to it, which determines paternity. **In short, there is no detectable DNA from a father. Judo says this is exactly what scientists might expect from a male born of a virgin.** *Apparently there is something like a one-in-a-hundred-billion chance of this. There is also some blood from a female.'*

Jane read on, *transfixed* by what followed - the results of laboratory tests. She could not take it in. She read the explanatory paragraph of the email again. It did say what she thought it had. The email then concluded:

'There is also evidence of a substance, possibly medicinal oil, in the particles of the cloth or fragment of robe. The colouring has faded but there are hints of purple. This may be the result of staining from acid peat, but we would expect that to be more reddish in colour. I have no idea where your cloth came from but it's undoubtedly **unique**. I think you can guess what I am trying to suggest. The coins are interesting, too; they are Roman, dating back to the first century AD. I'll tell you about them later. Strange that last Sunday was Palm Sunday. Happy Easter! Cheers, Luke.'

Jane's initial bewilderment was followed by a sharp quickening of her heartbeat. She did indeed understand what her friend Luke was hinting, a thought of such magnitude that surely there had to be a mistake. Her brain went into overdrive with wild, speculative thoughts and ideas; she could feel her heart pounding, giving her a distinctly scary feeling. The irony was not lost on her. She somehow sensed she was to remember this day for the rest of her life

Her mind racing, she returned to the sitting room to find them slumped down after their walk. Fortunately no one looked up; they were exhausted by their exertions and the bracing air, fuelled by the mulled wine. Jane slipped quietly out of the room, hastily scribbled a note to Mary, gathered her belongings, went out to her waiting car, and headed for home, thankful she had not had to explain the reasons for her sudden departure.

The blissful calm by the fireside was ended by the piercing ring of the old landline phone echoing through the tiled hall from the direction of the study. It was young Paul, immersed in a noisy and excited crowd in the Christchurch Botanic Gardens for an Easter barbecue party which would last well into the evening, accompanied by a massive display of fireworks ascending to the heavens. Mary answered, delighted to speak to her son, before passing over to Thomas, who had by now risen from his armchair. It was a brief conversation given the general cacophony of sound, and the crackling telephone line, inadvertently reflecting the tension between them. Neither made any mention of their previous altercation. All that was now outside Paul's compass - consigned to Norfolk on the other side of the globe. Neither of them had any inkling of the fireworks to come.

Chapter 6

The Cabinet Secretary has daily contact with the Prime Minister. Their relationship is a crucial one. There is within the Cabinet Office a mechanism to cope with emergencies. It is known as the Civil Contingencies Unit, part of the National Security Secretariat.

That evening, 6th April the Cabinet Secretary, Sir Julian Barclay, briefed Prime Minister Richard Benson. Other than the PM's Permanent Private Secretary they were alone, without aides.

'The Minister responsible for cyber security has received a surveillance report from our colleagues at GCHQ in Cheltenham about a potentially explosive archaeological discovery in Norwich. By "explosive" I mean its possible implications for the Christian concept of faith and, from that, the realm, our society and much else besides. **If** this report is confirmed, and hopefully it is a big "if", **and** it gets into the media, it could not only lead to mayhem in the religious communities, but also upset the whole constitutional balance between the State, the Church and the Monarchy.'

'You'd better explain that, Sir Julian; it all sounds a bit far-fetched to me,' replied the Prime Minister, a puzzled expression on his face.

'Well, sir, the Church is based on a calling. Theologians may well take the view that the crucial thing about faith is that it is voluntary, that there is the freedom to decide. Without this it could be argued that we are all clones, obliged to do God's will or face eternal damnation.'

'Sir Julian, you have omitted to tell me exactly what was found and why it should have such extreme repercussions.'

'My apologies, Prime Minister,' the Cabinet Secretary replied quietly but with conviction, 'I have here a transcript of the exchange of emails between an archivist and her colleague, an archaeologist, in which he describes the results from the laboratory tests which were carried out on some ancient artefacts found in an underground cellar in Norwich. I will read it to you.'

Before the Prime Minister could comment on what he had just heard, his Cabinet Secretary continued:

'Given the dramatic nature of the discovery, evidence of a virgin birth apparently with links to the Middle East, if it is confirmed that is, it could open up a whole can, or perhaps in this case, chalice, of ecclesiastical worms. I convened a meeting of my most senior civil servants. It's the duty of civil servants to plan for every eventuality. You did make that abundantly clear on a previous occasion. We quickly identified some problem areas. Firstly the Christian Church itself. It would have to completely reconstitute itself as the world's spiritual leader. Think what repercussions that would have around the world, especially in the Middle East. Also, its whole edifice is one built on a calling to faith, not its de-facto imposition. It certainly requires a fundamental re-write of its modus operandi…'

'Don't start on that Latin stuff. Remember, I didn't go to a posh school like you,' barked Prime Minister Benson. He was proud of his comprehensive school education, and always remained steadfastly loyal to his Northern roots as a native of Lancashire, born in Burnley. He could be a rather fearsome character, with his craggy, oval face, thick grey hair over his ears, and a deep, booming voice. He exuded authority and expected total loyalty from not only his team of civil servants, but also his fellow Cabinet ministers.

'I chose the buggers; they dance to my tune or they're out.'

'Which branch will set the new rulebook, the Catholics or the Anglicans?' added his Permanent Private Secretary, undaunted, and well-used to his superior's ways. 'We anticipate deeper than ever internecine conflict, especially between Rome and Canterbury, far more divisive even than their disputes over women bishops, homosexuality, and gay marriage.'

'Which brings me to a second concern,' interrupted the Cabinet Secretary, Sir Julian Barclay OBE, Eton and Oxford. He was a highly respected career civil servant who knew how to manipulate, or rather, exert influence over, as he preferred to put it, politicians of all parties. He did it so well and with such subtlety, they rarely noticed. Unlike Sir Christopher Perrin, the Prime Minister's Principal Private Secretary, Sir Julian never portrayed any feeling of superiority, no airs and graces. The Prime Minister rather liked him; 'Not bad for a "toff",' he would say to his wife. Likewise, Sir Julian would privately remark that Dick Benson was a good advertisement for a "pleb" who had made his way in life.

Sir Julian was keen to be in the driving seat. 'We foresee it could escalate into another much more fundamental disagreement over whose laws prevail,

Church or Parliament. The archbishops and their flock of followers could one day turn into unelected religious zealots, seeking to ride roughshod over our institutions, imposing what they interpret as God's will. What price our democracy?'

At last the Prime Minister had the chance to have his say.

'You're getting ahead of yourself, Sir Julian. Our increasingly secular country will never accept it, and I certainly won't,' he added emphatically, even dismissively; 'You're getting carried away; this is all wild and fanciful speculation.'

'Please hear me out. I accept this is all pure conjecture and it is only a possibility rather than a probability, but things have a habit of turning out worse than expected, so we should at least give some consideration to the worst-case scenario. You, perhaps rightly, often criticise your civil servants for not thinking things through, assessing all the consequences. This time I hope we have. Daniel Defoe apparently once said:

"And of all the plagues with which mankind are cursed, ecclesiastic tyranny's the worst."

'I have to remind you, Prime Minister, that the world has numerous historical precedents for this. Her Majesty could be in an impossible position as the Head of the Church and Head of State.'

'Tales of turbulent priests spring to mind,' murmured the Prime Minister, 'And all this coincides with the Easter weekend. Ridiculous!'

'Isn't it just? And how will other faiths react? Passive acceptance? No way,' continued the senior civil servant.

'We see it as a recipe for yet more conflict between religions, exacerbated, as always, by men and women of violence.' His tone was matter-of-fact, direct, convincing. The message was evidently beginning to alarm the Prime Minister as, arms folded on the table and fingers tapping, he stared anxiously into the void. He did not want all this on his watch, not on top of the financial crisis.

'You had better brief the Home Secretary, just in case we need to call a meeting of the Civil Contingencies Unit, and, one other thing you haven't told me: exactly why were we monitoring this professor's emails?'

★★★

In all her academic research of the old monastery records, Jane had not encountered anything with links to France or, indeed, continental Europe. If at all possible, she needed to establish some kind of timeframe to attribute to the writing on the parchment. That Good Friday evening she browsed through the book she had purchased in the cathedral gift-shop, also researching the Fighting Bishop on the internet. She learned that Henry Despenser, a 14th-century English nobleman and former Bishop of Norwich, had fought in Italy before being consecrated in 1370 by Pope Urban V, and had been a mercenary in the Vatican Army, subsequently leading an unsuccessful crusade to Flanders in 1383. Jane was aware that Norfolk had a vested interest in the outcome because of the previous trading links, with wool being exported and then woven into cloth.

'Flanders, some parts French-speaking,' she muttered, aware that western Flanders had been under French rule around that time. Had the Fighting Bishop been given the casket for safe keeping? Even if that were the case, why should it end up at the Old Monastery Hospital? Another possibility was that it had been brought to Norfolk by the Flemish weavers who had settled in Norwich around the time Henry became Bishop. She was soon head-down into her books and then onto the internet.

'*Some kind of medicinal oil*'; the comment fixated Jane. 'I wonder. It can't be what I think, surely?' She sat motionless, reflecting on what was flooding through her mind. Eventually she picked up her mobile.

'Sorry, Luke, but before you get caught up in family matters over the holiday, I can't get the oil out of my head. Do you know any archaeologists who researched in the Middle East or, say, at Qumran? Oh yes, and by the way, the blood from a female is probably mine.'

'You could try some research written by Professor Sir Philip Pyrford-Bolton about his time there. You should be able to Google him, and his colleague Jake McDonald,' came the reply.

She went into her study. It didn't take long to access Sir Philip's website. It was here she read about the 1988 discovery of a small jug at Qumran. The jug dated from Herodian times and had been wrapped in palm fibres. The website referred to speculation that it might have been used for balsam oil. This was an expensive substance, costing double its weight in silver and used for royal anointing. Many of the artefacts found around Qumran had come from Jerusalem and, indeed, the Temple itself. If they did indeed come from that part of the world, or even Jerusalem itself, how on earth could they have ended up in a trunk under a swan pit in Norwich?

Jane had a love of fine wines and had unwittingly chosen a white from the Languedoc region of France to accompany her take-away meal. She intended to refresh her memory about the swan pit and its origins – she was aware that there had been an earlier one in near proximity. But the combined effect of the fresh sea air and the wine overtook her, and she was soon asleep.

Chapter 7

After dinner on Good Friday evening, Carol announced that she had a headache and did not intend to stay up late. Mary, ever supportive of anyone, even of Carol, said she would go to bed too, disappointed at Jane's sudden departure. Thomas and Peter adjourned to the study with Peter's bottle of cask-strength malt as lubrication.

Thomas had studied Theology at university, gaining second-class honours, in contrast to his brother, Peter, who was awarded a first-class law degree. So far as Thomas was concerned, Peter was annoyingly clever. In his early years he trained as a banker, quickly rising through the ranks to become an area manager. Losing autonomy over his decision-making to the computers 'upstairs', and furious that technology overrode his own judgement, he soon fell out with his superiors and resigned. Turning to the law, he qualified as a solicitor and was subsequently called to the Bar as a barrister, where he could give free rein to his adversarial skills. He was by now a wealthy man. He also had the looks; a tall, handsome man with wavy grey hair, but more strongly built than his brother, giving him an air of authority and distinction, the kind of man women craved.

Mary knew that Thomas, despite his occasionally brazen exterior, was in awe of all this. She had tried to console her husband, quoting from the New Testament:

'The brother in humble circumstances may well be proud that God lifts him up; and the wealthy brother must find his pride in

being brought low. For the rich man will disappear like the flower of the field; once the sun is up with its scorching heat the flower withers, its petals fall, and what was lovely to look at is lost for ever. So shall the rich man wither away as he goes about his business.'

Peter had also been in his heyday - which Thomas thought had never ended - a fine sportsman; a rugby Blue at Cambridge University and no mean cricketer, on the fringes of County standard, until a knee injury ended that particular career. Thomas preferred the so-called 'lesser' sports of football, 'soccer', as Peter called it disparagingly, and tennis. Whilst Thomas had sung in the school choir, Peter had avoided activity of that sort like the plague.

When challenged, Thomas could be prickly and intolerant of opposing views, his tall but wiry frame shaking, his face reddening, and portraying unexpected animation.

It didn't take long for battle to commence. With alcohol taking hold, Thomas was challenged by his brother Peter to demonstrate his faith with a rebuttal of atheism. Thomas reluctantly agreed; reluctantly, because faith was not a matter for logical dissection - which Peter knew full well. He just could not resist a little bit of mischief over Easter.

'If your faith is so strong that it can move mountains, which it should be given your vocation (Thomas preferred "calling"), then you need to have at least read and understood the alternative point of view and be ready to convince the judge and jury, me in this case, of the veracity of your assertion that Jesus rose from the dead,' Peter had challenged. This was the barrister coming out in him. The trouble for Thomas was that he acknowledged only a higher authority, the Supreme Judge of all.

'Nevertheless, I can hardly ignore the challenge; that will only give him more ammunition,' reflected a doubting Thomas; 'He ought to take note of the *Book of Romans*:

"If a man is weak in his faith you must accept him without attempting to settle doubtful points."

Thomas stood up as if to leave, but then rounded on his brother, the unpredictable and volatile character, normally hidden, suddenly roused.

'Faith gives substance to our hopes, and makes us believe in things we do not see.'

'Like fantasies and fairies,' interrupted Peter.

'I know enough about your atheism to remind you that, whatever your books may say, you cannot prove that God doesn't exist. And, if God doesn't, how do you explain what is foretold in the *Book of Genesis*?'

'What? God made the world in seven days? I never took you to be a naïve creationist.'

'You know full well that I don't take the creation message literally. No, I am referring to the emergence of our world. It's all perfectly described in the first chapter and, what's more, its sequence has been subsequently proven by science,' exclaimed Thomas assertively.

'What on earth are you talking about, dear brother? Had too much whisky?' was Peter's retort, taken aback by his brother's unusual vehemence. He certainly seemed to be spiritually rejuvenated.

'I suggest you overcome your prejudice and read the Good Book again. You won't recall,' continued doubting Thomas, now launched into combat, 'God said: *"Let there be light, water, seeds of grass, the division of day and night, and let the waters bring forth the creatures that hath life, the great whales and every living creature after their kind."* I paraphrase, but it's all there.'

'What's all there?'

Thomas, just for once, had wrong-footed his elder brother. Introverted by nature, he had delivered this tirade as if he were in the pulpit, the one place he became more confident, even abrasive. He felt secure there; no one would answer back. He had only once been heckled and that had been by his son, Paul, at the time he was 'off the rails', as Thomas put it. Despite his many misgivings he was glad he had chosen the Church for his career. He was born under the star sign of Libra, but did not always conform to type. He found it difficult to balance the Libra scales, also the emblem of the accountancy body with which he started work as a trainee. Unsurprisingly he sank in a maze of debits and credits, always supposed to equal each other, but he found they never did. This career was not for him. As many young men did in those days, he had returned to his roots and followed his father into the priesthood.

Peter had not experienced such a highly-charged brother since their childhood, and rarely then; indeed, not since he had hidden Thomas' music score just prior to a choral recital. Reflecting on that, Peter had no time to don sackcloth and ashes as Thomas again launched forth.

'Your scientific friends now tell us, dear brother, that those events were set out in exactly the correct order and, indeed, they have attributed timescales to each, from the formation of the sun and the seas, the emergence of organisms and, crucially, the Cambrian explosion. That's the mass diversification of complex organisms over a short timescale in case you didn't know,' he added facetiously. 'Analysts claim there are a whole series of parallels between the Bible's sequential account of the creation and the modern scientific knowledge of our planet's life history. Whoever edited the various writings to produce the *Book of Genesis* was exactly right in his or her predictions, without any of the expertise we now have. Even you will have to admit that to be incredible guesswork in an era of limited scientific knowledge. And, Jane, who should know, tells me there is a lot of recently-discovered archaeological evidence for the historical truth of the Bible, the people, the places. As all that has proved to be accurately recorded, your beloved logic should lead you to acknowledge that divine acts may well also have happened.' Thomas paused to milk the occasion then continued his onslaught. Peter felt he was being lashed by a force-nine gale.

'Get your head round that! Yes, and I'll lend you a copy of the Bible - no doubt you have lost the one Dad gave you at your christening,' Thomas concluded, his voice suddenly triumphant. He liked to remind Peter of that event in his life. 'I'll read your books, you read mine!'

Chapter 8

Another glorious morning greeted Laura as she emerged from her cramped but cosy flat on the outskirts of Christchurch. One day she hoped she would have an apartment, or even a house, of her own. It was hard to accept the earthquake could actually have destroyed the centre of the city only a few miles away. It had been so full of life, the workers in their towering modern office blocks, the cafés and restaurants thronged with tourists. She reflected on the former majesty of the now-derelict cathedral, which had for so long watched over the busy central square. The remaining structure would soon be completely demolished to make it safe. 'So much death and destruction,' she thought, 'Courtesy of Mother Nature herself.'

With the morning sun beaming down on her, Laura threw off her moments of melancholy. The green Morris Minor convertible, roof folded back, with its quaint old number plate, JCS 212, purred into life, ready to take her to Paul's uncle's farm. With a mixture of mild apprehension and excitement she set off for the small town of Rangiora. She knew roughly where the farm was situated and, just before the turn-off, she stopped in a lay-by. Out came the make-up, another dab of what she knew to be an alluring, fragrant perfume, and a final check of her hair, blown about by the breeze.

The farm was set in gently undulating countryside, its link to the outside world being a large, gated road, with seven gates to negotiate. 'Not much fun on a wet, dank winter day,' she thought. The sheep bleated out their welcome.

Paul was outside the front door of the ranch-style farmhouse. He welcomed her in, the kettle having already boiled.

The initial slightly uncomfortable silence over coffee soon dissipated as Paul took her round the farm, the turquoise-blue water of the lake glistening in the New Zealand sunshine. The ever-cheerful bellbird sang its favourite little melody.

Seated under a gnarled old oak tree overlooking the lake, their conversation soon reverted back to the mysteries of the world.

'Elaborate on what you meant about your centuries-old predictions for the beginning of this century,' Laura asked, keen to get a conversation going.

'There are many such prophecies, emanating from diverse parts of the globe, but nearly all of them point to the first part of this century being some kind of watershed. Some suggest the end of civilisation as we know it, caused by war, famine, over-use of our natural resources or some natural catastrophe. Others talk of a subsequent renewal, with humanity adapting to survive whatever may have transpired. The most prominent coverage at the moment relates to the Mayan civilisation.'

Paul outlined the history of their civilisation, their mastery of mathematics and astronomy, their prophecies, their sudden disappearance. Very unusually for him, he kept it brief. He didn't wish her to find him boring.

'What caused the collapse of their society?' asked Laura, wanting to get him talking.

'One of the more current theories was they inadvertently poisoned their drinking water with human sacrifices to please the gods. Strangely, given their sophistication, they also practised extreme cruelty, including sacrifices, often of children,' Paul continued, his reticence now forgotten. 'It has happened before, most notably when the Islamic leader, Saladin, had overcome the Christians in a battle known as "Jacob's Ford", late 1100s, I believe. The bodies of the fallen were buried in pits, poisoning the water-table. That massacre was a portent of the unrelenting battles between Christianity and Islam which lay ahead.'

'This is all a bit grisly, Paul, spare me the detail.'

Ignoring her, Paul continued; he was launched into his favourite subject.

'Another theory, more fashionable today, is that some kind of climatic change led to their downfall. I don't hold with that explanation, as descendants became established only a few hundred miles away and climatic disasters would extend much further than that. Another is that they needed so much wood they eventually ran out of forest. They believed time happened in cycles, or ages; five ages, often called "suns". Each age ends with some kind of upheaval, followed by a new age. There are similar predictions throughout history; one that comes to mind was an old lady in ancient Rome, Sybil of Cumae, whose prophecies became known as "The Sibylline Leaves".'

'Is that why you can tell a fortune from tea leaves?' interjected Laura, trying to interrupt his remorseless flow.

'Could well be; she wrote her prophecies on oak leaves.'

At that moment a leaf fluttered down from the branch above, landing at Laura's feet. 'Like the one that's just fallen,' she suggested. 'Is that some kind of eerie sign?' she asked, feeling a pang of apprehension as she spoke.

'Not really; at least it wasn't a silver leaf – with a kiwi sitting on it.'

'Very funny.'

'Anyway, my interpretation is that the world enters a new phase, perhaps economic or social or spiritual. Others believe the transition is sudden, catastrophic.'

'You are going to tell me that the current "sun" finishes this December?'

'Yes, that is the popular view. It began on 13th August 3114 BC and, according to their very precise calculations, ends on 21st December 2012. But there is much more to it than that.'

'Much more to it? Elaborate.'

'Remarkably, and worryingly, I have to accept that the visions of dramatic change, or even catastrophe, sometime in this decade, apparently any time from December 2012 to December 2021, have received some validation. One prophecy was for a radical change in the sun's behaviour at the end of the long cycle, with potentially dramatic consequences. They believed the sun would receive some form of extra energy. NASA has confirmed that there will be a 30% to 50% increase in solar flares or bursts of radioactive particles this autumn. Some researchers predict that, sometime soon, there will be a complete polar shift; that is, magnetic pole reversal, which has happened before. Researchers have found evidence of a dramatic geological upheaval, mirrored in countries as far apart as Norway and Australia. Other writers have also predicted this. It's all to do with the seismic shift of tectonic plates, which cause…'

'Earthquakes,' interrupted Laura; 'Thanks for reminding me.'

'Sorry; I don't think before I speak, sometimes.'

'Obviously.'

'What's scary is that there is a galactic alignment of the sun with the centre of the Milky Way once every twenty-six thousand years.'

'Paul, please; can we talk about something else?' interjected Laura. It was her job to probe, but the subject was still too sensitive, the memories too raw.

'Oh, don't worry; there are various other predictions for 2014 and beyond, so no need to panic just yet!'

Trying to escape from Paul's gloomy prognosis, she picked up on an aside he had made which she hoped would get him on to a different tack, one that led in another direction.

'You mentioned Saladin. Do you know much about Islam?'

'I did a bit of religious history at university, but you don't want to hear about that.'

In fact she did. She tried again. 'Did you get any practical insight into Islam, meet its adherents, or experience their beliefs at first hand?'

'I learned most of that from my friend, Hussain.'

'I presume he's a Muslim. Tell me about him; you must have found it very interesting to obtain first-hand knowledge.'

'Oh, there's nothing much to tell really,' he replied dismissively. But was he being evasive?

Reluctantly, Laura decided not to push him; it could wait. Anxious to keep him talking, she asked:

'What other predictions have you found?'

'That many are eerily relevant to today. The Bible itself carries similar warnings. One prophecy is for the return of a Supreme Being.'

'The Second Coming?' Laura responded suspiciously.

'Listen to some of the others, which support my take on all this,' continued Paul. 'These refer to extreme materialism, otherwise known as greed, economic collapse, out-of-control advances in technology, damage caused to Mother Earth, changes in climate and ecology. 'Then there are the wars in the Middle East and the promises made to Abraham for the return of lands to Israel at the time of the Second Coming. You can see how all those signs are being manifested today and, combined with the financial and economic meltdown, they are all coming together in a perfect storm. And the predictions themselves come from not only the wretched Pagans, as my father calls them, but also from the Bible itself.'

They both fell silent, alone with their thoughts, before Laura spoke.

'It may be an uncanny reflection of our world, but no way am I going to be influenced by such crackpot ancient theories, at worst entire nonsense, at best entirely coincidental. They are like the Bible, open to any interpretation you may wish to make.'

'You can say that again.'

'You don't worry me, stranger,' she added defiantly, her slightly raised voice betraying her anxiety, trying but failing to hide her apprehension. Paul could see it in her face, now slightly flushed, full of emotion.

'I didn't mean to frighten you.'

'I presume you have been to the "Treaty House" up in Paihia, given your interest in the Maoris,' Laura replied, changing the subject.

'Obviously. It was the first visit on my itinerary.'

Taking no account of her sensitivities, Paul carried on regardless. She began to realise he was a great talker and was oblivious of anything else once under way. He had said his father was a preacher, so she assumed it was inherited. It would be some time before she found out the true source. Despite not much liking this trait, she realised it could prove fruitful to her assignment. He was soon riding his hobby-horse again; she decided to let him prattle on.

'Just look at 2011; a natural disaster pretty well every month.

'**January** – The Arctic conditions in the northern hemisphere, record rainfall in Australia. The river in Brisbane burst its banks, unleashing fifteen-foot-high floodwater, leaving twenty thousand homes inundated. To put that into perspective, that's three times the area of Great Britain.

'**February** – The largest ground motions in New Zealand's history.' He paused in embarrassment; 'I'm sorry, I didn't need to remind you of that.'

'Your brain can't keep up with your mouth, can it?'

Unperturbed, he carried on.

'**March** – The Japanese tsunami; immense waves travelling at five hundred miles an hour, ten billion tons of water. And don't forget the destruction of the nuclear plant, the fires, the radiation, now a total write off - a hammer-blow for the nuclear industry. A combination of the prophetic warnings - technological advances and a natural disaster all coming together,' continued Paul, disregarding Laura's scepticism; 'Don't you think that's scary?

'**April** - The two-hundred-foot tornados ripping through sixteen US states and, two weeks later, a further three hundred and thirty-six tornados in less than three days, a massive seven hundred and fifty-odd in total.

'**May** – A monster tornado which demolished the town of Joplin, winds rotating at two hundred miles an hour.

'**June** – A massive fireworks display in Chile – a volcanic eruption spewing out billions of particles and the resultant ash cloud.

'**August** – A hurricane batters the Bahamas and only a last-minute change of direction saves New York. 'Sixty-five million people were said to be at risk.

'**October** – Intense monsoon rains in Taiwan, much of Bangkok under water. Then the Turkey earthquake, 7.2 on the Richter scale. Next on the fault line is Istanbul, and my old university flatmate, Dr Miles Mulligan, a geologist, keeps going on about a threatened volcanic landslide from Mount Cumbre Vieja in the Canaries. That would apparently dwarf anything we have seen so far. Even my father's county in England experienced the worst drought for ninety years in 2011.'

'OK, Paul, I get the message,' Laura again interjected, voice raised, trying to stem the flow.

'Some would say these are warm-up acts for disasters to come, supporting evidence for the veracity of all those predictions. The timescale may not be as precise as some suggest. The warnings, if that is what they are, apply to the period of time measured in years but, if manifested, then God help us,' concluded Paul, still oblivious of the effect of his diatribe on Laura.

She had had enough. She leaped up from the bench and stormed off, startling the ducks on the lake which, squawking loudly, flew off in fright. She didn't know where she was headed, she didn't care. Tears again trickled down her face at the memory of her own natural disaster in February 2011, her lost friends and work colleagues. Paul, realising he had overstepped the mark, chased after her, but she angrily pushed him away, her face as scarlet as the enticing red dress which she gathered up above her knees, as she raced off down the track. She ran through a nearby gate, into the field beyond, coming to an abrupt halt as she found herself eye to eye with a large herd of cows staring at her in disbelief; and was that a bull amongst them? Feeling threatened, and suddenly aware of the colour of her dress, she panicked. The involuntary reflex to fear was to escape. She fled back towards the gate, imagining the Gadarene Swine in hot pursuit. She knew it was not a wise thing to do, to run away from a bull. In her haste she tripped on a protruding stone, stumbled and fell sideways onto the soft, muddy grass. Except it wasn't mud. She staggered back through the gate, her hair dishevelled, her heart pumping, suddenly noticing her dress, now no longer scarlet, and then her shoes. The evidence of where she had been was quickly apparent. Realising the state she was in, and out of breath but safe, she looked back over her shoulder. The cows were peacefully chewing the cud, oblivious of her plight. She could only laugh or cry. She decided the former was the best way out of the mire.

'Something about a red rag to a bull,' she shouted to Paul, as he pounded up towards her. Seeing her predicament, an anxious Paul caught the mood, laughed nervously, and put his arms round her to comfort her. The tears returned as she grappled with her emotions: fear, then relief, then shame for losing her cool; very unprofessional, she thought to herself. No word was said as he led her back to the farmhouse, showed her upstairs to the bathroom, found her a clean towel, discreetly took her shoes and set about cleaning them as he had never cleaned anything so carefully in his life. If she left, he knew he would never see her again. He imagined her naked body behind the shower screen, her curvaceous brown legs, those pert breasts being massaged by the sponge, soft with gel, under the warm spray of the shower. He tingled inside, and then down below, as he craved for an invitation to wash her down. She was tantalisingly close and he longed to take the opportunity with both hands. Sadly he knew he had done enough damage for one day. He realised it was now him who should tread more carefully. Besides, he still had the embarrassing problem of finding Laura something to wear. He prayed his uncle's wife, Kiwita, would be delayed at the supermarket. The last thing he wanted was for her to leave, but he also knew Kiwita was unlikely to believe their story; she was bound to assume they had been up to no good and most certainly would not approve.

He had not had much chance to talk to Kiwita about the Maoris and their history. He desperately hoped the incident with Laura would not scupper that line of research. He went downstairs and put the kettle on. He stood in silence as the steam began to rise from the bubbling waters surging to boiling point, in tandem with his own thoughts and desires for the girl upstairs.

Laura emerged refreshed after her shower. Paul had got under her skin; he was annoying, irritating, and yet, she rather liked him. Perhaps this assignment would be more rewarding than she expected. Now composed, and cosily wrapped in Paul's maroon dressing-gown, she walked tentatively down the carved wooden staircase, accepting the offer of a mug of hot coffee. Neither of them wished to speak first. The fire of sudden passion had seemed to burn Paul's throat, his voice stifled, no words coming out. Paul's doom-mongering occupied Laura's thoughts, reminding her of her quest for spiritual guidance, some kind of faith to hang on to.

She eventually asked: 'Does your father believe in a Second Coming?'

A first one would have been nice, Paul thought to himself, knowing full well she was referring to the Messiah and not to what he had in mind.

'I've never asked him. I don't discuss religion with my dad any more. As far as I understand it,' cautioned Paul consolingly, 'There is an interpretation that it may not be an actual physical return, but more a spiritual reincarnation of some kind. 'This does resonate with many religious teachings. Linked with this is the prophecy of "unity", the healing of sectarian divisions between faiths.'

'Do you have any kind of faith, Paul? Do you question your lack of belief? Is that why you have such suppressed anger?'

'If ever I had any faith, maybe when I was young, it's been drummed out of me. I hope I have left it behind in England.'

'Well, I am looking for it, hoping for it, needing it, whatever you say. By chance I read only the other day there is a "Council for a Parliament of world religions", promoting interfaith dialogue, and the Archbishop of Canterbury recently spoke of a quest for inter-religious dialogue via the "inter-faith initiative". He believes religions share a common quest and should not feel threatened by each other.'

'Well he would, wouldn't he?' said Paul, 'He's losing his priests to Rome in droves as we speak.'

The shrill tones of Laura's mobile interrupted them.

'It's the office. Something urgent has cropped up. I have to go. We'll have to leave the dolphins for another day - I'll call you.' With that she abruptly upped and left, still wearing his dressing gown. He went with her, dutifully opening the farm gates, then standing in awe watching her go. It was if she was slipping away on an ebb tide. Would he ever see her again?

'Why did they have to call me back now, just as I was getting to know him better?' she said to herself as she drove back down the dusty track, but also relieved that she had been forced to leave before Kiwita returned. Her relief was short-lived. Just as she turned on to the main road at the end of the farm track, Kiwita came in from the other direction. Seeing Laura in her open-top car, she spotted that she was wearing what looked like Paul's maroon dressing-gown.

'Was that your visitor in that Morris Minor convertible?' she asked, the moment she stepped in the door.

'Yes, you just missed her; she was called back to work.'

'In your maroon dressing-gown?' she asked quizzically; 'And why is the washing machine whirring in the utility room?'

Paul's heart sank. His explanation certainly did not persuade Kiwita, who was convinced he had not come clean. Once again Paul reflected ruefully that he had not come at all, despite what she might think.

A totally despondent Paul wasn't sure if it really was Laura's employers who had called, or had she used it as an excuse to leave? Somehow he had managed to prejudice his relationship with both women. Feeling isolated, he later sat down on the veranda with his Uncle Oliver as the sun set over the nearby hills. Over a cold beer, he hoped a 'man to man' talk would raise his spirits – and give him answers to his quest.

Laura, summoned back to her office, had been ordered to submit a report on her assignment by 9am the next day. It could not wait, they needed an update. She was fully aware that she had little to say; she had failed in

Napier and gleaned very little from their meetings at the Botanic Gardens and his uncle's farm.

David Buck

THE SWAN PIT
PART II

Beginning in April 2012
Ending on 25th December 2012

David Buck

Chapter 9

'Why were our security guys monitoring the professor's emails, Sir Julian?'

'We are watching some alleged Muslim activists in Norwich who have links to Pakistan. It seems they have seconded a young, impressionable Englishman to their ranks. This professor, with the fancy title of Jane Clifford-Oxley, is the young man's aunt *and benefactor*. She funded the youngster's recent trip to New Zealand, which happened to coincide with the visit of his Muslim friend, one of the Norwich cell. We believe they will be attending a training camp there, and are planning some kind of outrage in that city.'

'I certainly see what you're driving at, the reason for your concern. Keep the lid on this, and keep me informed of any further developments the moment they emerge, day or night. And keep tabs on that archivist.'

Jane Clifford-Oxbury, oblivious of the discussions in Whitehall, and unexpectedly home alone, had the whole weekend ahead of her. She decided she was too pre-occupied to return to the rectory and had made some excuse about not feeling well. Mary did not believe that for one moment, and was disappointed at her sister's sudden departure, guessing that it was something related to her phone call.

Jane had dropped the 'Oxbury' from her name back in her university days, not wishing her ancestral roots to prejudice the perception of her by fellow undergraduates.

She also wished to keep it hidden from her colleagues on the History degree course. By the time they found out, they were all firm friends, a situation which lasted a lifetime. There were annual reunions in hostelries close to historic or ancestral sites; contacts made provided useful associates for her work. She had never married. There had been someone special and marriage had been very much on the cards, but she had been talked out of it, regretting it for the rest of her life, and with good reason. She had joined the Norfolk Archaeology Service from university and had therefore been working in academia most of her life – not in the 'real world', her other acquaintances would jibe, particularly when discussions turned to the economy, the debt burden and the resultant strains on local authority finances. Most of them felt the Archivist Service was a most suitable candidate for cuts. Jane would counter by pointing out that, if the lessons of history are not learnt, they are repeated. She cited Iraq and Afghanistan as prime examples, telling them you can't expect to impose Western, or before that, Communist, ideals and values on peoples with long-standing and deep-rooted opposing ideologies.

Her professional services generally comprised enquiry and identification, often accompanied by translation onto archives which were accessible to students the world over on the internet. She also provided an ancillary service for archaeological finds, but did not expect to end up finding one herself. It somehow felt very different.

She had to find out how the casket had got there – preferably before she alerted anyone else to the nature of her discovery. She had no idea it would change her life for ever, or that her involvement was already on the radar of the Government agencies and the Prime Minister.

She thought about contacting the Bishop of Norwich, the Right Reverend Marcus Banham, but hardly over the Easter weekend? Whilst very appropriate in many ways, she needed more time to think and, in any case, he would be very busy. It was not the moment to re-enter his life. Not now. She would love to tell Thomas, her brother-in-law, of the discovery, especially as it was Easter, but there was work to be done and she did not relish him fussing all over her.

Sipping a glass of wine from Languedoc, she again picked up the book about the Fighting Bishop. She read that Henry Despenser had been accused by a Sir Thomas Bungay of involvement in a plot known as the 'Epiphany Rising' of January 1400. Henry had been summoned to Parliament in February for the case to be heard. Epiphany was a rather more appropriate description than she realised. Jane had a hunch and decided to check her archives for 1400. She found out that on 5th February, just before the summons to Parliament, Henry had appointed a John Derlyngton, the Archdeacon of Norwich, as his 'Vicar General' and, crucially, John Derlyngton was also a former Master of the Old Monastery Hospital, holding the post for four years. He also continued to live there for many years. Henry could have given the casket to John Derlyngton for safe keeping, given his own impending trial. Henry had subsequently been cleared and had died in Norwich in 1406.

This was a possible explanation, but was it likely that he would really have obtained it in Flanders? After all, that crusade had ended in ignominy and disgrace for the Bishop. Hardly realistic to surmise he would have been given precious artefacts in defeat and withdrawal. Again, with his Vatican connections, it was difficult to contemplate why the Catholic Church would countenance such precious possessions being taken out of their control.

She remembered the story of Joseph of Arimathea. He reputedly came to Britain accompanied by twelve apostles, their task being to establish Christianity on these far-off islands, the furthest from the heart of the Roman Empire. However, he had been to Glastonbury and had apparently planted a thorn from the crown of thorns worn by Christ. But she was not aware of any links to Norwich. These initial theories did not stack up. How else, then?

She resisted another glass in favour of a clear head. It was then that another thought occurred. She had read many books about the Knights Templar and she was therefore aware of some of their history. She had ceiling-to-floor mahogany bookshelves in her study where, unlike her desk, all her reading matter was neatly sectioned according to the respective subject matter. She read that the Knights Templar had originally been known as the 'Poor Knights of Christ', and their movement was founded in AD 1118.

She found out that the Knights Hospitaller was an Order attached to a hospital in Jerusalem, founded by the Blessed Gerard around 1023. It had previously been linked with an Amalfitan hospital in one of the old quarters of Jerusalem, its purpose being to care for the poor, sick or injured pilgrims to the Holy Land. If there were any truth in the story, this could be the source.

The number of coincidences began to play on her mind:

1) An old hospital in Jerusalem and an old hospital in Norwich.

2) She had received Luke's message on Good Friday and the Crucifixion was on this day.

3) Ridiculously, she was drinking a glass of wine from Languedoc, where the Knights Templar had been based.

'I don't believe in omens or anything like that, but it is a bit scary,' she muttered under her breath.

She knew the Templars had owned land and property across Europe and the Middle East and were renowned as men of faith. They were also warriors and crusaders, just like the Fighting Bishop. Were they also guardians of some of Christendom's inner secrets?

She looked them up on the internet. Where did they go after the fleet left La Rochelle? Could they have sailed to England or, perhaps, Scotland, as some rumours purported? She determined to find out. One other thought occurred to her - the mention of purple in the cloth. She recalled a discovery in 1939, when excavations thirty feet beneath the Basilica in Rome revealed ancient bricks and bones dating back to the time of Christ. The find had also included purple fibres. There had been intense speculation amongst archivists and archaeologists that they had found St Peter's burial place. As he was a disciple of Christ, was it yet another coincidence that there was evidence of purple in the cloth? Or was it simply degeneration over time?

Chapter 10

P aul and Laura spent the day at Laura's flat on the outskirts of Christchurch. The weeks had flown by; it would soon be time to return home. He had been mightily relieved to hear from her after that episode at his uncle's farm. The evening conversation with Oliver after Laura had left had not gone as he had hoped. It had started so well, his uncle giving him some suggestive looks making Paul blush in embarrassment. 'Pretty was she?' he had said. But his uncle clammed up the moment Paul asked what had made him emigrate to New Zealand all those years before. The subject never came up again. Paul sensed he had brought down an impenetrable barrier - his uncle became uncommunicative, avoiding any meaningful conversation, unless it was about Jane and her work or Mary's wellbeing.

Excited at the prospect of seeing Laura again, Paul took with him a peace offering, a very expensive bottle of perfume, with an enchanting fragrance, or so the shop assistant told him. He was no expert in such things and had chatted up the young lady in the pharmacy, who was delighted to sell him a high-quality, superior brand. He was amazed how much it cost for such a tiny bottle.

After a slightly hesitant welcoming peck on the cheek, they indulged in small talk, both unsure of how their day together would work out. She asked Paul if he had spoken to his parents over Easter. His reply was non-committal.

'I have left Easter behind; it's not on my radar.'

Laura, undeterred, and delighted she had got him onto the subject of religion, hoped it would lead in the direction of his friend, Hussain. She told Paul she did not believe in the biblical story of the Resurrection. Her investigative interest in the religious story, and her quest for faith, had led her to read numerous books - at least, that's what she told him.

'Christ himself said "I am human". Even the Bible states: *"Jesus made of the seed of David."* I am beginning to think that Jesus survived the crucifixion. Even Pilate himself was surprised he was dead, as if there had been some kind of cover-up. When Joseph of Arimathea asked for Jesus' body to be handed over to him, Pilate apparently thought the plan had failed.'

'I don't go along with that. What I have learned from my father, and my studies, is that there is more than sufficient historical and anecdotal evidence to be sure that the Crucifixion actually took place. No human could survive such brutality, such injuries. He couldn't have survived.'

'Christians, of course, agree with you; it's critical to their concept of faith, the Church's one foundation and all that. Sorry, I didn't mean to offend your delicate sensibilities,' she added sarcastically.

'Whether you did or didn't is irrelevant. You know my stance on that. Even if he didn't actually die, he suffered a barbaric and painful crucifixion, enough to render him unconscious, a near-death experience and, with no modern medicine he wouldn't have lived long. That he appeared again is the wonder of the Christian miracle - at least that's my father's belief.'

'But even if he came through it and lived and rose again, it doesn't necessarily destroy the significance of the message at all. Not for me anyway. He still suffered for us and sent this symbolic message. It demonstrates that we can all arise from our sins and start a new life. 'It doesn't matter to me if he died and was reincarnated or survived. And what does your friend Hussain have to say about that?' she added, knowing she had to lead the conversation in that direction.

Paul continued, seemingly ignoring her probe.

'What about the stone at the entrance of the cave being rolled away, up an incline, as I understand it, much too heavy for those women?' he challenged disdainfully; 'And the Roman seal was unbroken. You also ignore my point about what limited medicines they had then.'

'Someone in high places could have bribed some soldiers to move the stones and arranged for a replacement seal,' Laura replied, 'And, so far as medicine is concerned, they did have some quite sophisticated drugs and potions. The unusual thing is that the anointing was carried out by a woman rather than any officials. A *woman*, Paul, what do your Islamic friends make of that?' she added defiantly, again hoping to move the discussion on to Hussain.

'There is also speculation that Mary of Bethany was Mary Magdalene. The militant zealots, who hated the Romans, might even have called for Jesus to be crucified as a martyr. They were infuriated that he had told his people to pay their taxes. This alone gave Pilate reasons for not seeking his death,' cautioned Laura.

'That's all pure conjecture. Besides, he couldn't have survived on the cross for any length of time.'

'The Roman soldiers would often break the legs to hasten the end, an act of mercy. Jesus had apparently "died" much earlier, before this was necessary. He could have been drugged. It was not unknown to survive a crucifixion,' countered Laura. 'Someone called Josephus is supposed to have witnessed the survival of a man crucified on a cross. The scriptures did say that Jesus complained of being thirsty and he did have a sponge soaked in something passed up to him on the end of a reed. Usually it was vinegar to help revive the poor captive. But was it some form of anaesthetic? They did exist in those times in the Middle East.'

'You seem to know an awful lot about all this.'

Laura winced, realising she had let slip the extent of her knowledge.

'We all did "Divinity" at school. I think you English call it "Scripture". I remember a debate in school. I had to propose the motion that "*This class believes Jesus survived the resurrection*".'

This time Laura was rather pleased with her quick thinking. She was sure she had not given the game away, revealing too much of all that painstaking research she had done.

'These days it's called "Religious Studies", and what about the spear thrust into his side?' Paul asked. He was still far from convinced.

Neither spoke as they reflected on their respective uncertainties and beliefs, both also nervous about what they hoped lay ahead, apprehensive of making the first move.

'I actually believe Jesus Christ was a prophet,' announced Laura, breaking the uncomfortable silence between them. 'As I said before, perhaps it is the "Message" with which people should be more concerned, not the "Messenger". I do not mean to be blasphemous.' She hoped this time it would lead him in the right direction.

'Actually, that is what Muslims believe,' said Paul, adding, 'The Koran also states that they did not crucify him, interpreted as "they did not cause his death on the cross".'

'At last,' she thought to herself, 'I'm getting somewhere. He seems to know a great deal about the Koran.'

Paul then continued, 'The prophet Muhammad made it clear that he was indeed the Messenger and not the writer of the Koran. He emphasised that it was inspired by God's word, not his, and based on personal revelations from God. You will never see images of Muhammad because of this – that is anathema to Muslims. Unlike in Christianity, it was only God who should be worshipped, not His prophet. In Muhammad's case there was no miraculous birth and no resurrection. He was known as the Honest and the Truthful.'

'Who told you all this, your studies?'

'No,' replied Paul, seemingly innocently, 'It was my friend, Hussain, from university, the one I mentioned before who, by chance, is also in New Zealand. In fact it was he that I went to see in Wellington, also so I could be introduced to his acquaintances here. He is studying for a postgraduate degree in Religious History. He is very knowledgeable about Islam, proud of their history and their beliefs. I've known him for years. His parents live in East London, originally from Pakistan. In their early years in England they had to endure long years of racial prejudice, taunts about "Pakis" from white, shaven-haired thugs, often members of the National Front. I met his father once, a kind and spiritual man, a humble Muslim, proudly wearing his turban, with the almost obligatory grey beard. Hussain's uncle is still in Pakistan and he often goes back to see his family over there; just like I'm doing here in New Zealand. His uncle's an engineer and pretty wealthy. He paid for Hussain's trip over here. 'I'll introduce you to him one day. He has a pronounced Cockney accent, probably derived from his spare-time job as a runner at the old Smithfield Market.'

'I would like to meet him too,' affirmed Laura, aware Hussain had no rich relatives in Pakistan, but her request seemed to fall on deaf ears.

'Muhammad, a human being and a wise one, had several wives, at a time when their laws also forbade drinking wine and, more importantly, falsehood and fornication. That's why they had several wives,' added Paul, cheekily.

'Keep that for your dreams, Englishman,' replied Laura. 'How come your Muslim friend knows people here in New Zealand?'

'Oh, they have groups of like-minded friends all over the place. And of course these days they can easily communicate through Skype or chat rooms. But naturally they like to get together from time to time.'

'Presumably there are some amongst them who are anti-Western, more extreme, though not your friend, I imagine?' asked Laura, probing.

It was then that Laura sneezed. Groping into her handbag she pulled out a pack of tissues, dropping some of them on the floor. Paul, ever the courteous English gentleman, averted his gaze as he picked them up for her. He did not hear the very slight click as she put them back into her open handbag.

'Bless you,' he cried, leaving out the God bit. 'You were asking about my friends. They seemed pretty moderate to me; passive, simply following their beliefs in Allah to the letter. They do, you know, it's a way of life, like sleep, breakfast, lunch, etc. Prayer is an integral part of their day. I am full of admiration for their devotion to their cause.'

'Go on,' Laura encouraged him, hoping for a breakthrough.

'For them, Allah rules the people, whereas it is the people who provide rulers in our western democracies, not God. They passionately believe that it is God's will that one day the decadent West will fall and Britain will become an Islamic state. It's not that far-fetched – who would have believed what is happening in Egypt, the Middle East, and North Africa?'

'How did Hussain get to know his friends over here in the first place?' She knew it was a leading question, one she had to ask. 'I'm sorry; you have not told me their names. I really would like to meet them,' she then added inquisitively.

'Enough of all this – I'm boring the pants off you.' concluded Paul, slightly unnerved by her questioning. Seeing her there, beautiful, beguiling, her hair silky in the sunlight, he wished he could.

Chapter 11

With those thoughts and desires foremost in his mind, Paul left Laura alone in her flat and, urged on by her, reluctantly went off for his run. She needed to prepare herself for his return.

Paul was honing the fitness and speed which would later hold him in such good stead, preparing for an important cup match as a wing three-quarter in his uncle's local village rugby team. Paul was well aware that every Kiwi rugby match, whatever the level, would be keenly fought, and he was not going to let the side down. He did not have any reason to notice the man with binoculars observing Laura's flat. Nor did he see the flash of a camera held by a man called Farim, watching from further down the street. His mind and body were consumed with only one thought - the consummation. Would Laura respond?

Laura had teased him mercilessly about his new outfit; he had even kitted himself out in All Black running gear, adorned with the obligatory kiwi emblem and silver leaf. As she had watched him change, she knew the time was nigh to fulfil her professional duty – 'to get close', as her boss had put it. Unexpectedly, she had started to become rather fond of him, even fancying him, despite his bouts of verbal diarrhoea. She knew full well what she was supposed to do, it came with the territory, but there was something about this man, something that went beyond the requirements of her assignment. She wanted him but not out of a sense of duty. On previous assignments she had dreaded this moment, but not this time. The very thought aroused her, she could feel her breast tighten in anticipation; her pulse rate began to rise as if in tandem with Paul's heartbeat as he pounded the streets, then the nearby park. She had never experienced such longing before. Her whole body seemed to be on fire. She hoped he would not exhaust his energy supply; keep something in reserve for his return.

Paul arrived back at the flat, panting and breathing heavily. She feared he would not be up to what she had in mind for the afternoon. As well as applying the entrancing perfume he had given her, she had put on a CD of soft, soothing love songs, just in case her flat was bugged and Agent Neon was listening. She did not want that, not this first time. Her thoughts were interrupted when she noticed that Paul, recovering his breath, had a strange expression on his face, betraying a sense of unease, almost angst. 'What's the matter? I can tell there's something troubling that pea brain of yours.'

'I think there's been someone watching your flat. There was a man with binoculars sitting in a Toyota car out there. I'm sure they were trained on your flat. I half saw him when I opened the door earlier, but took no notice; he was still there when I got back. The car's gone now,' warned Paul, looking out of the window. 'It may be nothing, but please be careful. And that's not all. I was into the park and had just slowed for a breather when two hooded youths jumped out of a bush right in front of me; one had a knife. I was off like a shot across the grass and back to the path beyond them. No way could they catch me, but it fair put the wind up me. It was in a knife fight I got that scar on my shoulder in my teens - I saw you looking at it when I changed my top. I think we should call the police; others, perhaps some frail pensioner, may not be able to get away.'

'Oh, I wouldn't bother to do that,' countered Laura defensively, 'We get loads of muggings round here. I'm sorry; I ought to have warned you.'

She did not want the police involved, whatever may have happened. She guessed that Agent Neon was bound to be lurking nearby, and he would not like that one bit. But was anyone else out there, watching, perhaps waiting?

'I'm not happy about you being here alone. I have to make this trip to see my friends but, while I'm away, contact your office and tell them that you are taking some leave, and that's an order,' he announced with unusual authority. 'We'll go away, anywhere, out of harm's way. You know this island better than I do; think of a suitable place.'

He wanted to add: 'Preferably desolate, romantic, with a king-sized bed,' but dared not risk it.

'I'll do what I can - I do have a job, remember,' Laura replied, enjoying his display of masterly authority and knowing full well she would get permission.

He had not known how to make the first move. He had had fun at university but this girl was special. He had nearly, and pretty well literally, mucked it up that day at the farm, and he didn't want to get it wrong again. He did not realise then that part of his charm was his English reticence, his apparent innocence, his naivety. Laura too was holding back, hoping he would take the initiative.

Paul put his arm round her and spoke tenderly to her.

'I really am worried about you being here, and I meant it about taking you away.'

Laura smiled. She grabbed him and kissed him; at first gently, then passionately. That first kiss sent quivers all the way down her spine; her whole body had tingled with excitement as he responded, especially in her nether regions where she could feel the dampness of her love juices starting to flow. She was no virgin but this feeling, this intensity, she had never experienced before. She had expected to get close to him, go through the motions, but this sensation was not in her brief; it went deeper than that, well beyond 'job satisfaction'. He had penetrated her inner being. 'Should I have let it go this far?' But she knew the answer.

Later that afternoon, after his cooling shower and their parting kiss, now very much of the French variety, a totally exhausted Paul climbed into the old Jeep and drove off towards Waipara. The perfume had cost him dear, two whole days clipping sheep, but boy, had it been worth it. Never before had the release of the Exocet of love engulfed him, body and soul. He would remember that afternoon for the rest of his life.

Waipara was a wine-producing region one hour's drive north of Christchurch. Laura tried hard to persuade him to take her with him, not out of fear for her safety, nor because of her job, but just simply to be with him.

'Not this time, Laura; it just wouldn't be appropriate,' was his response. After he had gone she pondered his comment, especially the unexpectedly formal use of her name. Was it because he had switched into a secret world, one which she was not supposed to enter, one with sinister purposes? Perhaps it was because she was a female whose presence would be anathema to his friends. It was vital for all sorts of reasons that she found out.

Paul hoped to pick up a really special bottle of Sauvignon to take home to Aunt Jane, as he had promised before leaving Norwich. His destination was a café at Waipara Springs, on the main highway. He was in high spirits now that he had successfully bored the pants off her. He barely recognised Hussain, with his thick black hair tied in a pigtail, arriving with some fellow Muslims, all interested to meet Paul. It was the pigtail, together with the hairy stubble masquerading as an embryonic beard, which threw him. Somehow, too, he seemed different; his hazel-brown eyes lacked warmth, and he seemed nervous and distant, almost aloof. There was something almost sinister about him, yet this was a man he had known since he was a teenager. It made Paul feel edgy, ill at ease, yet this was his closest friend.

'We need to use him, capitalise on his family connections,' one of them, Farim, had said on their journey north. 'He also has a girlfriend with a flat in Christchurch; he was there only this afternoon.'

'Even better; he is less likely to attract the attention of the authorities if he is in a relationship. 'Hussain, be careful not to let on that we know about his afternoon activities.'

They ordered coffee and began to talk. Omar and Farim, who had never previously met Hussain, had often communicated with him via chat rooms, relying on modern technology for contact. Students, unless funded, could not generally afford to fly halfway round the globe, and Paul assumed they had rich uncles like Hussain; it seemed most of them did. They seemed especially keen to quiz Paul about England, a country about which they had heard so much, but usually only from fellow Muslims.

His initial apprehension had soon been dissipated; the conversation had been easy and Farim particularly had shown great interest in him and his home life. It was hard to get a word in as they questioned him about his homeland, its cultures, and its beliefs. In turn, Paul was seeking to learn more about Islamic culture, and he had enjoyed talking to Farim about how they hoped to integrate with the indigenous Maori population. Omar had said little but smiled a lot; perhaps shy, or his grasp of English was not good. Eventually Paul made excuses to leave; he was due back at the farm for supper and did not want to upset Kiwita by being late. His relationship with her had not recovered sufficiently from the earlier episode at the farm for him to glean much background information, but he certainly did not want to antagonise her.

He did not notice the well-dressed man with pointed chin and cold, staring eyes sitting a few tables away, apparently sipping some white wine, the glass half full, no longer chilled. This time he had no need of any binoculars.

Chapter 12

I n Norwich Jane read that Joseph of Arimathea was said to have been a custodian of the Holy Grail and had fled to Egypt, along with Mary Magdalene. They later left Egypt, along with Joseph, Martha and Lazarus, safely returned from 'the other side' and still restored to life, apparently travelling to France. There were also old legends linking Mary to southern France, where parchments were found, ostensibly written in Latin, but which were alleged to contain secret messages in French.

She had to conclude that it was indeed possible that the casket had travelled from Jerusalem to France. But an underground pit in Norwich?

What happened between 1307 and 1327 was still not clear to her, although there was evidence that in 1312 all property owned by the Knights Templar had been transferred to the Knights of St. John, called the *Hospitallers* by what was known as a 'papal bull'.

Historical records verified that the Knights of St. John had come to Leith, in Scotland, in 1327. That part of the Order was known as the *Hospitaller Sisters of St. John of Jerusalem* and, crucially, they were originally based at the Hospital of St. Mary Magdalene, Jerusalem.

'All these hospitals,' Jane thought, 'I'll probably end up in one quite soon.'

The town of Leith was known for its trade with Northern Europe. The coat of arms of Leith is an image of a Black Madonna. She read about the Tau Cross, named from the Hebrew alphabet's last letter, which was transcribed as a 'T' in Greek. The Tau, she discovered, is a figure constructed of five lines and was the symbol of the Knights Templar of St. Anthony of Leith.

The old grandfather clock in the hall struck midnight. Jane reluctantly closed her laptop. She needed her sleep. She had now traced a logical path from Jerusalem to Scotland. As yet there was still no obvious connection with Norwich. It all seemed tenuous, the stuff of dreams.

★★★

Mike Burrows was well aware of the risks of his job. He was sanctioned by his employer, *Britain on Sunday*, but accepted he was on his own if discovered. His task was to find, by fair means or foul, a scoop - or infer one if necessary. Since the 2011 debacle with *The News of the World*, the media witch-hunt which followed, the curbs on press immorality, he had kept a low profile. He was classified as a 'paid sleeper' by his editor, Joe Culverhouse.

Easter Monday morning was not likely to bring him much joy, but he was sufficiently disciplined to pursue his target of the weekend for one more day. It was Easter and it would be an appropriate time for some kind of revelation. Chuckling at the prospect, he tapped in to listen to any voice messages that came his way.

Jane knew she had to confide in someone. She was not trained for dealing with such matters. She was outwardly calm, but inside her stomach was churning. Luke Matthews was a possibility, but she did not wish to involve him further. Perhaps if she had, life would have not taken such a fatal course. There were two choices. After all, her sister Mary could be trusted with any secret, as had been proved over many years. But, although she was married to a priest, she could not imagine Thomas being able to deal with an issue of such magnitude. It would destroy him. It had to be someone she had known as a student at university, her former lover, the Bishop himself. It would be difficult for both of them, but she had no other option.

A recorded message answered her call. *'I am sorry that I am otherwise engaged. Please either phone again or you can leave a message on my voicemail and I will respond as soon as I can.'*

Jane, keen to unburden herself, left a message.

'I need to see you urgently, very urgently. I fear I may have come across something which embraces mankind and all that you stand for and, by the way, I know you studied the life of one of your predecessors, the Fighting Bishop. I should like to ask you about him. It is relevant. I have read a guide book about him which, quite by luck, I found in the Cathedral, but you may be able to provide a fresh insight into his life, where he travelled, particularly if he went to Scotland. Please call me back as soon as possible.' She added some brief details of her discovery then concluded the call. Had it not been for the splinter wound, she would not have gone to the Cathedral on her way to the pharmacy. Much to her surprise, she found herself thanking God for His 'Divine Intervention'.

Mike Burrows could not believe his good fortune. He had that evening heard from one of his past acquaintances, someone he had studied with at college. Judas Swan had studied as a trainee journalist, but later developed a keen interest in medical science and genetics, undertaking a degree course as a mature student, followed by a highly successful career working as a forensic scientist in Norwich. They had kept in touch only intermittently, so it was a surprise for Mike Burrows when he received the call.

'Mike, hello, how the hell are you? Still delving into the private lives of the rich and famous?'

'Judo, great to hear from you; all well in Norwich? How are Joanna and the boys?' He couldn't remember their names.

'They're fine thanks. Listen carefully, Mike; I have come across something which will interest you. On the Sunday before Easter I set up some DNA analysis for a colleague which has turned up something unique in my experience. It was a piece of cloth, with bloodstains, found in an underground cellar during the excavation of a medieval site for a new development, here in Norwich. Our forensic analysis reveals that the cloth was worn, or came into contact with, a male who had no paternal DNA.

'Some hairs found embedded in the cloth also had this unique characteristic. The chances of this happening naturally are so remote as to be irrelevant. Some pieces of parchment or scrolls were also sent for analysis by a Professor Jane Clifford-Oxbury, an archivist who works for the local authority. That's all I know, but you can guess what I'm thinking. She will have this report shortly, so leave it a day or so before you make any move. How on earth this has found its way to Norfolk God only knows, as it were. Over to you.'

'Bloody hell, Judo, are you quite sure?'

'Absolutely.'

'Cheers for this. I owe you one.'

Mike Burrows realised this could be the universal scoop of all time. This would be lauded for generations. He phoned his editor on his red personal mobile – rarely used. He did not want a record of the call circulating amongst his colleagues and fellow hacks. This being a Bank Holiday Monday, the day after publication, he guessed his editor would not be at work. That was the correct call. He was washing up the family meal – hardly imaginable. Perhaps Joe needed the practice, as he was rarely at home.

Joe listened intently. 'If true, it's too big a story, but you will understand that I need more. Pretend you are doing a feature. Find out about this professor, what her work entails. You said she is an archivist and, presumably, a historian as well. Do your research on her and then arrange to meet. This conversation has never taken place and I scarcely need to remind you of our constant companion, the Regulation of Investigatory Powers Act, not to mention the Leveson Inquiry. Neither do I have any wish to be summoned to appear before the Culture, Media and Sports Select Committee.'

★★★

Jane walked nervously through the main gate leading to Bishop's House. She turned left, following the signs to the Bishop's Office, the second door on the left. The subject matter of her visit was bad enough, without all the extra tension of meeting him again, the one love of her life. The buzz of the intercom sent a chilling quiver through her whole body. There was no going back now. His secretary let her in, then took her round to the main door of Bishop's House and through into the hallway, where she caught a glimpse of his wife at the end of the corridor. She knew 'that woman' had seen her, but neither acknowledged the other. That would never change.

By midday Jane was sitting in his study. They generally tried to avoid each other. It was easier that way. Their meetings were rare, and often difficult; there was so much history, too much endured between them, too many bitter memories. She recalled the last time she had been to see him. It had been tense; for a bishop from whose lips words usually flowed like a river in swell, he had dried to a trickle. There had been long silences.

The study walls were lined with books and DVDs; the desk was clear, save for one book, and it was not a Bible. Upside down across his desk it looked like a book about his predecessors. He never used to be that well organised, she recalled; it must be Rebecca's influence. Life might have been very different, very different indeed. Why had she held such sway over him?

Initially Bishop Marcus Banham was surprisingly calm and composed. She knew his faith had always been rock-solid, even when he was a student, and faith was crucial to his Church. He had once told her that proof, evidence of His existence, beyond doubt, would nullify faith as a concept, telling her that the foundations of the Christian Church were built on the dogma of faith, that people should come to it, find it for themselves, have a choice, earn their reward in eternity, not be simply told to toe the line as compliant automatons. 'Without faith we are nothing,' he had said.

It was evident to her that a whole new world could prevail, starting from this small room in Norwich. She thought about Thomas and his brother, one a priest, the other an atheist. She tried to imagine Peter swallowing large slices of humble pie, his world of logic turned upside down by the ultimate proof of an existence beyond reason.

Bishop Banham interrupted her train of thought.

'How are you, Jane? It's been a long time. 'It's been difficult, knowing you are here in Norwich. I hope life has not been too hard for you.' He said it kindly, trying to put her at ease, as if he really meant it.

'It's not easy, but we agreed it should be this way,' she replied coolly, instantly regretting her aloofness. It was a natural defence mechanism. She knew she was not good at such things - emotions were not her scene. She had discarded them to the annals of history, or thought she had.

Much to her surprise, his next words were: 'Shall we start with Henry Despenser?' Jane presumed it was to get this out of the way before he got on to the serious business of the consequences of her discovery. It also avoided any meaningless small talk as a cover for their discomfort. Or perhaps he was playing for time, anxious about what was to follow.

'As you know, he was Bishop here from 1370, when he was only twenty-seven, to the date of his death in 1406. You may also know that he combined, controversially, the role of a soldier with that of a priest, excelling at both. I expect you have also worked out that his confidant and close associate, John Derlyngton, supported him throughout that time. Like us, they were contemporaries at Oxford and both studied law.' He paused. He looked at her, to see her expression. She smiled; that warmth was still there.

'Henry's interest was civil law, and John's was canon law. John was his 'Vicar General' from 1371. They were very close. Henry came under threat of impeachment after a failed battle in Flanders under his command and, given what you said in your message, he might well have given some precious possessions to John Derlyngton. It is perfectly feasible, and he could well have hidden them at the monastery, given that he was Master there. As for Scotland, there is a potential link. In July 1385 Henry left Norwich to join the King's army, led by John of Gaunt, in its venture north to the Scottish borders. The Scottish army, aided and abetted by the French, was threatening an invasion of England.'

'Yes, and Henry loved a fight, didn't he?' added Jane.

'Indeed he did. He was soon at the forefront of the expedition, accompanied by his crusading banner. They crossed the border, and burnt down the Abbeys of Melrose and Newbattle. However, the Scots were nowhere to be seen. They had ventured south west down to Carlisle. Frustrated by lack of action, the English army resorted to the usual pursuits of a marauding bunch of soldiers, indulging in a campaign of rape and pillage.

'Henry wanted no part of this and returned home. However, before then, the army did get as far as Edinburgh and probably Leith, being so close. The Knights Templar of St. Anthony of Leith had been based there and founded a hospital.....'

'Another one,' interrupted Jane. 'Leith,' she thought, her blood pressure rising as she excitedly recalled that her own research had led her there.

'Again, it is perfectly possible that Henry took possession of some of their treasures, either by force or perhaps even by agreement, given his affinity to soldiering and their likely respect for the Knights Templar. Either way you have a possible trail to Norwich.'

At that point the Bishop again paused. 'Now tell me exactly what have you discovered that's so important?'

Jane gave a full description of what they had found in that ghostly old cellar beneath the swan pit – ironically just round the corner from his Palace. For the first time, she could see the flood-tide of emotion beginning to flow; the enormity of what she had described was weighing heavily upon him. This time she had transferred the burden of responsibility to him. Outwardly calm as ever, inside a maelstrom. She had seen it all before. The lines etched on his forehead were protruding, the wrinkles more and more prominent as their conversation developed. She could see his fingers had tightened; she had long forgotten, or suppressed, her memories of his only visible reactions to the impact of stress. It was there again now, plain to see, as she outlined what she had found in that eerie cellar. When she had finished the Bishop spoke slowly, gravely, carefully considering every word.

'Your discovery, here in this historic city, with its two cathedrals, one Catholic and the other Anglican, if authenticated, and I must emphasise that, will rock the religious community and the world beyond. It may never be the same. You might think I should be jumping for joy. In some ways I am, but the notion of faith has sustained us for centuries; the sense of finding it, the belief that comes with that personal revelation, is an integral part of coming to know God. If Jesus really is **proven** to be the product of a virgin birth, as your discovery suggests, the whole basis of our theology could be fundamentally changed. I have read that the odds of this occurring naturally are billions to one against. There are many in the Christian faith who do not necessarily believe in the virgin birth itself, but I can see that your discovery will be construed by many as evidence for God's existence. **For doubt and the wonder of faith, read certainty.** That is how it will be perceived in some quarters – a devastating blow to the concept of faith.' He paused before continuing: 'What about the implications for other faiths? It hardly bears thinking about. This is as sensitive an issue as it is possible for me to imagine. You will appreciate I have thought of nothing else since your call. It must be very carefully handled. Get your cloth re-tested by the laboratory as confirmation.'

'It's already under way.'

'Please then, speak to no one. As ever, I know I can rely on your discretion. You know how grateful I am for that. We will need to keep this information within a very small caucus, but that is a matter for the Archbishop of Canterbury. I will contact him as soon as we have finished. Should the blood tests be substantiated I expect he will inform York and, yes, the Archbishop of Westminster, to represent the Catholics. I am tempted to tell my counterpart at the Catholic Cathedral, but not until I get permission. The Archbishop of Canterbury will no doubt consult the Pope in the Vatican. The consequences are potentially so far-reaching that I anticipate the Prime Minister will have to be informed at an early stage.'

'And Her Majesty, as Head of the Church?'

'Yes indeed. Above all, this must be kept out of the media. Leave everything to me. You must get that confirmation from the laboratory as soon as possible, hopefully tomorrow. No delay. Please leave me now, I need time alone.'

Arriving home, Jane wished all this had never happened. Just as she collapsed into her armchair, drained and exhausted, the phone rang. Still in shock at the enormity of it all, she nervously picked up her landline receiver.

'Hello Aunt Jane, it's me, Paul. I just thought I'd see how you are. Enjoyed Easter?' he said, cheekily. 'In a coma after Dad's Good Friday sermon?' This was a little joke between them, illustrative of their mutual fondness.

'It's great here, the hills, the forests, the lakes, the mountains, even herding the sheep! You'd be in paradise sampling the wines, the nearest thing to heaven you'll ever find.'

'He's right about that,' she reflected, her family secret weighing heavily upon her. She could not imagine ever getting to a heaven which she had not believed existed.

'Everywhere you go there are vineyards, hundreds of them. The people are so friendly too; they really are sincere about where you come from, where you are visiting – none of that "have a nice day" stuff.'

'How about the young women?' asked Jane suggestively.

'They're OK,' replied Paul, in a tone of deliberate understatement.

'I see. Tell me about her when you get home. Not long now, is it?'

'No; flying back on Friday. First the short flight from Christchurch to Auckland, then on to Hong Kong, then to Heathrow.'

'Cattle class, I presume, unless you've met a millionaire's daughter.'

'Fat chance of that,' Paul replied, suddenly thinking he knew little of Laura's background.

'Have a safe flight,' concluded Jane. Having been caught unawares she had not asked about her brother, Oliver, or his wife with the funny name.

Paul was left with a sense of unease. Why was Laura less than forthcoming about her family? He knew that would be the first thing his aunt would ask on his return, and he would have little to say.

Within moments of Jane putting down the phone its shrill tone again interrupted her thoughts. 'Not now. I don't want to speak to anyone; I need some space.'

'This is an urgent message. Please listen carefully. You still have time left to claim a refund of premiums on your payment protection plan. The banks have recently lost a case in the high court, etc., etc.,' concluding, *'Please press five to speak to an adviser.'*

'Go away!' she shouted down the phone at the pre-recorded message. No sooner had she slammed down the receiver than it rang again. Jane was tempted not to answer, but it was a different number. Gingerly she listened.

'Is that Jane Clifford-Oxbury? My name is Mike Burrows; I'm a journalist, researching a piece on

"Archaeology and the Church". I would very much appreciate an interview, just a few minutes of your time.'

This was the last thing she wanted, particularly just now.

'Surely you should interview an archaeologist, not an archivist?'

'I'm looking for a different slant; you must have come across some interesting records, or indeed prepared them yourself. I have seen your online work for the Old Monastery Hospital in Norwich covering several centuries. It's very impressive, absolutely fascinating. It's definitely you I wish to see.'

He knew flattery would get him everywhere; it always did.

'I'm extremely busy at the moment…'

Burrows would not take 'no' for an answer.

'Look, by chance, I'm in Norwich on Wednesday. It won't take more than one hour, that's a promise. I'll call back later to make the arrangements. No, actually, it's best if we make them now. I know where you live. 'I'll call on Wednesday around 7pm. Many thanks Jane.'

With that, the phone went dead. She did not like his familiarity, and she would have preferred to meet elsewhere. She tried 'ring-back' but the number was withheld. She assumed he had got her address from the electoral roll, or even the phone directory. There was nothing she could do other than be out, but that would only defer the inevitable; journalists, she reckoned, were more difficult than salesmen to rebuff. The appointment was made; she would have to go through with it, and she never could resist talking about her work. She hoped it would restore a sense of normality to her life. She was mistaken.

Chapter 13

T he Rt Revd Marcus Banham, Bishop of Norwich, was aware that the Church of England was not structured for a high-profile crisis, one which required immediate leadership and decision-making. Its procedures and protocols had existed for centuries and were instituted for an earlier age. None of its venerable institutions or councils was designed for instant crisis management or the unrelenting glare of the 24/7 media circus.

In common with other senior bishops, he had a private line to the Archbishop of Canterbury, to be used only *in extremis*. Their conversation was brief and to the point. His instruction was to submit a report from Professor Jane Clifford-Oxbury detailing her discovery, including the authenticated DNA report. Until then, he must not confide in anyone.

Alone at home, and fearful of speaking to anyone, Jane heard her computer ping once more to denote an incoming email. It was from Luke.

'Jane, I've attached the second DNA report from Judas at the laboratory. *It confirms the first one.*'

It was not what Jane really wanted to hear. Whilst she felt it would be a godsend to get publicity for her work in the face of potentially swingeing cuts to her department's budget, she had quickly dismissed that line of thought. She much preferred obscurity to the dazzling glare of the searchlights which she now suspected would be coming her way. She also had another fear. She had never married, but was no virgin. The days, or rather nights, at university had seen to that. Had it been love or infatuation, her fling with Marcus Banham? Either way, the end of that relationship had left her devastated. She had never been able to cross that particular threshold again, but here he was again, back in her life, with another shared secret between them. The flame, so long extinguished, was sparking inside, threatening to re-ignite that long-forgotten passion. She was spending too much time on her own, she knew that, but she had no choice.

Nervously, her fingers shaking, taking an age to type the momentous message, then another pause before pressing 'send', Jane emailed her report to the Bishop, including the DNA confirmation. He forwarded it to the Archbishop's private email address. With the aid of his secretary, he sent it encrypted.

The civil servants at the Cyber Surveillance Centre at GCHQ in Cheltenham intercepted the two emails, one from Jane, the other from the Bishop, using their sophisticated echelon system designed to protect the nation's security. It was not difficult for the experts to decipher the encryption code used by the Bishop. The Head of Security at GCHQ immediately contacted the minister in charge of cyber security at the Cabinet Office.

★★★

On Wednesday afternoon, Mike Burrows knocked on Jane's door. She showed him into her sitting room. He spotted her desk in the corner, papers all over it. He accepted the offer of tea. As she disappeared to the kitchen he seized his chance. He tiptoed stealthily across the faded Persian carpet towards her desk, careful not to trip over its frayed edges. It was worth a try. There on the desk, to his great excitement, was a copy of the confirmatory DNA report which she had innocently printed off for her file. Although a regular user of IT technology, she still preferred paper storage at home. And this was so important that she just had to keep a paper copy in case of any technology failure or worse. On this occasion she had decided to take the hard copy print to her office to scan it into her system herself, rather than risk an email which might be read by the local authority security team.

It took him only moments to pick up the document, take photographs on his mobile, and return to his chair as the old-fashioned kettle whistled its warning of her impending return. He was sitting comfortably when she arrived, tea tray in hand. Afterwards, as he got back into his car, he congratulated himself on how he had conducted the interview. It had not been difficult; a few questions here, a few prompts there, and she was telling him all about the marvellously preserved records of the Old Hospital, how they had survived through hundreds of years. He knew all that before he arrived, having spent the day on the internet site where her work was available for all to see. It had been a useful distraction for Jane and, once started, she felt it had gone well and looked forward to an article which never materialised.

That night, alone in her bed but not in her thoughts, Jane was convinced she heard a whispered voice from outside. She tensed and crept to the window, carefully peeling back the curtain. Nothing untoward, she got back into bed. Her mind was in a whirl and now she was imagining things in the dead of night. Sleep would not return. She tossed to and fro, her toiling mind beset with anxiety, even fear of what lay ahead. Then she heard a whistling sound – wind, a bird, or perhaps a cat?

She managed to doze. Next morning, brewing her habitual mug of caffeine, she opened the front door to pick up the milk. Her mind elsewhere, she knocked the bottle over, spilling the contents, a trail of milk oozing into the rose bed. She froze. There were scuffed but distinct footprints around 'Mary's Roses', as she called them, just to the right of the door. They had not been left by an animal. She knew at once that this had to be connected to her discovery. She sensed she was heading towards a dark tunnel. It was chilling, frightening, like something out of a novel, unreal. She rarely read fiction, but now she felt immersed in it.

'They are watching my every move. I am alone. I cannot talk to anyone, not even Marcus.' She wanted to phone him, even to warn him, but she knew she should not. He had enough to contend with without her insecurities. Besides, 'that woman' might well answer the phone. What had he seen in her? She still could not understand. A lot of things seem to be beyond understanding. She worked with the past. She dreaded the future.

★★★

'Prime Minister, you will recall that conversation about the archaeological find in Norfolk. Well, I have more bad news. A new flurry of emails between the archivist professor and the Bishop of Norwich, including the Archbishop of Canterbury, suggests the find has been authenticated; meaning the person to whom it belonged was born of a virgin. The emails also suggest links have been made with a Middle Eastern origin.'

'Holy Moses!' exclaimed the Prime Minister.

After a short pause for reflection, Prime Minister Benson addressed the Cabinet Secretary, his baritone voice stern, but measured.

'Sir Julian, call an emergency meeting. Not in the MOD bunker; out of town, but not Chequers - too obvious; perhaps Churchill's place, Chartwell.' He liked the sound of Chartwell, it had a certain aura about it. 'There must be as few people in the loop as possible: the Deputy PM, the Home Secretary, my Permanent Private Secretary, the Head of the Civil Service, the Commissioner of the Metropolitan Police, the Archbishops of Canterbury and Westminster, and their confidential aides. It must be held in secret. Tomorrow at 7.30pm. Instruct them to cancel any other commitment. Dress it up as a dinner party in case of leaks, black tie and all that malarkey. And get that bloody cloth independently analysed in one of our own laboratories.'

'Already in hand, sir'.

It became clear to those attending that this matter was potentially too controversial to become public knowledge at this early stage. Crucially, once in the public domain, it was felt that any perception of this alleged Truth could become very inflammatory in a multicultural society, regardless of its validity. Even if the further tests came back negative, the Prime Minister realised that once a rumour had started it could spread like wildfire in a world of instant global communication. The Cabinet Secretary's warning was pertinent: 'So many assertions nowadays are presented as fact that before long everyone believes them, Prime Minister.'

Denials or confirmations would both be viewed with scepticism and suspicion by the various factions. He was haunted by the words of his Cabinet Secretary on a previous occasion: 'Perception is everything, Prime Minister.'

He envisaged all sorts of scenarios, some potentially alarming. It seemed odd to him that such an apparently wondrous moment for Christianity could have such potentially dire consequences. Nonetheless, the initial briefing and the clandestine meeting instilled these fears deep within the Prime Minister's mind. The Archbishops had requested more time to conclude their discussions with each other and with the Papal authorities. They would meet again on 14th April.

★★★

Jane was unable to concentrate on her day job. By mid-morning she decided to take some long-overdue leave. She returned home to take stock of the enormity of the discovery in the grounds of the Old Monastery Hospital. In the turmoil of events, she had forgotten to take her diary to work. Neither had she noticed the date, Friday 13th, the date the Templars fled La Rochelle. Entering her study she did not notice that it was on the top of a pile of papers on her desk. When she had left in the early morning it had been underneath – which was why she had overlooked taking it with her. Picking it up, she checked her arrangements for the weekend. She looked forward to the concert in the grounds of the Anglican Cathedral on Saturday evening. Without thinking, she telephoned the Bishop's Palace to check the time, expecting a secretary to answer. But it was his wife who answered, her tone wary, realising who was calling;

Jane, the woman she knew to be her husband's former lover.

'What can I do for you?' she asked, curtly. They had never seen eye to eye. Rebecca had come into the Bishop's life after he left university. They had met at theological college, thrown together in thought, word and, presumably, deed. They had inevitably met a few times and Rebecca had seemed cold, even hostile. Perhaps it was simply some kind of defence mechanism in her presence. Jane had to acknowledge that Rebecca's gregarious nature enabled her to get on with most people she met – except her. As a more introverted academic, Jane knew also that she was not cut out to be a bishop's wife. But, back then, no one knew he would become a bishop.

Preoccupied with the underlying tension of speaking to each other, neither heard the slight click as Jane replaced her handset. Other than attending the concert, her time was her own this weekend – or so she thought.

★★★

Her brother-in-law, Revd Thomas Morgan, alone in his study now that Peter and his wife had gone home, summoned the enthusiasm to pick up one of his brother's books. Mary was at her very expensive hair salon (at least Thomas thought so) for he was born of a generation of men who begrudged even the cost of a light trim. The rectory was cold and austere, with large rooms and high ceilings. It was too expensive to update with modern furnishings and, in any case, it did not belong to them. They (in reality Mary) had tried to redecorate once, but the wallpaper soon peeled off the damp surface. Thomas was not a natural when it came to DIY. He stood idly by, issuing instructions with no clue how to implement them.

He looked at the pile of books Peter had lent him. He felt the books staring back at him, daring him to pick them up. He did, but felt like a heretic. Inside was a message from Peter. It read:

'Well done, dear brother, you have started on a journey which will prove your faith is a delusion. Good luck!'

It took Thomas a few minutes to calm down. 'Is my faith really a delusion?' Thomas wondered, not for the first time. He checked his English dictionary. It declared starkly: *'Delusion is a false opinion or idea, a false, unshakeable belief indicating a severe mental disorder.'*

That last part really shook him. He knew of suffering priests for whom the Church provided a safety net, more reassuringly known as a 'retreat'. Except that he suspected many such places were really psychiatric hospitals and it wouldn't do to let these lost souls loose on the unsuspecting public. An ageing priest he had much admired, even revered, had gone to one of them after being accused of 'inappropriate behaviour'. Thomas knew it had been hushed up. Thomas, suffering one of his spells of depression, felt vulnerable.

He chose not to believe the literal truth of all the biblical stories. He had read somewhere that the chance of a virgin birth was so against the odds that many believed it belonged to the world of fantasy. But miracles do happen, he accepted. In any case, belief did not rely on chance. He had long felt, unlike his brother, that the beauty of the Creation, of nature, could not have happened by accident. The 'chance' versus 'design' debate did not worry him unduly. Both relied on outlandish odds. Nor indeed did the theory of evolution and Darwin's theory of natural selection. Like the theists, he believed survival of the fittest to be God's way of developing His creation, even if it took millennia to do it. He was well aware that his personal view was open to challenge by Peter and his not-very-merry band of atheists. After all, Peter had once disdainfully said to him that, if you believe in God, you couldn't lose! It sustained you during your lifetime and you would never know if you were wrong. His brother considered that hypocritical, indicating a flawed faith. But he would, wouldn't he?

'The man's beyond redemption,' Thomas would mutter in exasperation.

He heard the crunch of car tyres on the shingled drive. He quickly turned down the stove, gathered up his brother's books, opened the window so the room would cool, and settled himself by the wood-fired oven in the kitchen to await Mary's arrival. It did not occur to him that the old three-bar electric stove which had been warming his study was nearly as expensive as Mary's stylist. She was fully aware of her husband's little antics, and certainly did not begrudge herself the monthly pampering. She joked with her sister Jane about her 'great escape', as she called it. After all, she was the vicar's wife; would he notice or, even better, compliment her? She knew the answer.

Living with Thomas was not an easy existence - he could be tetchy and irritable. He was fussy, too, about his food, about cleanliness, about crooked electrical sockets and pictures not straight after Mary had dusted them. Then the old standard lamp over his chair would not function because the plug had been removed when Mary had been busy vacuuming the carpet. It seemed sometimes as if she spent her domestic life treading on eggshells.

His irritation would usually surface as the prelude to a period of depression which would last for days. He would say little, only speaking when spoken to, quiet as a church mouse, no guffaws of nervous laughter to be heard. But she understood; she knew the reasons, and not all were derived from his religious insecurities. He felt ashamed, guilty about the deception to which he was party, but it was not his fault and she always tried to reassure him of that. If anything, she would tell him in her fiercely supportive way: 'You are the Good Samaritan in all this.' At other times, when relaxed and at ease with himself, he would be kind, gentle and thoughtful. Generally, he kept his thoughts to himself.

Mary busied herself with her charity interests, particularly *Save the Children*, working tirelessly with their fundraising, as well as helping out at the Cathedral gift shop. One of the few attractions of Thomas' calling, and the old rectory that came with it, was the chance to restore the overgrown grass tennis-court near her much-cherished rose garden. She had been no mean player herself, having competed as a junior in the local tournaments from genteel Frinton in Essex, to Cromer and Hunstanton in her native Norfolk. She also hoped Paul would find the time to visit the Botanic Gardens in Christchurch, with their famed collection of roses, and send through some pictures. Despite years of devoted care, it was rare to find a day when the east wind or dampness of the grass, or latterly the moles, allowed her to set foot on her beloved court. She fought a running battle with the little furry creatures, liking neither traps nor poison as a deterrent. Unfortunately, her husband had neither the expertise of a John McEnroe on the court, nor that of a pest controller off it.

Mary Morgan was not afraid to confront difficult issues. Her tireless work for the homeless bore testament to that. She would fight for what she believed in, and that included her husband. In all her endeavours she was well aware that life had been kind to her, but some sixth sense seemed to be warning her it would not last.

★★★

Late in the afternoon of 14th April the bombshell dropped. *Britain on Sunday* contacted the Downing Street Press Office to advise them they had heard rumours of secret meetings. They had a story which hit at the heart of Christianity and intended to publish the next day, Sunday 15th April. The Press Office informed the Cabinet Secretary, who contacted the Prime Minister by telephone. His Permanent Private Secretary was unable to take any calls – it being Saturday, he was 'working-out' at his local health centre. This was how he portrayed it. He was actually stretched out in the steam room, awaiting his turn in the sauna.

'Prime Minister, we have a problem,' announced the Cabinet Secretary. 'We don't know the full extent of their story or how they got it, but my advice is we cannot take the risk of publication.'

'Do whatever is necessary – meet the Editor, get an injunction, whatever it takes. This must not get into the public domain.'

'Yes, sir,' replied Sir Julian. 'There's a second problem. The cloth has gone missing in transit between the Norwich laboratory and our own in London.'

'How do you mean, "Gone missing"?'

'The scientists in Norwich gave it to a courier on a motor bike. Apparently he seemed to have all the right credentials, showed some ID and signed for the package. He has never turned up. The ID given was false.'

He could not believe his ears. 'What sort of crass arrangement is that? It should have been in an armoured car, police escort, blue lights flashing,' he exclaimed, his tone frustrated, turning to anger. 'Get it found,' he said sharply, 'And have this archivist brought to London for questioning and, perhaps, for her safety.'

It was too late. Jane Clifford-Oxbury had left home in the early evening of Saturday, 14th April to attend the performance of Handel's *Messiah* in the Cathedral grounds. Aware that she had grown into the stereotypical portrayal of an ageing professor, with pale complexion, and hair stiff and wiry from long personal neglect, she had been to the beauty salon and had her hair dyed back to its natural auburn colour, shedding the grey which had taken over. She had never bothered much about her looks in recent years. She had admitted to herself the transformation was entirely due to meeting Marcus again. She realised it was childish, but it did give her a lift. Besides, her find meant she was likely to have a more public profile in the coming days or weeks.

It was only a short walk to the Cathedral. A car with blacked-out windows pulled up beside her; two burly men grabbed her, bundling her into the back between them. It happened in seconds. There was no time to react.

To the relief of those members of the Government in the know, *Britain on Sunday* had, at the last moment, agreed not to publish 'in the national interest'. Mike

Burrows was denied his moment of glory, at least for now.

The Bishop of Norwich was not invited to the meeting that Saturday evening. The whole issue was out of his hands and he could be relied upon to keep his own counsel.

He had months ago been asked to say a few words of welcome to the musicians and the audience who were now assembling for a concert on the Cathedral lawns. It was overcast, but rain was not expected. Bishop Banham was well-known for his easy style. His pithy and humorous words of welcome got the evening off to a relaxed start:

'My Lord Mayor, The Lord Mayor's Escort, or rather, Consort, I should say, (to suppressed chuckles all around), fellow concert-goers; it is my great pleasure to welcome you all to the grounds of this magnificent cathedral. We are privileged to have with us the *Norwich Broadland Orchestra*, all the way from their rehearsal at St Andrew's Hall, and a special welcome to our soloists, Barbaroni Hubbard and Antonio Busselli, whose voices will echo round the cloisters. You will be delighted to learn I will not be singing tonight. My text this evening…, no, it's not a sermon, is taken from a "sent message" to the Almighty on my tablet, the current version of the ones Moses used in Sinai. I have requested a fine evening for the *Messiah* to visit our cathedral. Lord, hear our prayer!' At that very moment the irritating jingle of a mobile phone pierced the silence, interrupting the Bishop's address. The Bishop paused, looking not a little displeased. He was not used to an intrusion when in full flow. As the mobile's shrill tune echoed round the cloisters, it dawned on Bishop Banham that the sound was rather familiar and from near at hand. Very near in fact, he realised, as he desperately fumbled inside his regalia to find the offending object. Putting on a brave face, he calmly held the phone to his ear before replacing it into his nearest pocket.

'It's a message from God, replying to my text. You will be delighted to hear it's not going to rain this evening. Now, let's hear the orchestra,' he concluded. With that, the Bishop handed over to the conductor to commence proceedings.

'He could talk for England,' whispered Thomas, in the midst of the audience.

'You're just jealous,' whispered Mary; 'And where's Jane? She promised to be here.'

They had been due to meet beforehand. Afterwards, Bishop Banham wondered how the clandestine governmental meeting was going. He also wondered what had happened to Jane. He had expected to see her during the wine-and-canapé reception after the concert. Her sister, Mary, accompanied by Thomas, had come through for drinks, but Jane had not been with them. She had certainly been invited and he had welcomed all the guests, but she had not been among them. Later, back in his study, he rang her mobile. No reply. He had no rational grounds for alarm, but he did have a niggling apprehension.

During the course of that evening two men entered Jane's apartment. Under cover of darkness they removed her computer and any papers or documents they could find. The burglary, if that is what it was, had been meticulously planned and executed with extreme professionalism.

That Saturday, from the Pope to the President, to the Secretary General, the members of the inner cabal in the Vatican City were aware their long-held status as guardians of the faith, maintained through generations, could soon cease. If this English find were to be authenticated, as now seemed likely, 'faith' as a concept would be in jeopardy. On the other hand, those who truly believed, and who did not rely on faith, would continue to believe, undeterred by the apparent decline of faith.

Their initial request to delay the London meeting had reflected the controversy within the Vatican. Some held the view that God wanted believers to come to Him through faith, some that the discovery must herald His second coming. Others relished the power their status would bring, sensing that a new age would dawn with the Christian church in the vanguard. The moment had come; although it wasn't epiphany, the inevitable 'revelation' was imminent. The Vatican Press Office would reveal all. It would get in first.

In Rome, a coded message was circulating. It was short and to the point, simply stating: 'The Kingdom of Heaven is at Hand'. It had been circulated by the 'Prefect of the Congregation for the Doctrine of Faith'. The Archbishop of Westminster received the message; his Church was ready to act. Were the Anglicans?

Chapter 14

After the incident with the man with binoculars, Laura had made the arrangements to get away for a few days. She had suggested a trip south to Queenstown, provided it was in her car and not the rusty old banger that Paul drove. They headed south on the main highway SH1, passing through a colourful patchwork of hills, with the peaks of the Southern Alps in the distance.

'What do you know about the Vatican?' asked Laura, probing, hoping he would let something slip; reveal his motives. 'You studied aspects of religious history at university.'

'You know full well I came over here to get away from all that,' he replied testily.

'Just for my own curiosity, Paul, my spiritual search; the Vatican is central to the Christian faith, after all.'

This time, in the happy anticipation of a few days away together, Paul was altogether more relaxed and responsive; 'A good omen,' thought Laura.

'It's the spiritual nerve centre of the Roman Catholic Church. It is the smallest independent State in the world, outside Italian jurisdiction. It maintains the highest security, with some two hundred and fifty Papal Swiss Guards and a similar number of CCTV cameras. Some thirty thousand people visit every day. They have been particularly sensitive since Pope John Paul was shot from within the crowd in 1981. It has its own radio station. 'It's almost impossible for journalists to gain access. It covers about one hundred and ten acres and has thousands of employees – even women,' he added mischievously.

'There must be a lot to hide; treasures, secrets.'

'Indeed there are. I believe their archives are held underground on the northern side of the city.'

'Do you know what treasures they hold?'

'No one outside the Vatican really knows. There are rumoured to be thousands of sacred objects gathered over the centuries, many from holy sites. Some were seized by Napoleon and taken to Paris. Others were rumoured to have been taken by the Knights Templar. When Napoleon's empire crumbled, there were just too many to take back to Rome, and many treasures were lost or destroyed. I think I'm right in saying there are some fifty-nine miles of corridors in the Museum, all climate-controlled.'

'Sorry to keep asking questions, but I'm intrigued with what secrets they hold.'

'Laura, do I really have to compete with *Abba*? Can't you turn it down a bit?'

'Sorry, but I get carsick sometimes on long journeys; it helps keep my mind off it,' Laura replied, unconvincingly. At least, with her sitting beside him in the passenger seat, he could not see the guilty expression on her face. Laura did not like telling lies, nor did she like the prospect of that creep, Agent Neon, listening to every word.

'You will soon be able to find out quite a bit more. Although no archives are made public until seventy-five years after a Pope's death, some one hundred of the most significant documents held in their secret archives are now on public display in Rome's Capitoline Museums, until September, I believe.'

'No doubt these particular records will have been carefully selected to portray the Catholic Church in its best light,' added Laura.

'That goes without saying. But even so, they do apparently contain some interesting documents, spanning from the eighth century to modern times.'

'But not from the first century? The gospels of Thomas or Mary Magdalene will not be among them, then?' Laura asked. Paul paused, thinking it bizarre that his parents were Thomas and Mary, before answering her question.

'No, but we don't know what the butler saw.'

'How do you mean?'

'The Pope's personal butler has allegedly copied numerous documents; whether they will surface somewhere, who knows? Anyway my Aunt Jane, who is an archivist, believes there are plans to digitalise much of it and make it available online. Even now, the Museum displays will throw light on many historical characters and events, including the Knights Templar, the heresy trial of Galileo, who had the audacity to claim the earth revolved around the sun, and also Martin Luther and Henry VIII, to name but a few. Never before have such important documents been allowed to leave the Vatican, albeit for a short time only.'

'Except some pieces of the Turin Shroud,' interjected Laura. She had always been intrigued by that piece of cloth. 'Is it a fake or a fraud, Paul?'

'That's another story altogether,' concluded Paul, and then suddenly screaming, 'Shit!' as he braked, swearing loudly, using words she had not heard coming out of his mouth before. He swerved sideways to avoid a gleaming, chrome-fronted 1960's trucker lorry, with its large, protruding engine casing in the front, heading straight towards them in the middle of the highway. In hindsight, Paul reflected that it was a good thing that they drove on the left, as in England, otherwise his instinctive reaction might not have kicked in to save them from a nasty collision, more likely worse. Shaken, but impressed with Paul's manoeuvre, Laura suggested they stop at a roadside restaurant for a coffee, which became a light lunch as they talked, their conversation drowned by the ceaseless monotone of popular music from the loudspeakers nearby.

The incident with the truck disturbed Laura. Was it deliberate? Who could it have been? Surely not her own side? Or had she been rumbled by Paul's Muslim friends, identified as a spy? Were both their lives in danger? She tried not to let her anxiety show.

Queenstown was bathed in blue skies for the duration of their stay. They ate and slept, laughed and loved, besotted with each other, oblivious of those around them. They strolled around the waterside, took a trip on the lake, and scared the living daylights out of each other on a jet-boat ride. After the exhilaration of the descent in the skyline gondola, they particularly enjoyed a supper at a nearby bistro, a meal of marinated olives, chorizo, pumpkin with feta, and pork belly roast for Paul, fresh fish for Laura, accompanied by her favourite lyonnaise potatoes adorned with crispy green mange-tout. Somehow they sensed they should savour every precious moment away from normality and lost to the outside world, or so Paul thought. Laura suspected otherwise but simply did not care. The man with the piercing eyes kept well hidden. Even Laura, infatuated as she was, did not spot him. An evening in an alehouse was particularly memorable, surrounded by hordes of boisterous rugby fans glued to the television screens showing the latest international against the Australian Wallabies, so busy shouting and drinking that half of them missed the only try of the game, as did Paul and Laura, straining to get a glimpse of the replay.

The end of their romantic escape came too quickly. On the long drive back to Christchurch there were long silences, with only small talk to fill the void, both mindful of Paul's impending flight back to England. It was tedious listening for Agent Neon, and often impossible with the music blaring.

'Turn the bloody thing off, girl; you should know better. Just wait till I next see you,' he shouted in frustration.

Arriving back in Christchurch, Paul was relieved to see there was no sign of the man with the binoculars. Entering her flat, he asked again: 'You've still not told me much about your family, your background, your childhood.'

Laura had long dreaded that question. Evasively, she reminded Paul he was supposed to be meeting someone that evening.

'Who's the lucky person you're seeing? she asked, although she already knew the answer.

'Hussain; and maybe some of his friends, the ones I met at the café. Promise me you will tell me about your family next time,' added Paul as he headed for the door. 'You also promised a swim with the dolphins. I can't go back home without at least one swim.'

'I promise. It's only about an hour's drive. There's a deserted scenic road back round the mountain, with lots of secluded stopping-places,' she concluded. The seductive tone to her voice was not lost on Paul, stoking the fire inside him. Although time was running out, she felt that would provide a better opportunity to find out more about Hussain Barzal and his colleagues.

'Can't wait, but I must go; I'll call you later.' And with that he was gone.

The lambing season was long over and there was nothing Paul could usefully do to earn money on the farm. His visit was at an end. He had repaired fences, rebuilt stone walls, but he could not break down the wall of silence about the past; his relationship with Kiwita and Oliver had remained strained.

Laura had not gleaned much at all from her target. It worried her that Paul revealed so little about his Muslim friends. She could so easily have planted a listening device in his mobile, but had buckled at such an act of betrayal. Had this been a bad mistake – another one? This lack of information would not go down well with her superiors.

Paul's flight had been booked and he would be flying back overnight. Laura took the short afternoon flight with him from Christchurch to Auckland, telling him it was funded from her Trust. She felt ashamed at telling another lie.

They were both all too aware that they had little time left together. Laura had suggested a seafood restaurant on

Princes Wharf overlooking the harbour. She had booked a table on the veranda overlooking flotillas of luxury yachts, a multitude of brightly-coloured hulls, halliards tinkling in the breeze. It was tailor-made for a romantic evening, the gentle ripple of the quiet, still waters lapping round the craft moored along the quayside, illuminated by the silvery light of the full moon above. Paul half expected some Oscar-winning film star to wander by, with curvaceous blonde attached. But he knew that was being greedy; he had one opposite him, one he wanted to take home to keep but couldn't.

Paul had a large lamb-shank, wondering if it had been one he had tended at Oliver's farm. Laura pushed the boat out and had lemon sole. As they ate they looked out over the harbour bathed in the eerie light of the moon, alone in their thoughts. Their conversation had always come so naturally, but now it was like their first meeting at the ranch; neither knew quite what to say. Sadly there had been no time for the swim with the dolphins, or the scenic road back. Perhaps too much time had been spent on their debates about God and the Church. Much was still unexplained or unresolved. Paul knew it was logical to believe that, living on opposite sides of the globe, they were unlikely to meet again. Laura knew otherwise, but could not say so, nor could she admit that any future flight to England would be on her expenses claim, any more than she confessed that their trip to Queenstown or that night's expensive dinner would not be paid from her trust fund. She had swallowed hard and taken a deep breath when she had paid the bill, and Paul had thanked her so profusely for her generosity.

The meal over, Paul tried to conceal the feeling of melancholy which had enveloped him, clearly sad at the prospect of losing her. He was frustrated, too, realising that with no employment, no immediate prospects, he was not an attractive proposition. He so wanted to repay her hospitality. He could only do that in kind, and how long could that be the basis of a long-lasting relationship?

'It's our last evening together; one last drink before I go,' hoping to prolong the evening until the very last moment; 'I'll have loads of time to sleep on the plane.'

Once he was gone she would find someone else. She was young, beautiful, and had a good job with prospects, or so he thought. She would find a new love. He was unaware that Laura was in turmoil, but for different reasons.

They walked slowly away from the restaurant bathed in the moonlight. A bar was open nearby. Paul ordered a cold beer for himself and a glass of wine for Laura, angrily declining her offer to pay, then regretting his sudden spark of temper, betraying that other side of his character. Laura understood where he was coming from; she liked a man with fire in his belly, even if it was mostly hidden. She said nothing, thinking: 'I love this man, but I still want to scream at him sometimes.'

Paul broke the stifling silence hanging over them.

'Actually, I find the moon and stars very intriguing, and so might you if you had time to study them. There are aspects which trigger the debate about God so dear to your heart.'

'You men and your space games. Well, I suppose you all come from Mars anyway.'

'And you from Venus?'

It was small talk, an effort to hide the tension of parting.

'It's a strange fact that the diameter of the sun is four hundred times that of the moon, and the moon's distance from us is one four-hundredth our distance from the sun.

'A bit like life on earth being by chance,' said Laura.

'The millions of coincidences needed to provide us with life on our planet defy anyone to argue against some kind of intelligent design,' Paul replied, seemingly unaware of the implications of his comment.

'You imply the same thing with the position of the moon. Did you hear what you said? You are pointing me in the direction of God!'

'That's why the moon is so fascinating. Amazing that it controls our seas, our tides, not to mention your menstrual cycle. It certainly contributes to the issue of God's existence. But there are counter-arguments that there are multi-universes; so many, in fact, that the odds are that one, ours, happens to have the right characteristics to support life, or the origins of it. It then took millennia to evolve through what Darwin called "Natural Selection".'

There was a silence; Laura was losing interest, but Paul then continued: 'Churchill once described the moon as a riddle wrapped in a mystery inside an enigma. Even the code-breakers at Bletchley failed to crack it.'

'Bloody hell, Paul, stop rabbiting on about the moon,' interrupted Laura, 'It's our last night together! You really do frustrate the hell out of me sometimes.' Despite that, all she wanted to do was grab him, hold him, and stop him leaving, this hopelessly naïve and kindly Englishman who came into her life from the other side of the world. But, to her annoyance, Paul continued, desperate to prolong the conversation, to avoid the pain of his departure.

'I cannot see that scientific research will ever resolve any God debate. The essential prerequisite for God is belief, or not knowing; that is, faith. If He was proved either to exist or not to exist, I wonder what that would do for the concept of faith?'

They had no idea how prescient that comment was, what turmoil was unravelling on the other side of the globe, *at that very moment.*

The awkward silence returned. Paul looked across at Laura. She was deep in thought, unaware of his gaze. He studied her silky, blonde hair, centrally parted, trailing round her sweet, oval face with those azure-blue eyes and, below, her perfectly formed mouth, with lips born to kiss. It must be zillions to one that they should have met in that hotel in Napier, and then again in Christchurch. Had their meeting been chance or design? And if by design, by whom?

He was blissfully unaware that Laura knew the answer. Her loyalties were becoming agonisingly divided between her professional and personal lives. Reluctantly, she knew she must try once more, while there was the opportunity.

'How did your meeting go with Hussain? Did you discover anything interesting?'

'Oh, the usual stuff about fundamentalist ideals, the next outrage, suicide bombing, that sort of thing.'

His tone was jocular, but was that a front, Laura later wondered, as she walked slowly back to her hotel. Both had suppressed their emotions, indulged in small talk, neither able to find the right words, neither wanting to upset the other, Paul unsure if they would ever meet again, Laura unable to escape the lingering and painful anxiety of her breach of trust. After their strained farewell embrace as Paul got into his waiting taxi, she watched until it was out of sight, taking him off to the airport and his overnight flight. Her only relief from the pain of parting was she had managed to avoid any further discussion about her work or her background.

Chapter 15

The Prime Minister's emergency meeting did not go well. Professor Jane Clifford-Oxbury had disappeared off the face of the earth. All attempts to trace her had failed. Her home had yielded no clues and her computer, mobile phone and laptop had all gone missing. There was no movement on her bank accounts, no phone calls to trace her. The security services and the police had drawn a complete blank, infuriating the beleaguered Prime Minister. The Archbishop of Westminster had blown the Government's containment strategy apart. His contacts in Rome had informed him just one hour previously that, following an emergency meeting of the Sacred College of Cardinals, in part by telephone conference, the Vatican had decided to go public. The message was that public exposure was inevitable in today's world of instant communication. Once out there, it argued, whether as rumour or fact, any distinction between them would become blurred. The two would become entwined, tangled up together such that no man, or even woman, could put asunder. The Roman Catholic Church, despite its misgivings over the adequacy of the evidence, was going to seize the initiative, take the leading role. The meeting closed within the hour. The Government and the Church had work to do. Coordinated press statements would have to be issued the moment the news broke. At midnight the Vatican issued a press release.

'*The Kingdom of Heaven is with us as Christians. If, as is now being alleged, we have proof that Jesus was born of a virgin, this vindicates the centuries-old Christian message. This is a momentous revelation for all mankind – redemption's happy dawn. We urge all peoples to embrace with us in the unity of the worship of Christ, our Saviour. We thank God for this long-awaited moment, and for His trust in recognising us as His spiritual leaders, bestowing upon us the privilege to take forward the message of peace and reconciliation for all. The light of the world shines upon us. The Lord is with you,'* and so forth.

Within seconds the news was circulating the globe, from East to West, West to East, North to South and South to North. Messages in various time zones circulated via mobile phones, via satellite, on Twitter, on Facebook, and the rest. By morning, most networks in England and around the world were overwhelmed. The Vatican had been right about the frenzied reaction.

The Prime Minister had little faith in the Anglican Church providing the necessary religious leadership – 'After all, look at the mess they got into over a few tents outside St. Paul's,' he exclaimed; 'There must have been an unholy row in the inner sanctum and, most likely, another one now. They had days to reflect then; now they have a few hours for divine guidance, at best,' bellowed Richard Benson.

The Prime Minister, his Permanent Secretary and the Home Secretary, in the company of their aides, had to be ready for all the demands of the media when dawn broke. It was a late night in the well-appointed cabinet room at No. 10 Downing Street. At 9am next morning, a clearly overawed Norfolk County Archaeologist, Luke Matthews, issued a press release to a hastily arranged news conference, his voice shaking with the enormity of it all:

'We have carried out extensive forensic testing of the cloth found in a casket buried in the grounds of a medieval site in Norwich. Using the very latest techniques of radio carbon-dating, we have established to our complete satisfaction that the cloth dates from the first century AD. More significantly, based on extensive forensic analysis, using established DNA sequencing techniques, the DNA profile of a speck of blood on the material shows, beyond reasonable doubt, that it was worn by a male who had no paternal DNA. The chance of this happening is infinitesimal, such that it must be considered to be unique. Further forensic testing will be carried out by an independent agency, but we have no doubt that such tests will only serve to corroborate our findings. We also have it on good authority that some of the coins found in the underground cellar date from the first century AD. We have no further comment to make at this stage. Thank you for listening.'

With that, a clearly nervous Luke Matthews stood up, declining to answer any questions, and left the room, much to the fury of the assembled newshounds. It was obvious the poor man was overawed by the gravity of his predicament. No mention was made of the untimely disappearance of the cloth, nor of the missing professor.

Midnight in Europe was eleven or so hours behind New Zealand, where the news broke during mid-morning. Laura heard it on television, frantically tried to call Paul but there was no mobile coverage. What on earth would he make of this, given his scepticism? How weird that they had been discussing faith and the Vatican only yesterday. And what would his Muslim friends make of this development?

★★★

In Norfolk, Revd Thomas Morgan was nonplussed at the news. He initially thought the local radio station was involved in a prank. Then the bombshell exploded. The discovery had been here in his home city of Norwich. Mary heard his piercing, high-pitched shout echo around the old rectory with its high ceilings and stone floors. The animation in his voice, its sheer intensity, left her in no doubt that something serious had happened. She ran down the hall to find him in the study, spellbound as he listened to his still-functioning portable radio, his eyes staring ahead in disbelief. It was not yet revealed who had been involved in the find, that piece of information would come soon enough. What it did imply was that he was 'Doubting Thomas' no more.

A special weekday edition of *Britain on Sunday* was published the following day. They could not contact the elusive Jane Clifford-Oxbury for another attempt at an interview, nor even a quote. Mike Burrows was beside himself. Where was she?

★★★

Paul's flight from Auckland had arrived safely into a foggy Hong Kong. There was a short break before the onward flight to Heathrow. Heading to the washroom, Paul caught a glimpse of the news headlines on a television monitor in the transit lounge. He stood transfixed, eyes focused on the screen, which had suddenly gone blank. He thought it had said something about God, but he did not have time to read it. And then the departure screens also went blank. He soon dismissed the news headline from his thoughts, mindful that his father would soon fill him in if there was anything to it.

It was not the global media frenzy that blanked the screens. Air traffic controllers were expressing concern over the safety of in-flight communications. Within minutes the departure boards reappeared showing dozens of delays, but not so the television screens. They remained blank, with no breaking news stories at all. No news did not feel like good news. His flight had a new departure time, a possible wait of several hours. Mobiles not receiving signals left the passengers in the transit lounge effectively cut off from the world, and they could have been in outer space. They assumed it was censorship of some sort.

Paul's delayed flight arrived at Heathrow late on the Saturday evening, the conclusion of eleven hours of flying time from the Hong Kong stop-over. By now he was dog-tired, exhausted by sitting in a cramped seat for so long, sat between a large, grumpy businessman on the aisle seat, with a nasty cough, and a twelve-year-old boy in the window seat, continually playing with his in-flight games console or clambering onto the seat to talk to his sister in the row behind. Just as Paul found sleep he would be woken by the boy climbing over him on his way to the toilet. The man beside him also had the irritating habit of glancing over at Paul's reading material throughout the flight, and often engaging in conversation with the man adjacent to him, seated on the end of the same row of the central aisle of the aircraft. The second man, of thin build and with slightly receding hairline but piercing eyes and pointed jaw, was dressed in rather a smart suit for a Standard-class flight, looking out of place away from Business class, head in his laptop. He also had a raking cough. There was something familiar about him, Paul felt.

The landing was smooth, straight out of the textbook. Leaving the airport terminal, he staggered down to the Underground station looking like a hunchback under the bulk of his massive backpack. He was convinced its weight had increased in flight, but knew that it was really a symptom of his tiredness. At Liverpool Street Station he boarded the last train of the day to Norwich and, by Brentwood the gentle rhythm of the train soon lulled him into a deep sleep, all the way to Norwich, where he awoke with a start. He still had some English money and was straight into a taxi and back to his flat. Collapsing onto his bed, he fumbled in his pockets to locate his mobile and ring his parents but, oblivious of the drama soon to engulf his family, sleep overcame him.

★★★

That evening, the Downing Street Press Office received some leaked information. Another special edition was to be published by *Britain on Sunday* – '*The Story of the Missing Professor*'. By then the Prime Minister and his colleagues had been fully briefed about her; her life history, her work, her family, her illegitimate child, and her student fling with the current Bishop of Norwich. Was he implicated in her disappearance? How much did the newspaper know?

Chapter 16

The media erupted. *'God Exists'* and *'New Evidence for the Existence of God,'* screamed the headlines around the globe. They were referring to the Christian God. *'Jesus, The Son of God,'* was the only story in town, and would be for the rest of the year. 'Or until perhaps 21st December,' thought Paul, on reading the newspapers later that day, or could it really herald the long-awaited Second Coming?

That Sunday morning, as the hastily revised editions hit the news vendors, the shops and the media, Paul's mobile rang out, at first dimly, then more loudly, as consciousness gradually returned, an unwelcome intrusion into his dream. He was back in New Zealand, high up, circling the snowy peaks above Franz Josef Glacier, swooping down low, then soaring like an eagle, piloting a helicopter on a rollercoaster ride with Laura beside him, scared out of her wits, screaming at him to land. Waking, he reached for his now-silent mobile. The call had been from his father, and he or, more likely, Mary, had sent a message.

'Paul, you haven't phoned; we hope you got back safely. Please call as soon as you hear this, it's urgent.'

'A bit strange, Dad should be preparing for the 8am Holy Communion service,' he thought, noticing the time, 'It must be important.' He phoned back. After a few moments of conversation his drowsy state had evaporated, his father's news an immediate cure for jet-lag. Jane, his beloved aunt, had gone missing. His father told him the police had woken them in the early hours, the banging on the front door of the rectory scaring the living daylights out of them. His mother had panicked on seeing two police officers at the front door, one male, one female, assuming the worst, and that something terrible had happened to young Paul on his journey from New Zealand. He had not phoned to say he was home as she had asked. But it was not about Paul, it was about her sister, and she was being informed as her closest relative. Aunt Jane was at the centre of a global news storm which had reverberated round the globe in ever-increasing circles, the epicentre being his home city of Norwich. Paul could hardly absorb it, acutely aware he had spoken to Aunt Jane only shortly before his return. His mother then spoke, telling him not to worry, her initial panic now translated into her more customary gentle, soothing manner, the force behind his father's throne or, in his case, pulpit. 'She is so good at hiding her emotions,' thought Paul, knowing that inside she would be in turmoil.

Paul was shocked by the revelation. From what he had gleaned, his father's beliefs had been vindicated. A flicker of a smile crossed his face as he speculated how Uncle Peter would react. He had only once seen the great man brought down. His golden retriever had been run over outside his London home; Peter had been bereft, moved to tears.

What would be the effect on Laura in her search for faith? He also thought of his recent phone conversation with Aunt Jane. His call must have been in the midst of all this but she had revealed nothing, apparently calm and collected, just like her sister. He realised how fortunate he had been to have those rocks of stability around him as he grew up, particularly thinking of his aunt, who had turned his young life around at such a crucial time in his adolescence. Had it not been for her he would have very likely ended up the same way as his friend, Danny. He could still vividly recall that night when he found him dead, slumped on the floor, surrounded by needles, overcome by his addictions.

Shaking himself free of his morbid memories he thought about his aunt, the irony of it all, she being a non-believer. Nor was she an atheist, frequently reminding Peter, as her brother-in-law had done, that he had no evidence that God did not exist. In that way she had been a reassuring presence in those sibling skirmishes, a buffer between his father and uncle.

Paul knew he should be with his parents at such a time. He dressed, grabbed a stale biscuit from an unsealed tin, wondering where he had left the car keys before his departure. The biscuit tin reminded him. Yes, there were his keys, hidden in a cornflake wrapper in the bottom of a cereal packet. His faithful old Fiesta was still parked in the street outside, a ticket attached to the windscreen - he realised he had forgotten to renew his parking permit before he left – but he was not going to lose sleep over that, not with everything else going on. He thrust the key into the ignition. After an initial groan his trusty servant spluttered into life and he headed straight over to his parents, wondering how they would cope with Morning Service. He need not have worried. Despite his concern for his wife and her sister, the renewed and invigorated Revd Thomas Morgan was at his best that morning.

★★★

Endless discussions took place in studios all over the world. Christians, non-Christian faiths, other religions, demanded more proof, deeply suspicious of the Vatican's motives. In the UK the media loved it. There was a plethora of chat shows, political discussions, churchmen and churchwomen paraded between studios. Only Her Majesty the Queen kept silent, staying above the fray, keeping her own, dignified counsel.Behind the scenes there were more meetings. Prime Minister Dick Benson called a meeting of COBRA, the name given to the Government's emergency committee which meets in Cabinet Office Briefing Room 'A', to discuss matters of national importance, a room awash with laptop computers and banks of television monitors.

'Where are the results of the independent testing of the cloth?' demanded the Prime Minister.

'The cloth's still missing, sir,' replied Frank Hussler, the Permanent Private Secretary's underling.

'It's a f...stitch-up,' yelled the Prime Minister, not in sufficiently good humour to notice the pun.

'We just don't know at this stage but, with respect, sir, it's too late in any case; the genie is out of the bottle. The truth is out there; that's what many believe.'

'Or the lie is out there,' added the Prime Minister, more in hope than expectation.

'That's as maybe, Prime Minister, but we have to consider all eventualities,' interjected Frank's boss, in a remark more addressed to the attendees.

Despite the absence of more definitive proof, and given the frenzy developing around them, he stressed they had a responsibility to plan for every conceivable possibility on the basis of the evidence so far. There was a suggestion that the Church, asserting its new-found dominance, might challenge Parliament or, indeed, even dispute the Queen's position as Head of the Church. Not yet, perhaps, but it was not an inconceivable outcome in the medium term. Whilst most of those attending regarded it as somewhat far-fetched, others, including Prime Minister Benson, accused the civil servants of scaremongering.

'What a load of tosh,' interrupted the Prime Minister, his irritation a measure of his growing concern. The ever-rational and unruffled Cabinet Secretary ignored his superior's intervention. Sir Julian Barclay discreetly pointed out that the Government had been at loggerheads with the Anglican Church for some time, the Prime Minister and Archbishop being barely on speaking terms. The Archbishop had been wading into political waters, scornfully commenting on issues the politicians regarded as outside his remit. He had no compunction about speaking out to defend the poor and the weak as they faced the full brunt of Government cutbacks. Would the Monarch, as Head of State, survive such a challenge if, but more likely, they suggested, when, it came? If Church and State came into conflict, whose laws would prevail, those of God or those of the State? Would republicans make this the moment to once again press for the abolition of the Monarchy? It had happened centuries before. Prime Minister Benson was more concerned than most, as this was all happening under his watch. He worried that it would only take something minor to go wrong for the mood to change from celebration to castigation, or worse. He was well aware that some small, trivial incident could quickly be transformed into a riot, and then whipped up by vested interests into an inferno, as it had been with the riots of the previous summer. Perhaps it wasn't such an implausible scenario after all.

The media, the press and internet sites were trying to fathom out where it would all lead. Editorials in the broadsheet newspapers speculated as to what would be the implications for the other faiths. The Muslim leaders, imams and elders alike, were defiant, not accepting the Christians' unproven assertions, but were privately expressing concern to Ministers about how some sections of society might respond to them, using the opportunity to pursue a racist agenda. They particularly feared the groups of so-called Christian Fundamentalists who, ominously, were rumoured to be establishing militias to pursue their agendas.

If any civil unrest emerged, everyone now knew how quickly it could get out of hand, echoing the concerns expressed at the COBRA meeting. After all, they reflected, the riots of the previous summer started with a simple arrest and the police had lost control over events within hours. Some Christians were spreading alarmist talk that recent events were a portent for the second coming of Christ, and they linked this to the alarming frequency and scale of natural disasters unfolding round the globe, warning those who would listen that 'The end of days' which the ancient cultures and the scriptures had predicted, was indeed coming to pass. Revd Thomas Morgan echoed these sentiments in his selection of the Reading for his Sunday service, taken from the *Second Letter of Paul to the Thessalonians*, on the subject of Hope and Discipline:

'And now Brothers, about the coming of our Lord Jesus Christ and his gathering of us to himself: I beg you, do not suddenly lose your heads or alarm yourselves, whether at some

particular utterance, or pronouncement, or some letter purporting to come from us, alleging that the Day of The Lord is already here. Let no one deceive you in any way whatsoever.......'

There were as many as twenty souls in the congregation that day, instead of the usual five; a welcome boost to the collection.

★★★

It seemed the tectonic plates were already shifting, but they were not only of the geological variety. It didn't take long for the questions.

'Whose God is it?'

'What or who is God?'

'Where is God?'

'Who made God in the first place?'

'Why now?'

The ultimate 'reality' show had begun. Catholic and Protestant Church congregations soared, and priests were unable to cope. Some believed it to be true; others, unsure, went to church 'just in case'. Church services seemed outdated for this new world. The public demanded spiritual leadership. The Anglican Church had been caught out and was desperately trying to respond. Its structures and procedures were not designed to cope with a maelstrom like this. The sudden revelation, whether for better or worse, portrayed another world altogether, its implications far more instantaneous and of such magnitude that they dwarfed the prolonged and unhurried series of debates about women bishops and gay marriage.

Sinners sought repentance in confessionals, seeking to unburden themselves. There were not enough priests to go round. Despite this, the Christian evangelicals lobbied for priests to be assigned to all state schools to promote religious observance. The 1970s were revisited by some: 'Live life in the present.' Musical gigs and open-air concerts became free-love festivals as they had before. 'Live now, for tomorrow we sinners are doomed.' They did not heed the message of Salvation.

Archivist Jane would not have been one of those claiming to have seen God. Many people did indeed make such claims. From the River Jordan to the Thames, from the Severn Estuary to the Ribble Valley, visions of God were reported. Many of these tales were similar. They spoke about a whirlwind, a great cloud with plumes of fire, and out of the amber glow came the likeness of a man, sparkling like brass. Sometimes it was 'men', in the plural. In most reports they then disappeared up to heaven in a craft with wheels.

The press enjoyed the stories, and so did their readers. It was akin to all those UFO sightings, but now far more newsworthy. No concrete evidence was produced. Grainy pictures on You-Tube circulated on the internet. There was, however, one rather more plausible sighting. A coach carrying Peter Morgan, along with a group of fellow atheists, on their way to an 'emergency' secular conference in Harrogate, was travelling across the Yorkshire Moors on the A65 when the sky suddenly lit up. The weather was appalling - wild, wet and a lashing gale. Astonished, they reported seeing fire engulfing very human forms, wrapped in what looked like orange cloaks, silhouetted in the glow, heading skywards. It certainly caused quite a stir as they tried to analyse their sighting in the next day's open forum.

Revd Thomas Morgan read the newspaper reports of the unexplained incident and was amazed as to how closely the reports echoed Chapter I of the *Book of Ezekiel*, the prophet.

'And I looked, and behold, a whirlwind came out of the north, a great cloud, and a fire unfolded itself, and brightness was about it, and out of the midst as the colour of amber, out of the midst of the fire. And also out of the midst thereof came the likeness of four living creatures. And this was their appearance; they had the likeness of a man.'

He did not know many atheists who had much in-depth knowledge of the Bible except, perhaps, his brother. Peter Morgan had the Good Book rammed down his throat when he was a youngster, a significant factor in his subsequent study of it as an adult, applying his analytical mindset. He had ended up denigrating it. Peter had also read numerous related books and publications in order to augment his disbelief, many of which were now sitting uncomfortably in Thomas' study. He had particularly enjoyed pretending to Thomas that he had misplaced the very special edition of the Bible his father had given him on that fateful day of his Christening.

If Peter could remember that passage, surely it would shake even his non-belief? But with Peter he could never be quite sure; it was always possible much of what he said was to wind up his younger brother.

Driven by press speculation allied to constant chatter on social media, it didn't take long for the mood to turn ugly. Those who grieved, those who suffered misfortune, even the sick, the downtrodden members of society, they cried out, demanding to know why God had left them to suffer. All over the United Kingdom people took to the streets carrying placards. **'God, why have you forsaken us?'** and, in search of the ultimate proof: **'We want miracles,'** or **'We are not prophets - why should we bear the sins of the world?'** Predominantly peaceful, they stopped traffic in cities, blocked entrances and exits to motorways, and besieged churches each Sunday, which became labelled as 'Demonstration Day'.

The Church tried to respond with the message, repeated in sermons all round the country, that we were given freedom to evolve, the opportunity to make choices in our lives, and with that came risks. God placed us in a context where there is birth, death, growth, decline, random happenings and natural disasters. To be free from bad news would mean the absence of human existence. We would not then know love, desire, virtue, or the corollaries, hatred and mistrust. We would be robots or zombies programmed by God to sing his praises.

'Is this not what we have now become?' was the obvious response. The Church represented faith, and this was gone. The new truth, for that is how it was perceived in many quarters, met with outright denial by other faiths and religious movements. The spectre of further strife and, worse, the prospect of new tensions between the religions of the world, worried the politicians.

A Home Affairs Select Committee requested the Archbishop of Canterbury to appear before them. The Archbishop declined, sending a clear signal that he was not beholden to Parliament. A collision course between Church and State really did now seem to be developing.

It was at this point that the Prime Minister summoned the Cabinet Secretary as Head of the Civil Service, and his Principal Private Secretary. Sir Christopher was known to have close links with the Archbishop; they had been to the same public school and then on to Oxford University together, sharing digs. Mr Benson did not much like Sir Christopher, with his cut-glass upper-class accent, his first-class degree at Oxford, his love of rugby, cricket and tennis. He was a debenture-holder at Twickenham and Wimbledon, and a member of the MCC at Lord's. He regarded his seats at the Centre Court at Wimbledon as a well-merited perk.

Sir Christopher had no interest in the Prime Minister's first love, football, and particularly 'Tottenham Hotspurs', in the plural, as Sir Christopher insisted upon calling them, but known as 'Spurs' to Mr Benson. When in his Burnley constituency, also his home town, he would support Burnley FC whenever he could, but that was not often these days. He would lapse into his old Lancastrian accent whenever he talked of home. The two of them came from totally different backgrounds and had nothing in common – except this crisis. The Prime Minister needed an ally, a go-between with Church leaders, and he reluctantly appointed the senior civil servant to this important role.

Bodies like the Council for Christian Unity of the Church of England and the Inter Faith Network for the UK also wrestled with the problem. The Network was firmly committed to the principle that dialogue and cooperation could only prosper if they were rooted in respectful relationships between the various religious interests. Their message fell on stony ground.

Christianity's resurgence inevitably led to renewed interest in the so-called Turin Shroud. It had not been widely known that 4th May is celebrated by the Roman Catholic Church as 'The Day of the Shroud'. Revd Thomas Morgan was one of many who had watched the *Panorama* special documentary that evening, an investigation into the mystery of the images detected in the Shroud of Turin. The programme included speculation that the shroud might have been one of the Templars' treasures which left La Rochelle on 13th October 1307. Jane, in captivity, did not see the broadcast.

Chapter 17

Behind the scenes, the Archbishop of Canterbury was at loggerheads with the Vatican as well as the politicians. He was particularly miffed about the defection of his priests to the 'Ordinariate' in Rome, the body set up by the Pope to accommodate the disaffected Anglican clergy within the Catholic Church. He most certainly did not approve of this poisoned chalice being offered to his priests, especially as its original announcement coincided with the Pope's visit to Britain, thereby restricting him to stifled platitudes of protest in order to avoid the visit becoming a public relations disaster. In February, the General Synod had rejected special provisions for local parishes that refused to accept women bishops on theological grounds. The House of Bishops would have to think again. There was also the problem of homosexuality. Paul regarded the inter-faith initiatives as a smokescreen to divert attention from these divisive issues. In a facetious email to Laura he pronounced:

'Typical of the Church of England to split itself apart just as God took centre stage. No doubt He will in due course pronounce on these issues in a judgement that would rank above any European Court. There will be no right of appeal and no gravy train for lawyers in that particular case. Poor Uncle Peter! That awful new wife of his will have to go without the latest fur coat or leather handbag. I can't wait to confront him on all this - an extra ingredient for his annual jousting match with Dad.' Then he thought of Aunt Jane and added: 'Sadly, we have heard nothing at all about my aunt, whether she is alive or dead.

Mum is trying not to show it but I, as well as Dad, who never notices anything, can tell that she's worried sick.'

An inter-faith network based in the UK, soon to lose the word 'faith' from its title, amended its 'Act of Commitment':

'In a world scarred by the evils of war, racism, injustice and poverty, we offer this joint Act of Commitment as we look to our shared future.'

The Statement read:

'We commit ourselves as people of many religious backgrounds (replacing faiths) to work together for the common good, for unity to build a better society, grounded on values and ideals we share, namely community, personal integrity, a sense of right and wrong, learning, wisdom and the love of truth. We must show compassion, justice and peace, respect for one another and for the earth and its creatures.'

The Statement was met with derision by non-Christians. They were not going to abandon their beliefs on the basis of the flimsy evidence produced so far. Adherents to other faiths vented their fury at what they perceived to be the arrogance of the Christian Church, engaging in some kind of deception to promote its ownership of God. The more militant amongst them besieged Catholic and Anglican cathedrals, setting up yet more tented communities outside, forcing clergy to pass through picket lines, and barracking services with trumpets, rock music, jazz, anything loud enough to disrupt the services. Thomas watched the news coverage, simmering with anger when the normally quiet and peaceful city of Norwich, with its two cathedrals, one Catholic, one Anglican, once again became the fulcrum of the drama. He feared the contagion might spread to the other churches scattered throughout the city, Norwich at one time having had the reputation as having more than any other city in England, fifty-two in total, one for each week of the year. He discussed with Mary what precautions he should take if a camp were set up outside one of his own churches. He sought guidance from the local Diocese, but none was forthcoming.

Paul too watched the news bulletins with deep concern. In response to the attacks on the churches, a racist backlash began to emerge from the lunatic fringe, always looking for a cause, who regarded this as an opportunity to vent their rage upon the immigrant communities, most of whom they perceived to be non-Christians. In a text to Laura he berated these hooligans and misfits, as he saw them; 'With friends like them, my father's Church is really in deep trouble,' he lamented. Paul was worried on two counts: what might happen to the churches in his father's diocese, and would Hussain be safe? He could not track him down, and he was not answering his mobile. Paul mistakenly assumed he had gone to ground for his own safety. In fact they were planning, plotting, preparing for the conclusion of 'Operation Trojan Horse'.

The people and the Government looked on in ever-increasing concern as the inevitable and much-predicted unrest spilled over on to the streets of Britain. Gangs of youths attacked each other using the troubles as a means to establish their 'street cred', their place in the hierarchy. Cars were burnt out, and shops set alight. Most of it had little to do with religion. Many different people were angry about many different things: the prolonged recession, the cuts, the need for food banks; the soaring cost of heating, the morality of the rich avoiding their taxes, the bankers and their fat bonuses and high-flyers with their pay-offs for failure. Such topics were the talk of social networks, journalists, and bars in those pubs that had not yet closed. All manner of things were coming together in a contagion of mistrust; a tidal wave of anger was gathering pace, threatening a tsunami which, if unchecked, would engulf Britain, a society potentially in meltdown. The police struggled to maintain order and tanks appeared near city centres, heralding the arrival of the Army. Politicians appeared impotent in the face of the troubles. Prime Minister Benson was desperate for the Army presence to be short-lived. Could he, or his Government, retain control over the Army if it became an established presence on the streets of Britain? Would the generals in charge of operations at some stage ignore the dictates of their elected leaders? Fears of a military coup had not circulated since the 1970s, but were creeping back in to conversations around the dinner tables of the chattering classes.

'We politicians may be regarded as rogues, especially after the expenses fiasco, but generals can be killers,' Mr Benson told his ministers.

In his fretful half-sleep the Prime Minister had a dream - visions of tanks and armoured cars crashing through the gates of Downing Street, soldiers breaking down the famous door of Number Ten. Then he could see the tank commander, a Hitler look-alike, moustache bristling with anticipation, striding into the Cabinet Room, pistol in his hand. Then he could feel the muzzle, cold and menacing, on his neck. He awoke with a start, knowing he was due to make an unprecedented televised address to the nation, to reassure the public, but perhaps not himself.

'*The Army has moved in on a temporary basis to maintain stability in the face of an undemocratic minority who are determined to undermine our way of life. These people will not be tolerated on our streets and we will stop at nothing to maintain law and order. Night-time curfews will be imposed wherever necessary. I must stress that this a purely short-term measure to ensure public safety, and we anticipate a speedy return to normality in the coming days. Thank you for listening.*'

Some, a tiny minority, speculated that the Church, with its new-found authority, would align itself with the generals. Prime Minister Benson dismissed this out of hand at a press briefing following his broadcast. No way could he imagine the Church wanting to be seen taking up arms in the twenty-first century. Others thought that the Queen would have to step in, but that would undoubtedly lead to the very constitutional crisis envisaged by Prime Minister Benson and his colleagues at the outset. Others argued that, although the Queen theoretically had all the constitutional powers as Head of State, the Church and Parliament, and as Commander in Chief of the armed forces, in reality she had no capacity to exercise any powers at all. Who will govern Britain?

Chapter 18

J ane Clifford-Oxbury had been well treated in her captivity. All attempts to locate her had failed. She had had no idea where she was. Initially she had been drugged, so she had no perception of travel or surroundings. She could be anywhere. She was not allowed access to television, radio, or newspapers, only books, scrutinised in advance by her captors. However, one seemingly academic book slipped through the net, one about the history of mute swans in Norfolk. She read that the first proper account of swan ownership on the old hospital site was around 1589/90, and the original swan pit must presumably have been constructed at a similar time.

Her frustration mounted at her inability to remember what her own archives revealed about any construction costs or trading patterns in swan sales. Disappointingly, the book made no mention of any underground cellar.

She had no idea of the turbulence in the world outside which she had unwittingly unleashed. She had given up speculating about her captors. They spoke English, but were not English, and gave little away. Their demeanour, their jet-black hair and swarthy complexion had a hint of the Mediterranean – Spanish, perhaps Italian? Her surroundings gave her few clues as to her whereabouts. The room was quite spacious, with a single bed in the corner up against a side wall. There was a high-backed armchair which was perfectly comfortable. There was a table, and even an en-suite shower with toilet built into the corner behind the door. The walls were a pale cream, with bluish-green carpet, almost turquoise. There was a radiator blasting out warm air under the window. Sadly this was boarded on the outside so there was no incoming light. She was desperate to see the sun, blue skies, or even dark clouds laden with rain. She wanted to smell the fragrant scent of spring flowers, to see the bees and butterflies, any evidence of nature's existence, the world she knew and had left behind, perhaps even for ever. The prospect horrified her. She suspected her room was sound-proofed. She assumed there was a camera somewhere, eyeing her every move. Not that she could do much other than read the vetted books given to her. There was no sound whatever, other than from her captors outside her door. She looked forward to the changing of the guard, probably more than the Queen. It meant human, well almost human, company. Her most frequent visitor was a burly man, who brought her meals on a tray, saying little, but when he did speak the tone was brusque and unfriendly.

Breakfast was cereal, in the early days soft rather than crisp, presumably the remnants of a long-opened container, followed by burnt toast, a frozen slab of butter, a small jar of marmalade, and what passed for coffee. It was the breakfast cereal and the marmalade which suggested she was at least in the British Isles. Lunch varied from cottage pie or shepherd's pie to fish pie. She worked out that the latter came once a week, which she presumed to be a Friday. Lunch was invariably accompanied by two boiled potatoes, two vegetables and too much gravy, generally cold and congealed by the time it arrived. Occasionally there would be a piece of ham or beef instead of pie, but this would only be a temporary reprieve. The pudding would then be apple pie or apricot pie. She would never eat another pie in her life, even one of Mary's. In the evening it was soup and a curled-up sandwich. She had to be in England.

She had read about a rumoured secret underground government city near Bath and, despite the apparently boarded window, wondered if she was there. What was it called - Corsham, or something like that? Or was she being held by some extremist group? Although it seemed unlikely, the latter possibility really scared her. In her agonised mind she conjured up the word 'fundamentalist'. It sent shivers up her spine.

The end to this solitary confinement came suddenly. A tall, grey-haired gentleman, beautifully manicured and dressed in an expensively-tailored blue pinstripe suit, crisp white shirt and maroon tie, entered her room. He was accompanied by a priest, one clearly of some standing; a cardinal perhaps? A thought crossed her brain like an electric charge, panic, and then an all-consuming fear swamped her whole being – surely not the last rites?

In measured, upper-class tones the tall man, unmistakably English, quietly explained that he was a senior government civil servant, and he certainly looked the part, simply stating that she would now be under their protection. He outlined worldwide events. She had been held for her own safety. It was not appropriate for him to tell her by whom, and she would not be able to resume normal life.

'But why have you taken me? What about the archaeologists? They were on the scene before me.'

'They simply did the analysis, the dating. You were the one who examined the parchment and were responsible for tracing the link back to Jerusalem. We can't have you out there writing books or detailing your research on the internet for the world to see. You will be released to a safe house under an assumed name with a new life history.'

'Ironic that an archivist should have a *new history*,' she thought. She would be 'required' to sign a declaration accepting this.

'And if I refuse?'

'You will not refuse,' Sir Christopher replied firmly, menacingly.

'What about my...,' she hesitated, 'My family? I cannot cut my ties with them.'

'I understand your difficulty, but you have no choice,' he replied firmly.

She could not be sure if he really understood or not, but he had that air about him which said, loud and clear: 'Don't mess with me.'

It was evident life could never be the same, and she did not relish the celebrity status the media would confer on her. But not to see her family? All kinds of images flashed through her mind: her sister beside her on the walk along the Norfolk beach, Paul back from New Zealand, not to mention Bishop Marcus. She wondered if this was like experiencing news of imminent death, the last moments on this earth with, for some, only a void beyond. Sadly, tearfully, thinking of loved ones she might never see again, and after a prolonged silence, Jane grudgingly accepted there was no alternative. She signed the declaration consigning her past to history and adopting a new one.

Sir Christopher had not mentioned the meeting to his boss, the Prime Minister. It had all happened under the cloak of great secrecy, the result of his well-honed negotiating skills and his close relationship with the Archbishop, and he would delight in taking the credit when the time was right. Until now it had not been appropriate to involve meddling politicians.

What Jane did not know was that she had been kidnapped by agents of the Vatican and, after highly secretive negotiations, handed over to the jurisdiction of MI5. Fortunately, the journalist from *Britain on Sunday* discovered neither this nor another closely guarded secret, one relating to her family.

Prime Minister Benson had been apoplectic with fury when he discovered that the archivist had been in the hands of the Vatican, and held in London too. He was only informed after her release to another safe house. It had been dealt with on a 'need to know' basis and he, the Prime Minister, had been excluded. Undoubtedly someone would soon be in the Prime Minister's firing line, and most certainly Sir Christopher, should his deception come to light. It would not be a good place to be – the Prime Minister had once been an Army reservist and knew how to point a gun - and fire it.

'And those Catholics knew all the time; no wonder that cardinal said nought. Who runs this bloody country?' he bellowed.

'I'm afraid it's the Civil Service,' volunteered young Frank, rather bravely, 'A Prime Minister is merely a fig leaf for democracy!' Frank Hussler was the PM's Assistant Private Secretary, but he was unlikely to become a permanent one.

After much discussion amongst Sir Christopher's colleagues, senior civil servants and representatives of the Security Services, and endorsed by Nigella Blackburn, the Home Secretary, a decision had been reached in early June, now that the violence had subsided and become much more sporadic, that sporting events like Henley, Ascot and Wimbledon should go ahead as planned. They would inform the Prime Minister of their decision. He was hardly likely to disagree. Too bad if he was miffed at not being involved but, after all, he had enough on his plate - they made sure of that. The tourism industry had lobbied hard to maintain an image of normality to counteract the adverse publicity generated by the civil unrest. Although he had no interest in tennis, which he had always considered to be elitist, The Prime Minister had mentioned his view that a successful event at Wimbledon, and the following summer schedule soon after, would capture the public mood, take the focus off the troubles and, most importantly, send a message that 'Britain was open for business as usual'. He was desperately hoping for British triumphs to occupy the headline writers.

Taking his cue from the Prime Minister, on the first Thursday of the Wimbledon fortnight Sir Christopher was enjoying a glass of champagne in the Debenture-holders' lounge, as a guest of the New Zealand Ambassador. The invitation had followed a meeting with the Ambassador and the Director-General of MI5 about the covertly organised spread of fundamentalist threats to the United Kingdom, including an update over some leads they were following with links to both countries. He had no conscience about enjoying the excellent hospitality on offer. After all, he had sorted out the problem of the Professor and that was now out of his hands. He had not informed the Prime Minister of his role in her release, but why should he? Neither would the Prime Minister be party to his talks with the Ambassador; such discussions were for civil servants, certainly not ministers. Sir Christopher knew next day he would have a long day in Canterbury on his mission for the Prime Minister. Usually he could persuade the Archbishop to join him for a lengthy lunch, washed down with fine claret, but he knew his friend would be much too busy in present circumstances.

He relished the afternoon ahead; it would be good to get away from the Westminster village for a few hours. He considered his presence would be in tune with the policy decision to proceed with the tournament, and he would find the opportunity for a press interview to take the credit.

Much to his embarrassment he, and the other guests clinking their glasses around him, heard the tone of his Blackberry, a considerable breach of etiquette in such august company, but he was required to have it switched on at all times, except perhaps in a church. It was his Secretary, Jill Gilbert.

'Trouble at mosque, sir,' she said simply.

★★★

With Paul the other side of the world, Laura busied herself in her work. There were endless training sessions, workshops and tense meetings to analyse her sketchy and limited reports. She was then sent on another assignment, taking her to Wellington and Cambridge in North Island, and Dunedin, a city in South Island. When in Wellington, she had spent time at the Museum which had so enthralled Paul. She had then been sent along with a group of tourists to 'Doubtful Sound', a remote, sometimes sinister fjord in the South West, accessible only by boat and mountain bus. She was also tasked with trying to find the whereabouts of a secret Fundamentalist training centre in the region. Looking like a student, dressed in faded jeans, laden with a backpack, and the inevitable smartphone, she had sat close to three dark-skinned young men, bearded, of Middle East complexion and certainly not native to the Island. Just as in the café in Waipara, preoccupied by their conversation, they took no notice of anybody else, even the pretty young woman sitting nearby. Neither, fortunately, did Farim recognise her; she had dyed her hair and was no longer the blonde he had seen that day hidden outside her flat. It was not difficult for someone with Laura's training to extract a cabin key from an anorak laid on the seat as she passed, cleverly distracting them by asking one of them to mind her backpack as she went to the toilet.

'It's that purple one on the seat over there,' was all she needed to say so that they averted their gaze in that direction. She then slipped it back on her return, thanking them for their kindness and, under her breath, their naivety. Now she did not need to be too close to them - both the coat and the cabin were in earshot as she apparently listened to music on her earpiece. She could always roll out the seasickness excuse if challenged for being so obsessed with her music rather than admiring the scenery. The only time she could not hear them was when they dived off the back of the boat to swim with the dolphins. Poor Paul had missed out on that. She thought of Paul often; too often, probably, longing for him to be sharing her cabin, the comforting feel of his body beside her; but she knew she could not let her thoughts of him distract her from this mission. She had not done well in

Napier and she was determined to make a success of this surveillance assignment. She realised she had performed well with Paul, but not her employers.

★★★

Sir Christopher Perrin had left Wimbledon without seeing a single game, or sampling a single strawberry. The Blackberry took precedence. He also anticipated a dressing-down from the Prime Minister, who was waiting for him in the Cabinet Room, probably not pleased to learn that the reason for his absence from the office was a jolly at Wimbledon. Sir Christopher received the anticipated withering look as he found his seat. Present were the Acting Commissioner of the Metropolitan Police, Steve Copas, the Commissioner of the City of London Police, the Solicitor-General, the Director-General of MI5, the Home Secretary, the Foreign Secretary, the Mayor of London and some aides and assistants. There was also a man with a long, pointed beard, tinged with grey, and adorned in white garments, whom Sir Christopher did not recognise under the obligatory turban. Also present, on secondment from Wales, was Detective Chief Inspector Joshua Lyon, head of the Metropolitan Police Religious Violence Unit, and who was first to speak.

'A tip-off has been received that a bomb has been placed at a mosque somewhere in central London. Search teams with sniffer dogs have been dispatched to potential targets. I know we have had these attacks before, but in these particular times we cannot afford to inflame racial tensions still further. The warning implies that the bomb will be detonated tomorrow at 11am. Intelligence reports suggest the most likely target is the mosque in Whitechapel, on Christian Street, of all places.' The irony was not lost on them. 'This operation is particularly sensitive, as some very senior imams will be visiting for Friday prayers.'

'Gentlemen;' the Prime Minister spoke, his manner gruff, his voice stern, 'The backlash we anticipated against our Muslim friends has begun in earnest. These extremist attacks could soon spread, whether perpetrated by Christian fundamentalists or militant Islamists. Both are espousing a cause which is a betrayal of Islam and peaceful and law-abiding Muslims, who give so much to our country. They are as much a part of our community as anyone else, and we will do everything in our power to protect them.'

'The problem, Prime Minister, so far as the Jihadists are concerned, is that the conviction of the righteousness of their cause is so indoctrinated in them that they really do believe they are carrying out God's instructions, just as the early crusaders perpetrated all kind of barbaric crimes when they seized control of Jerusalem after four hundred years of Muslim occupation.' interrupted Sir Gordon Bamford, Director-General of MI5. 'That is what makes our job so difficult; for them it is a just war. Our 'invasion', as they see it, of Iraq and Afghanistan justifies their actions,' he concluded with a barely disguised glare at the Foreign Secretary, a long-time adversary.

'Nevertheless, it only takes a spark to ignite an inferno,' added Prime Minister Benson. 'I know that the Chancellor of The Exchequer is desperate that nothing happens to undermine his attempts to make London into a leading centre of Islamic finance, given the growing market for their investment into this country, possibly even the launch of an Islamic index on the stock market.'

'Do we have any intelligence leads? I guess you wouldn't tell me anyway,' he added, his tone laden with sarcasm, then concluding: 'It is vital this bomb is found, today, this evening, tonight, as soon as. Keep me informed.'

As they all left the room the Prime Minister walked slowly round the long Cabinet table, accidentally knocking into one of the sabre-legged chairs, then finding himself staring out of one of the shuttered windows, the view through to Horse Guards Parade and St James' Park obscured by the frenzy in his mind as his onerous predicament engulfed his thoughts like a spinning top. The dark clouds hovering ominously overhead seemed like an omen as to what might lie ahead. He knew he had hawks in his cabinet that opposed multiculturism and were lobbying behind his back for greater immigration controls. He pictured Sir Christopher's belated entry to the meeting, the smug expression on his face as if he were actually enjoying the situation, and wondered whether he was encouraging them. Although much tempted, he felt it was hardly the right time to issue a rollicking to Sir Christopher for his various deceptions. He was aware that Perrin was due to visit the Archbishop on his behalf the following day, and he could ill afford to prejudice that attempt to foster improved relations.

There were some intelligence leads, but Acting Commissioner Steve Copas had said nothing - better to announce a *fait accompli*, mission achieved, than to raise false hopes now. He wanted that promotion, the top job, but he and his team had little time to locate and defuse the bomb. The clock was still ticking.

Chapter 19

The Rt Revd Marcus Banham, Bishop of Norwich, was well aware of the procedures in his Church. The Church of England's General Synod legislates by 'Measure and Canon', using powers inherited from the former Church Assembly and the Convocations, the provincial synods. Measures need approval by both Houses of Parliament, then Royal Assent, before they become law. Bishop Marcus regarded the whole process as cumbersome and outdated, the crisis enveloping the Church requiring a considered but speedy response.

The Archbishop of Canterbury convened an emergency and unprecedented 'Lambeth Conference' of his fellow Bishops. The Bishop of Norwich had been briefed beforehand, and advised what he could reveal in any discourse. He had been grilled by the security people and they had eliminated him from suspicion in relation to the missing archivist. The notice convening the event promoted it as a 'conference' as distinct from a formal 'meeting'. Members of the laity were allowed to be present for consultation but on this occasion, controversially, they would have no vote. No media or television crews were admitted. There was strict security.

They endorsed the statement issued by the formerly titled 'Inter-Faith Network'. It was renamed the 'Inter-Church Network'. They commissioned a website for citizens to sign up to the statement or, as it became more commonly known, 'Declaration'. People would be encouraged to wear badges, emblazoned with a cross whenever practicable, to signify their adherence to the 'Declaration'.

Emboldened by its stated position as God's representative on earth, the Church began to push its 'ethics agenda'. This was interpreted as a code for 'bash the bankers'. This was not a true reflection of the initiative, but it resonated with the public mood. The anti-capitalist movement, with its humble beginnings as a tented community outside St Paul's the year before, had spread throughout the Western world, finding allies in Islamic and other non-Christian communities throughout the United Kingdom. In what appeared to be an attempt to mollify the protesters one senior banker, based at the Bank of England, even went so far as to praise them for their role in helping to instigate what he called a 'reformation of finance'.

The spectre of public and sovereign debt still hung over Europe and the United States of America. In consequence, growth remained around zero, or below, which signalled recession. The London FTSE 100 continued to fluctuate, sensitive to any news, good or bad. The 'ethical and moral crusade', whilst officially welcomed and, indeed, extolled by members of both parts of the Coalition Government, caused considerable concern within the business community. Financiers recognised the Church was flexing its muscles and using its new-found authority to challenge business ethics, even, in some quarters, capitalism itself. This did nothing to settle market nerves.

'God rid us of these turbulent priests,' cried voices in the City, echoing the Prime Minister's private aside. But these voices had not been universal. There were such people as Christian bankers. There were also many

Muslims who worked in the City. They were employees of the numerous law and accountancy firms, the stockbrokers, the commercial and investment banks who littered the high streets. It had been their practice on Fridays to hurry through the streets of Spitalfields to their nearest mosque, for the most important prayer of the week. Indeed, so great were their numbers that many resorted to worshipping in the streets, protecting their pinstriped knees with tarpaulins. The public and the police had previously turned a blind eye to these gatherings. On that particular Friday morning they were out in force from early morning, watching like hawks, desperate to avoid any confrontation or worse, mindful of the threatened attack on the mosque in Christian Street. The time-bomb for Acting Commissioner Copas and his team was ticking.

'Will they now be asked to move on?' was the question asked in some quarters. The Home Secretary utterly refused to countenance any such suggestion.

'They are as entitled as anyone else to follow their beliefs, just so long as they do not cause nuisance or disruption.'

The Church of England was sympathetic to their plight. It remembered all too well the pressure it had been under before the recent revelations, the banning of prayers in council meetings and the restrictions on wearing crosses at work.

The failure of a private security firm to recruit sufficient staff for the summer's sporting events had given the Prime Minister cover to bring in the troops, but this time without the tanks and armoured cars. This temporarily kept the troublemakers away and reassured the public. He was also mightily relieved that the bomb found at the mosque in Christian Street had been successfully located and defused. He was amongst the first to congratulate the Acting Commissioner. What worried him and fellow Ministers was the oxygen of publicity given to it by the press and the media, and the encouragement it might give others to follow suit. Hussain and his pals had their own thoughts as they scoured the news bulletins. Lessons needed to be learned before 'Operation Trojan Horse' could be brought to its conclusion.

***

In Norfolk, Peter and Thomas were together for a summer weekend at the rectory. It was fine and warm, one of the few balmy evenings Norfolk enjoyed that year. Peter was delegated by Mary to look after the barbecue; 'A man thing' she said, but not a role Thomas was normally equipped to perform unless they required burnt offerings. Mary came into the garden, the food prepared, ready to indulge in Peter's claret. Like her absent sister she was partial to a fine wine, but seldom were they in evidence unless he was present. Peter was resplendent in coloured shorts with matching tee-shirt, as if in Hawaii, displaying his still-handsome physique, especially those legs that women would die for. Following his recent holiday he wore an outrageous sunhat, straight from the Australian outback. Mary expected to find Thomas in long, white trousers, plain, open-necked shirt, and an ancient straw hat, slightly tatty now, and which Peter would have recognised to have been their father's. But no, here he was in shorts and casual shirt, purple as the priesthood, and, unbelievably, sandals. The straw hat had survived the makeover. The only area left for her to work on was the socks. She was also surprised to find Thomas had asserted his authority as host and was standing over the barbecue, willing the reluctant coals to light and turn to ash, in readiness for the cremation to follow.

The conversation echoed the national debate. This time there was another participant, young Paul, but no Jane. It was a potent mixture. Thomas was reinvigorated, a clergyman with new-found confidence. Peter, the seemingly avowed atheist, remained sceptical about Jane's discovery, and Paul was full of the ideals of youth.

Thomas, without doubt, was on the front foot, teasing Peter about the vision of God he had seen on the Yorkshire moors. He then launched forth into the political arena.

'We need business to take on a new moral dimension, to recognise that worship of shareholder value is not God's way. We must never again allow the greed of the few to destroy the finances of the many. The city types have learned nothing; they still take their massive bonuses, buying second homes here in Norfolk, forcing up prices so that local people can't afford homes of their own. And this is at a time when the vast majority have had their pay or benefits frozen or, worse, cut,' he cried out belligerently, as if in his pulpit.

'You've been listening too much to your boss in Canterbury. Yes, I heard what the Archbishop said. But you have to accept, Thomas, we need businesses to flourish and make profits. Only by making profit can we invest for the future, and they can only do that if supported by a thriving banking sector. We have to create wealth if we are to deliver jobs and generate revenue through taxation to satisfy the demands of the public purse,' retorted Peter.

Paul was waiting his turn, but had to interject. 'Politicians are liars if they peddle the line that we can balance the books. We have to adapt our society to expect less. We can never expect to raise the sums needed to finance the aged as they live into their nineties and beyond, their associated healthcare, and all the other demands on the state. But I do agree with Dad, we must clip the wings of the greedy bankers,' provocatively adding: 'And lawyers. Remember this, Uncle, and yes, it's from the Good Book:

"Brothers, you must never disparage one another. He who disparages a brother or passes judgement on his brother disparages the law."

'And,' Thomas interrupted, 'There is only one lawyer and judge, the One who is able to save life and destroy it. And that is not you, Brother!' he proclaimed defiantly.

'It's no use pretending that soaking the rich, to use popular parlance, will ever come close to raising the funds needed; there just aren't enough of them. It would be counter-productive in any case. Some would emigrate, but those that remain would not have the resources to invest for the future either,' responded Peter, adding authoritatively: 'The market economy has proved the most successful mechanism yet devised for raising living standards. The home comforts today for the average citizen are immeasurably better than fifty years ago. Our father was brought up in an age when the toilet was at the bottom of the garden, and there was no such thing as central heating.'

'Nevertheless,' responded Thomas, 'The inequality between rich and poor is as wide as ever, and widening fast. People like you, Peter, just don't realise how difficult it is to cope with ever-escalating energy prices that never come down, food prices increasing week by week. I'm sure you identify with that, boy, having your own flat and limited resources.'

'What we need is socially responsible capitalism,' added Paul supportively.

'Fine words, Paul, but probably unachievable,' was Peter's response.

'I have more fine words, Uncle. You should listen, both of you, to the words of my *First Letter to the Corinthians*,' he said cheekily:

"I appeal to you, brothers: agree amongst yourselves, and avoid division; be firmly joined in unity of mind and thought!", or words to that effect.' He missed out the reference to *'in the name of Jesus Christ'* - that would have been too much for Peter.

'Fine words indeed, Paul, but probably unachievable,' was Peter's deliberately repeated response.

'It had better be achievable, Uncle, otherwise there will be yet more social upheaval, far more threatening than the current debacle supposedly about religious faith. I bet they are preparing for it as we speak; after all, the troops are already guarding sporting events, probably to get us used to the idea for later.'

Thomas, as usual, was left feeling deflated, his new-found confidence on the wane. It was an intractable problem. The world of business and profit he knew little about, yet he could not avoid them if he was to provide spiritual guidance and inspiration to his congregation as they faced these issues in their daily lives.

The Church did not need much encouragement in its determination to take the high ground. In a packed Canterbury Cathedral the resurgent Archbishop delivered a high-profile sermon announcing a whole series of new 'policy initiatives', interpreted as 'demands' in Downing Street. He breathed new life into the 'Keep Sunday Special' movement. He called for immediate legislation to restrict Sunday working to the essential services. He demanded changes to the Employment Equality (Religion or Belief) Act and its provisions that employers must justify Sunday working as a legitimate business need.

'The right to worship must be paramount, ahead of commercial requirements. Shops, offices, businesses, should be banned from opening before 2pm so that people can worship without hindrance. I admit I find it difficult to resist calling for an all-day ban. A recent poll found that eighty-seven per cent of the British public believed a common day off is important for family stability and community life.'

He knew this would chime with similar Government pronouncements. He made no mention that there were not enough priests to cover all the churches in their parishes. He further called for new legislation so that all public-sector meetings should begin with prayers, and this should be an agenda item. He also pressed for this to be extended to all formal business meetings and that it should become a requirement for charity trustees, with confirmation of compliance in annual reports.

He spoke about forgiveness of sins, calling for earlier parole for repenting prisoners.

'I shall lobby for a new third upper chamber in Parliament, composed of a built-in majority of Church representatives, who will scrutinise all legislation to ensure religious compliance. This will enable Her Majesty to combine her roles as head of the Church and Head of State when she gives the Royal Assent. In effect, she will wear two hats, or perhaps crowns,' he added, the only attempt at humour in his very lengthy address.

That Sunday evening, news of the sermon set alarm bells ringing for Government Ministers.

'He thinks he has some God-given right to lecture us, a democratically elected Government,' bemoaned a frustrated Prime Minister.

It delighted members of the trades union movement, who had long supported workers in their fight to not work, or be 'persuaded' to work, on Sundays. A clever cartoonist for a major broadsheet depicted a church with a notice attached to the porch door – *"Closed on Sundays"*.

Paul, with his sense of social justice, felt all this meant nothing to average citizens. They simply wanted roofs over their heads, and for food, electricity and gas to be affordable. In a message to Laura he proclaimed in indignation:

'I want to catch a train to London and walk the streets outside Uncle Peter's chambers, parading a sandwich board, and perhaps even join the tented community outside St Paul's Cathedral. I fear that would be a step too far; it would upset both my father and uncle in one go!'

The normality of Paul's message left Laura confused. It arrived just after she had listened to one of the recorded conversations of the Muslim lads on Doubtful Sound. It was Farim speaking.

'We have gleaned a lot from Hussain, aided and abetted by his friend, the English kid, and we will learn a lot more when Malik's cell goes active. Our brothers should be able to put this knowledge to good effect here in New Zealand, although the task at Christchurch has already been done for us. Allahu Akbar!' he exclaimed triumphantly. 'We are all very grateful to Hussain, and particularly for all the valuable information the English boy has given us. And I don't half fancy his bit of stuff.'

'You know that kind of reward comes later, once the job is done.'

It left Laura embarrassed and bemused, and, crucially, with many unanswered questions about Paul. What Farim had said about Paul's provision of information shook her rigid. And she had been observed without her realising, and on that occasion it had not been Agent Neon. Thank God she had changed her hairstyle for the trip to Doubtful Sound. As for Paul, her quarry, her prey, her lover; could she trust him? Was he friend or foe?

Chapter 20

In late August mobs, communicating through social media sites and the new generation of smartphones, were once again on the streets. This time they were besieging Muslim, Sikh, Hindu and Buddhist communities, amongst others, and their places of worship, citing any non-Christian faith as a mask for indiscriminate racial violence.

On what became known as 'Black Friday', from the suburbs of London to Leicester and north to Bradford, the streets again became battlegrounds between riot police and petrol-bombers and looters, this time around burning mosques.

'Where is your Allah now?' they shouted, as they launched their missiles. There was not much to loot, because mosques are places of devout worship rather than ornate shrines of gold. As the fire-fighters tried to deal with the burning buildings they were attacked by rioters, causing the police to go to their rescue. These diversionary tactics left other areas with only limited numbers and resources, leaving the coast clear for looters to ransack retail premises and the much-hated high street banks and financial institutions. One brave Christian woman was lauded as a heroine for tackling a rioter as he launched a petrol bomb towards a mosque in the Prime Minister's home town of Burnley, chasing him down the street wielding her umbrella. As with the 2011 riots, the original cause was soon overtaken by the opportunity to engage in mob rule. This time, however, rioters were much more aware and kept their heads well covered, out of the sight of police helicopter cameras.

'We must not vent our anger on the peaceful and law-abiding Muslim members of our society. As with all those cowards who engage in these disgraceful acts of violence, we will seek them out; there will be no hiding-place, and they will face the full rigour of the law,' declared the Prime Minister at a press briefing outside the front door of 10 Downing Street.

'*Who Rules Britain?*' screamed *Britain on Sunday*, along with its competitors, intensely irritating Prime Minister Benson. Britain was not a happy place. Every aspect, every angle, was covered by the television crews and beamed around the world. The pictures were reminiscent of the Arab Spring and its aftermath, far from the seismic divisions of the Middle East – but Prime Minister Benson was all too aware that the dividing line between law and order and anarchy was a thin one- could such turmoil happen under his watch in the green and pleasant land of his home country?

Britain was not alone in facing the crisis; it had spread through the whole of the western world in varying degrees but, as yet, none matched the level of the disruption in the United Kingdom. Prime Minister Benson blamed the media for exaggerating the scale of the unrest. Where it did manifest itself he attributed this to the fact that the archaeological discovery had been made in his country and this had acted as a catalyst to inflame the deep and divisive fault lines in British society. Middle Eastern countries simply preferred to carry on fighting each other, within or without their borders, regardless of the 'mischievous' claims of the Christian Church. The last thing they would do is embrace the now-resurgent

Christian religion. They did not believe the veracity of the discoveries in England, nor was it in their interests to do so.

***

Jane, hidden away in her safe house, now had access to television and radio as well as the internet, but no access to social media. She was incredulous that the cellar beneath that medieval swan-pit had unleashed such tumultuous consequences. She longed to make contact with her family, but she had signed the declaration under oath and was sworn to maintain her secrecy. It was impossible to erase her past; she wondered if Paul had brought his girlfriend back to England, how her stoical sister would be coping. Her thoughts turned too to Bishop Marcus and the special bond between them, so recently re-kindled but now extinguished.

She had been given a new 'sister', in reality her guard. Edith was kindly enough, understanding and supportive, a widow with no immediate family, but she could never be a substitute for her real family. They went on shopping expeditions together and visited historic properties but, as yet, Jane was not allowed out alone.

'Can someone at least tell my sister I am safe, alive and well?' she implored, but to no avail.

Paul was missing his aunt, not knowing if she was dead or alive. Her disappearance brought home how much she meant to him. He was also increasingly concerned for the wellbeing of his friend Hussain. He could easily become a target for the mindless idiots flocking to a cause they knew nothing about. Had he known that Hussain and his pals, as trained operatives, were well able to look after themselves, and it was he who was their unsuspecting informer, he would have been more careful, more circumspect. He innocently made sure they got together regularly during this period in cafés, on campus, or in flats or bed-sits. Sometimes it was just the two of them but, on several occasions, Hussain's friends, Abdul, Malik, and Jarmal joined them. They portrayed an insatiable thirst for knowledge about their adopted country, its customs, its heritage. They told him they wanted to learn from an Englishman's perspective, as their own views reflected those of their friends and peers. They would also talk to Paul about the usual subjects such as sport, politics, and women. Occasionally would they stray into religion, asking Paul all sorts of questions about Christianity. Sometimes they would speak of their friends from Tower Hamlets College, how they all believed that one day they would see Islam achieve political supremacy over Western ideology and Communism. Initially Paul was not fazed by this as it was natural, with their background, they should think that way. On one occasion, however, he noticed a cutting edge in their voices which had not been evident before, except perhaps when he had met Hussain and his friends in New Zealand. Since the failed attack on the mosque in Christian Street they had become argumentative rather than analytical, angry rather than reasoned. Afterwards this did play on his mind; he belatedly began to suspect that they were using religion, and even democracy itself, as a Trojan Horse to further their political aims; a cover for a more draconian regime to follow. It never crossed his mind that he was complicit, giving them the access they sought for their plans.

Whilst driving out to see some dinosaur remains found on the North Norfolk coast, Paul wondered if they were trying to convert him. He soon dismissed the thought. He had no desire to commit to any faith, Muslim, Christian, or any other. He was on the road to Cromer, not Damascus. But, more and more, Paul began to feel uneasy in their company; he had the distinct impression they were holding back from telling him things. From the questions they asked him he almost felt he was being used, especially when, knowing his father to be a priest, they got on to the subject of church procedures, their patterns of worship, and showed what he felt to be an unhealthy interest in the workings and practices within Norwich Cathedral itself and, he recalled later, often arranging to meet for coffee in the refectory.

'He provides us with cover, he's well-known here, no one will be suspicious,' Malik said repeatedly when Paul was out of earshot.

On one occasion his increasing anxiety turned to alarm as their discussion turned to the thwarted bombing of the mosque in Christian street, Whitechapel, in London. Like many of their peers, Hussain's friends appeared to blame the attempted attack on Christians, in turn giving them an excuse to retaliate against the Christian religion, regardless of who had actually perpetrated the violence. The word 'retribution' had not been used in his company, but he could not get the thought out of his mind. And Hussain's anger apparently had some justification, given that his father worshipped at the mosque. Should he warn the authorities? But Hussain was his best friend, and Paul was reassured that Uncle Peter had once told him that 'mere speculation' was not the same as 'suspicion'. Perhaps he should confront his friend in the first instance.

Paul did not know that, shortly after he left, Malik received orders to stand down 'Operation Trojan Horse' because of the heightened publicity surrounding the thwarted bombing in Christian Street and also as rumours began to circulate in certain circles as to the identity of those behind the plot.

It was a time of ever-increasing numbers of natural disasters – floods, storms, hurricanes, forest fires, drought in Africa, ash clouds from volcanoes. Concerns were mounting about the San Andreas fault, so long dormant, and the volcano, Cumbre Vieja, in the Canaries. Paul knew this had the potential to create a tsunami which would devastate the Eastern Seaboard of the United States.

There had been extreme weather conditions in northern England. The Revd Thomas Morgan opened his morning newspaper to read press reports of an inquest into the deaths of four council workmen in Harrogate, North Yorkshire. Tragically, they had perished in a freak tornado high on the moors when they were thrown clear from their van after it exploded and was sucked into the air in flames. They were wearing orange boiler-suits. He wondered if Peter, having witnessed the mysterious incident, had seen the article. He rather hoped not; 'Leave him to fret about what he saw.'

Paul observed all these apparently natural phenomena with mounting apprehension. His friend Miles Mulligan had again been in touch. He had referred sceptically to mounting panic in the United States as December approached, saying a poll had revealed that some twenty per cent of Americans feared the world would end, if not then, then sometime in the next few years.

'People are stockpiling food, water and fuel, storing petrol in giant jerrycans in their garages in order to feed their giant cars, even building underground bunkers equipped with everything needed to survive for months on end. Many US citizens have been reluctant to adapt to climate change and recent global catastrophies. Scarce resources, political and religious instability at home and abroad, especially in oil producing regions, are now threatening their much-cherished way of life. The world would reap what it had sown,' he concluded.

Paul had immersed himself in reading about the many prophecies handed down from ancient cultures from all parts of the world, by Hindus, Egyptians, Romans and Greeks, as well as the South Americans. Their messages, all incredibly similar, did not necessarily speak of global extinction in the era 2012 to 2020, but of the dawning of a new golden age. What amazed him was how they all seemed to focus on the same short but precise timescale. These predictions were consistent with his less dramatic interpretation of the ancient codes - as one cycle ends another starts. Nevertheless, he still harboured some concerns, perhaps unintentionally fuelled by his geologist friend, Miles Mulligan, that he might be wrong and that something more cataclysmic could occur, if not this December, then sometime this decade. He thought of Laura all those miles away on the other side of the world. Everything - the turmoil, the widespread climatic disasters, the financial meltdown, pointed to the fulfilment of ancient prophecies, one way or another. Once again he remonstrated with his father.

'Even the sayings of your namesake, St Thomas, who was so close to Jesus, are full of proverbs, parables and prophecies. So what if those ancient Mayans were pagans, Father? You can't just ignore their prophecies because their beliefs were different from yours. Scientific evidence is all around which validates many of those claims, just like you say it has in the first chapter of *Genesis*. Yes, Uncle Peter told me about your little rant at Easter. Can't you see that they are aligned to the Bible itself, given its warnings in the *Book of Revelations* – which even describes itself as a "Book of Prophecies" with its visions of "The End"?'

Paul was becoming anxious about Laura. Her texts had been subdued and seemed not to come from the Laura he knew. It was easy to assume she was deeply worried about the state of the world, the decline in natural resources, and the potential for catastrophic climatic change. He realised it was natural for her to be fearful, given her own experiences. It was he who had introduced her to all this; it was largely his fault. He should have been more mindful of her sensitivities, given what had happened in Napier and Christchurch. He also knew she was under stress in her work but, as she would not reveal anything much about it, he found it difficult to sympathise or offer encouragement. But was there something else? The enthusiasm had gone from her texts; they seemed too matter-of-fact, without warmth, as if something was troubling her. Had she found some handsome, swashbuckling rugby-player to share her evenings and, much worse, nights? Her remoteness was getting to him. He had to find a way of getting Laura to England before 21st December, in time for Christmas.

***

Described as 'irresponsible' by the Prime Minister, the newspapers were cataloguing events demonstrating how, taken together, they were consistent with the forecasts of all the harbingers of doom, of whom there were many. They listed a lethal, worldwide cocktail of riots, debt crises, famines, species extinction, and the widespread breakdown in social fabric, the Arab Spring, the rise in religious tensions, the territorial wars and the frightening acceleration of technological advances. Scare stories like these were a golden opportunity to sell newspapers. '*Will God protect his people, or is it the End of Days?*' they asked. The newspapers were full of ancient prophecies, attributing every aspect to current events. They trotted out the scientific data for raised solar activity, spoke of meteorites heading for Earth. The stories were laden with doom-mongering in order to create a public frenzy, and therefore sell more and more copies.

Paul had become sanguine about the apparent geological threats. Laura clearly was not. There had been tragedies before, and she feared another. One evening, in a rare phone call, it all spilled out in a flood-tide of emotion, gushing forth like a surging torrent in flash floods. It was as if a Pandora's Box of Paul's dire warnings had burst open. Quoting from the Bible, she warned:

'"*You must face the fact: the final age of this world is to be a time of troubles. Men will love nothing but money and self; they will be arrogant, boastful and abusive,*" etc, etc. It's all coming true, and you said it yourself!'

Paul tried to reassure Laura that it was far from conclusive that the end of the Long Count, the Mayan's thirteenth baktun, on 21st December would bring disaster, as some claimed. He reminded her it could simply herald some kind of new age of spiritual awareness.

'Come to England for Christmas; take an extended holiday; we can be together for whatever happens. Please, you sound so depressed, I'm sure I can find something to raise your spirits. Please!'

Mary did not often openly disagree with her husband. News that Paul's friend from New Zealand was coming for Christmas filled her with delight, but there was a practical problem to resolve.

'You've been polishing and cleaning the guest bedroom rather than preparing the two single bedrooms. I'm not having them sharing a room in my house. We don't even know her.'

'Oh, for goodness' sake, Thomas, this is the twenty-first century in case you haven't noticed. Trust me, they are deeply in love, and haven't seen each other for months. Do you really want Paul sneaking between bedrooms at the dead of night? You're a light sleeper at the best of times, so what will you do if you hear those creaky old floorboards at 2am in the morning - go and create a scene? All they would do is up and leave, then you may have lost Paul for ever. Despite everything, you don't want that to happen, do you? I remember all too well your last altercation.'

'I will not allow fornication under my roof. This is a rectory, not a whorehouse!' he shouted, face reddening as the blood rushed to his cheeks, anger mixed with embarrassment at the prospect. With that, he stormed out of the house and into the garden, something he usually did when faced with the frustration of a losing battle with his wife.

'It's freezing cold; you might need your coat, in case you haven't noticed,' Mary shouted after him, infuriating Thomas all the more. Once out there, the problem was how to return without loss of face. This time he slunk back into his study, later emerging as if nothing had happened.

Her trust funds enabled Laura to fly Air New Zealand to the UK in mid-December. At least, that is what she told Paul. Permission was a foregone conclusion; it was just what her boss wanted. He had no difficulty in persuading his English counterparts. She arrived tired but safe to a foggy and damp Heathrow. With her diplomatic immunity she was able to pass speedily through Customs, quickly locating her luggage, and then reunite with her lover waiting anxiously in the arrivals area. She hardly recognised him at first. The frizzy hair had gone and had been replaced with straight, blond hair, quite short, and ending in a fringe. She said it was a great improvement from that spiky, boyish look, more mature. They spent the rest of the week together, their bodies and souls entwined, convulsed in love. Paul's flat was even more cramped than Laura's, but that was of no concern to either. He had tidied up as best he could, even dusted what little furniture he had and borrowed his mother's vacuum cleaner. He need not have bothered. He had hardly led her through the front door before she loosened her skirt and let it fall gracefully to the floor, then enticing him to remove her frilly lace panties, revealing that golden-brown skin, soft as velvet. Unclasping her bra strap as she did so, she pulled him down on to the welcoming sofa, providing a whole new experience for the coiled springs below. It would be altogether different once they got to the old rectory.

On 15th December Thomas pulled no punches as he addressed his congregation that Sunday, his text taken from the *New Testament*, the *First Letter of Peter*.

'Dear friends, do not be bewildered by the fiery ordeal that is upon you. It will give you a share in Christ's sufferings, and that is cause for joy. If Christ's name is flung in your teeth as an insult,

count yourselves happy, the spirit of God is resting upon you. The time has come for the judgement to begin; it is beginning with God's own household, here in this church. If it is hard for the righteous to be saved, what will become of the impious and the sinful? If you commit your soul to God, your maker will not fail you.

'*Awake, be on the alert! Your enemy, the devil, like a roaring lion, prowls round looking for someone to devour. Stand up to him in faith!*'

With that he came slowly down the steps from the pulpit, smiled triumphantly at his congregation as if he knew what lay ahead in the coming days, and announced the next hymn: '*Great is thy faithfulness, Lord unto me.*'

The message he conveyed was all too clear. Laura clutched Paul tightly, her fears reignited.

***

The exhortations of Prime Minister Benson and his Cabinet colleagues had no chance of calming nerves. Hysteria ruled, fuelled by the media moguls. Many felt they might as well go out with a bang and arrangements were being made for firework parties on the evening of 20th December.

That evening the Revd Thomas Morgan, alone in his chilly study, recalled how Noah warned about the unseen future, took good heed and built the Ark to save his household and, as things were in Noah's days, so would they be when the Son of Man returned. Later, in a fitful sleep, he had a dream. He was the saviour of mankind as, after morning service, he shepherded his flock from the church into the waiting space shuttle parked outside. He let them on two by two, even finding room for their treasured pets. Then he was into the cockpit, up and away, rising from the dread, and free from earthly danger.

21st December soon came. Those old enough vividly remembered the fear, the apprehension, the night before the Cuban missile crisis reached its climax, particularly in East Anglia, then jammed full of American missiles. A nuclear holocaust, Armageddon, was only then avoided at the very last moment. Fifty years before, it was Man that had the finger on the trigger; this time it might be Mother Nature.

As Paul, Laura, and the rest of the world held their collective breaths, they were unaware that two suicidal scientists were hiding a momentous secret. Their prank had got out of hand so quickly that they were scared to come forward. Luke had not been able to resist playing one last practical joke on his old school friend. The coincidence had been too great to ignore. The day he had set up the tests on the cloth containing the palm fibres had been 1st April, known to many as 'April Fools' Day', also fittingly Palm Sunday. He had also known that Jane Clifford-Oxbury was a non-believer. It had seemed fun at the time to send a hoax email to her on 6th April, Good Friday, as it coincided with Easter weekend and the celebration of the Resurrection. He had persuaded his scientific colleague, the aptly named Judas Swan, who had undertaken the blood tests, to join in the prank, re-living their mischievous teenage tricks on classmates and teachers alike. Consumed by their childish naivety, they had manipulated the DNA report, never considering for a moment it would crucify Jane's career, let alone their own, and result in such worldwide repercussions. Judas, caught up in the excitement of their betrayal, had been unable to resist the challenge of winding up journalist

Mike Burrows, his acquaintance from university, just for the hell of it. The phone call to Mike had been such a brilliant piece of acting that he felt he had missed a career in that profession. The cloth never left their laboratory for independent analysis. It had all got out of hand, gone too far, and the shame, the implications for their families, their careers, was too much to bear. They had despairingly asked themselves why they hadn't come clean when they issued the second confirmation. The enormity of it all engulfed their troubled souls. There was only one end to their nightmare. They left notes confirming there was nothing notable about the ancient cloth, or the casket, or that grim underground cellar beneath the swan pit. The writing on the parchment was indeed ancient French, but there was no more to it than that. The apparent confirmation of God's existence was no longer sustainable. **The concept of 'Faith' had survived**.

Within twenty-four hours Mary received a telephone call from a Sir Christopher Perrin, a high-ranking civil servant. Her sister would be returning home in time for Christmas - as soon as she had been de-briefed by the authorities.

THE SWAN PIT
PART III

WHAT IF THERE HAD BEEN A DIFFERENT TURN OF EVENTS?
'THE ALTERNATIVE SCENARIO'

Beginning on 6th April 2012
Ending on 21st December 2012

David Buck

Chapter 21 – April 2012 – The Alternative Scenario Unfolds

I t was 6th April, Good Friday of the Easter weekend, and the beginning of a new tax year. Jane Clifford-Oxbury was to remember this day for the rest of her life. Accompanied by her colleague, Luke Matthews, she had examined the fragments of parchment found in a cellar under the grounds of the old monastery in Norwich, and they had sent them, along with the other artefacts, including the silver rings and coins, for analysis.

After a bracing walk by the sea, the Morgan family had settled down in front of the warming fire. Jane was woken from her reverie by the vibration of her mobile. It was Luke. Suddenly wide awake, she hurried through to the study.

'Apologies for calling you over the holiday, but I have some interesting results from the tests carried out at the University research laboratory on your piece of cloth and the accompanying artefacts. I've put it all into an email, so have a look and see what you think.' With that he put the phone down. Jane opened the inbox on her smartphone.

'Hi Jane; I had a lot of work on so I went over to the lab last Sunday, Palm Sunday, to get the testing on your cloth under way. The fragments of wood or thorns have no special characteristics. However, there were some spots of blood on the cloth matched by the DNA we were able to extract from some follicles of human hair and fingernails. There were also traces of sand on the fingernails. Tests show they came from a human, not an animal,

with perfectly normal male DNA. They are approximately two thousand years old and show features which suggest a Middle East origin. The coins found in the casket date from Roman times and one is particularly notable. It has on its reverse side a triumphal arch from Rome with a statue of an emperor, presumed to be Claudius, riding on horseback. I am getting Judas to research its origin. My guess is the hair and fingernails come from somewhere south of Sidan, probably what was Galilee or Samaria, perhaps even Jerusalem itself,' he added, *'But don't take that as gospel. 'There is also evidence of some kind of oil, perhaps medicinal oil, and fibres in the cloth. I suspect they could be palm fibres. I have securely stored the parchment in your office safe using the password you gave me. I thought I would call you straight away as I will be involved with the family over the weekend.'*

Jane was intrigued. Her brain went into overdrive with speculative ideas. The fact that it was Good Friday certainly quickened the pulse. Leaving the others to their slumbers, she scribbled a message of apology to her sister and, quickly gathering her belongings from her room, slipped out of the rectory and returned home.

She recalled the 1988 discovery of a small jug in that part of the world dating back to those times, which archaeologists thought had been used for medicinal purposes. She soon found reference to it on the internet. What triggered her rapt attention was that the jug had been *'wrapped in palm fibres'*, just like those in the cloth. No doubt, she thought, there would have been many such wrappings in those days, but she could not dismiss the connection from her mind. She still had the parchment to decipher, stored securely in an airtight container in a safe in her office designed specifically for temporary retention of any such records. She decided that she would go to her office in the County Records Department the next morning.

After a fitful night's sleep, beset with bizarre dreams, the next day, 'Black Saturday', as it is sometimes described, Jane was in her office. It was eerily quiet, being the holiday weekend, with the exception of the finance department.

'Of course, the end of the fiscal year – they will be at it all weekend, poor darlings.' Jane was not remotely interested in the world of finance, except when there were threats of budget cuts. For her the date was only notable because she knew she had funding in place for the year ahead. She knew her brother-in-law would also cherish the date, and not only because it was Easter. The Revd Thomas Morgan had years before abandoned his fledgling career in accountancy; nevertheless, he always remembered this particular day – the opportunity for the Treasurer of the Parochial Church Council to generate much-needed funds from the deed of covenant tax reclaims.

She put on her plastic gloves and carefully examined the parchment. Her knowledge of French was sufficient to translate many words, but not all were familiar. Quite unexpectedly, she came across a piece of parchment containing Aramaic writing. It looked like an important document, still just about legible despite its age. There were other documents behind it, barely decipherable.

Jane had a distinct advantage. Both her Oxford degree and her professional career had included studies on the Aramaic language, common in the Middle East some two thousand years ago, *matching the time period postulated for the cloth and coins*. Excitedly, she examined the first document.

It was what today would be described as a certificate of some sort. She then did a double take. It referred to a couple, a *'Jesus Kristos'* and a *'Mary Magdalene'*. The inference was clear; the document was nothing other than some kind of official recognition of a marriage between them. In it, Jesus was described as *'Son of Joseph'*. **Son!**

Then came another bombshell; the other documents appeared to be recording the birth of children. She looked at the first one. The date, and the name of the baby were indecipherable, but she could make out that the parents were a *'Jesus'* and a *'Mary'*. She studied the second document, also with the same named parents. Again the child's name was difficult to decipher; it could, she thought, be construed as *'Josephes'* but she could not be certain. On this one she noticed a date which, under the glare of her portable microscope, suggested what Jane, with her specialist knowledge, interpreted as AD44. The third document was almost completely illegible, but again there was a date, the equivalent of AD 37.

Was this child named Sarah as some have claimed? Sadly, it was indecipherable.

'Hell's teeth!' she exclaimed; 'Black Saturday or not,' she shouted out ironically, 'I must call Luke.'

Luke answered. She explained what she had discovered.

'You must come over and see for yourself.'

Much though he loved them, he was pleased to escape the grandchildren for a few minutes. The call turned out to be less than that. It took some moments to find his car keys - a male thing, his wife frequently reminded him.

Jane and Luke studied the documents, and just looked at each other without speaking.

'Are you thinking what I am thinking?' asked Jane, tentatively. Luke simply nodded. 'What was the date of the Crucifixion?'

'I'm not sure; I thought around AD 33.'

Luke went onto an internet search engine, entering: *'Date of the Crucifixion'*.

'It's still subject to debate and speculation, but there certainly does seem to be a consensus for AD 33. And two certificates,' as they began to describe them, 'Appear to be dated **afterwards**!'

Alarmed by the momentous possibilities, they calmed themselves with the probability they were mistaken, especially as they were in the county of Norfolk in England, with no realistic likelihood of a link with Jerusalem, Bethlehem, or the Middle East.

'If these documents are what we think they are, how on earth did the casket find its way to Norwich?'

'That's for you to puzzle over,' replied Luke. 'I will have tests carried out on the certificates as soon as possible. I know Judo will do what he has to do while it's quiet over the Bank Holiday. I'll call you when I'm back at work on Tuesday. Keep all this to yourself.'

Jane spent the weekend surfing the net. She researched the history of the swan pit, recalling from her previous research that swans had been kept under licence at the old hospital for centuries but, as it had for the swans swimming above, that line of investigation into the ancient cellar ended only with a brick wall.

Looking for historical links, she entered *Joseph of Arimathea*, supposed custodian of the Holy Grail, into her search engine. Again no trails led to Norwich. She followed the Templars' trail from Jerusalem to the South of France. She discovered that 'property' possessed by the Templars had been given to the Knights of St. John and that they in turn had travelled to Leith in Scotland. Further, that the particular Order was known as the *Hospitaller Sisters of St. John of Jerusalem* and, crucially, that they had been based at the hospital of St. Mary Magdalene – in Jerusalem.

Jane was aware of all the conjecture and rumour which had persisted in recent years concerning a possible relationship between Jesus and Mary Magdalene. It would not have been a surprise to her had they been married and had children. Books had been written and articles posted on the internet to this effect. There was also much written concerning the searches for the Holy Grail. Some thought it was the chalice used in the Last Supper, others that the blood of Christ was secretly stored somewhere. Jane was also aware that France and Scotland figured prominently in much of the speculation. Nothing had ever been proven - until, perhaps, now. It would be ridiculous if she, a humble archivist in Norwich, not looking for anything, should stumble upon something so controversial by chance. Given the magnitude of the discovery, she could not put it out of her mind, and she just had to find out if there was any kind of link from Leith in Scotland to Norfolk.

★★★

That miscreant journalist, Mike Burrows, was looking for material to justify his covert existence. It made no difference to him that it was Easter. One of his many unknowing 'sources' was the forensic scientist, Judas Swan, from whom he had extracted useful information in the past, and who was totally unaware his phone was being tapped by the hacker at *Britain on Sunday.*

At 2.55pm on Tuesday, 10th April, Judas left a voicemail message for Luke Matthews. He had gone into work over Easter to undertake the further tests on the documents. He had been happy to have an excuse to avoid a house full of teenagers, especially seeing his daughter hand-in-hand with a youth in torn jeans, with tatty trainers and a baseball hat, peak at the back. His late father-in-law would not have let him in the house dressed like that when he was dating Emily.

'There is both male and female DNA on the blood smudges on the marriage document, and that of the male matches the blood specimens on the cloth, as well as the hair and nails. It's impossible to be precise about the dates but, using our very sophisticated method of carbon dating, we think they were probably first century AD, and the birth certificates, as we would describe them, later than the marriage document, assuming that is what it is, which is probably towards the second half. I can also confirm the silver coins also date from that time, my research suggests from around AD 46/7. It does seem likely that this was after the date of the Crucifixion, which corroborates the dates you have tried to decipher. From the DNA profile, the male was not the product of a virgin birth. That of itself may be of great interest to you. As for the other documents, the allegedly earlier birth confirmation, well, it has the same imprints but has suffered considerable degradation and needs more analysis.

'You don't need me to tell you that all this could have significant implications for the beliefs of the Christian Church,' he said, making this profound exclamation in a matter-of-fact

tone, his voice showing no emotion whatsoever, a master of understatement.

'My role is one of painstaking analysis, of ascertaining facts, and certainly not engaging in speculative leaps of faith,' he pronounced, not realising what he had said. *'I am committed to confidentiality, as are my colleagues. I can't deny that I shall follow any further developments with particular interest.'* That was the nearest he got to any expression of excitement or, indeed, amazement.

'But you can rely on me – integrity is my watchword,' he concluded.

Luke Matthews was thunderstruck to hear the message from Judas Swan. So indeed was Mike Burrows, listening-in shortly afterwards. He called his editor on the secure personal mobile. There was silence at the end of the phone. The response, when it came, was terse and to the point. 'Meet me at 7pm at *The Two Fishes*, the pub near St. Paul's.'

★★★

Judas Swan did not live up to his lofty ideals. He could not resist confiding in his close friend and former colleague, Jake McDonald, a jovial Scotsman who was by chance out in the Middle East working on an archaeological dig close to Qumran. Jake was in his mid-fifties, tall and handsome, a lovable rogue whose ginger-haired legs were much admired by the ladies when displayed under his ancestors' tartan kilt. He had a large scar above his right eyebrow; the story was that he had fallen into a ditch and hit his head on a jagged stone on his return from a night's drinking at his local pub. He had been found the next morning, bloody and bruised, with a severe headache which he later attributed to the fall, rather than the whisky. When he was upright his rusty, straggly beard and wrinkled face gave the appearance of a man of some distinction, one not to underestimate. He had always had a fascination with the so-called missing years in the life of Jesus. He had long believed that Jesus must have been married, and he knew it would have been most unusual in those days for that not to have been the case. He had heard rumours that Jesus had three children. Judas was well aware of his friend's interest from their years together at university. The temptation to tell his friend of the discovery in Norwich was just too great. He sent an email to say he had some staggering news, and asked Jake to phone when he had a moment alone.

'You really aren't joking, are you? Here am I near Christ's birthplace, doing all the hard work, covered head to foot in dust and sand, sweltering in the sticky heat of the eastern Mediterranean, and you tell me you have his marriage document sitting in your safe in Norfolk. You jammy bugger! I have to get a flight to Norwich to see this for myself.'

'Sorry, Jake; no way. This is one hundred and fifty per cent confidential and must stay that way; my job, my mortgage, depend upon it. When you have time to think you will understand exactly why. And, don't get pissed one night and tell everybody.'

'Yeah, OK, I get the picture. I promise to be the soul of discretion.'

They then exchanged some information by email, later finding an opportunity to speak again.

★★★

Later that evening, Jane spoke to Luke. She told him of her emotions, of excitement, of apprehension, and certainly of fear. Luke said nothing to alleviate her discomfort.

'I'd better speak to Bishop Banham; I know him well. We were at Oxford together. We were close. If I had ever married it would have been him. It was not the right time, we were too young. Then he married Rebecca.'

She left it at that, as she always did. The Easter holiday was over. Bishop Banham could well be having an evening at home in the Palace after such a busy weekend. She did not relish dropping this on him – at least it was after Easter she reflected, with some relief at the timing.

★★★

Journalist and editor looked for a quiet spot in the bar of *The Two Fishes*. There was a corner seat with padded cushions, upright wooden backs, dim lighting and a small table. On the table were two pints of the local ale, brewed in the pub's own microbrewery, in what had once been stables at the back of the inn. There were beer mats on the table, each depicting five loaves of bread and two fishes. Mike Burrows had the transcript in his pocket and showed it to Joe Culverhouse.

'There's long been speculation about a relationship with Mary. Until now, perhaps, there has never been any proof. I'll need to go right to the top with this one, call the proprietor himself. But first there is a major problem - our source. We cannot be perceived to have got this by illegal means, not after last year and the problems at *NOW (News of the World)*. I don't see enough of my kids as it is – I have no wish to spend the next ten years in jail.'

'This professor - what do you think she will do with this information? Find out more about her.'

'I have made a start,' responded Mike Burrows.

'Anything useful?'

'I believe so. She studied at Oxford at the same time as the Bishop of Norwich. A source at the University said there were rumours they were an item. They were certainly seen together quite often.'

'And what would be the obvious thing to do?'

'Confide in the Bishop, I guess,' said Joe.

'Got it in one,' replied Mike.

'You know what to do. Something may crop up to enable us to go to print. Draft the article so it's ready for publication.'

Within twenty-four hours their luck was in.

★★★

A nervous Jane Clifford-Oxbury was shown through to the Bishop's study. He had spent the hour before her arrival reviewing the life of his predecessor, Henry Despenser, the 'Fighting Bishop'. He already knew a great deal about him; he had a wall chart hanging in his study showing the previous bishops of his diocese, which went way back, even to Bishop Walter de Suffield, the founder of the Old Monastery Hospital, now the Monastic Leisure complex.

He wondered what Jane wanted to tell him. She had said it was a matter of extreme delicacy but wouldn't say anything further, other than to ask if he knew much about the Fighting Bishop. He was about to find out.

'How are you, Jane? Please have a seat.' He paused, looking at her, thinking of the past. 'It's been a long time; it's been difficult, knowing you are living and working here in Norwich.'

'I know; I understand, but we agreed it should be this way.'

'And how is young Paul, if I may ask?'

'He's in New Zealand doing some exploring.'

It was a long time since they had been alone together. There had been, and would always be, this special bond between them.

Jane had decided to start with the medieval bishop, who combined the cloth of his calling with the blood of soldiering. Most apt, she thought - the cloth and the blood. She knew once she got on to the marriage document the historical link would be of less consequence to Bishop Banham. He would be totally focused on the end, not the means. But Jane wanted to fill in the missing piece of her jigsaw puzzle.

Bishop Banham told the story of his predecessor Henry Despenser, otherwise known as the Fighting Bishop. He told Jane about the expedition to Scotland and, likely, Leith.

'His closest confidant was a John Derlyngton - and he was Master of the Old Monastery Hospital. It's intriguing, too, that there are historical links for this bishopric with the founding bishop of the Old Hospital, one hundred and fifty years before. It seems we are both inextricably linked to that old monastery. Now tell me what this is all about.'

Her emotions running high with the enormity of it all, Jane explained about the swan pit excavation, the digger, the discovery and the documents. Bishop Banham was rarely lost for words but he said nothing for some minutes, visibly shaken. Only once before, all those years before, had she seen him so distressed.

'Can you rely on the veracity and confidentiality of those scientists?' he finally asked. She could see the tell-tale signs of tension, soon so intense that the lines on his forehead began to redden and protrude.

'Certainly; I've known Luke and Judo for years, even before you, Marcus,' she replied, unaware that they had an assistant technician to help them.

So she did have a previous boyfriend, thought the Bishop, before continuing: 'I will need to speak to the Archbishop and warn him of these developments.'

He glanced apprehensively down at his special red smartphone. 'Where are the pieces of parchment?'

'After I had examined them, Luke took them over to be stored in the University science laboratory under Judas Swan's personal supervision. They have special facilities there, totally secure, with temperature and humidity controls. My colleagues are sworn to secrecy. I have had these copies taken under laboratory conditions so as not to damage the parchment. They are as distinct as I can make them, given the condition of the original documents.'

'Email a report to me so I can forward it on to him – encrypt it as well, just in case.'

When she had gone, Bishop Banham reflected for half an hour. This was the most momentous thing he had ever had to do. He illuminated the '**Do not Disturb**' sign on his study door. The past and future of the Christian Message, the Bible itself, could be at stake. It was surely unlikely but...

He looked anxiously at his special red smartphone, only to be used to speak directly to the Archbishop of Canterbury. It had rarely been used. His hands began to quiver and then he noticed they were shaking. Would he remember how 'The Holy Line', as he called it, worked? He was supposed to memorise the input code but his brain stubbornly refused to activate it. He had so many others, he could not pin it down. It was the stress, he knew that. He tried to sit calmly, hoping the grey cells in his brain would respond. All this reminded him of the Cold War hotline. He thought about the confrontation over the blockade of Cuba fifty years before, the edge of a precipice for mankind. He was old enough to remember Kennedy and Khrushchev, fingers closing on the nuclear button, ready to unleash Armageddon. The straying thoughts cleared his brain. He picked up the phone and successfully dialled the Archbishop, who would phone back. It was the longest wait of his life. He jumped when it eventually rang. He briefly warned of the nature of Jane's report, which he would forward within the hour.

The Vatican is not so holy that it is immune from illicit activity - quite the opposite. Its agents are everywhere, watching, listening. They have to protect the Catholic Church and all its secrets. All senior English bishops are monitored, even the supposedly secure 'hot-lines'. There is no such thing as 'confidentiality'. The phone hack brought consternation and, indeed, panic to those inside the Vatican. Their belief in the uniqueness and divinity of Christ was in jeopardy – an unstable situation. The world would claim their whole edifice to be built on a myth, one they had carefully nurtured for centuries. Very few souls were trusted with the explosive secret.

The call brought a similar reaction inside the hallowed precincts of Canterbury, and from the listening security officers inside GCHQ at Cheltenham. In so doing they had exceeded their official powers. But the Ecclesiastical Monitoring Division, mindful of the divide between Church and State, was simply piloting anticipated new procedures under the provisions of the draft Communications Bill currently under parliamentary scrutiny.

That evening, 12th April, the Cabinet Secretary briefed the Prime Minister. Other than the PM's Permanent Private Secretary they were alone, without aides.

'The Minister for Cyber Security has received a surveillance report from our friends at GCHQ in Cheltenham about a potentially explosive archaeological discovery in Norwich. By 'explosive' I mean its possible implications for the Christian concept of faith, and from that the Realm, our society and much else besides. If this report is confirmed, and hopefully it is a big 'if', **and** it gets into the media, it could lead to mayhem in the religious communities, and upset the whole constitutional balance between the State, the Church and the Monarchy.'

'You'd better explain that, Sir Julian; it all sounds a bit far-fetched to me,' replied the Prime Minister, a puzzled expression on his face.

★★★

The next day, Science Laboratory Twelve at the University was blown apart. It was a massive explosion. Judas Swan, his colleague Luke Matthews, and their assistant were killed outright. In the charred remains of the laboratory the bodies were barely identifiable, and then only through their dental records. It was initially assumed that animal rights activists were responsible, but had got the wrong laboratory. At least that's the line that was spun to the media. It was never established for certain who was responsible. Some, including Prime Minister Benson, privately speculated that MI5 was a potential perpetrator.

The Prime Minister and his colleagues agreed it would not be in the national interest for the discovery beneath the swan pit at the old monastery hospital to reach the public domain; not yet, anyway. A secular world, and other religions, would relish the opportunity to denigrate the Christian faith. The potential implications needed serious thought. A containment strategy needed to be agreed. Involving so many parties, the Anglican Church, the Government and the State, not to mention Her Majesty as Head of them all, this would take time. Not to mention the Vatican and an ageing cardinal, the Pope. How long had they got before the story leaked out?

Chapter 22

B ishop Banham felt very protective towards Jane. He could see how stressed she was about the potentially momentous nature of the discovery. Not for the first time, he was concerned for her welfare. His wife, Rebecca, thought too much so. Did he still fancy Jane, even after all these years? Rebecca had long felt her husband was holding something back, some inner demon. Even bishops were not immune from them. She felt its ghostly presence watching over them, permeating through their marriage, but she did not have the powers of exorcism.

The anxious bishop phoned Jane on her mobile. No answer. He tried the landline. Again there was no reply. The bishop was right to be worried. At much the same time, Jane Clifford-Oxbury left home to collect her daily paper and some fresh bread. She did not return. The local newsagent was the last person to see her.

It was not long afterwards that colleagues reported that Jane Clifford-Oxbury had disappeared, taking her secrets with her - what she had seen, what she knew. No one had any idea where she had gone, or who had taken her. The Bishop of Norwich kept his concerns to himself, at least for the time being. Inside, his stomach was churning and it was not all to do with religion. Was their shared personal secret safe?

What had happened to Jane? Who would do this? He wanted to do something, anything to help her; if necessary become *the 'Interfering Bishop',* but that was not possible. He had just read, with increasing trepidation, about the laboratory explosion and it seemed too much of a coincidence. *'Am I next?'* In the event he could do nothing except pray.

Jane's home had been entered and all her documents and manuscripts taken, including her computer, laptop and all means of storage and communication. But who took them? One person put two and two together and came very close to four. Mike Burrows again met his editor, but not this time at *The Two Fishes*. On this occasion they chose a corner in a busy supermarket 'restaurant'. Hardly a fitting description, thought Mike, more of a café. This time no beer, just tasteless, cheap, black coffee. He also smoked and, fittingly, drank like the fish on the beer mats at *The Two Fishes* pub. Unlike the fish, it was rarely water that he drank - unless drowned in whisky. He was not a healthy individual, not that it worried him.

'What have you got?' asked Joe Culverhouse.

'Don't you think it a bit strange that the laboratory explosion happened within hours of that conversation?'

'I expected you to link the two. I have no doubt you are right. Sinister forces are at work, especially as it seems the professor has gone AWOL.'

'We could print a story speculating that a secret experiment had taken place at the laboratory – one that proved explosive in more ways than one!'

'It will be a matter of record that the forensic scientist and his colleague were working on Easter weekend, so give the story some kind of religious inference.'

'Let's run with that – I'll speak to the Governor', as the proprietor of *Britain on Sunday* was known.

★★★

There are moles in all sorts of unexpected places. There was one at the offices of *Britain on Sunday*. Like most moles he kept his head down, and no one knew who the supergrass was, even his paymaster. The call to Sir Julian Barclay, the Cabinet Secretary, much to his intense annoyance, was anonymous and untraceable.

'Bad news, Prime Minister; very bad news – the people at *Britain on Sunday* are running with a story this weekend which threatens to reveal all. We don't know exactly how much they know or how they got it. We have to plan for this to be public knowledge, perhaps within hours or days.'

'The bastards. How did they get this? Beyond the law, I'll bet. Call a clandestine meeting, somewhere away from Downing Street. Include the Bishop of Norwich, given his intimate knowledge of events, and include the archivist lady.'

'I'm afraid not her, Prime Minister – she's gone missing.'

'How the hell did that happen? I thought we had her under surveillance.'

'It appears we were beaten to it.'

'If *Britain on Sunday* know that, their story will have even more credence – get an injunction, stop them, do whatever it takes. We, and certainly the archbishops, need more time.'

In Rome, the hierarchy in the Vatican were only too well aware of recent events. Their sources, both legitimate and illegitimate, had kept them informed. They had their own moles at *Britain on Sunday*. They knew full well public exposure was imminent. They, unlike everyone else, had feared this moment – '*The Doomsday Revelation*', as it was known. Their long-held secrets, kept through generations, could no longer be preserved. As far as they were concerned, with Jesus Christ exposed as a mere mortal and married as well, the Church's one foundation, their faith, could hardly survive in its present form. The Bible story would be dead in the water, engulfed in a flood tide, and this time there would be no reincarnation of Moses to part the waves of destruction. What was worse was that other religions, faiths, would surely flourish, filling the spiritual void left by the Christians. It was suggested their only, barely plausible, recourse might be to rely on the words in *Romans* Chapter 1 verse 3. '*Concerning his son Jesus Christ our Lord, which was made of the seed of David according to the flesh...*' His very survival of the Crucifixion, and the Resurrection which followed, could be still be classified as the miracle on which the faith was based. His alleged marriage after the Crucifixion demonstrated his human weakness, but that showed He was among us, with us, in thought word and deed. Some might even have to abandon their long-held abhorrence of the role of women in the church to enable the Catholic Church to survive. Priests would be allowed to marry. The Vatican State and its message hitherto, were in severe jeopardy. They were well aware that any defence was full of holes that scholars would take little time to expose. On the other hand, there were numerous validations of the historical accuracy of the accounts of the Resurrection, not least the five hundred eyewitnesses recorded in *Paul's*

Gospel. The conclusion was that they should stick rigidly to the assertion that the validity of the documents was unproven. It was not a very different story in the heart of the cathedral precincts in Canterbury, or at Lambeth Palace.

★★★

Another meeting took place that evening. It was held in a rented flat in Elvaston Mews, in the heart of South Kensington, London SW7. The three participants arrived separately, unremarkable in their conventional city suits. Their leader spoke first in a strong, Italian accent.

'One left – he must be taken out.'

'What exactly do you mean: "taken out?"' enquired a second man, this time with an English accent. He continued: 'He is one of us.'

'Only loosely,' replied the third man.

'Yes, but we risk another schism in the Church if this gets out.'

'It must not "get out" as you put it. Indeed, no one would suspect us to eliminate one of our own.' The leader continued: 'Our intelligence reports suggest a secret Ministerial meeting has been arranged. Normally these are held in Downing Street. This one may be elsewhere, which may make it easier for us. Our target must not, in whatever circumstances, attend that meeting.'

They left the flat separately, on foot, never to return, having agreed what was to be done. It mattered little where the Government meeting was held, provided it was in or near London. Given the likely attendees, they would not travel too far from Downing Street or too far out of London.

★★★

Early on Saturday afternoon a shiny black Daimler car drove up to the front door of the Bishop's Palace in Norwich, arriving earlier than expected, apparently for security reasons. It had been dispatched to collect the Bishop, driven by a uniformed security man from MI5, the security service for the Government based at Thames House in London. The driver of 'AOC1', the codeword for the Archbishop's official car, rang the bell, showed his credentials and ushered the Bishop into the spacious, leather back seat. It was fitted out with a TV monitor, an alarm button, a drinks cupboard and a coffee dispenser. There was an intercom connection with the driver's compartment. The fact that it had blacked-out windows did not worry Bishop Banham as he settled down, thinking about the meeting ahead, and also Sunday's sermon. He should be back by 11am next morning. He placed his attaché case containing the precious copies of the documents on the seat beside him. For security reasons, the driver himself did not know their destination. He advised they would be routed by the specially programmed satellite navigation system as the journey progressed.

The journey down the A11 and the M11 was uneventful. They joined the M25 at Junction 27 and headed south-east towards the Dartford crossing. It was a gusty late afternoon, but not gale force, as they crossed the Thames over the Queen Elizabeth Bridge. Bishop Marcus looked down at the river below and spotted the tide was on the turn, a reflection of his own thoughts; was it going in or out?

The driver went straight through the toll booths without stopping. He assumed they had a special dispensation. The black Daimler, now accompanied by a police motor cyclist with flashing blue light, then unexpectedly pulled up on the left-hand side area directly beyond the toll. The intercom crackled, the driver informing the Bishop that he would now swap into an unmarked saloon car, a black BMW, which had drawn up alongside. This would take him to the destination.

A tall, dark man, of swarthy build and complexion, opened the car door and escorted Bishop Banham to the back seat of the waiting BMW, putting his jacket in the boot.

'Routine security switch, sir,' was all he said. As the BMW disappeared from view heading south on the M25, the Daimler also headed south, then turned off at Junction 1A on to the A226 towards the aptly-named Gravesend, and a decaying street of derelict warehouses. A short while later there was a loud explosion. The black Daimler, assumed to be 'AOC1' was no more. The real official car had just arrived at the Bishop's Palace, only to find he had already left.

★★★

In her home city of Christchurch, Laura's religious research, her search for life's truths, veered off at a tangent. She spotted a book on mysticism and voices from the spirits. The blurb on the back spoke of miracles, an immanent force, messages, omens and signs, available to us all if only we would look. She wondered if the book was speaking to her. Out of curiosity she decided to make the purchase.

'Probably cranky,' she surmised, 'Good job Paul can't see me.'

★★★

Paul had returned to his uncle's farm to collect his things in readiness to return home. The end of Paul's visit had come upon them quickly, the lambing season was long over and there was nothing he could usefully do to earn money. He was dreading leaving Laura behind. He had found his soul mate and now it seemed inevitable he would lose her. He thought of their lovemaking, the trip to Queenstown, the consummation in her flat, now about to become but mere memories.

Laura, waiting for him to arrive at her flat to share her bed for one last time, reflected that, despite the several occasions he had been with his Muslim friends, she had not gleaned much at all from him. This would not go down well with her employers.

The next day they took the short flight to Auckland, Laura telling him her ticket was funded from her trust. After their moonlit dinner in Auckland harbour, the mood seemed to change in an instant, their final hug strained, as if all that had gone before was no more. Her less-than-passionate kiss lingered with him as he travelled to the airport. It had been no way to conclude his visit, leaving him to travel halfway round the world distraught at the manner of their parting, alone with his thoughts and memories.

Neither had seen the dark-suited man with a receding hairline and pointed chin, once again lurking on a street corner nearby, watching every move Laura made as Paul disappeared in his taxi. She walked disconcertedly back to her hotel, her loyalties divided, her mind in turmoil. She sent a brief message to her employer confirming her target's departure. They already knew.

Back home in her flat the next day she picked up the mystical book and, seeking distraction from her angst, immersed herself in the strange world of spirits and alleged communications with the 'far world'. She was intrigued to read of references to 'divine forces' and wondered if any had been present in her life. In some strange way, all this wondering and worrying led her back to her college days, the letter 'w'. She had once attended a course on public speaking. One of the routines was for a fellow student to place an object in a brown paper bag. She remembered you had to take it out, not knowing what it was in advance. You then had to speak for two minutes, non-stop, and without deviation or repetition, about the object. She recalled the pot of honey and the muddle she got into as to whether the honey or the bees came first. She also recalled other less innocent objects, chuckling at the recollection of the packet of condoms. Another student had a hand on the buzzer, and pressed it when you hesitated, repeated or deviated. The 'err' meter, they called it. 'Why on earth don't professional newsreaders and reporters and their ilk have such training? Some of them are really terrible,' she reflected.

She remembered that she only began to succeed with this daunting little exercise if she worked with the 'w' letter - what, why, where, whom, which, etc. She was thrown back to her search for some meaning in life.

Who am I?
Where do I come from?
What is the purpose?
Where am I in time?
Where do I go next?

Who is God?
What is God?
Which God?
Where is God?

She had so many questions. She read passages from a book about the value of faith. 'Faith sees the invisible' was a phrase that stuck in her mind. It talked about Judaism, Islam and Christianity all being monotheist religions – one true God.

There was reference to a passage from *Joel* Chapter II, verses 28-30, which declared that old men will dream dreams and young men see visions. She checked her Bible. Scarily, it went on to say: *'The sun shall be turned into darkness and the moon into blood, before the great and the terrible day of the Lord come.'* She thought of Paul and his predictions. She decided to read no further.

That night she did indeed dream. She was having an audience with a dark-haired old lady, a mystic.

'You are a sensitive girl. You are looking for peace of mind. You will find it. Your great-grandparents are watching over you. They are safe. The rest of your year is bound up with numbers.'

When she awoke, and most of the next day, she thought about the dream. It was reassuring about her great-grandparents, 'But was that my wishful thinking?' The numbers thing was curious. Late in the afternoon she got out her Bible. This time she opened it at the fourth book of Moses, otherwise known as *Numbers*.

It didn't make any sense to her. It talked about people in the wilderness. 'Well that could be me,' she thought. It talked about the order of tribes in their tents. The St.

Paul's protesters came to mind. She put her Bible away, exasperated. Nothing there spoke to her.

★★★

That Saturday evening there was yet another meeting. It did not take place in Cabinet Office Briefing Room 'A'. It was somewhere in the tranquillity of the Kent countryside. Those attending were the Prime Minister, Dick Benson, the Deputy Prime Minister, the Home Secretary, the Chairman of the secretive Joint Intelligence Committee, and their private secretaries. Also present were the Archbishop of Canterbury and his trusted aides, representing the Anglican Church, and the Archbishop of Westminster, accompanied by Cardinal Napoliano, who had flown in from Rome, to represent the Catholic Church. The Acting Commissioner of the Metropolitan Police had also been summoned, the Commissioner himself having recently resigned. There was no sign of Bishop Banham.

'Ladies and Gentlemen,' the Prime Minister began in his gravelly tone reserved for such occasions, his demeanour exuding gravitas and importance, as he paused to look round the attendees. He proffered apologies for the missing bishop. In his deep, authoritative voice he outlined the predicament they faced.

'We face a grave situation, with the possibility of severe unrest and disturbance. That is assuming that the Catholic Church and the Anglican Church are to be discredited and potentially face meltdown. We could well face a constitutional crisis.'

'There is no need for this to happen,' interjected the Archbishop of Westminster, 'The alleged documents perished in the laboratory fire.'

'Surely you would not stand in the way of the truth, Archbishop?'

'We don't yet know it is the truth. The story is nothing without testimony from Bishop Banham and the archivist. And where is the Bishop? Is he not supposed to be attending this meeting?'

'I, we, have not seen the documents. Their veracity cannot be proven,' interrupted the Cardinal.

'Even the story itself will be enough to cause massive derision. Denial, warranted or not, will only exacerbate the situation,' retorted the Prime Minister.

At this point an aide to the Home Secretary knocked and entered the room.

'I need to inform you of bad news. Firstly, sir, the car bringing the Bishop of Norwich has been found in a derelict area in Gravesend just off the M25, wrecked by an explosion, a massive fireball. We have no news of the Bishop. There is more, Prime Minister.'

'What else can there be?'

'That car was not the official Daimler dispatched to collect him; someone else got there first.'

'I want an immediate investigation. We have to know who has inside knowledge, not tomorrow, now! Anything else?'

'I'm afraid there is, Prime Minister. Our attempt to get an injunction to prevent *Britain on Sunday* from publishing has failed. It will publish tomorrow morning.'

'And be damned!' shouted one of the archbishops angrily.

'Archbishop, please!' interjected the Home Secretary.

The hearing had taken place in camera. Justice Nicholas Squires, very reluctantly, as a lifelong Christian himself, placed the requirements of the law first, notwithstanding the potential damage to his Church.

He held the publication to be 'in the national interest'. 'The Churches have the resources to defend their own interests,' he declared. He did not know that the Vatican, despite its untold wealth, was running at a budgeted loss for the third year running. Its treasures did not pay bills. Unlike governments, it would not readily sell the 'family gold' to balance the books.

There was little else they could do other than prepare for the morning. It was a long night at Lambeth Palace and in the Vatican. The news bulletins reported that a street in Gravesend had been cordoned off after an explosion. The Government had the luxury of a day's grace to see what emerged. The Prime Minister would deliver a statement to the House of Commons on Monday.

When the men and women of religion had left, the Prime Minister remarked to his colleagues: 'The Catholics didn't have much to say. The Cardinal hardly said a word. It makes you wonder if they already knew something. After all, it is well known that they hold archives full of ancient documents and papers.'

'They probably have the bloodline on an Excel spreadsheet,' remarked the Home Secretary dryly, 'And their own copies of the documents.'

The remaining participants then broke for refreshment, coffee and strong drinks, brandy or fine malt, with or without water, before reconvening at 9.30pm. They had no doubt that belief in a Christian God would be lost in many quarters. Their concerns were the possibility of civil unrest, the security of the clergy and its estate, the many irreplaceable historic buildings, and what might become of Christians themselves.

The black BMW with blacked-out windows had sped south on the M25 before turning right at Junction 4 towards Croydon, and then to South London. By this time Bishop Banham had descended into a drowsy stupor. He knew nothing of the subsequent transfer to a very plain, unmarked Ford Focus, or of his destination.

***

'Good morning, Bishop. I hope you slept soundly.'

The Bishop awoke with a start. His head was heavy as he raised it from the pillow. He was in a light, airy room with pastel-blue curtains. He could hear the birds singing outside and, in the distance, the chime of church bells. He was sure it was not Heaven, but it was pleasant enough. Or was it a dream? The apparition at the end of his bed became clearer as his eyes came into focus and he recognised the portly gentleman at the end of his bed. It was Cardinal Napoliano.

'My attaché case – where is it? I have a sermon to preach.'

'It may be some time before you deliver your sermon. You will have no need for your briefcase. We have taken the documents for safe keeping. I suggest you take a shower, refresh yourself. A light buffet breakfast will be provided shortly.'

'Where am I? Why are you holding me? Is Jane here as well?' asked the Bishop indignantly.

'I think you know full well why you are here. We will ask the questions. You will answer them,' was the rather menacing reply. With that, Cardinal Napoliano left the room. The Bishop sat on his bed, bewildered that he should be treated so disdainfully by a fellow churchman. Especially one with whom he had walked 'the holy mile' at Little Walsingham, the shrine in Norfolk, where it was customary for representatives of both Anglican and Catholic Churches to walk together in a rare show of unity.

Unbeknown to Bishop Banham his first love was nearby, further down the corridor, just as she had been in the student Halls of Residence all those years before. Except then he had been to her room, many times, and many nights.

★★★

In Christchurch Laura saw a wall poster advertising the visit of Lucinda Palmer, New Zealand's best-known mystic. The poster gave an invitation to make a personal appointment. The lady had clearly not predicted the Christchurch earthquake, thought Laura sceptically but, nevertheless, she was fascinated and, remembering her dream, plucked up the courage to fix an appointment. They met in a corner of the local Community Centre.

'Relax, dear,' said the mystic, Lucinda. 'I can see you have not come to one of these before.'

'How does she know?' pondered Laura.

'Let me hold your hand.' Lucinda examined her palm lines. 'You are troubled by family misfortunes and your treatment of someone dear to you. You are searching for solutions.'

'Easy that; aren't we all?' thought Laura, but the accuracy of her comment was chilling. Lucinda continued:

'You were born in the second month.'

'How on earth…?'

Lucinda interrupted: 'Not on earth, dear; I can tap into another dimension. I can access the world of the spirits. It's a resource available to everyone, if they open up their senses. You are troubled by the sudden death of family relatives. Not your father, no; further back. They are still alive. They have simply left their bodies behind. Their souls are immortal. Do not fret over them. Watch out for signs, for omens, for messages. They are always there, but people don't see them. Nothing remains the same for very long; the universe is constantly evolving under the guidance of a divine hand. You see, the essence of life is the spirit.'

'You believe in God?'

'Of course; God is the ultimate source of all things, but not in the conventional, religious sense.'

'The Christian faith?' asked Laura.

'God is out there – traditional faiths are mostly based on rules, rituals, dogmas, ideologies, often flawed by politics of one kind or another. God transcends all that and is the source, the love, the light, behind all religions. It is frailties of the human kind that diminish religion in the eyes of the world.

'My fellow spiritualists speak of an immanent "revelation". God is available to you, Laura. Do not fall for the constraints of a religious club. The Roman Catholic Church, for example, controls its members, does not approve of a personal relationship with God, other than through itself. Other faiths are similar.'

'I had this strange dream,' interjected Laura, anxious to resolve this mystery.

'Dreams are often an expression of inner thoughts, the gateway to your innermost being. They are a means of connecting with your *"Source Field"*, the conduit for your spiritual life and guidance. Don't fall into the idea that we have no control over our lives, our life beyond. Maintain a positive attitude. Hold my hand while I immerse myself with you.'

There was a prolonged silence. For Laura it felt like an eternity. Perhaps Lucinda had gone there.

'Your dream; there are numbers involved, but not the Bible's book in the First Testament. Before you were born there used to be a number to call to trace relatives in an emergency. Although it was based at Scotland Yard in London, it was known the world over. It was long before mobile phones and computers. It was "Whitehall 1212". That's where you need to look.'

'The numbers one and two again,' exclaimed Laura.

'Precisely, my dear.'

Still puzzled, but even more intrigued, Laura thanked her and left. The meeting prompted her to undertake further research into her ancestry. With the aid of one of the many internet sites, and a partially-completed family tree borrowed years earlier from old Uncle Noel, she pieced together many of the missing links. She should not have embarked on this journey back to the past. It struck her like a thunderbolt. She looked again. 'Oh no, it cannot be!' Trembling with anxiety, she feared the worst.

Chapter 23 – April 2012 – The Alternative Scenario Unfolds

'Christianity a Fraud.'
'Jesus Not Divine.'
'Jesus married Mary.'
'Mary not a virgin.'
'Jesus, son of Man, not God.'

Thus screamed the news headlines in *Britain on Sunday*.

'Rumours of a royal wedding bar none are circulating the globe this morning. We have it on good authority from "informed sources" that messages are circulating in high places that Christ's wedding certificate has been found. This appears to corroborate the considerable speculation which has circulated on internet sites in recent years. What will stun the world is that the wedding is thought to have taken place after the crucifixion. There are also rumours that there is yet further documentation to suggest they had children. He cannot have ascended up to heaven, unless you believe in instantaneous reincarnation. This begs the question that the faith on which the Christian Church is built is based, if not on a lie, then on a false premise. The Church's one foundation is shattered into tiny pieces. Readers will be immediately aware of the implications. Those who alleged that this was a Christian country have had the rug pulled from under them. The Christian festivals of Christmas and Easter will be gone for ever, to become but receding memories of naïve mysticism. Churches will become community hubs, post offices, shops, cafés, frequented by the many

rather than the few. The ramifications will be enormous and threaten the very fabric of our increasingly secular society.'

So ran the story. Inside, editorials speculated on the implications.

The newspaper had been meticulous in founding its story on 'rumours'. With all the modern means of communication, rumours could come from anywhere. There would be no need to reveal the real source. It was a short journey from rumour to perception to fact in the public mind, exacerbated by users of Facebook, Twitter, I-pads, smartphones and the like.

The Vatican was, however, well-prepared, and issued a statement via its Press Office just as morning Mass began. It read as follows:

'The Catholic Church totally refutes the malicious and scurrilous rumours being spread by a British Sunday newspaper. The story is without foundation. We have seen no evidence of any marriage of our Lord Jesus Christ, and nor is there any. We urge Christians, wherever they may be, to disassociate themselves from such mischievous nonsense. We intend to make no further statement on the matter.'

The Archbishop of Canterbury quickly followed the Papal lead, stating his endorsement of the Vatican's statement.

This was not sufficient to stem the tide. Chatter on social media reached a crescendo. *Britain on Sunday* simply screamed:

'Church in denial of Jesus story - Christianity's Cover up?'

All this had the effect of spreading the contagion, dwarfing any statement from the Church.

Thomas was dumbfounded by the news, broken to him by a worried parishioner just before morning service. He asked his congregation for support and guidance, attempting to reassure them it was mischievous nonsense. Distraught and unbelieving, he devoured the newspapers on his return home. He fielded telephone calls from his flock, refusing to answer one from his brother. He could imagine Peter gloating at the other end of the phone. After that he took the phone off the hook. Paul, too, was astonished to hear the news on his return from New Zealand.

The Monday-morning press was saturated with speculation concerning Jesus' survival of the crucifixion. There were conflicting opinions expressed by medical experts on both sides of the argument. Articles were published in specialist medical magazines over the next few days as to the likelihood of a family and, inevitably, on to the bloodline and the DNA structure. A retired doctor claimed to have a spreadsheet of Jesus' family tree adorning the walls of his downstairs toilet. Another claimed to have matched the mitochondrial DNA of a mother with the DNA profile specified in an article in *GP News*. He could not release his results on the grounds of patient confidentiality. She was a staunch Catholic and her permission was withheld.

Then, for Christians, came questions of the purpose of human existence. Without a Creator, a guiding hand, there was a spiritual void.

Other religions proclaimed their various faiths, disassociating themselves from, and in many cases celebrating, the apparent meltdown in the Christian Church. Conversion to their faiths would soon, no doubt, strengthen their position further. It was this backlash, and the threat of Sharia Law, that the Prime Minister and his inner sanctum feared most. There were numerous groups, more commonly described as 'cells', talking, plotting, planning, and turning the situation to their advantage. Paul's friends Hussain, Malik, Abdul and Jamal were no exception – Malik was a member of the Sharia Islamic Law Committee; he was working on a draft of their UK penal code, whilst also lobbying for their laws to be recognised within the British legal system.

At Buckingham Palace, Her Majesty's advisers were discussing The Royal Prerogative at that very moment. If a constitutional crisis between Church and State emerged, to what extent could, or should, she exercise it? It was a vexed question, perhaps remote, but no stone should be left unturned. There was no written constitution. Her normal recourse would be to call a meeting of the Privy Council, but many of its members were politicians, so would they be able to give impartial advice? With her encyclopaedic knowledge of parliamentary affairs she was well aware of pressure for the use of the Prerogative to be reduced or amended. She readily recalled the 2009 *Government Review of Executive Royal Prerogative Powers*, which called for wide-scale reform.

Should she relinquish her position as Head of the apparently discredited Church? The disestablishment movement was led by secularists, who had been flexing their muscles before this crisis emerged. They sought to challenge what they regarded as the highly privileged status of the Church of England in what they considered to be a secular state. They argued that other faiths did not have such a position in our multicultural society, nor should they. They cited the example of Norway, where the Government was in the process of passing a constitutional amendment severing all ties with the Church. The secularists were threatening to use the new e-petition arrangements to raise the hundred thousand votes needed to pressurise the Government.

Prime Minister Benson was reminded by his advisers of the 1929 attempt to revise the *Book of Common Prayer*. This failed, but back then there were renewed calls for the separation of Church and State, so as to prevent parliamentary interference in matters of worship.

'I suppose the boot's on the other foot now. We may need to do something to prevent religious interference in matters of government!' he exclaimed.

'Sir, that is exactly what the National Secular Society says,' replied the Cabinet Secretary. 'Apparently we are the only Western democracy to have church representatives in our legislature as a right, rather than through the ballot box.'

'I find that staggering; we are the only ones, yet we invented democracy in the first place. Just like football - we start the whole thing then lose our way, become second-rate.'

'Unlike rugby, where we are still at the top table,' ventured Sir Christopher, in a superior tone.

'And what about you civil servants? We delegate to you to implement our policies and you simply set your own agenda, regardless, knowing we soon won't be around to complain. And, no one ever elected you!' he proclaimed, having the last word as always. That was his Prerogative.

With that, he was off on his bike, past the security guards at the end of Downing Street and on to the House of Commons. The Prime Minister liked to occasionally display his green credentials, not perhaps appreciating that the team of security officers on their motor bikes, desperately trying to provide the necessary level of protection, were damaging the environment more than he was saving it. It was the message which mattered more than the cost, he stated a year later, when called before the House of Commons Select Committee.

The Prime Minister played a straight bat in the Commons on that Monday afternoon. The Government had no time for rumour and unsubstantiated allegations in relation to issues facing the religious community. Her Majesty's Government must continue to focus on the economic situation and the reduction of the national debt. The Church of England had issued a statement and it was not for Her Majesty's Government to comment on ecclesiastical matters.

The Prime Minister had been somewhat disingenuous. He had not said anything that could be construed as misleading Parliament. He, and his advisers, did realise the seriousness of the situation. They had no wish to sound any public alarm bells; they were playing for time.

A meeting of COBRA was called. This time there were no representatives from the Vatican, but the Bishop of London was invited, as well as the two Anglican archbishops from York and Canterbury. Their concern was for the security of the clergy and the Church's many historical buildings.

The riots of the previous year were fresh in the mind. It would be a national, not purely religious, disaster if buildings embodying the national heritage should be destroyed in acts of vengeance against the Christians. Whilst there had long been rumours, conjecture, that Jesus had survived the Crucifixion, rumours of bloodlines, the DNA reports, had the effect of transforming speculation into fact. This became the public perception. People were all too readily discarding the religious fairy tales, the fanciful talk of miracles and eternal life. A devastated Thomas Morgan saw his congregation dwindle yet further. The bishops steadfastly expressed their determination to maintain the position of the Church of England. The last thing they and the remaining adherents to Christianity wanted was further corroboration of the DNA evidence. It arrived suddenly, without warning, from an unexpected source.

Chapter 24 – The Alternative Scenario Unfolds

T he unwelcome corroboration for the veracity of the discovery in Norwich came with the arrival of the head of Special Branch of the Metropolitan Police, Elizabeth Langley, accompanied by the head of MI5, Sir Gordon Bamford, to see the Prime Minister. They had requested an urgent meeting with him and his Cabinet Secretary. Sir Christopher Perrin, in his capacity of the PM's Principal Private Secretary, also attended. Elizabeth Langley, tall, elegant in a blue cotton dress, with immaculately coiffed, greying hair, took centre stage.

'Thank you for seeing us, Prime Minister. I have important information of which you need to be made aware.'

'So I am to be included in the loop this time,' retorted the PM sarcastically, still smarting at his exclusion from information hidden from him by his civil servants. 'Forgive my cynicism, Miss, err, Mrs, Ms Langley; please carry on.'

No one had thought to mention her marital status; a pet hate of his, this dilemma of how to address women without causing offence. 'Just how do these women expect us to know if they don't tell us?' he mumbled under his breath. He could sense the pompous Sir Christopher enjoying his discomfort.

'There is, was, this archaeologist, a Scotsman by the name of Jake McDonald, who was on an assignment in the Middle East, near the ancient city of Qumran. In case you were not aware, Prime Minister, it is an area rich with ancient religious relics and artefacts.'

'Yes, yes I am fully aware of that; please get to the point.'

'This professor, a bit of an eccentric by all accounts, had recently returned to this country to convalesce after a severe bout of malaria. Sadly, he passed away last week.'

'Another bloody professor,' mumbled the irritable PM under his breath. Elizabeth Langley continued unabated, her voice smooth, confident, unruffled by the Prime Minister's intake of breath. He decided he should not dismiss this woman lightly; she had an aura about her that demanded respect. He remembered being lectured at school not to read between the lines before he had read them; he would pay attention to Ms Langley.

'His relatives discovered a voicemail message, one of the last ones he received when in Qumran. It was from a former colleague of his, a Mr Judas Swan, the scientist killed in the laboratory explosion.'

The Prime Minister sat bolt upright, now listening intently.

Gordon Bamford then interceded. 'We have a transcript of their conversation, which we obtained from the mobile phone company. It goes like this,' he declared, reading from his laptop:

'You really aren't joking, are you? Here am I near Christ's birthplace, doing all the hard work, covered head to foot in dust and sand, sweltering in the sticky heat of the eastern

Mediterranean, and you tell me you have his marriage certificate sitting in your safe in Norfolk. You jammy bugger! I have to get a flight to Norwich to see this for myself.'

'Sorry, Jake, no way. This is one hundred and fifty per cent confidential and must stay that way; my job, my mortgage, depend upon it. When you have time to think you will understand exactly why. And, don't get pissed one night and tell everybody.'

'Yeah, OK, I get the picture. I promise to be the soul of discretion.'

Mr Bamford then addressed the Prime Minister. 'They then exchanged some information by email. It is this I need to tell you about. Some of the characteristics of the DNA sequence of the fibres of cloth and human hair, referred to in their exchange of information, closely match that of some skeletal remains found at Qumran and the rumoured burial place of Christ. And, to add to that, further analysis showed evidence of "endogenous retroviruses".'

'And what the hell are those?' demanded Prime Minister Benson, butting in before the civil servant could continue. Undeterred, he continued.

'They are ancient viruses hard-wired into DNA structures, possibly the root cause of modern diseases such as AIDS and some cancers. The particular strain identified matches others found in that Middle-Eastern region. It also seems the coins found in Norwich are of Roman origin, dating from around AD 46. The scientists do comment that the DNA samples of the remains at Qumran must be assessed alongside the genealogical and genetic evidence, and they also have confirmed that the bones found there indicate what they describe as "humiliation injuries" consistent with a crucifixion and also a sword wound. Unfortunately there is insufficient evidence to say whether these injuries would have been fatal. There certainly seems to be a more than circumstantial case which can be made for the cloth and presumably, therefore, the documents, to have come from that region.'

Elizabeth Langley then chipped in. 'Clearly, in the absence of the documents which, together with the Norwich scientists, perished in the fire, we cannot now verify the DNA comparison, but one has to admit it is some coincidence. It's not conclusive, but it does give added credence to the Norwich discovery. We also spoke, in complete confidence, to a colleague of his, Sir Philip Pyrford-Bolton, but he claimed he had not had any recent contact with the late Jake McDonald. It seems they fell out over a game of chess.'

'His death seems somewhat inconvenient. Any suspicious circumstances?' asked the Prime Minister.

'It seems genuine enough; the Coroner was satisfied that he succumbed to the infection. However, crucially, the viral illness that killed Professor McDonald is thought to be the modern derivative of the ancient one identified in the Norwich discovery.'

'This is all very interesting but, in the absence of the documents, the evidence from these emails is purely circumstantial, albeit pretty convincing. For that reason I propose we keep it confidential and hope those bloody journalists have not got wind of it, especially *Britain on Sunday*. They seem to know most things before we do,' the PM added facetiously. 'If there are any leaks the culprit will be hung, drawn and quartered - just like those poor bloody Norfolk swans,' decreed the Prime Minister. His tone was fearsome and unmistakable.

'Is the Archbishop aware of this development?' asked Sir Christopher.

'Get the bishops together again. We'd better tell them before it leaks out,' the PM barked, looking straight at Sir Christopher, his emissary and confidant of the Archbishop of Canterbury.

★★★

Bishop Banham was in no position to help his Church. He had been interviewed many times by local radio and television networks, and the local press. He had, however, never been interrogated. He suspected it would not be pleasant. On the other hand he was, he assumed, in the hands of fellow Christians. His sense of foreboding was exacerbated by his knowledge of history and the fact that he had been moved to a darkened room, with its windows boarded. Churches of all kinds had never been reluctant to use intimidating tactics, even force when it suited them. He thought of his predecessor, the Fighting Bishop. He must show the same resolve under duress. He could feel his temple beginning to tense and swell, the wrinkles on his forehead tightening as if a tight noose had been applied. He had rarely experienced apprehension like this, even fear. Fear for Jane, and also, unworthily, for himself. He thought, too, of his estranged son, who would have no knowledge of his father's predicament. A relief perhaps? Remembering his calling, mindful of the need for faith in the face of adversity, he steeled himself to face the suffering he expected to be visited upon him.

To the Bishop's surprise, Cardinal Napoliano was accompanied by a female, very smart, wearing a black suit, probably late twenties or early thirties. He surmised she must be some kind of administrative assistant. She could hardly be a cleric of the religious kind. Nor, he presumed, was the burly man with enormous hands, hovering ominously in front of the door, the only means of escape.

'Bishop Marcus, you are being held in what we might describe as "protective custody". Now, I assume you have seen the original documents? The copies you had with you tell us nothing which can be construed as evidence.'

'I have not seen the originals, Cardinal. Jane Clifford-Oxbury simply came to see me to tell me about them.'

'Did you not even ask to see them?'

'She had arranged for them to be securely stored at the laboratory. I asked her to have them re-tested to ensure their authenticity.'

'That was very remiss of you, Bishop. I, we,' he glanced at his young assistant, 'Would have expected you to want to see them straight away.'

The Bishop again sensed the menace in the Cardinal's voice. His hands were becoming clammy, sticky, and he could feel the nausea in his stomach. He wanted to mop his brow; wipe the sweat from his forehead. It was hard not to reveal his anxiety.

'As I said, I considered it wise for them to be stored securely under laboratory conditions.'

'Well, it wasn't very secure, was it? They perished in the explosion.'

'I can hardly have anticipated that, Cardinal.'

The Bishop was sorely tempted to suggest that Cardinal Napoliano knew everything there was to know about the cause of the explosion and, indeed, about the disappearance of his former lover, but knew that would not be wise. Instead he rather lamely stated that he had no knowledge that phones were being hacked and emails intercepted.

'Very naïve of you, Bishop. You have not been a very helpful witness.'

'That's as maybe, but I am, like you, a man of the cloth. I would not lie to you.'

'No, perhaps not, but you might be ecumenical with the truth.'

At this point the young assistant said her first words. 'The Cardinal's grasp of the English language is not complete. He means "economical".'

'Please describe the whole sequence of events to us.' It was more of a command than a request. Bishop Banham felt a fevered flush engulfing him. Unconsciously mopping his brow with his purple handkerchief, the Bishop summoned up some courage to complain.

'I demand to speak to the Archbishop of Canterbury; you have no right to hold me like this.'

'You have no such option; now tell me all you know.'

The Bishop duly related the whole story. He hoped it would tally with Jane's version, for he was now more convinced than ever they were holding her, either under the same roof or, perhaps, in Rome.

'This is all most unsatisfactory. By the way, the Daimler in which you travelled to London has been blown up in an explosion. You will be assumed to have perished inside. It was a massive fireball. Your jacket and, indeed, your attaché case were left in the back of the Daimler for good measure, so the forensic evidence will suggest you were still in the car. The motor cyclist was not an officer of Her Majesty's Constabulary. The spot where you changed cars was carefully chosen, away from the watchful eyes of the cameras. They will not have known whether or not you were inside because the car had blacked-out windows. They will have assumed the fire was no accident, but we expect them to cover it up. They would not want any publicity. They have said so far only that you have gone missing. When it is revealed after lengthy forensic investigation that you perished in a road traffic accident, no doubt your memorial service will be televised. If you co-operate we might let you watch it, "live", as it were,' sneered the Cardinal.

'And what happens to me after that?'

The reply was chilling.

'Remember the story of the sacrificial lamb?'

With those final words he turned towards the door and marched out, followed by his assistant. The burly man gave him a parting stare, as if to warn him not to try anything even if the opportunity arose.

Jane, close by, knew nothing of this. She had eventually acclimatised to her new life. Initially it had been frightening, then tedious, and now suffocating in its remorseless routine. There were no Friday nights, or weekends to look forward to; every day was the same, and they all felt like Mondays. She longed for the great outdoors, to smell freshly-mown grass, hear the birdsong, to see the sun go down, even to walk along the dunes beside a remote, windy and sand-swept Norfolk beach in the depth of winter. She was allowed library books of her choice, but knew they were vetted before she got them. She wondered how young Paul, presumably now back from New Zealand, was getting on. She had always kept an eye on him and was not around to do so. At least she could rely on Mary. There was no radio or television. Her two guards were a diversion, one an older woman, courteous and quite friendly, the other a burly, intimidating presence, younger, but abrupt, rude and sullen. She named them 'Jekyll and Hyde'.

★★★

The Church was already in a dark place. It had not taken kindly to being challenged by the judiciary the previous February. A test case had been brought by the National Secular Society in an attempt to ban prayers at the beginning of local authority meetings. This ruling had been upheld by a judge in the High Court in London. The Archbishop of Canterbury had testily challenged the politicians by asking if the next step was the scrapping of prayers at the start of the parliamentary day, or, indeed, would prayers be banned in his cathedral and in churches across the land? Next stop the European Court of Human Rights? 'Is that a higher "God"?' he sarcastically asked.

A former Archbishop of Canterbury had been vociferous in calling for Christians to be given greater legal protection in the wake of cases where women had been disciplined or dismissed from employment for practising their faith, whether they were Christians, Muslims, Hindus, or, indeed, of any religious persuasion. At this particular time it was especially brave, if not foolhardy, to wear a cross at work.

A Government Minister, the Communities Secretary, defended the right to worship as a fundamental liberty.

Others argued it was no role of the state and the judiciary to defend that liberty in a country whose people had a thousand gods instead of one. The press asked what part the beleaguered Christian Church could play in such discussions. The Church argued that a poll taken just before the Norwich discovery had indicated that some seventy per cent of the population professed to be Christian at heart but chose not to show it. The Law Society advised its members not to require clients or members of the public to swear under oath clutching a Bible. Judges continued to adopt the practice in their courts, defying the public mood, asserting their independence.

The prayer issue was not, however, confined to the Christian Church. An Islamic charity angrily denounced the court judgment as an attack on all faiths. Hussain, Malik and the others reacted with fury, perceiving much of what was being said as an attack on Muhammad. Paul had been with Hussain and his friends when the verdict was announced, and they then asked him to leave. Hurt and bewildered that his friend Hussain should treat him in this way, Paul, not for the first time, began to harbour serious doubts about their intentions.

The Anglican Church was resisting the notion that its places of worship should be turned into armed fortresses. Ministers wondered how many worshippers there would actually be to need protection. Or had the Government suddenly become a preservation society for the clergy and their precious buildings?

The Church, in the absence of any proof, given the disappearance of the archivist, the Bishop and the document, or documents, stoutly defended its position.

That some kind of crisis would emerge seemed highly likely, but what form would it take?

Numerous attempts were made to trace the bloodline of Jesus. Some, like the good Doctor's, were well researched and plausible, some totally specious. A fortune awaited anyone with proof. Without the cloth or the marriage document, there could be none. The DNA samples had perished in the fire. The Christian faith could survive in the absence of proof; it always had. The coincidental discovery by the Scotsman Jake McDonald was not in the public domain.

It was fortunate for Jane Clifford-Oxbury that neither the Church nor the Government wanted her to surface. There had as yet been no publicity concerning her disappearance; she was simply a missing person. She would not have wanted to take centre stage in such a controversy but she had seen the documents, was convinced of their authenticity, and was the one witness who could potentially blow apart the stance taken by the Church to counter her 'revelations'.

In Christchurch, Laura was shocked at the news headlines. 'No God,' she wondered, 'Or just no Christian God? And some kind of birth certificate?' From what Paul had told her the similarities with Muhammad were striking. After all, he had married and had children. 'What would Paul's dad make of that?' she wondered. She tried to contact Paul but her mobile network was temporarily down - again. It was unable to cope with the sheer volume of traffic circulating the globe.

The last message Paul had received before his calls were suspended was from his geologist friend, Miles

Mulligan, with his posh title of Dr Mulligan. The text message alarmed Paul.

Chapter 25 - The Alternative Scenario Unfolds

T he media, the talk shows, and the television studios were majoring on the faith debate. Mystic Lucinda Palmer had been particularly vocal in giving her spiritual views. Based on her personal experiences, the existence of God in some spiritual form was clearly beyond doubt. She also reported receiving messages carrying dire warnings of times to come.

The evening television news programme joined in the fray by arranging a secure line, at considerable cost, between its studio in London and the *Canterbury Television Centre* in Christchurch, New Zealand. The original CTV building, a towering office block near Cathedral Square, had been demolished in the earthquake of February 2011, with the loss of one hundred and fifteen lives. Its new broadcasting centre was located in the *Mainland Press* Building in the suburb of Harewood. Lucinda Palmer, in Christchurch, would debate the 'God issue' with Simone White, a well-known writer and philosopher, in the London studio.

The presenter, Jeremy Edwards, began by welcoming viewers and the participants to this special international edition of the programme.

Lucinda Palmer was larger than life, both in character and body. She was well-endowed, with her bosom prominently displayed under a green jumper, and adorned by flowing, black hair down to her shoulders. She wore a crimson scarf which most viewers thought clashed terribly with a deep-purple skirt down to her knees, pink tights and shoes with worn-out black soles.

'Lucinda, let me begin by asking if your well-documented belief in God still stands, given recent revelations.'

'Of course, absolutely beyond doubt, and let me explain. My belief is not derived from a single faith or religious code. When we engage in a divine communication it is a dialogue with the spirit, a word derived from the Latin word, "spirare", which means "to breathe".'

'You are saying you have spoken with God?' interjected Jeremy Edwards, somewhat incredulous at the prospect.

'Of course, in a manner of speaking; regularly, every day. The Divine Spirit is always there with me, guiding my inner being, leading the way. I see things, experience things, pick up messages that most people do not see, because they are not looking.'

'So you don't believe in one God for all.'

'All our interaction with God is personal, not prescribed by man-made orthodoxies.'

'That I take to be a reference to the Christian Church.'

'That and the others.'

'Simone, is it correct that you are an atheist?'

'No, certainly not; I am an agnostic. I keep an open mind but I remain sceptical. As Plato said, religion provides mythical clothing and authority for a morality that already exists. Religion is an authoritarian code that compels people to obey dogma established for the preservation of certain questionable ideals and the wealth that goes with it.'

'Good Lord,' said the interviewer, 'It seems you both agree about some aspects of religion. That wasn't in my script at all.'

'Much too tame, Jeremy; more drama, engender more controversy.' Those were the words Mr Edwards heard in his earpiece.

'Let's move on to God then. Simone, one of the major theories for the existence of God is one of mathematical probability. You cannot seriously believe that complex mathematical relationships, some gigantic cosmic lottery, provided us with the perfect position for the Sun and the Moon in relation to Earth, or that the incredible complexity of DNA that provides life, the beauty of nature, all happened by a chance of zillions to one, surely?'

'I find anthropic reasoning does not provide a satisfactory way of explaining improbable events,' she replied, in a haughty tone. She appeared to be a very driven woman, highly articulate, but giving no hint of warmth or humour.

'I think you had better explain what that means for our viewers.'

'Essentially, that line of enquiry places Man at the centre of the universe. I cannot subscribe to the view that a Creator made this Earth and our tiny, sustainable place in the universe, simply for our benefit - that we are some marvellous experiment watched over by some God.'

'I guess neither of you believes in a vision of some crusty old man in the sky. Lucinda, do you agree with the widely accepted Big Bang theory for our beginning?'

'I do not find it inconsistent with belief in God.'

'If something arranged or ordered the Big Bang,' interposed Simone, 'Who made that thing or, to put it another way, who made God? Something cannot come out of nothing. It was once said that a nothing will serve just as well as something about which nothing can be said.'

'I think you have lost us there, Simone,' commented the interviewer.

Viewers detected that the academic was finding it tiresome to conduct a debate at such a mundane level.

'My God is not a thing, neither a something nor none thing, as you put it,' interjected Lucinda vociferously. 'My God is not a physical object. He is spiritual, of the mind, of consciousness. Consciousness is the basis of all being, one whom we call the Godhead. Because He is not tangible, it does not follow that He does not exist.'

Jeremy Edwards paused, noticing the edge in her voice, then spoke again to Lucinda.

'Charles Darwin and his generally-accepted Theory of Evolution, surely mean that life on our planet has advanced naturally, adapting to the surrounding conditions, rather than being guided by an unseen God.'

'Not at all,' responded Lucinda; 'Evolution is entirely consistent with a concept of God having given us freedom of choice. It does not serve His purpose for us to be on this earth simply to be clones, or zombies.'

'The "Deist" view,' said Edwards. 'We are left to get on with it. I presume Darwin's theory would only fail if it could be shown that our complex molecular structure was **not** formed by a numerous series of tiny modifications taking place over millennia.'

He had clearly done some research before the programme.

'It's a bit ironic that most believers have no choice about their approach to worship,' added Simone. 'If they belong to a Church or religious movement they have, in effect, become clones who have to follow the rules or they are out – excommunicated or, often, worse. 'Furthermore, if God gave us the ability to think and analyse, and doesn't want us to be zombies, why is it unacceptable to challenge religious dogma or the manner in which the message is delivered?'

'Perhaps recent events have laid that particular dogma to rest, at least so far as Christians are concerned,' interrupted Jeremy Edwards. 'We had hoped to have a representative of the Church here with us, but the interview was declined at the last minute, for which I apologise to viewers.' He then turned to Simone.

'How do you explain consciousness, emotion, love, likes and dislikes, hatred? They are not things.'

'These experiences are intertwined with our physical being. Come now, Jeremy,' her tone now condescending, 'If you get an erection, is that not a manifestation of your desire? You cannot separate the sensual from the physical.'

'There isn't much association in your case,' thought Mr Edwards, managing to keep it unsaid and off air.

'It follows that if the body is destroyed, so is the soul or, in your terminology, Lucinda, the ghost, both within us, and without,' continued Simone.

'Ah, you are referring to what people call "the ghost in the machine" concept. So there can be no afterlife?' responded Jeremy Edwards, again evidencing the fruits of his homework.

'Precisely so.'

'Lucinda?'

'There is absolutely no scientific basis for that assertion. We all have a soul. It watches over us, guides us towards our purpose in this life, *and the next*,' she stated emphatically. I know there is an afterlife. 'Physical death is simply another form of evolution to the next phase. I communicate regularly with the souls or spirits of those who have passed on. Many people I have met will bear witness to that contact. How else could I tell them about their families, their inner secrets, information I could not possibly know unless provided from the other side? And I am not alone in this. My fellow mystics are doing this day in and day out.'

Simone interjected: 'How can God, if He exists, allow such suffering, disease, starvation, cancers, sex pests preying on children, all these destructive forces?' She knew the answer but hoped, but failed, to wrong-foot the mystic.

'That's the reality of our freedom, that we do not live in a controlled environment,' responded Lucinda.

'Religion itself is the source of much of the suffering in our world,' said Simone.

'Indeed,' replied Lucinda. 'That is the influence derived from the weakness of Man following politically-motivated aims or other agendas and using religion as the justification for them. You philosophers often try to advance this argument – you rarely mention the good things done in the name of religion or, rather, God.'

'I presume you believe in Heaven?' countered Simone.

'Yes, not as a place, but as an individual, spiritual existence. Since you haven't persuaded any of God's representatives on earth to appear in this programme, may I at least quote one passage from the Bible?'

'Certainly, Lucinda, please go ahead, but don't take all night; our time is limited.'

'Thank you, it's quite brief actually. It's the less well known "Saying 108" of the *Gospel of Thomas*: "*Salvation is personal and found through spiritual introspection*".'

★★★

Thomas, watching at home, sat bolt upright, reflecting on his own troubled journey through life. Mary whispered to her husband: 'See, you must keep the faith.'

★★★

'I fear I would find Heaven, or the infinity of eternity, rather boring,' interjected Simone. Jeremy Edwards then turned to her, thinking that he would find the prospect of spending eternity in her company also somewhat wearing.

'Talking of spiritual matters, Simone, most human beings find the need for some kind of spiritual awareness, or even fulfilment, in their lives. Many find this through religion. How do you replace God in your life?'

'I do not replace God; He was never there in the first place,' she replied testily.

'*More like it Jeremy, get them worked up!*' were the words in his earpiece.

'I find inner contentment through the arts, literature, music, if that's what you mean,' responded Simone, noticing Mr Edwards' momentary distraction.

'Then you are a spiritual being after all, Ms White,' interjected Lucinda. 'The harvest of the spirit is love, joy, peace, patience, kindness, goodness, fidelity, gentleness and self-control. The spirit is the source of our life.'

'Indeed it is,' thought Mr Edwards irreverently, his mind on the scotch he would need at the end of the programme.

'Can you foresee the future, Lucinda?'

'Not in specific terms, but I have had messages which speak of turbulent times ahead.'

'Such as? And what timescale are you talking about?' probed Jeremy Edwards.

'They relate to later this decade and beyond. I envisage massive floods, not only in the Aegean, but also in your homeland, Jeremy, an Al-Qua'ida attack on a United States naval base, akin to Pearl Harbor, and our treatment of the planet reaching crisis point.'

'Bravo,' interrupted Simone White, 'Even I can predict all that!'

'If you let me continue; there are others. There will be a crisis in the Catholic Church which…' Again Simone chipped in: 'We have that already.'

'Simone, please; let the lady finish.'

'I am led to believe that later this decade there will be an attack by religious fundamentalists on Southern France, with suicidal extremists releasing biochemical infections all round the globe at the same time. Then, around the end of the decade, there will be undersea volcanic activity on a massive scale, tsunamis, earthquakes, the like of which have never been experienced before. In December 2021 the sun will go down in the early morning and darkness will follow. Even if our planet survives beyond that, it may not be long before the demise of our civilisation, as has happened before with the Romans, the Mayans and many others. The demand for food and water will outstrip supply as populations expand and resources diminish. This, allied to climate change, will lead to massive human displacement, war and eventual collapse. Just look at what has already been happening in the Californian Central Valley. Its appetite for water could not be sustained, great industries dying, and the land will return to desert. That is as specific as I can be, but do not take it as gospel,' she added, mischievously and irreverently.

There was a stunned silence before Mr Edwards responded, addressing Lucinda:

'You obviously believe in miracles. How do you explain them?'

'Miracles are generally an exaggeration or wishful thinking,' responded Simone, again interrupting.

'Whilst I would agree that many so-called miracles fall into that category, others provide one of the strongest reasons for a personal faith,' countered Lucinda Palmer. 'The evidence comes from my own personal experience and the testimonies of my clients. It is well documented, for example, that people who have been seriously ill, perhaps in a coma, when they recover or awake, have been known to speak several different languages, ones not attributed as being known to them at all. As a matter of fact,' she added, pausing for emphasis, 'I could relate many examples from my client meetings.'

'Please do, briefly, Lucinda.'

'I would need permission.'

'What? Who from? Surely not from God?'

'I am bound by client confidentiality.'

'Surely you can give us some general examples?'

At which point, television screens went blank.

The transmission had failed. This was not at all unusual in present circumstances. Back in London, the interviewer rather mischievously asked if the mystic had somehow arranged that, or at least knew in advance that it would let her off the hook.

Laura watched the programme fascinated. She thought about evolution and the evidence all around her. She wondered whether the mind or spirit could also evolve, perhaps to the extent that it no longer needed a human form wrapped around it – some kind of metamorphosis, as happens in nature. Religion might be one way, but not necessarily the only one, of enabling, or preparing the soul for this afterlife. She found it hard to accept that all the mystical experiences she had read about, and indeed gleaned from her own meeting with Lucinda Palmer, were imaginary, coincidences, or downright lies. She was reminded by the television interview, if indeed that was necessary, that she had better work out what the numbers represented. She had avoided facing up to this until now. She had been haunted by the dates in the family tree. Every female had been born in January or February, and the most common month of their deaths was…December. Months one, two and twelve; or, 1,2,12. These were exactly the same numbers that Lucinda Palmer had advised her to research, and was she alluding to 21.12.12, or perhaps 21.12.21, as another flashpoint?

Paul had also watched the broadcast, spellbound that the mystic should echo so plainly his own anxieties about the imminent demise of life on planet Earth. Like his lover halfway round the world, he was also worrying about some numbers, emailed to him by Miles Mulligan. But these were of the geological variety, readings from GPS sensors, giving warnings about increased underground activity on the island of Las Palmas in the Canaries. His friend had previously warned him that a massive slab of rock, twice the volume of the Isle of Man, could, or indeed would, one day break away and slide into the Atlantic Ocean. He had been told of the computer model which predicted that the resultant tidal wave, or tsunami, would travel west at a speed of some five hundred miles per hour, not much less than a jet plane. It would take eight to nine hours to cross the Atlantic to Florida. On reaching the Americas it would devastate the coastline and sweep inland, covering the seaboard from Canada down to South America. Millions would lose their lives. Evacuation zone plans for New York indicated it would take sixteen hours minimum to evacuate the city - too long. Even if there were some warning of the imminent catastrophe, it was unlikely to be a full sixteen hours, and would the Mayor of New York really have the courage to evacuate the city based on an unconfirmed prediction?

Not only would the huge wall of water potentially annihilate every coastal city on the eastern seaboard of the Americas, it would also devastate the Bahamas. Florida would be submerged. Miles also predicted the tsunami would reach North Africa within sixty minutes and the English Channel not too much later. He was not to know that the Mayor would soon have a full-scale dress rehearsal to contend with, but this would be a hurricane, not a tsunami.

Who was he to dispute "Metric Miles" calculations? Paul knew his friend had contacts in the Research Centre in the University of London and also with members of the United States Geological Survey. Data had been fed into a computer from the Boxing Day tsunami in 2004. Its predictions had matched the reality and should, therefore, be taken seriously.

Questioned, even pestered, by Laura, Paul had once asked his friend Miles why earthquakes could not be predicted. The spectre of a repeat of the California 'quake of 1906 worried many people in the United States, although Miles confirmed every fault was mapped and monitored using GPS satellite technology. Paul thought that was not much consolation to Laura in Christchurch.

Paul had read that earthquakes could be preceded by weird animal behaviour, particularly by snakes, which were known as 'earth dragons' for that reason. The last eruption on Mount Cumbre Vieja had been in 1949, when a fissure three kilometres long had been created. Miles had also said that a sister volcano had apparently erupted some half a million years ago, causing untold devastation. Was it about to happen again? If Laura accepted his proposal, they would certainly not be holidaying in the Canaries.

Chapter 26 – The Alternative Scenario Unfolds

When Paul Morgan received the news of the disappearance of his aunt it had troubled him greatly. 'Who could have taken her? All she does is live in a remote world of antiquities, far removed from life in the twenty-first century. She doesn't deserve this. It doesn't make sense.'

He must share his anxiety with Laura. He sent a text. Phoning was too expensive. He hoped it would get through: *'Hi special 1, luv u, aunt J gone awol. C web big story big worry. Need u, miss u, P xxx.'*

It made him feel better. He needed to tell her in advance of the publicity which he knew to be imminent.

★★★

Detective Inspector Bob Morley banged his fist on the desk in frustration. He had hardly been able to touch the surface of this investigation. It did not help that the piping-hot plastic beaker, discarded as too hot to hold, and filled with something labelled as coffee, had now upturned over his files. He was set in his ways and still preferred to read files in the way he had always done, rather than stare incessantly at the screen on his monitor. His team of detectives, working closely with forensics, had found no clues as to the perpetrators of the explosion in the laboratory. Dental records had confirmed the identities of the dead scientists. That was about all there was. He could find nothing untoward in their backgrounds. He owed it to their relatives to obtain justice. He was a diligent and thorough officer, with thirty years' experience, and this was his highest-profile case. His name was in the national press. Now he was being taken off the enquiries, removed from the investigation. The Metropolitan Police would take over. Clearly the team from Norwich was to be sidelined. They had also intervened in two other investigations, those of the missing archivist and the missing bishop.

Bob Morley had quickly assumed the three incidents were linked, as did *Britain on Sunday*.

Following up its stories about the 'God' issue, the front page now speculated about events in Norwich and the University of East Anglia.

'The strange case of the Bishop, the missing Professor and her links with murdered scientists.'

'Rumours abound….We have it on good authority….'

Once again they hid behind the cloak of speculative rumour-mongering. What was new was the connection of events and the the word **'murdered'**. Up to now the laboratory explosion had been either an accident in a laboratory or an animal rights issue, or perhaps even the work of a terrorist cell. It all made a good story. The local police force and the Metropolitan Police both declined to comment. These incidents were part of their ongoing enquiries.

Acting Commissioner Steve Copas was on his way to Rome. He had risen quickly through the ranks, was thought to be squeaky clean with no hints or even suggestions of impropriety to his name. He was highly respected by his peers, almost revered in some quarters, and many expected him to be the automatic choice for promotion to the summit of his profession following the latest top rank resignation. He had been dispatched by Special Branch, with the full covert support of MI5 and MI6, following the COBRA meeting. His task was, ostensibly, to discuss security issues with his counterpart in the Vatican. His real mission was to find out if they held two missing persons, and whether they were responsible for the bomb that destroyed the evidence contained in the documents.

As ever, the hackers at *Britain on Sunday*, or their police informants, were not far behind. Commissioner Copas, trying to glean some useful Italian phrases other than the somewhat unsavoury ones he had picked up as a former international rugby referee, did not appear to spot the smartly-dressed businessman a few seats behind him on the scheduled flight from London's Gatwick Airport.

Steve Copas arrived safely at Rome Airport. It was thought less suspicious if he went through the normal Customs checks on arrival along with the other passengers. This made life easy for the suited man behind him in the queue at Passport Control. The Acting Commissioner was met by his Italian counterpart. He did not see the taxi following not far behind the unmarked Fiat in which he was travelling – he was deep in conversation with his Italian colleague. Nor did he know that he was photographed by an unseen camera as he arrived at the Vatican. He would be staying at the *Domus Sanctae Marthae*, a five-storey building for the use of visiting emissaries.

'*Cop Copas at Vatican?!*' screamed the headlines in the next edition of *Britain on Sunday*. Was it a fraud investigation into the Church, or had it got something to do with the missing professor or even the bishop?

This was another scoop. Circulation for the newspaper was on the increase. The Editor was happy, and so were the moguls who owned the newspaper. Acting Commissioner Steve Copas was less happy. His all-expenses paid trip to Rome finished before it started. He was recalled to London due to the adverse publicity. Would it cost him his promotion?

★★★

Mary was worried sick about her sister. Thomas, for once, acutely aware of his wife's torment, could not stand idly by and became desperate to do something to help. Their frustration at the lack of information, and apparent inaction of the police, led Thomas to launch a public appeal for information. There was coverage on all main news programmes. The family was offering a staggering £50,000 reward for information leading to the release of Jane Clifford-Oxbury and the arrest of her captors. Mary had been both delighted and surprised that her brother-in-law had been prepared to make the funds available. It was only later she found out that her husband had been instrumental in persuading his brother to finance the campaign. It had not been difficult - Peter had been growing tired of the financial demands of his new wife. It would frustrate and annoy her if he diverted funds elsewhere, and especially to his Norfolk family. The glamour of her lifestyle was not for him. He began to doubt the marriage would last. He was very fond of Jane, the sacrifices she had made years before and how she and Mary had transformed Thomas' life, at least superficially. He also valued her intellectual ability, her capacity to challenge him without emotion or malice. Mary, too, had been such a pillar of support for Thomas throughout the years, beyond the calling of a dutiful wife.

There was no such campaign for the missing bishop. It was not considered appropriate to allocate church resources to such a mission. Despite his apparent demise in the explosion at Gravesend, there had as yet been no funeral for Bishop Banham. Technically he was still a 'missing person'.

★★★

The national media were raking up everything they could find about the hidden agendas of the Catholic and Protestant Churches. They wrote about the prejudice against women and their suppression. They majored on Christ's love of the company of women, which fitted neatly into the story of his subsequent marriage. In the broadsheets they talked about goddesses and Asherah, the so-called intermediary between gods, mentioned some forty times in the Bible. Laura read that there was also evidence of a strong feminine presence in ancient Israelite worships. There were suggestions of a relationship between the Israelite God, Yahweh, and Asherah. They published previously-forgotten stories about relics which had been dug up depicting a wife of God. Inscriptions on pottery found in 1975 at an ancient travellers' site were apparently still being guarded by the Egyptian Army. These were said to include a large pot depicting Arway and Asherah entwined together. It was reported that the Camp David Accords, signed in September 1978 following thirteen days of secret negotiations, provided for the relics to be returned to Egyptian control.

There was further speculation that missing artefacts had been found following the Arab uprisings of 2011 and the Egyptian revolution.

Articles speculating about the ancient Israelites' belief that God had a wife or consort were unacceptable to Catholics and Protestant alike. In Laura's mind this soon turned the debate into one about religious discrimination against women. She was no feminist, but certainly believed strongly in women's rights. Some made comparisons with Muhammad and his perfectly normal relations with women, his several wives, his children, in the way that Paul had. On the other hand the treatment of women in some Middle Eastern countries was, in her view, deplorable. She would have relished the opportunity to challenge Hussain and his friends, tell them what she thought, but she had not been allowed near them. But she knew it would have been a waste of time and could have jeopardised her job - and her relationship with Paul. 'Whose side is he really on?' she wondered, 'Is he really more important to me than my work?' This dilemma continued to haunt her every day, every night.

The newspaper editorials and columnists majored on the apparent gulf between what was now known about Jesus the man, and the depiction of Jesus historically portrayed by the Church. They shouted loud and clear that the Vatican had maintained its position through suppression and manipulation of the truth.

The perception of 'No God', although hotly disputed by a largely discredited Christian Church, had become all too readily accepted in the public mind, and was eagerly embraced by secularists, atheists and, more importantly, agnostics.

The apparently defrauded former adherents to Christianity in the United Kingdom were furious at the apparent deception perpetrated against them. In June they gathered to protest outside Canterbury Cathedral and St. Paul's, which was once again in the limelight.

Anxious priests were forced to run the gauntlet of picket lines formed outside churches. Thomas was fortunate that because Norwich had so many churches, his country parish was spared - at least for the time being. Inevitably, other religious organisations joined in and it wasn't long before fundamentalists, aided and abetted by 'yobs and hooligans', as the Prime Minister described them, were whipping up the fervour. It was a God-given opportunity to vent their fury at the Christians, who were now in full retreat. The water in the church fonts evaporated as the number of christenings reduced to a trickle. Christian funerals were rare, with the exception of a few diehards. Those services which did take place were monthly or quarterly, and church revenues were declining fast, causing consternation to treasurers on Parochial Church Councils and, in turn, for their Diocesan Boards. Income from investments was also in freefall as interest rates remained close to zero.

The first petrol bomb was thrown into early-morning Mass at a church in the East Midlands. Other sporadic outbursts soon followed. An Anglican priest was killed by a bomb hidden under the pulpit. The elders in the Muslim community joined in the condemnation of the outrage, as did the Home Secretary, who was quick to visit the scene.

The Prime Minister chaired another emergency meeting of COBRA that evening, attended by the Home Secretary, the head of MI5, the Commissioner of Police, the Bishop of London and the Mayor of London. The security services had anticipated problems. The trouble was they didn't have the resources to police thousands of churches around the country just to protect the few selected targets. In scenes reminiscent of the days of King Henry VIII, church buildings were set alight and burned. Some were irretrievably damaged, leaving charred ruins of once-majestic buildings.

***

'We need to be ready, Hussain. I have the equipment, the explosives. All is in place. Use code words for any mobile phone conversation. We succeeded before, we will do so again. The English boy, our Trojan Horse, has given us crucial information; his knowledge of church procedures has been invaluable. The time has now come. Allah is with us.'

'Malik, I am ready. It's our destiny,' replied Hussain. The moment was nigh; 'Operation Trojan Horse' was imminent.

They were unaware of the microphone in the internet café where they frequently met.

***

In his naivety, Paul was also blissfully unaware of what his friends were plotting, what their plans were for his home city. Alone in his first-floor flat, not far from the city centre, he looked down at the murky waters of the River Wensum flowing slowly below, as it had for centuries. There was something reassuring about its continuous motion, a never-ending cycle which, should it ever cease, would signal Doomsday. It reminded him, too, of the power of the Earth's sun and moon, how they controlled so much of life on Earth, and inevitably, too, of those reflections with Laura on that last night in Auckland.

He worried about the mayhem in his father's beloved Church, becoming increasingly concerned for his father's welfare, his safety, his vocation. His dad did not have the emotional stability of his brother, and he wondered how that distinction had originated from the same upbringing, the same surroundings and the same parents. He knew his mother would be enduring her husband's anxiety, quietly, stoically, supportively.

Paul devoted his energies to finding out more about the real causes of the riots, which sectors of society were in the forefront. He devoured the newspapers, attended rallies and went to public meetings, carefully observing the motives and hidden agendas, unaware he, too, was being observed. He spent time with his friend Hussain and his fellow Muslims in his university lodgings, meeting their friends from the London colleges who often came to stay. Their talk was of creating their own states, whether in the Middle East, Palestine or now, North Africa. They were emboldened by the apparent demise of the Church of England and Christianity. They talked of the opportunities this presented. Much of this he understood to be a perfectly reasonable reaction, but there was at times an edge to their conversation he did not like. He would unwittingly send texts to Laura spelling out some of the things he had heard, some potentially incriminating. He was disappointed at the non-committal nature of her responses.

★★★

Her Majesty the Queen, making a rare televised address to the nation, appealed for calm, as did Church leaders, but no one took much notice. The 'Sunday Riots', as they became known, were costing many thousands of pounds in police overtime. With the country struggling to come out of recession, the Government could ill afford any increase in public expenditure. These were grim times, and the unseasonable wind and rain, accompanied by hurricane-force winds in the west, did little to lighten the mood. It was rare indeed for the Meteorological Office to issue Red Alerts, the highest warning level. There were fatalities as racing yachts capsized in the English Channel. Uprooted trees fell on cars across the land, rivers burst their banks and towns in the West of England and Wales were once again flooded, with high streets under water. Many homes were still not habitable from the previous time. Some of those who disputed the so-called discovery in Norwich regarded the floods as the retribution of a God spurned. They also talked of renewed plagues against mankind, citing devastating fires in Asia, extreme weather conditions, droughts, ferocious storms, the spread of AIDS, and the increasing and disturbing resistance of infections to antibiotics. All this coincided with the apparent increase in sightings of unidentified flying objects, and all manner of extreme natural events. Did this portend the implosion of the world, of the return of The Supreme Being? In the minds of some, they were portrayed as a warning of the forthcoming demise of this civilisation, as Paul noted had happened to the hierarchies of the long-lost past. He reflected on the collapses of so many established empires which he had studied so assiduously as part of his degree course. Would Man through his excesses, his greed, his selfishness, determine the end of days, or would God, whoever He might be? Much to his surprise, he found himself wondering if some sort of faith were preferable to the empty void, the spiritual vacuum around him.

The police had adopted a more aggressive approach following the Ministerial and media criticism of their initially muted response to the August 2011 riots. They had learned some important lessons. The Police National Information Coordination Centre was much more streamlined, and there was no shortage of riot gear and vehicles, but even this proved inadequate - these vital pieces of equipment always seemed to be in the wrong place as rioters and looters coordinated using their smartphones and all manner of modern gadgetry, switching targets with alacrity.

News broadcasts showed bloody scenes of clashes between police and rioters. This time police protected by riot shields used water cannons, tear gas, stun guns and even Cessna 4 spy planes. The Army was called in to guard sacred monuments and to provide a flexible response unit. In echoes of the 2011 riots, when Magistrates' Courts sat over weekends, extra custody suites were laid on, in some areas using local church buildings.

Concerned politicians had debates in both Houses. The Speaker was forced to intervene to calm bitter exchanges between the Prime Minister and the Leader of the Opposition, goaded by their baying MPs, which dominated Prime Minister's Questions. That evening, a weary Prime Minister retreated to his Downing Street living quarters and collapsed into his favourite armchair, one from which it would be pleasurably hard to escape. It had been a long day.

'What are you doing about the National Anthem, Dick?' asked his wife, Denise, out of the blue.

'What about it?'

'Can the National Anthem really be appropriate any more; *God Save the Queen*, in present circumstances?'

'Oh my Lord,' exclaimed the Prime Minister ill-advisedly, 'How come no one has raised that one before now?'

'That's obvious, my dear. They are either frightened of mentioning it, which I doubt, or they are already in consultation with her advisers and wish to present you with a *fait accompli.*'

'Or they haven't thought of it at all,' he chipped in disdainfully.

'I expect your friend Sir Christopher has had an audience with her already, as well as the Archbishop. You've often admitted you are the last to know.'

Mr Benson looked daggers at his wife then relented, his irritation subsiding. She was his one faithful ally, the one person who had the temerity to get away with a remark like that.

Next day he summoned the Cabinet Secretary, his Principal Private Secretary and the Home Secretary, Nigella Blackburn, to his private office.

'Nigella; how, in God's name, do we discuss this with Her Majesty?'

'Hardly in God's name, Prime Minister! You have your weekly audience tomorrow,' proffered Sir Christopher. The Home Secretary intervened.

'This needs to be resolved quickly. It's sung or played on so many different occasions. You will be attending the Last Night of the Promenade Concerts in her presence. You cannot risk any show of dissent or derision, if not there, somewhere else. You must not allow yourself to be put in that position, Prime Minister.'

He did not know if the civil servants had previously identified the issue or were waiting for him to raise it; or worse, hoping for him to be embarrassed. He was aware that relations with Her Majesty's Civil Service were at a new low, following cuts in departments, restrictions on pensions and a pay freeze.

The weekly audience now took place on Wednesdays at 6.30pm prompt. One must not be kept waiting. A former Prime Minister had put this back from the conventional Tuesday to give him more time to prepare for PM's Questions in the Commons. This was in response to the fact that it was now live on television. He must project the right image.

Prime Minister Benson knew that Her Majesty was an avid reader of the 'Red Book', the weekly intelligence summary. A former Prime Minister had apparently once remarked that Her Majesty the Queen was one of the best-informed people in the world.

'Get the Minister for Religion to speak to the Queen's Private Secretary at Buckingham Palace,' he barked. This was a new appointment, perceived by many as a panic response to the crisis.

'I am afraid the Minister for Religion is off sick with stress, Prime Minister. He is worried about losing his job. He knows you are likely to appoint a Muslim to the post.'

'Then it falls to you, Home Secretary. I want this sorted before I get to the Palace.'

'Surely this is one for the Communities Secretary?' Nigella replied, hastily passing the buck.

'No not him. I want you to see to it.'

'How about Sir Christopher? He's very good at this sort of thing.'

'An excellent suggestion,' he replied gleefully, delighted that the burden should fall on his nemesis.

'Are you sure, sir? I can think of people much more suitable,' countered Sir Christopher, squirming uncomfortably in his green, leather-backed chair.

'Absolutely sure; you're so good at this kind of thing.'

Sir Christopher was not at all sure it was a compliment.

'Serve him right; he's always creeping about talking behind people's backs. Now he can use his experience on my behalf,' he chuckled, as his PPS shuffled out of the room. He then wondered if his wife had been right all along.

The last thing he wanted was a showdown with Her Majesty. He could imagine the conversation.

'Let me remind you, Prime Minister, that under our constitution the Monarch is both the Head of the Church and the Head of State;' and his lame reply, 'Yes, Your Majesty.' It must not come to that.

Chapter 27 – The Alternative Scenario Unfolds

The historical spectre of the dissolution of the monasteries loomed large. Local communities pitched in to protect their much-loved, but now rarely used, parish churches. In increasing numbers, redundant churches once again became a pivotal hub for village communities, who formed co-operatives to run post offices, convenience stores, coffee mornings, even sharing books, CDs and DVDs in the absence of local libraries lost to the cuts. There were toddler groups, village book clubs and even, read a chuckling Peter, investment clubs. Thomas Morgan did not believe such an invasion would happen in his parish. He remarked to Mary one evening that his parishioners were much too loyal for that.

The communities' usage of parish churches, and the sense of identity it engendered, ultimately proved the most effective deterrent against the mobsters and looters. The Prime Minister lauded this as an example of the 'Big Society' at work. He was utterly frustrated at the Church's lack of direction as conflicting messages emanated from a disillusioned clergy. He decided to do their job for them. He publicly rebuked the Church for its lack of decisive leadership in a speech to his constituency party. It seemed to be more addressed to the newshounds at the back of the hall. The Prime Minister reminded everyone of his call the previous December, for the Archbishop of Canterbury to lead a return to the moral code of the Bible.

'If the Church does not accept the veracity of recent revelations then it should proclaim its position from the rooftops. In the face of adversity and mistrust, surely the Church should be up front in preaching a clear message of right and wrong? The Bible has helped to give Britain a set of values which we should stand up and defend.'

He chose not to mention that much of the moral teaching as prescribed in the Bible, particularly the Old Testament, but also the New, was not a legitimate basis for any attempt to establish some modern code of conduct. It would not be acceptable today to bring back the death penalty for committing adultery, working on a Sunday, or being a homosexual. Nor did he mention that the vast majority of non-religious citizens lived perfectly moral lives in the absence of religious teachings.

There was no place for 'live and let live' becoming 'do what you please'. The Prime Minister was, by inference, attacking the hand-wringing pronouncements of senior churchmen, human rights apologists and even some politicians, who refused to condemn lawbreaking by rioters. The right-wing press lauded his message and the left derided it. A senior rabbi issued a rallying call in defence of faith, saying that without it there would be a serious breakdown in trust affecting all sectors of society, adding that when trust is eroded, the institutions at the heart of British life would also enter into terminal decline. The secularists, Peter Morgan amongst them, vehemently disagreed, enraging his brother Thomas.

There was a general unwillingness to challenge militant Islam – a very real threat, given the apparent demise of Christianity. Hussain and Malik echoed the views of their fellow fundamentalists, seeing it as a 'God-given' opportunity to espouse their cause and impose their will on the 'Disunited' Kingdom, which would lead to the imposition of Sharia Law, initially in Muslim communities and ultimately throughout the land. Then the Bible would be replaced by the Koran and the five pillars of faith.

Hussain's father, one of many less vociferous Muslims, was highly suspicious of the motives of the fundamentalists. Their values, their teachings were not, in his view, consistent with the preaching of Muhammad. He argued passionately with his son on one of his increasingly rare home visits.

'Of course I am enthusiastic to welcome new adherents to our faith, but I accept peaceful co-existence with others. You and your brothers project a false image of our religion. I, and my fellow Muslims, want nothing to do with violence as a means of promoting our faith.'

'Father, you are out of touch. It is our chance, a once-in-a-lifetime opportunity, to Islamise this country, to replace the laws of the English infidels with our Sharia Law, to make this an Islamic state. In order to achieve this we must replace the teachings of the Bible with those of the Koran. It is the duty of every Muslim to work to achieve this aim. All means to support our cause are justified by God.'

'No, my son. The Koran states "Whoever kills an innocent person, it is as though he has killed humanity." It also says people should have the freedom of religion. You are adapting our sacred teachings to fit your revolutionary agenda. Violence is abhorrent.'

'Humanity is not important. It is the will of Allah we must follow. You are not a true Muslim, Father.'

His father knew that his son was insinuating he was what some Islamists called 'Partial Muslims', those who kept their religion within the confines of prayer and piety.

Hussain left his parents house that day vowing never to return until his father saw the light. Such contrasting views were typical of the internal strife between moderates and fundamentalists. It was not new. For years the rival factions had been engaged in an acrimonious power struggle, even to the extent that the Metropolitan Police had intervened to keep them apart. A young 'Cop Copas' had been one of those who saw at first hand the utter hostility between fellow Islamists back in the late 1980s. It was an experience he never forgot. The atheists and agnostics cited the current turmoil as a further example of the damage caused by religion and its ethics, or lack of them.

***

Laura was horrified to see television news broadcasts showing the violence, the riots in the UK.

'Men playing war games in the name of religion, just as Lucinda had said,' she exclaimed resignedly. 'When will they ever learn?' echoing the protest song of the 1960s.

New Zealand could not expect to remain immune from the religious pandemic sweeping not only across Britain, but also Italy, Spain and the rest of Europe, to varying degrees. She just hoped the rural nature of her country, the tiny population, would provide less appetite and opportunity for violence. Regardless of religious beliefs, people were still numbed by the aftermath of the Christchurch earthquake and had no real desire for confrontation. They had been devastated at the loss of their Cathedral and the city centre itself through an *'Act of*

God' as the insurance companies described it in their small print. In England, all this was happening as an *'Act of Man'*, or perhaps, even, *'Woman'*. Like Eve, they would undoubtedly get the blame, thought Laura, as she pondered the destruction of Christ's Church in her city.

She trembled at another thought, remembering how Paul's recent messages about the potential for collapse in society mirrored those of the mystic, perhaps heralding a 'second coming'. After all, the Maori culture had lost its former dominance in her own country, gradually becoming subsumed into a western way of life. That had taken well over a century, but what was that in relation to time itself?

She found herself praying that all this violence and vandalism would not spread to her beautiful country. To whom she prayed she did not know. Although she had never met him, she felt sympathy for Paul's father - a lost soul, his life's work in tatters, his 'calling' unheard; a cry in the wilderness.

The Prime Minister's audience with Her Majesty had gone unexpectedly well. He was not sure if it was the Queen herself, or her advisers, who had come up with a typically adroit compromise. She had let it be known that One would find *Rule Britannia* an acceptable alternative to the National Anthem. The Prime Minister was delighted to accept her proposal, knowing that many Royalists in the population wanted the change in any case. It was later revealed by Dame Pauline King, Lady-in-Waiting to the Queen, in her autobiography entitled *King and Queen*, that she had advised Her Majesty not to consult with her eldest son in case he only made matters worse, speculating that he might have suggested a 1960s hit should be re-released with the amended title, *Step Aside Love*.

Prime Minister Benson returned to Downing Street from his audience with Her Majesty in triumphant mood. It darkened slightly when his wily Cabinet Secretary pointed out that Her Majesty, as ever, might be one step ahead.

'What on earth do you mean, Sir Julian?' he asked impatiently.

'She may be putting down a marker for the rare issue of a Royal Prerogative on behalf of the Crown, in the event of any constitutional issues; *Rule Britannia. "Rule"*, Prime Minister; do you get my drift?'

Now it was the Prime Minister who was not amused.

★★★

The Government COBRA Committee had sanctioned the creation of a new 'think tank'. Its remit was to come up with a moral and ethical code which citizens could adopt in the absence of spiritual guidance from the country's predominant religion. 'The Moral Imperative' as it was called, became the new name for 'The Big Society'. It had to be framed so as not to offend the Muslim community particularly, and other faiths generally, whose beliefs had survived the catastrophe which had befallen the Church of England. This new Government initiative had a second purpose – the more that individuals, voluntary groups and charities supported worthy causes, the more the scope for reducing duplicated local authority services, thereby enabling the cunning Chancellor to reduce public expenditure by stealth.

The civil servants handed this urgent task did not have sufficient time to debate the philosophical distinction between morals and ethics. They would have to combine the two in this endeavour. Professor Simone White and her fellow philosophers would no doubt debate, attack, and denigrate whatever code they produced.

As the 'think tank' laboured to come up with a new code of 'citizenship', a multitude of citizens became amateur philosophers overnight. They grappled with leading questions:

Why be good? People asked for what reason should they behave well? Why resist temptation if there is no Godly punishment? Why not put myself first?

Goaded by a telephone call from his brother, Thomas Morgan belligerently challenged his parishioners to abide by the Ten Commandments, following up his sermon with an article in *Parish News*. Few listened.

Some scribes argued that life's experiences had taught us to respect others, not some biblical code. Simone White, the philosopher, argued in a newspaper article that social culture, rather than God, determined behaviour. She also argued that the only true personal freedom was the right to choose, to make one's own decisions unencumbered by threats of damnation or promises of eternal life.

Simone became a household name, expanding her theories, frequently appearing on radio and television, intensely irritating Thomas. For most people the ethical debate was beyond understanding. But they were aware that the code of instructions embodied in the Bible and the Ten Commandments were now in many ways obsolete or, at the very least, needed updating. Before, those who had obeyed would have had their rewards in Heaven, and those who disobeyed could look forward to the fiery furnace of an eternal Hell. But what would happen now?

The 'think tank' focus group comprised the Home Secretary, her Permanent Private Secretary, Sir Christopher Perrin and his team of civil servants, and Simone White, the philosopher. It was thought preferable to have her on board, but if they thought they could muzzle her they were much mistaken. No church representatives were invited as it was considered they had too much of a vested interest to contribute objectively. The remit was to produce a charter for social cohesion and morality in the absence of Christianity. They were given one month to produce a first draft to Cabinet. They did not get off to an encouraging start to their deliberations.

'What is already in place internationally that we could latch on to?' asked the Home Secretary. 'There are a myriad of agreements and declarations,' replied Sir Christopher Perrin, that academic high in the ranks of the Civil Service.

'We have the United Nations General Assembly and its *Universal Declaration of Human Rights* dated 10th December 1948, with its thirty *Articles of Basic Rights*. We have the *European Convention on Human Rights 1950*. There is an *International Bill of Human Rights*, an *International Covenant on Economic Social and Cultural Rights* and an *International Covenant on Civil and Political Rights*. Then there is the *Charter of Fundamental Rights of the European Church 2000*. Would you like me to summarise each one for you, Home Secretary?'

'Thank you, Sir Christopher, that will not be necessary,' replied the Home Secretary.

'We are bound by European law in any case,' added a Whitehall mandarin.

'We are back to square one – we can't formulate a UK charter because of the European Union,' interjected the Home Secretary. 'This will take months.'

'There is another problem, Home Secretary,' said Sir Christopher.

'I don't want problems - I want solutions.'

'Well, madam; you, we, need to take account of the burgeoning Muslim population within the UK. They do not accept these Declarations and Charters. They have their own *Cairo Declaration on Human Rights*. Their view is that all the other conventions have no validity because they take no account of Sharia Law.

'All these electoral successes will only encourage further demands by Muslims to adopt their laws in their own communities around the globe, and especially here in the United Kingdom. Indeed, you will be aware that the Muslim Councils are already pressing for this. This task is potentially more divisive than the problems we are trying to solve, Home Secretary,' he concluded.

'Perhaps we should take our cue from the Bible?' added young Frank Hussler facetiously, and with a confidence beyond his position. 'It has served as a benchmark for human behaviour for centuries.' He got a withering look from Simone. It was the opportunity she had been waiting for. She jumped in, all guns blazing.

'We are in a new world now. The Bible is no longer our reference point. I am sure I hardly need to remind you of the manifold sins and wickedness perpetrated in the name of that book. Take Moses in *Exodus*, for example, he who managed to drop the tablets of stone containing the Commandments and then, having dealt with the golden calf, instructed all the tribe to kill as many people as possible. What about the ethnic cleansing, the massacres in *Joshua*, or the absurdity of visiting the sins of the fathers on their children? I could go on with a whole litany of examples.'

'We get the point, Professor, you wish us also to drop the tablets of stone.'

'Into little tiny pieces, preferably,' she concluded vehemently, the atmosphere now tense and febrile.

With that the meeting broke up in disarray. The civil servants were all too aware that the failure to reach a solution would not go down well with the Prime Minister.

Chapter 28 – The Alternative Scenario Unfolds

Bishop Banham was growing increasingly restless, denied any news of the drama he had left behind, and what had become of Jane. He was tiring of his daily diet of academic books, crosswords, code-words, puzzles, sudoku, and especially the plain food; all those pies, not even a glass of communion wine to savour. He dreamed a lot, particularly of his son whom he rarely saw, and then only at a distance. It only increased his feeling of depression.

'My God, why have you forsaken me?' he was tempted to cry out, but he did not because he knew he was not without sin and deserved his punishment; perhaps divine retribution was what he was experiencing now. He knew his deception was unlikely to be forgiven by his estranged son should he ever put the family bloodline together on some ancestry website. Alone in captivity, with few distractions, the pain gnawed away at him, consuming his tortured soul like some flesh-eating bug.

He was not to know that the Christian Church was clinging steadfastly to its assertion that, as Jesus' alleged wedding document and the apparent birth records could not be produced, the Christian message, although in great jeopardy, remained intact. Bishop Banham was not there to reveal anything of his meeting with Jane Clifford-Oxbury, or what followed. Neither was she. Sitting alone in captivity he believed his personal knowledge must make his position as a bishop untenable. He tormented himself with an acute dilemma: 'Which is stronger, my religious faith or my faith in Jane's judgement?' He had not personally seen the documents but they had been seen by Jane, whom he trusted implicitly, and had also been scientifically authenticated, or so he assumed. Resignation for personal reasons was one option, but this could unlock a whole series of clergy resignations, and yet more adverse publicity for the Church. The other option was even less palatable. He could reveal his own inner torment, confess his sins, but the personal cost was perhaps too high to contemplate, not only for him, but for others. Here he was, a man of the cloth, a bishop, and he was not willing or able to embrace the truth, make the ultimate personal revelation. One day he knew he would reap what he had sown. It weighed heavily upon him.

He was also aware that many priests in his diocese would have their faith destroyed by the revelations. He imagined them clinging to office in the hope of receiving large redundancy cheques. He did not know that one errant vicar was suing his employers for 'wrongful employment'. If the case reached the House of Lords before the bishops were booted out, they would have to abstain.

There was also a developing scandal concerning another errant vicar - a much-respected country priest who presided over a parish on the outskirts of King's Lynn, a town in West Norfolk bordering the Wash. Journalist Mike Burrows and his colleagues had once again been busy. *Britain on Sunday* had led with the story. It had been leaked to them by 'Moaning Martha', a local prostitute, who described herself as an 'escort' in the hope of going up-market. She had allegedly been visited by this rampant cleric on several occasions in recent weeks. It seemed, set free from the shackles of his calling, he was ready to give rein to a long-suppressed desire which had long consumed his soul; a chance to savour the delights of the flesh. She quoted him as saying, 'What the hell, there is no God, so I'm going to make up for lost time; enjoy what time I have left.'

The Press could not resist a story of that kind and moved in *en masse* to the lane running through the picturesque rural village. There were picture-postcard cottages overhung with colourful displays of still-flowering roses, gardens bedecked with geraniums and orange-red fuchsias, and walls fronted with colourful hanging baskets, all bordering an attractive village green. The vicarage overlooked the north end of the green, beyond the village sign which welcomed visitors to their little oasis of tranquillity. The vicar's wife did not offer much of a welcome to the pack of newshounds relentlessly chasing their quarry, hoping for a quote. There were no cups of tea offered to the waiting media - she simply issued a brief statement through her solicitor in which he announced that the wayward vicar had gone on holiday.

'Bangkok, is it?' someone shouted - others mischievously misspelled it in their reports.

★★★

The Revd Thomas Morgan was one of many priests who had no idea what the future would hold. He dreaded the prospect of Christmas and New Year all the more this year. He wondered how many would turn up for Midnight Mass. Peter would doubtless revel in innuendos about 'Doubting Thomas', telling him there was no place for doubt now, nothing to look forward to, no eternal life. Thomas' lifelong hopes were dashed; also his faith and his position in society. He had never thought that mattered – until now. They had been the pillars supporting his life; without them the edifice he had built would come crashing down around him. It would be cowardly to cancel the annual invitation to Peter and his harlot, Caroline. He knew it was an unworthy description of her, but he now felt less restrained by the protocols of goodwill to all men, or women or, in this case, just her. Thomas regarded marriage as being a life-long commitment and hence utterly disapproved of Peter and Caroline's second-time-around marriage, declining to attend the wedding 'on principle' after Peter ignored Thomas' passionate plea against their union.

'If your brother commits a sin, go and take the matter up with him, strictly between yourselves and, if he listens to you, you have won your brother over. If he will not listen, take one or two others with you, so that all the facts may be duly established on the evidence of two or three witnesses. If he refuses to listen, report the matter to the congregation; and if he will not listen even to the congregation, you must treat him as a pagan or a tax gatherer.'

It had taken all Mary's considerable powers of persuasion to prevail upon her husband not to find or, God forbid, fabricate, some unjust impediment to prevent the union.

Paul had been continually reminding his father about the ancient predictions, their talk of the disintegration of society, of economic collapse, and also of recurrent and world-wide natural disasters. Perhaps, thought Thomas, sitting one afternoon in his study, those primitive and ungodly pagans did have a point. If the world did end on 21st December it would save him from a mauling from

Peter at the very least. A cockerel crowed outside in the meadow. Was it three times?

On the following Sunday morning the Revd Thomas Morgan's first thought on waking was how many communicants he would actually have at the 8am service. It was a gloomy, damp morning, in tune with his mood. This early service was not normally well attended; perhaps five or six greying parishioners.

But now, perhaps only a couple? he thought despairingly.

As he strolled down the lane towards the church he could hear the sound of voices coming from the churchyard. His spirits rose.

But where is the peal of bells? he wondered.

Rounding the final bend, he reached the gates of his beloved church. There were people everywhere. It was quickly evident they were not there to partake of bread and wine. He approached the heavy, iron-clad main door. He entered and stood transfixed, overcome by shock. The church had been stripped bare, the pews were stacked round the sides, and there was a short mat bowls alley down the aisle. The vestry was kitted out with a bank of computers each, he assumed, occupied by an internet surfer. Mary had explained what that meant. She had also shown him how to download sermons from the internet, but he doubted that was the subject matter on their screens. Decking had been laid in the chancel to provide a stage.

'Good Morning, Vicar,' someone shouted. Thomas recognised the voice straight away. It was Herbert Fletcher, chair of the New Village Hall Committee, a man he did not like one little bit. They had crossed swords many times.

'Sorry Vic,' he began, a form of address he knew irritated the Reverend, 'This is a church no longer. We are putting the money raised for the new village hall into renovating and refurbishing this building instead, with the post office in the vestry. This will save us thousands compared with a new build. You will naturally be delighted that this building will be at the heart of community life; the first time in years. Come and have a look round,' he added triumphantly; 'In fact, the newly formed "Community Investment Club" is having its inaugural meeting.' Wistfully, he reflected Peter had been right all along; his temple was now the domain of the money-changers.

'The toddlers group, the Women's Institute, have all signed up, and we will shortly be opening a community food bank.'

"Vic", crestfallen and shaking with emotion, could at first only muster a muted response. Then, as the reality of how they had debased his church hit home, he screamed defiantly, vocal chords stretched to their limit: 'Scripture says, *"My house shall be called a house of prayer: but you are making it a robber's cage!"'* Sadly, although the church was for once brimming with people, few listened.

To much laughter and some heckling, he turned and abruptly left. He thought about all the years of devoted service, the sermons, the sweet singing in the choir. It was all gone in an instant. He would fight back. He needed a good lawyer, but the best one was hardly likely to take such a case – if anything, he would represent the defendants. Thomas decided he would bypass the

Parochial Church Council and phone the Bishop - except that Bishop Banham would not be there to take the call.

It would have to be the Diocesan Board, but his hopes were not high that they would achieve much, if anything.

★★★

That same morning Paul walked past the crumbling outer wall of the ancient city of Norwich. There were, or had been, more churches in this ancient city than anywhere else in England and, possibly, Europe. Fortunately, only a few had been razed to the ground, ironically, thought Paul, St. Peter's being one of them.

Suddenly the ground shook; windows rattled and shattered fragments of glass landed around him. Paul felt himself swaying, as if he had had one too many, almost losing his balance. There seemed to be no serious damage but even minor quakes, if that is what it was, were unusual in Eastern England, especially in Norwich. Inevitably his thoughts turned to Laura's experience in Christchurch, how the path in front of her had suddenly disappeared, and what she must have been through.

He missed her, their conversations, their fun, laughter and, of course, the bedroom. The very thought aroused him. He needed her, to have and to hold. He could sense the fragrance of that alluring perfume he had bought so expensively, and how it had served its purpose, drawing him to her like a bee to a flower, then the taste of nectar and the soft, sticky stamen inside.

Despite the debilitating memory of that cool farewell, and the apparent aloofness of her messages, he, there and then, decided to invite her for Christmas. Money should be no object; she had her trust fund. As an afterthought he realised her presence might also restrain Uncle Peter from an otherwise certain 'I told you so' rant against his dad. He wondered when would be the best time to make his proposal.

Unbeknown to him, Laura had been summoned to a meeting with her departmental boss. She was to be sent to the United Kingdom on a follow-up assignment. It was to be based in Norwich. She would be coming anyway.

It subsequently turned out that the tremor in Norwich was not an earthquake, at least not in the conventional sense. At that time no one was aware of the highly secretive 'fracking' operation being conducted a few miles from the city of Norwich and well away from the beady eyes of the environmentalist lobby. This had been authorised by the Government as one of many initiatives to reduce imported energy costs, but there were those who expressed concerns that such operations would poison drinking water and, much worse, would cause earthquakes. He never mentioned the incident to her - she might not come for Christmas.

***

The future seemed bleak for Aunt Jane. She had no idea the tabloids were clamouring for results in the hunt for her, or that Peter had put up so much money in the search for information. She had been well treated and spent her time devouring the supply of books and magazines she had requested, all carefully vetted. She missed the wealth of information normally available to her over the internet, although she did have her almanac for company. She read about the revolt in AD 66 against one hundred and thirty years of Roman occupation. She learned about the destruction of the Temple in Jerusalem by the Romans in retaliation, and the stories of Jesus' escape through ancient tunnels and sewers. It was only one day's travel to the caves of Qumran.

Her captors wanted to preserve the old *status quo* and she was the only surviving witness to have actually seen the documents and the cloth, assumed burnt to cinders in the laboratory explosion. She was unaware that her friend and confidant, the Bishop, was also missing. He, meanwhile, was still sweating at the alarming prospect of becoming a sacrificial lamb to save the Catholic Church.

There had been no response to the public appeal for information. Peter would have to find a new home for his money. The police seemed to be stonewalling all questions. The Metropolitan Police simply stated that they had been taken by persons unknown, and they had no information as to whether they were dead or alive.

'*Cover Up!*' screamed the headlines.

The few remaining Christian people of Norwich wanted to pray for the safe return of their bishop, but of what relevance was prayer now?

Chapter 29 – Autumn/Winter – The Alternative Scenario Unfolds

L aura was in her 'counting house' counting all the numbers. That is how she liked to recall it. She was determined to solve the numerical puzzle set by the mystic. At least she now knew it was not a biblical reference to the fourth book of Moses called *Numbers*.

After fifty minutes of getting nowhere she spotted a book on messages, oracles and omens, the book she had purchased earlier in the year, before the session with Lucinda Palmer. She placed it on her kitchen table. Waiting for the coffee to percolate, she recalled the mystic's reference to 'Whitehall 1212', or perhaps it was code for 12th December. She did not know that would be the day when she would fly to England.

She concentrated on combinations of the numbers one, two, twelve, twenty-one and twenty-two. As she scribbled various dates down on her writing pad, her interest began to mount. There were some remarkable coincidences, significant events in her life which were based on those numbers. She wrote them down in chronological order, starting with her birth date:

Her birthday – 12th February – (12.2)

Christchurch earthquake -22nd February (22.2)

Her car registration number –JCS 212

She recalled, too, the eerie numerical dates in her family tree, all those births and deaths in January, February, November or December. In her excitement she missed two other potentially significant dates.

She turned to the book. Her attention was drawn to a chapter on 'life numbers', and a chart allocating nine numbers to all the letters of the alphabet. Before trying the chart she tried alphabetically sequenced numbers common to Laura and Paul. They both had an A, an L and a U. These were represented by 12:1:21. Turning then to the chart, she allocated the numbers to the letters comprising – 'Laura loves Paul A Morgan': $(3+1+3+9+1) + (3+6+4+5+1) + (7+1+3+3) + (1) + (4+6+9+7+1+5) = 83$. It then said to add them together: $8+3 = 11$. 'More "ones",' she thought. Reading on about life numbers, her pulse began to quicken. "Eleven" was described as the "double digit master". It was extra-special and also known as the "Master Psychic". It was held to represent someone with great spiritual and theological interests.

'Wow; that's me - *in one!*' she exclaimed in amazement. 'How crazy is that?'

★★★

The Friday security briefing was being held in Downing Street. Sir Gordon Bamford was accompanied by Nigella Blackburn, the Prime Minister's astute Home Secretary. The Prime Minister's Principal Private Secretary was also in attendance.

'Prime Minister,' announced the man from MI5, 'There have been some new developments about the Norwich explosion. We now suspect that it was perpetrated by an Islamic fundamentalist cell based in that city. They have been sleepers for some years, model students at the university, academic, bright and seemingly reputable. Thanks to our friends at GCHQ we have been keeping tabs on them. We don't know how they knew about the documents being in the laboratory, but it is quite a coincidence, there being a cell already there with the requisite knowledge to detonate a bomb. We are focusing particularly on the lives, contacts and careers of the three scientists, but currently no evidence has emerged to link any of them with Islamic radicals.

'Why would they want to destroy the evidence? Surely it would have served their interests to preserve it?' interjected the Prime Minister testily.

'Well, they may have feared the evidence would be discredited at some stage. After all, none of us can be entirely certain of the authenticity of these documents. This way the confusion, the doubts would be permanent. And boy, haven't they been proved right? In any case, we eavesdropped on a recent conversation in which they intimated that they were on alert for an attack, this time on a Norwich Cathedral. There are two in that city, one Catholic, one Anglican. We are pretty convinced it will be the latter. We have advised the Dean and he is co-operating with us.'

'Perhaps you may recall, sir,' chipped in Sir Christopher Perrin, 'That one of the participants is an Englishman, the son of a parson. The others are Islamic activists trained in Pakistan. We have been watching them for some time, including in New Zealand, from where they seem to be controlled; probably to avoid suspicion, as they know communications with Pakistan are closely monitored. I must stress that this is a joint operation in conjunction with our colleagues in the New Zealand Intelligence Service based in Wellington.'

'So, that's why you have been wining and dining with the Ambassador. How long have you known about this, Sir Christopher?'

'Only quite recently, sir,' replied his Principal Private Secretary.

'Thank you, gentlemen;' murmuring, 'Bloody liar' under his breath.

Prime Minister Benson eagerly awaited the Home Secretary's report from her 'think tank', expecting it to have produced some kind of universal 'civil code' for citizens to adopt. She would be reporting back in a few minutes.

The Home Secretary entered the Prime Minister's study with some trepidation.

'You have a solution,' said the Prime Minister, motioning her to a chair opposite his desk.

'It's a minefield.'

'Undoubtedly – that's why we have highly-remunerated civil servants with their million-pound pension pots to do our bidding.' He chose to overlook the generous retirement benefits receivable by a Prime Minister. In his mind it was justified as a compensation for his ridiculously low salary.

'Spell it out,' he barked.

'Well, it's like this, Prime Minister. We already have the *UN Declaration of Human Rights*, the *European Convention on Human Rights*, the…'

'Get to the point.'

'Let me finish, Prime Minister. In essence, we cannot reinvent the wheel. We are bound by our treaties.'

'Bloody European Union, again,' the Prime Minister interjected.

The initiative would have to be tossed into the long grass. The Prime Minister was not at all happy that he, as head of the Government, could not claim a new *'Richard Benson Declaration'* to be remembered for all time. As the Home Secretary left, the Prime Minister's Principal Private Secretary entered, and confirmed the remaining timetable for the morning.

'At 10am you have a deputation lobbying for the abolition of the Monarchy. They have the requisite one hundred thousand signatures on an e-petition.'

'That's all I need. Why the hell did we implement this procedure? I know, open government, before you say anything. It's a pain in the neck. First I lose a bishop, next my Queen.'

'I suspect you are not a very good chess-player, Prime Minister,' he replied, his tone smug.

'No doubt he's a bloody Grand Master,' Dick Benson thought to himself.

'After coffee and chocolate biscuits at 10.20 (surviving the cuts at the PM's insistence) you did originally have a meeting at 10.40 with the Minister for Religion. Unfortunately he has cancelled, still off with stress. Later, of course, you have Prime Minister's Questions and the daunting weekly audience with Her Majesty.'

★★★

Sitting in her 'counting house' in Christchurch, New Zealand, Laura heard the familiar tune of sheep bleating from her handbag. She had changed the tones after her visit to Paul's uncle's sheep farm. It denoted a text from Paul.

'gr8 2 hear from U. Will call soon, P xxx.'

Paul would only phone for a special reason. She sat by the mobile in anticipation. A few minutes seemed like an hour. She could not wait to hear that lovely English accent flavoured with a dialect Paul told her was 'Norfolk'. Their phone calls were few and far between. Texting was cheaper, but not so intimate. Besides, she did not know who might be listening in to their phone calls nor, certainly, did he.

The tones announced Paul was on the line.

'Our number's up,' he exclaimed, with a hint of a chuckle.

'How come?' replied Laura.

'The numerical connotations you put together are eerie enough, but you didn't spot potentially the most dangerous ones, especially with your history.'

'What on earth do you mean by that? You'll have to explain - my brain is addled by numbers.'

'21st December 2012 – 21.12.12 or, reversed, 21st December 2021 - 21.12.21, as some predict for the end of the world; a numerical shift perhaps coinciding with a polar reversal, like with the numbers!'

'Oh God - those dates again! That bloody prophecy of yours.'

'Not just *a* prophecy.'

'OK, prophecies.'

'Twenty-one in total; twenty-one, Laura,' he added for emphasis.

'Forget it, Paul; you're just trying to wind me up!'

Typically, Paul ignored the edge in her voice.

'Reverse twenty-one, and you get twelve.'

'So?'

'Prophecy number twelve is for "a new enlightenment". Remember? I mentioned that before. It speaks about the need for a radical shift, a reversal in our relationship with nature and the world around us.'

'There'll be a radical shift in our relationship if you carry on much longer.'

Paul hesitated. He wanted to talk about issues like carbon emissions, global warming, and suchlike. But he sensed that she would not share his enthusiasm for Miles' theories. He could not resist one more aside.

'In India, the Hindu Kalki teaches about the onset of enlightenment of humanity early this century. Note the word "onset" - the beginning of the transformation. The Hindus also spoke of an "age of darkness and destruction" in this decade, which will mark the end of an era. All these climactic events around the globe could mark the beginning of the end. Even that nutty friend of yours, Lucinda Palmer, spoke in her TV interview of catastrophic events throughout this decade. And you'll like this, given your love of that weirdo psychic; eastern mysticism also speaks of an awakening to the truth as part of a new enlightenment. Oh, and there's one more which will intrigue you - you got a 2:1 degree. End of messages!' concluded Paul, with a laugh.

'It's not funny, Paul; I find it all very frightening. It's getting to me; hardly likely they are all coincidences. There are just too many. I read in the papers only yesterday what some old priest, apparently a descendant of one of your early civilisations, said quite recently, in 1998, I believe. His warning was certainly ominous:

'There have been many destroyers, of peace, of the environment, of the beauty of the earth, even pollution of space. We do not have much time left. Then peace will prevail because Man will be no more.'

By now Laura was full of foreboding. 'See what you have done to me? This numbers thing is a warning – a prophecy of doom for me.'

'At least there won't be a day of judgement presided over by some absolute deity, as my father would have had me believe,' added Paul, failing to placate her.

'That frightens me even more – no final resting-place, no reunion with my father or my great- grandparents, my ancestors, no spiritual heaven – just a bleak nothing.'

'And no supply of virgins for me, then,' lamented Paul, trying to lighten the tone, realising he had once again gone too far.

'Paul Anthony Morgan; too late for such thoughts! Anyway, I don't want to face "nothingness",' she added, reverting to her state of anxiety.

'What about your mystic friend? You had some faith that she was able to communicate with people's relatives,' replied Paul, trying to comfort her.

'Don't go back to that word "faith" again – it's destroyed as a concept.'

'Only so far as Christians are concerned. Nothing in all this turmoil rules out an enduring spiritual existence, you said that yourself. Laura, you must not despair,' he uttered, in an attempt to console her. He didn't usually call her by her Christian name, but he wanted to shake her out of the melancholy he had brought upon her. This call was going to cost him a fortune, but he couldn't leave it there. He knew he had got carried away, sent the wrong vibes, hardly encouraging her to want to come to England to be with him.

'I'm sorry, I haven't handled this well,' he blurted out, 'I really don't want to be away from you in December. Come over here for Christmas. That's what I was really trying to lead up to.'

Laura deliberately paused, pretending he had put her off, just to let him suffer for his outburst.

'Are you still there?' Paul asked anxiously.

'Of course I'll come,' she eventually replied.

'Can you really get the time off work?'

'That's no problem.'

After the call, remembering her brief, her mind dwelt on the seemingly light-hearted quip about a supply of virgins – that was what suicide bombers believed would be their reward. Why had he let that remark slip? Why was it in his mind? Had this come from Hussain? Now she was worried for altogether different reasons, alarm bells ringing.

The invitation was just what she had been waiting for, but it left her with a heavy heart, her enthusiasm tempered by the intensity of her guilt; their love built on a cruel deception. Hers, certainly; but his as well?

Chapter 30 – The Alternative Scenario Unfolds

The news media were sending teams of reporters to all corners of the globe. There were hurricanes in the Gulf of Mexico, forest fires whipped up by high winds in Canada, and yet more floods in Australia. In the British Isles the rain continued unabated despite the heroic efforts of the newly-appointed Minister for Climatic Affairs, who confusingly confirmed that the hosepipe ban would remain in force for the time being, 'come hell or high water'. For many, both seemed to apply.

It was an exaggeration to say that half of Europe was under water, but it seemed like it. The floods deluged several cities in Austria, Germany and the Czech Republic. Many areas were inaccessible on foot, electricity supplies were down and drains overwhelmed. Most remarkably, the rains also spread to the African continent, providing much-needed water, but ruining crops. Numerous heart-rending appeals were launched.

On Tuesday, 31st October, the Mayor of New York's unplanned rehearsal began as America braced itself for the arrival of another hurricane, this time a real monster. There was mass evacuation across towns and cities all along the eastern seaboard, freeways jammed with departing cars, camper vans, trucks and all manner of transport, leaving behind deserted roads, abandoned houses, and ghost towns at Halloween. Even the airports, *John F Kennedy* and *La Guardia*, were closed, causing the cancellation of thousands of flights. Some sixty million people were thought to be at risk, including in Delaware, Virginia, Maine, Pennsylvania and Rhode Island. Residents hunkered down in readiness. New York State was divided into zones or evacuation areas, each dependent on the scale of the fury to be unleashed in what became known as a 'frankenstorm'.

Paul watched the television news reports transfixed. He had also read that it could well prove to be the wettest year in the UK since records began. Paul sent a message to Miles Mulligan. It was a crafty way of making Miles pay for the call, but 'hey, his phone is paid for anyway,' chuckled Paul.

'Please find time to call me when convenient.'

When the call came, Miles implied that the extreme flooding was all a consequence of climate change, and the UK should expect more such deluges in the coming years. To which Paul replied:

'Metric, let me remind you of Mayan prophecy number sixteen, which warned of the impact of climate change and destruction in the run-up to the end of the five-thousand-year cycle,' reiterated Paul, in a tone befitting the 'anorak' he had now become. 'Perhaps this storm is a blessing in disguise, a chance to put into practice all the arrangements and procedures for a greater disaster if Mount Cumbre Vieja in the Canaries erupts as you predict,' Paul added for good measure.

'Actually, your Mayan cycle ended on 26th December 2004. They didn't correctly factor in the leap years,' Miles replied, tongue in cheek, but not showing it. 'If you divide the number of days into years and deduct the leap years, of which there were seven hundred and thirty-two, you bring forward the date to 26ᵗʰ December 2004. And what happened on that day?'

'The Boxing Day tsunami!' Paul exclaimed, fascinated.

'Precisely. A quarter of a million people died as a result.'

'That will make him think,' thought Miles Mulligan. 'Cheeky bugger, trying to avoid paying for the call.'

★★★

The onset of a secular Christmas was a depressing spectacle for Christians. The spiritual vacuum left them in a state of dark depression. The Church struggled on, but congregations and communicants were likely to be few and far between. They were ridiculed in their communities. There were also very few carol services and choral festivals. There was no *Hark the Herald Angels Sing*. Perhaps, thought Paul mischievously, *In the Bleak Midwinter* followed by *Silent Night* would have been more appropriate.

The young felt it more than most, as did the elderly, having been brought up in the traditional Christian faith all their lives. Mary Morgan likened it to going through some kind of bereavement, a bleak emptiness pervading all the corners of this life - and the prospects for the next. It was hard, too, for the children who had looked forward to dressing-up as angels, shepherds and wise men and, nowadays, wise women, for the nativity plays at the end of term. But all this was as nothing compared with the void experienced by the Revd Thomas Morgan, his life's work in tatters, the annual celebration of the birth of Christ now only enjoyed by those whose belief was strong enough to preserve their faith. There were not likely to be enough of these to fill his chilly and desecrated church on Christmas Eve for the midnight service, so Thomas welcomed a few hardy souls to the rectory for a blessing – he could not face seeing his church bedecked with computers and all the trappings of the kind of modern society he so despised.

'Father Christmas' survived the maelstrom. His prevailing message was the glory of presents in colourful wrappings, bedecked with glitter. That epitomised society's run-up to Christmas in the towns and shopping malls of Britain.

The 'Anti-God' movement pervaded all sections of society; even, much to Mary's dismay, the Girl Guides and Brownies were caught up in the crisis. The Girl Guides Association had been considering dropping the pledge for devotion to God in the Promise on joining. It had been said that the pledge discriminated against non-believers. Tellingly, one parent had said they were bringing up their children with strong morals, but without religious beliefs, resonating with the new code of conduct being debated by the politicians. The issue had been on the agenda of the Girl Guides' executive committee since 2011, well before the current crisis. The public mood was now such that it was resolved to remove all references to God in the Promise.

It was then that another bombshell hit the Anglican Church. It was not this time an incendiary device - it was a piece of paper. To compound matters its issue was highly publicised. A news conference was called by representatives of a Christian Fellowship group, only there was no evidence of fellowship at all, quite the opposite.

A statement was read to the assembled throng of journalists and television reporters. A solicitor acting for the group made the following announcement:

'Members of the Worshipful Society of Norwich Christians have today submitted a claim for compensatory damages against the Bishop of Norwich, joined with the Archbishop of Canterbury as head cleric of the Anglican Church in England. The claim is in respect of the misrepresentation and deceit perpetrated by the Church against members of the Society. The claim is for pecuniary damages, being compensation for collection monies contributed under religious duress, charitable donations made, and costs incurred as a result of such misrepresentation, extending to lost time, personal affront and breach of human rights, as a consequence of the Church's "religious coercion" in its advocacy of a God and Saviour that it ought to have known, or reasonably to have known, was false. No further statements will be made, as the matter will be subject to due legal process through the courts. Thank you for listening.'

It was clear the claimants would seek to demonstrate that the Church ought reasonably to have known that the Christian message and exhortation to faith was based on a fanciful supposition and relied upon a false premise.

'How much is your claim?' was the obvious cry from one intrepid reporter. 'Is this a test case?'

'Profit from false Prophets - Make your claim today!' screamed the newspapers and news media that evening and the next morning.

The Chancellor of the Exchequer rubbed his hands gleefully at the prospect of clawing back all the tax relief he had handed out in good faith, but which, in its absence, should now be recoverable – plus interest, pointing out that those taxpayers affected could well have a valid counter-claim against the Church for misrepresentation.

Within days, irritating telephone messages plagued those poor souls on church electoral rolls:

'Let us reclaim your donations and collection monies, no win, no fee. Call now for your refund.'

The Church, shocked at this betrayal by the 'Turncoats of Norwich', put forward a spokesperson, who simply declared that the Diocese had received the claim and that it had no foundation, and would be utterly and totally refuted. It was clear that its defence would be the lack of evidence in support of the alleged misrepresentation, especially in the absence of the original birth and marriage documents.

There was one person who could be a crucial witness in this drama. The media speculated that she might be produced if she were still alive. Rebecca, the Bishop's wife, was beside herself, desperately anxious for her husband's well-being but also now deeply suspicious of his possible betrayal by 'that professor'.

The Revd Thomas Morgan was dumbfounded when he watched the news conference on the local news bulletin that night. He recognised many of the people present. He had known them well and had counted them as friends. He was amazed that they should do this in the absence of their much-loved Bishop, who was not there to defend himself or his faith. Thomas did not consider they had a cat in hell's chance of succeeding with the claim, until someone he spotted on the news clip made him do a double-take – there was a familiar figure hovering near the back of the hall. It was enough to shatter his confidence in any rebuttal of the claim.

'No, surely not? Please God, no,' he exclaimed then, turning to Mary, 'And they had the gall to hire a church hall for the press conference. *Alas for you, lawyers and Pharisees, hypocrites!*' he shouted at the television.

A few minutes later the telephone rang. Mary shouted: 'I think it's Peter on his mobile - it's a bit indistinct; it sounds from the general hubbub as if the call is from a crowded room somewhere.'

Chapter 31 – Winter – The Alternative Scenario Unfolds

The clamour for news, information as to the whereabouts of both the missing archivist and the bishop, which had rumbled on throughout the summer, was now again on the front pages.

Acting Commissioner Steve Copas and his team, after his fruitless trip to Rome, had spent hours of overtime desperately trying to solve the riddle. The trouble was they had precious little to go on, given the severity of the fire at the laboratory, the lack of any decipherable DNA or incriminating fingerprints in the archivist's home emanating from the so-called 'robbery'. There were no official comments at all about the cause of the fire which destroyed the replica Daimler AOC 1. The Metropolitan Police were by now under instruction to work harmoniously with the local police in Norwich headed by Detective Inspector Bob Morley, but their extensive enquiries led nowhere.

For Jane, the chance to get help, when it came, was sudden and unexpected.

She had no obvious means of escape. Even if she could, she had no documents, no passport, and no suitable clothing. Whilst this was not exactly a prison camp like Guantanamo Bay, neither did she have any knowledge of her surroundings or her location. She suspected, too, that archivist professors were hardly cut out for such escapades. What she had gleaned from the odd novel or film was that the chances of finding some way out were often the result of befriending the guards. She did not smoke, so she couldn't bribe them with cigarettes, but she would keep alert for any opportunity that presented itself.

She did not have to wait long. One afternoon, the duty 'minder' dropped his guard. He had replaced his moody counterpart, so intimidating with his fearsome large hands and burly frame, some weeks previously, and was much more amenable. He was gentle, almost charming; she guessed he was approaching retirement. He was really quite laid back; not quite horizontal, but clearly content in his work. It was not particularly arduous. Although she had lost track of the days of the week, she had developed a system of counting them as they passed. First thing in the morning she opened a new page in a book she had requested, an almanac, just the kind of book an academic might be expected to read. It served two useful purposes, one educational and interesting, even stimulating, and the other, day measurement. No one would be expected to read a reference book all the way through so, if she looked up anything in particular, she always ensured the book was closed on the same page as her starting point. Each morning she moved one page further into the almanac. That particular October day, page one hundred and ninety-five in the almanac, the guard had removed his jacket in the warmth of her overheated room and slung it on a hook behind the door. Jane had established that he had a love of English tea. He always poured her more than one cup, all very proper on a saucer, and filled from an old, brown, enamel, Victorian teapot. After more than one refill he answered the call of nature, leaving the room and his jacket. Jane leapt up from her chair and rifled the pockets. The mobile was there and switched on. She guessed she had only sixty seconds or so. She knew the Bishop of Norwich's private phone number by heart by now but, this time, dialling it caused an even greater quickening of her heartbeat. She could feel the thumping sensation in her chest as she quickly typed a text message, cursing her mistakes, and sweating profusely as she hurried. *'I'm alive, can you trace me?'* When the guard returned he could see nothing untoward. Jane hoped he would not look at his 'sent items' but, even if he did, she had nothing to lose. After all, she was in solitary confinement already. A beating perhaps, but it was worth sending it. She felt they did not intend to kill her. She need not have worried. That particular message was never received by her friend, the Bishop. She could have shouted to him down the corridor, but she did not know that. The mobile phone no longer existed. All relevant information had been extracted from it. It had then been destroyed. If only she had sent it to someone else, her sister especially. It was no breakthrough, a missed chance; her hopes of rescue were gone. The best she could hope for was to try again if the opportunity presented itself - this time she would phone Mary. Jane decided that to try to escape would be futile. In any case, where would she go?

★★★

A government quango then waded into the ongoing speculation about Church and Faith schools. The Charity Commission released, without fanfare, a 'guidance note' that a decision on the charitable status of these schools would be made by the end of the year. The fundamental problem was a requirement for charities to define how they acted in the public interest, as part of their Annual Report. It was patently clear that Christian-faith schools could no longer, in the absence of their faith, be said to act in the public interest.

The Charity Commission proposals caused consternation for these charities, their governors and trustees. They would lose their special tax breaks and this would be disastrous in such desperate economic conditions. The Treasury and the Chancellor of the Exchequer relished the prospect. Mary, as a governor of a local faith school, was, very unusually for her, livid. Thomas, also unusually, perceived her fury. Sympathising with her he cried out in frustration: *'There used to be faith, hope and charity. Now there is no faith, no hope and no charity!'*

The decline in support for Christianity and, with that, the potential for the advance of political Islam in the countries bordering the Mediterranean, caused considerable anxiety in Britain and Europe. The aftermath of the Arab Spring of 2011 brought with it a very real threat of new, democratically elected Islamic governments throughout the Arab world. In Egypt, the Muslim Brotherhood looked like it was winning the election but, assuming it did, Paul wondered if it would be able to wrestle control away from the army and its generals, and, if so, for how long? Syria was in the throes of a bloody revolution, with cities in turmoil and hundreds of innocent lives lost.

Paul, Malik and Hussain met on several occasions, debating the potential outcomes.

'Our brothers are everywhere,' proclaimed Hussain, 'They have infiltrated, sorry, joined, the professions, the armed forces, the media, and the public sector, especially state schools; even the civil service and the scientific fraternity. Our numbers will grow tenfold, a thousand times in the coming months and years, as your peoples seek spiritual guidance, salvation. It is a human need which only Allah can provide.'

Paul naively responded that he welcomed the fact that Muslims had become integrated into the various sectors of society. That, he said, was healthy; they were playing their part in community life. He referred to this in one of his messages to Laura. The casual use of the word '*infiltrated*' troubled her deeply, and not only her. Hussain, when alone with Paul, was deliberately more conciliatory, telling him he envisaged history repeating itself, as the Islamic revolution would again spread from the African continent to Southern Spain, France and then on through the Mediterranean countries. He speculated that this would only increase the divide between the southern and northern countries in the European Union. He made no mention that this was part of their hidden agenda, to bring down the Euro and de-stabilise the region. He said nothing, either, of Malik's contribution to the drafting of the Islamic penal code for Britain.

When Paul was not present, Hussain and Malik did not hold back in their excitement that the tide was turning in their favour - at last. Much though they abhorred democracy, they would use it as a stalking horse to assume power, followed by its dissolution and replacement by Islamic laws. They were careful not to reveal the full extent of their hopes and aspirations to Paul, their unsuspecting Trojan Horse.

Paul did not read the signs, perhaps did not want to; his trust in his friend was too deep-rooted.

The elders, imams, in the mainstream Muslim community, with Hussain's father in the vanguard, condemned the violence perpetrated against Christians. They knew it could prove counter-productive to their long-term goal – the peaceful and gradual conversion of Britain into an Islamic state. Relations between Hussain and his father had now broken down completely, it seemed irreversibly.

The 'Near Neighbour Fund' had been established by the Government specifically to assist bringing communities together. The fund was administered by the Church Urban Fund and was available to applicants of all faiths. Clearly the money could not now be used to rebuild church property damaged in the riots, as Christianity was likely no longer to be deemed to be a 'faith'.

This presented a unique opportunity for the Muslim elders, including Hussain's estranged father. They lobbied privately for an approach to the Archbishop of Canterbury, should his post remain in existence, for a 'merger' with the Church of England. As in business, they used that word although some, the more extreme, really meant a 'take-over', akin to acquiring an ailing business on the cheap - in this case the Anglican Church. The opportunity to acquire the numerous church buildings still standing, and the many magnificent cathedrals, together with the funds to repair them, was an enticing prospect. There were precedents for such acquisitions. They quoted, amongst others, the example of the mosque in London's Brick Lane which still had pews on the first floor. Originally it had been built by the Huguenots and then later converted to a Jewish synagogue, before finally becoming a mosque.

Hussain and his fundamentalist friends would have no truck with this. It was anathema for them to join together with the infidels. They did not have the patience to wait and maybe lose the opportunity which had, by the grace of Allah, presented itself. 'Strike while the iron is hot!' they cried. They were ready to impose Sharia Law, create *'Islamic Britain'*. Their lands had been invaded by Western forces, their boot-prints all over Iraq and Afganhastan, and they were now sending drones into their midst, killing fellow Muslims, including women and children, even, in some reported cases, mutilating their bodies. They had no time for excuses like 'collateral damage.'

★★★

There was still no rescue for the archivist from Norwich. Detective Inspector Bob Morley was convinced of a cover-up at the highest level of the Government and/or the Vatican. One well-publicised development was news of a dawn raid on the offices of *Britain on Sunday*, part of Operation 'Weeting'. Computers, phone records, files were seen being loaded into the backs of a fleet of police vans. Simultaneously the Editor, Joe Culverhouse, and journalist, Mike Burrows, awoke to the sound of battering-rams, shouting, and barking dogs, as their front doors were smashed to pieces, all but demolished. They were arrested and taken into custody. Their houses were searched and items removed. There was little in the way of explanation given to the two bemused wives and their teenage children. Painstaking and thorough though the search was, nothing was found that helped locate the missing professor. Plenty was found to incriminate *Britain on Sunday*, including evidence of illicit payments to Metropolitan Police officers.

★★★

Alone in her cell, Jane could only assume that the Bishop had not received her text message or, alarmingly, was he even party to her kidnap, to protect his faith? 'What kind of Church is that?' she thought. As her security guard entered the room to check on her she heard a sound through the open door, one which stirred her memory, causing her heart to flutter. It was not New Year, but someone was whistling *Auld Lang Syne*. Only one person she knew used to do that, long ago in the Halls of Residence at Oxford University. He never realised he was doing it. Her initial pang of excitement was short-lived, soon turning to anger at her betrayal. He, the Bishop, was in the building, her captor. He had left her to carry the can before, and now he was doing it again. How could he?

She was wrong; he was also a captive, trying to attract her attention; guessing, hoping, that she might be there too; just trying to let her know he was nearby.

★★★

By late November the Press and the media were majoring on the potential for cataclysmic events on 21st December. Will it be the End of Days? Paul thought not, but he was far from sure. He remained convinced that the end of the Mayan cycle signified a spiritual awakening, a renewed recognition of the need to restrain greed, especially after the events of 2008 and their financial aftermath, and to conserve the Earth's natural resources in the face of climate change. He expected the change to be gradual, over a period of years, and not necessarily a climactic event or catastrophe. However, he had been sufficiently duped by his friend, Miles, to retreat into his own counting house. Playing with the numbers, he came up with another scenario. This equated to a revised date of December 2014 for the end of the cycle – plenty of time for yet more floods, earthquakes, perhaps even a plague, if not of locusts, then of untimely deaths from the increasing failure of antibiotics, or something like that. 'A new Black Death,' he thought morbidly. He sent a message to Laura, and copied it to Miles.

'I believe everyone has been misled; we are looking at 2014 for the potential End of Days, or the beginning of a new age, not this December!'

Miles' reply shocked him.

'You need to look further ahead than that. Going back to AD33, on 3rd April to be precise, there was a massive eclipse of the sun, accompanied by earthquakes. The eclipse occurred at noon, **and coincided with the most widely accepted date, and time, of Jesus' crucifixion.** 'What was also of interest to people like me was that it was **not a normal eclipse**, as it could not have been caused by the moon.

'We can only speculate as to whether it was an asteroid near-miss or some strange, gravitational pull. Your father may have another explanation, one beyond my understanding. There is a total solar eclipse due in December 2021, and you'll need to be up early; in Norwich it is forecast to begin between 5.30am and 9.38am. Perhaps that gives you something to ponder!'

'December 2021 again,' Paul reflected; 'Just as Laura's mystic predicted.'

★★★

In early December, the Census results were announced. Thomas was in his study, staring out of the window, his mind apparently elsewhere. He had that strange sense of bad news to come. A crow, menacing and forbidding, black and sinister, swooped low as it headed for its target. The sparrows, hovering round the feeder like Harrier jets waiting to land, dispersed in panic. The crow, unable to perch on the feeder, flew back to a nearby chimney-pot and glowered down in frustration.

Thomas' thoughts were interrupted by a shout from Mary in the kitchen. She could not believe what she had heard from her newly-acquired television, which Thomas so disliked, on the kitchen sideboard. Like the Prime Minister he abhorred the creeping, all-consuming presence of technology in every corner of modern life, and now his own parish church. That really got to him.

'Thomas, have you heard what they have revealed about Norwich?'

'No, dear; what about Norwich?'

'It's just been reported that our home city is the most Godless in England, with the highest proportion of people reporting "no religion".'

Thomas was aghast. The evening television news reiterated the sobering news, including a statement from the Venerable Archdeacon of Norwich, in which she expressed shock and amazement, citing that this city had a church on every corner. Peter happened to hear the same broadcast. He reacted differently from his brother, gleefully letting out howls of laughter.

'So much for the success of their ministry,' he trumpeted with unrestrained delight; 'Carol had been right to call it a Godforsaken place after all,' he chuckled, congratulating the people of Norwich for their intelligence and wisdom. Peter was disappointed he would not be at the rectory for Christmas; there would be no opportunity to offer his condolences to Thomas on the demise of faith in his home city. Peter and his wife were not expected this year. Since that telephone call to Thomas he considered it inappropriate to come, given the nature of his current case. Thomas had indeed been correct in recognising his brother in the legal team at the back of that church hall.

★★★

Paul assumed that her trust fund enabled Laura to fly to the UK in mid-December. Despite his limited financial resources he had offered to contribute, but she had told him not to worry, she would make the arrangements. In fact, they had been made for her. She was under orders to watch Paul Morgan like a hawk, report to her superior daily. She was the one person who could act as their eyes and ears 24/7. It was a risk, given her obvious infatuation with him, but she was a trained agent and was all they had who could get that close to their target and his associates. Mike Tucker had not told her about the threatened plot, not yet. They wanted her to find out for herself and report back. Her performance was under the microscope. They particularly wanted first-hand corroboration of their surveillance reports about the impending threat to the Norwich cathedral.

It was only when airborne that she had thought about the date and time of her flight – noon on 12th December – 12.12.12.12. Only slightly delayed, she was reunited with her lover at Heathrow's new terminal building.

The airport would soon be stretched to capacity, with passengers flying to be with their loved ones. This year it was not only for Christmas. For many it was to be together on 21st December – or '21.12.12', as Paul and Laura referred to it.

20th December was a day neither Paul nor Laura would ever forget. They had enjoyed a long, afternoon walk in the weakening winter sunshine, deep in the Norfolk countryside. The few remaining autumn leaves danced cheerfully in the breeze, before falling gently to earth, leaving their mother trees looking desolate and austere, deprived of their clothing, snatched away by the easterly wind. Paul touched Laura gently on the arm, his fingers to her lips to silence her as pointed upwards to the sky. There, in the distance, a marsh harrier hovered, suddenly diving to earth its supper to devour, a life to steal. The unspoken thought between them, and countless others across the land, around the globe, was: 'How many lives would be lost that night?'

In the evening they went to a small, intimate restaurant overlooking the still water of a nearby broad, the Norfolk term for a small lake. The water glistened as they drank an aperitif, a warming red-wine punch, on the floodlit decking which separated the water from the diners behind them.

'Maybe our last supper,' suggested Paul, as they found their table. He did not know if he was joking or not. However, regardless, his proposal was accepted. By the light of the silvery moon she tried on the diamond ring, which seemed to sparkle with excitement, reminding them both of Auckland Harbour, the other side of the world. By this time New Zealand would already be facing up to 21st December. Paul vowed their union would be for ever, whether for minutes, hours, days, decades or eternity.

That fearful evening much of the population had no idea to whom to pray, or even if they should pray at all. The gathering clouds and promise of thunderstorms only heightened the sense of anxiety.

Thomas, not believing the dire expectations of those dastardly pagans, nor indeed fully accepting the alleged demise of his God, prepared an impassioned sermon, one he would deliver to a nearby parish - one of many whose vicars had resigned the priesthood. He took his text from the *Book of Hebrews*:

'You need endurance if you are to do God's will and win what he has promised. For soon, very soon, he is to come, will come; he will not delay; and by faith my righteous servant shall find life. We have the faith to make life our own.'

Mary wondered if he was really addressing the congregation, or was the exhortation more personal?

Thomas also sent the text to his brother, again quoting from the *Second Letter to Peter*- *'the remedy for doubt'*. Mary sent it, at her husband's behest, such a task still apparently being beyond his capabilities but, more likely, the consequences of his dislike of modern means of instant communication. She copied it to Paul.

'Note this first, in the last days there will come men who scoff at religion and live self indulgent lives, and they will say: "Where is now the promise of his coming? Our fathers have been laid to rest, but still everything continues exactly as it has always been since the world began." In taking this view they lose sight of the fact that there were heavens and earth long ago, created by God's word out of water and with water; and by water that first world was destroyed, the water of the deluge. And the present heavens and earth, again by God's word, have been kept in store for burning; they are being reserved until the day of judgement when

the godless will be destroyed....But the day of the Lord will come; it will come unexpectedly as a thief. On that day the heavens will disappear with a great rushing sound, the elements will disintegrate in flames, and the earth with all that is in it will be laid bare. Since the whole universe is to break up in this way think what sort of person you should be, what devout and dedicated lives you should live!' - 'Beware, Brother!'

On receipt, Paul mischievously forwarded his own message to Uncle Peter.

'You have only a short time to reform, until 2014, or perhaps 2021, the more likely dates for the end of the world, or transition to the next age, unless some rogue nuclear state gets there first. I never said that 21st December 2012 was 'D' day, my description for Doomsday. 'There are those who equally expect a transition to the so-called golden age to start in 2014, concluding by 2021. This has long been predicted by Hindus, Egyptians, Greeks and Romans, to name but a few. Their predictions are similar to those of the Mayans, all derived from the signs of the zodiac, the end of the twelve ages of two thousand one hundred and sixty years. On 14th July 2014, the procession of the equinoxes reaches its climax when the Sun, the Moon, and Jupiter meet in the same quadrant as the Tisha constellation. And in 2021 there will be a total eclipse – of you if you don't reform. Good luck, Uncle, with your new, devout life!'

Mary said her own prayer that night: *'There are some doubting souls who need your pity; snatch them from the flames and save them.'*

★★★

Prime Minister Dick Benson was woken early on the morning of Friday, 21st December. He feared the worst.

He was bleary-eyed from a late night, waiting and watching, listening to the rain lashing the windows, finally lapsing into a deep sleep. A voice spoke to him. He was still of this world, it had not ended. He realised it was not his wife - she was at home, well away from Downing Street, alone with the children and the security guard, even separated from him by the demands of office on this night of all nights. But he recognised who it was. It was his duplicitous Principal Private Secretary.

'I'm sorry to disturb you so early, sir. I have urgent news. It's about God. It is conclusively proven that…' An almighty crash drowned out his voice and, simultaneously, the lights went out, so he did not see the pained expression on Sir Christopher's face. He simply could not come to terms with addressing Mr Benson as 'sir'; it should be the other way round - he was the one who had been knighted.

The crack of thunder which had interrupted the Prime Minister's early awakening had fused the lights. The emergency generator kicked in within moments. His Permanent Private Secretary was evidently the harbinger of dramatic news.

'As I was about to say, Prime Minister, earlier this week the executors of the will of the scientist Judas Swan, who perished in the laboratory explosion, visited the local branch of his bank in Norwich. What I have been told is that the bank manager, having given them all the requisite details of the bank accounts, savings accounts, ISAs, etc., then made one further pronouncement.

'"*Gentlemen, there is one more thing. The late Mr Swan has a safety deposit box. I suggest it is opened in your presence.*"

'The bank manager fetched the key and opened the box. There were several items inside. He lifted them carefully out and placed them on the desk. **They were pieces of ageing parchment which looked like ancient documents.** They quickly realised exactly what they were and where they had come from. Only the scientists had perished - the attempt to destroy the evidence had failed.'

Extremely urgent scientific testing in two independent laboratories, both undertaken under the strictest security, revealed them to be fourteenth-century fakes. They certainly did not date back to Jesus of Nazareth. The carbon-dating technique had proved unreliable before, most notably with respect to the Turin Shroud. The discovery beneath the swan pit in Norwich had no religious legitimacy. All the mayhem about the destruction of the Christian Church had been completely unfounded. This revelation, announced overnight on verification of the results, coincided with the discovery of two missing persons, one a bishop and the other an archivist, found in the grounds of Kensington Gardens in London by a security guard, drugged and disoriented, but alive, well and reunited. It was later revealed they had been released on condition they signed a 'non-disclosure agreement', which included confirmation that they had been well treated and confined purely for their own protection, and had not been under duress of any kind. It was not long afterwards that Cardinal Napoliano returned to Rome, transferred to a new post. Hussain, Malik and Omar were distraught at the news, furious that the laboratory explosion had not succeeded in its objective. They would get their revenge on the Christians- 'Operation Trojan Horse' must be executed without delay.

The crisis in the Anglican Church was over. ***Their faith was restored***.

'*Now Thank We All Our God,*' was all the Prime Minister could say.

Chapter 32

On Saturday morning the Revd Thomas Morgan, his wife Mary, Paul and Laura awoke to find the world had not ended. The ferocious thunderstorms and Force nine gales of the previous night had passed. The sky was a perfect blue and the birds were singing some glorious melody, as if in celebration.

A momentous revelation was circulating the globe, heralded as '*breaking news*' on the sub-titles running across the bottom of plasma screens. Open spaces, town squares and public meeting places began to fill with people as Christians enthusiastically received the glad tidings. It was as if every football team had won the World Cup, as cars sounded their horns and the morning bulletins screamed out their headlines:

'**God survives**' and '**Jesus Lives On**' and '**Faith Restored**'.

It was just in time for Christmas but, ironically, too late for *Britain on Sunday* to print a special edition of the story. Its offices were shut down to enable police investigators to sift through all its computer files and paperwork.

On Christmas Eve a purposeful Thomas strode down to his church and placed an eviction notice on the old oak door. The Village Hall Committee had seven days to return his church to its former glory.

When Christmas Day arrived, once the morning service at another church in the parish was over, as was customary, all were assembled in the Revd Thomas Morgan's sitting room. A fire burned softly in the grate. The alcove beside was beset with holly, adorned by numerous glistening red berries, depicting the harsh winter to come. As the Herald Angels sang, church bells rang out throughout the land in celebration, not only of Christ's birth but also of the recent announcements from the Vatican and the Anglican Church trumpeting the restoration of 'Faith'. The contrasting stories of God's existence or His non-existence were no more.

Mary had received the telephone call she had so long hoped to receive. Her sister had been debriefed by the security services and would be able to join them for Christmas. Peter would be coming too, but without Carol, who would be with the children from her first marriage; anything to avoid the probability, as she saw it, of a cold and damp few days in that rectory in the wilds of Norfolk.

Mary was happier than she had been for a very long time. Paul had found a lovely young lady, and her first instincts were that Laura would at last help her son to settle down. Mary realised he might end up half way across the world in New Zealand, but that concern was, at least for now, a long way off. Jane was safe and well and coming for Christmas. Her brother, Oliver, it seemed, and much to her relief, had not spilt the beans, revealed the family secrets. It would be good, too, to see Peter without that wretched woman, with all her fancy airs and graces, draped on his arm. It was rare for Mary to think unkindly of anyone. She kept these thoughts private, but felt guilty she should have them.

The morning services were over, sermons delivered. The only fly in the ointment had, potentially, been Peter. To Thomas' surprise Peter had gone with them to church, no doubt to dissect every word, find ammunition for later. 'The enemy within,' thought Thomas.

Christmas Day afternoon was cold and frosty, but gloriously sunny. It was deep, crisp and even. Thomas, Peter and Paul went outside to inhale some fresh, Norfolk air ahead of the evening's festivities. Looking out over the marshes from the rectory terrace, Peter turned to Thomas.

'It's been a tumultuous year. There's been a lot to think about. I think we all need time to reflect. Now, about 'faith' itself; I...' At that moment, their conversation was drowned out by a cacophony of sound, rising to a crescendo, somewhere above them. Then, approaching from the west, came a majestic flypast, as thousands of pink-footed geese flew over, one leading, the rest in perfect formation like squadrons of the *Red Arrows*, with that familiar v-shape, honking loudly as if trumpeting the good news, then displaying a tapestry of oscillating lines woven into the sky, places exchanged as a new leader took over. Then they soared away to the horizon, and all that remained were shrouds of faint, white cloud streaked across the sky - a vapour trail in their wake. As they gloried in the wonder of nature, they heard Mary shouting from the open kitchen window.

'Thomas! Kettle on, please, we're preparing the Christmas dinner; you make the tea.'

Off he went like a startled rabbit, wondering what Peter had been about to say.

That evening, sustained by Mary's sumptuous Christmas dinner, washed down with two bottles of vintage champagne, courtesy of Peter, and Paul's bottle of Sauvignon all the way from New Zealand, the women settled down by the embers of the fire. It was Jane's first chance to meet Paul's girlfriend, and they had a lot to talk about. Fearing this, Thomas, Peter and Paul retired to the study armed with port glasses and a decanter, ready to let that deep-red liquid do its worst. They reviewed their long-held opposing beliefs in the context of recent events, and the lessons learnt from the deception bequeathed by the fraudsters. Peter could not resist reminding Thomas that he and his fellow priests would have their work cut out to bring God back to Norwich in time for the next census. Paul, sensing the possibility of the speedy end to the fragile ceasefire, the threat of renewed hostilities between them, quickly intervened.

'It's an appropriate time to remind you of the amazingly prescient ancient prophecies of a new spiritual awakening. Coincidence or not, you have to admit the timing is impeccable, coinciding with this week's news - unbelievably released on the morning of 21st December.'

Thomas and Peter looked at each other - but said nothing. A temporary silence prevailed. Then Paul, recalling the Bible-reading classes of his childhood, spoke again, looking at each one in turn.

'*…you, sir, why do you pass judgement on your brother?*

'*And you, sir, why do you hold your brother in contempt?*

'*Let us therefore cease judging one another, but rather make this simple judgement: that no obstacle or stumbling block be placed in a brother's way.*

'Let us then pursue the things that make for peace and build up the common life.'

Then he concluded in his own words: 'Peace be with you!'

They looked at young Paul in astonishment, but his words had sunk in. In their subsequent conversation they reached a mutual understanding that a world without faith, of whatever creed, might create more problems than it solved. They, even Peter, no longer confrontational, questioned whether God's existence could be regarded as a matter of scientific evidence that could be settled in a laboratory.

'There may well be some force which is beyond our understanding,' he acknowledged gracefully.

'Alleluia!' cried Thomas.

They agreed that those who express a religious faith, however diverse, should be respected and tolerated provided it was peaceable and not promoted by force, intimidation, or threat of any kind. Equally, those with faith should respect those who have none. They accepted that everyone should have the right to the freedom of making their own choice, of following their own beliefs. Peter acknowledged that secularism should not necessarily be regarded as an enemy of religion. They agreed that there was little point in maintaining their long-held polarised opinions because, however intensive the debate, *neither could ever win the argument.*

Heading towards the kitchen for their second bottle of port, they found the women had not gone to bed but were still deep in conversation; they joined them in the sitting room.

'I see you've managed to let the fire go out,' spluttered Thomas, swaying on his feet, words slurred. Mary gave Jane a knowing wink; it was good to see him enjoying himself, especially so in Peter's company.

'I see you three have been enjoying the port,' Jane responded.

'Is he often like this?' asked Laura bravely, and to which Peter responded:

'Every Sunday, my dear, after he has polished off the communion wine.'

Paul, looking at Jane, intervened.

'You've not done so badly yourselves. Do you like the new wine glasses Mum bought especially with you in mind?' He knew how particular Jane was when it came to her passion for drinking fine wines. It seemed like a good time to make the announcement. He looked at Laura for reassurance.

'What I was going to say was, having just experienced my father and uncle actually see eye to eye on something, maybe those ancient soothsayers were right after all and we are at the beginning of a new golden age of enlightenment! Well, **we** certainly are!' he announced triumphantly, putting his arm round Laura. 'We are engaged to be married.'

Mary was the first to react. 'Congratulations, both of you; wonderful news, I'm so pleased.'

The others soon followed. They did not notice Jane's wistful expression, almost sad, as if her happiness were, for some reason, not complete.

'This Christmas is certainly one to remember,' reflected Mary, Thomas then chipping in indecipherably. It sounded like 'Faul, petch annuver dwink.'

'One to remember, or rather one-two remember!' pronounced Laura, thinking of her numbers, adding that the 'new age of enlightenment' was prophecy number 'one two', otherwise known as twelve!

'I was consumed by doom and overlooked that message of hope - the mystery of the numbers is solved!' she cried out, in a mixture of delight, excitement and relief. In the heady atmosphere of Paul's family, her worries seemed far away.

It was at that moment that they decided to finish the evening by watching the late-night repeat version of Her Majesty's hastily re-written televised Christmas broadcast which had gone out that afternoon. In many ways the theme echoed the discussions in the Morgan family. At its conclusion, coverage switched to the hastily reconvened 'all faiths' multi-denominational choir in Norwich Cathedral. Led by Bishop Banham, back from his morning sermon at the Queen's Sandringham estate, they were singing **Oh Come All Ye Faithful**.

PART IV

THE COMBINED CONCLUSION TO PARTS TWO AND THREE

David Buck

Chapter 33

The happy couple enjoyed a blissfully happy January, walks over snow-covered fields, tours of North Norfolk, a walk to the remote headland of Blakeney Point, and visits to the many bird reserves. There was also a drive to Horsey to see the seals, the next year's litter.

Lovemaking at the rectory was discreet and inhibited – they knew any such activity did not meet with his father's approval, despite their engagement at Christmas. It was a great relief when they moved on to Paul's flat. It was freedom at last, far away from the creaking floorboards of the old rectory, which had prevented any attempt at such unrestrained activity.

Late one evening Paul talked more in hope than expectation, about starting their own family.

'Not yet, Paul; we need to establish ourselves, have stability.'

Laura had also fallen in love with the medieval city of Norwich with its two cathedrals, its winding streets, some still paved with cobblestone, and its many renowned historic sites, collectively known as the 'Norwich 12', comprising the UK's finest collection of heritage buildings, from Norman to Medieval, some Georgian, some Victorian, as well as the most modern. Paul delighted in taking her on a journey through a thousand years of history in the 'English City', once the second city in England, to such fascinating places as Dragon Hall, the Guildhall, the Assembly House, St James' House, the

City Hall and the architecturally stunning Forum, rebuilt out of the ashes of the former library. Laura was enthralled that so much had survived the ravages of the centuries. They attended a concert in St Andrew's Hall and studied the portraits of the great and good in Blackfriars' Hall. She could not believe that one city could have so many iconic buildings, and with them such a heritage.

They had gone swimming in the new leisure centre and then raved at a disco in the grounds of the Old Medieval Hospital, with part of the site still roped off, the legacy of that now notorious discovery. Paul showed Laura the derelict pit where the swans had flown in to meet their maker, and which had caused such mayhem for his family - the Roman baths and steam room remained an architect's plan. The Chief Executive of Monastic Leisure Limited wanted to turn it into a tourist attraction, a potential source of extra funds to help cover their legal fees in the ongoing disputes over the delay in completion and the rightful recipient of what he regarded as the 'treasure trove' of Roman silver found on the site.

Laura had told Paul she had been granted some long-overdue leave, a sabbatical but, on 12th February, her birthday, the message she received was not a celebratory one. It was the summons she had dreaded, but knew was coming. She was instructed to return to New Zealand. Local agents could now take over. Her work was done. Despite everything it was odd that Paul, despite her best efforts, had still seemed very reluctant to introduce her to Hussain. It was a niggling worry but, nonetheless, she did not feel there was a hidden agenda, anything she should report. She had been diligent in sending daily reports, often when in the toilet, one of the few places of privacy from her lover and fiancé. She had, however, been economical with the truth, unconvinced that Paul was a participant in anything untoward. The authorities knew otherwise, or thought they did.

Paul had thought it strange that Laura qualified for a sabbatical, as she was only just twenty-seven. He did not pursue the point. All he wanted was to have her in England, or anywhere else for that matter, and especially on her birthday.

'Paul, I have to go back to my job, something urgent has cropped up. We both knew I would have to go back sometime.'

'Laura, hang your job; stay, you'll soon find something here,' Paul replied despairingly.

'Mine is not the kind of work you can just resign from and walk away. I don't have a valid visa to stay here, and besides, we need the money. I have employment and you don't.'

'Ouch!' exclaimed Paul, reluctant to accept the inevitable. 'I'll go back with you. You can lend me the money for the flight. I could live in your flat and look for a job.'

'Later, Paul; there are things I have to do.'

'And you don't want me hanging around, do you?'

'I didn't say that.'

Paul recognised there was a steely determination in Laura's eyes. It was disconcerting and he accepted he couldn't push her further. He tried another tack.

'What about the wedding plans, fixing a date?'

'Plenty of time for that,' replied Laura evasively, 'And in any case, we haven't discussed which side of the world it will be. I believe it's the bride's prerogative and I need to discuss it with my mother. Remember you will have to ask her for permission.'

There was something about her demeanour, a distance, a remoteness that Paul could not fathom. Paul had eventually found out that Laura's father had died quite young. He found it difficult to accept that Laura would want, or need, to discuss it with her mother, an alcoholic. He had given no thought to asking her mother - the prospect scared him. Was he supposed to do this over the telephone, with someone he had never met? He began to wonder if that aside was a smokescreen, particularly as her warmth towards him seemed to have suddenly evaporated. 'Ever since the call from her employer,' Paul muttered to himself afterwards.

Their parting at Heathrow was tense and strained, the final hug hesitant, the kisses without their normal passion, those magnetic blue eyes somehow anguished, no longer sparkling, her face a shallow, pale complexion, almost ghostly. Gone was the radiance, the unrestrained affection, even perhaps the love? Paul walked dejectedly back to his car, unable to comprehend the complete change in her. It was a re-run of his departure from Auckland. Laura, through Customs and into the departure lounge, found a seat in an empty row, threw down her back-pack in frustration and promptly burst into tears, then sobbed quietly, awaiting the call for boarding.

Three days after leaving Heathrow, Laura was back in her apartment in Christchurch. She had been ordered to see her boss, Mike Tucker, at 10.30am.

She had never really liked him, nobody much did. He could be brusque and abrupt, to the point of rudeness. No one disputed that he was good at his job, always focused, a totally driven man. Like her colleagues, she wondered if he had a life outside, a wife or partner. No one seemed to know. He was as secretive as his work.

Laura nervously counted the clock down towards the time of her appointment. As 10.30am approached she walked slowly down the long, carpeted corridor on the third floor of the temporary offices now occupied by the intelligence services, following their forced relocation after the earthquake.

'Come in,' he bellowed, as she knocked tentatively. Mike Tucker motioned to her to take a seat in the leather-upholstered chair opposite him. There was only the one file on his desk and she could see it was simply entitled **'Paul Anthony Morgan'**. The room was forbidding, austere, no clutter and no family photographs, just two large maps behind him, one of North Island, the other of South Island. Feeling distinctly ill at ease, she spotted red dots over Napier, Wellington and Christchurch. It was not an environment to make a subordinate feel at ease.

Mike Tucker looked piercingly at Laura. The look was hostile, unfriendly.

'I've read your reports, Miss Francis, and I am underwhelmed. They do not tell the whole story, and you have left out important details, suppressed others. For example, when Morgan visited your flat, sometimes you switched on your tape-recorder, but you clearly did not on other occasions when you were together. Or you made sure there was music to hide your conversation. We know that from observations made by Agent Neon, your minder. You became protective of your target. I want you to think carefully before we go further. I need more information.'

Laura blushed, thinking of Neon listening to their lovemaking. At the time she had blocked him out from her mind but now, the very thought of his unseen presence revolted her, the wonderful moments of intimacy sullied and soiled, perhaps for ever tarnished. Her betrayal of Paul weighed heavily upon her; her eyes moistened, she felt sickened as she held back the tears. She also sensed this interview was not likely to have a happy ending. What more could she tell him to save her career going into freefall?

★★★

Paul had driven despairingly back round the M25 motorway from Heathrow, his mind elsewhere, in some kind of trance, oblivious of the customary stop, start, hold-ups which so irritated the other motorists. He certainly did not notice the blue Ford Focus a few cars behind. He was in such a daze he missed the M11 turn-off north to Cambridge, having to settle for the A12 dual carriageway to Chelmsford, then Colchester, next Ipswich and finally the slow crawl up the A140 to Norwich. He phoned his parents to confirm he was safely home. In need of company he also phoned Hussain, who declined to join him, making some excuse he was working on an assignment. He reluctantly settled for a take-away pizza and a few beers, to drown his sorrows, then to bed.

The next morning began early, around 5am. It was the deafening crash as the door to his flat door burst open that awoke him. Hung over and bewildered, he found himself staring at three uniformed police officers in full riot gear demanding him not to move. They tore off the bedding, leaving him lying prone, half naked on his mattress, and simply stood there, guns drawn. It felt like a movie. He soon heard the sound of drawers being opened; it was evident they were pulling his flat apart. He was told to dress and was then immediately handcuffed, before being led out past the splintered wooden panels, the last vestiges of his broken front door, and out to the back seat of a waiting police vehicle. There was also a van, which was being loaded with his computer, laptop, the old memory-stick and all his lever-arch files and paperwork. It was then off in the bright yellow-and-blue car, speeding through the deserted streets, siren blazing, lights flashing, and down the A11 to the Police Operations Centre at Wymondham.

'How crazy is this? I would have come willingly, without all this palaver, had they simply asked and told me what they wanted,' he muttered, as he sat pinned in the back seat between two surly, unspeaking police officers.

For the next two days, Interview Room 3B became his new home; it seemed like that, anyway. It was sparse, with a concrete floor carpeted only under the table in the centre. There were four chairs and a tape-recorder and a small, grilled window. He was interrogated by a thin, well-dressed man with a receding hairline and pointed chin, not in uniform and wearing a smart suit, and one overweight detective. The main focus of their questions was Hussain, but it was also clear they were holding his friends, Malik, Abdul and Jarmal.

'How long have you known Hussain Barzal?'

'Where did you first meet?'

'What were your discussions about?'

'What did he tell you about his parents, his family?'

'Who funded his trips to Pakistan?'

'Who were his friends?'

'Why did you spend so much time with them?'

'Why did you go to New Zealand to meet them?'

'What did they tell you about Abu Nawaz?'

The questions were endless, repetitive, and remorseless. He felt they were trying to trip him up, tie him in knots; and who was Abu Nawaz? It was also evident to Paul that they knew a great deal about him, where he had been, whom he had met, and when. He now began to realise what this was about but, alarmingly, when it came to New Zealand, they did not seem to accept his protestations of having being an innocent abroad. They knew what books he had taken from the local library, and had trawled through all his internet visits. This worried him; over the months and years he had visited so many sites as part of his studies that he could envisage how this could be misinterpreted. The bombshell came when they told him Hussain had no rich uncle in Pakistan. The frequent visits there were not to see his family.

'All this so-called research is a cover for your real purpose. Spare us all a waste of time and admit it,' they demanded. He had nothing to confess.

He spent the intervening night in a police cell, fearful for his future. He became increasingly scared. Would the questioning get aggressive? How could he prove his innocence? In the middle of a long, sleepless night his mind began to play tricks, his imagination starting to run riot. He began to panic. They had seized his passport. Would he be extradited to the United States or, worse, sent to Guantanamo Bay? He knew something about what that entailed; the misery, the hardship, in some cases, according to Hussain, torture.

The puzzle was unravelling now, clues he should have spotted - like Hussain knowing someone, or of someone, inside that ghastly detention camp. There was something, too, about one of his interrogators, the one he knew as 'Thin' and who had that irritating cough. It eventually dawned on him. He had been too shocked to think straight – the suited man was the man on the plane, and he was the man with the laptop in the café in Waipara. Then he could picture the fellow photographer in the rose garden. How could he have been so blind? But there were other things they seemed to know, *some very personal, even intimate*.

By morning of day two of his interrogation Paul had realised the origin of much of the information the police and the man, presumably from MI5 or MI6, he couldn't remember which was which, had obtained. There could only be one source. He screamed out loud.

'Duplicitous, double-crossing bitch,' he shouted, furious at her deception; 'A fucking honey-trap! How was I so stupid?' The jigsaw was coming together now, the pieces beginning to fit; she worked for the security services, nothing short of a spy. 'Now I know why she left like she did, so suddenly; mission accomplished.' He felt used and dirty, ashamed to have been seduced by it all.

★★★

'Now, Miss Francis,' Mike Tucker barked, bringing her back to earth with a jump, 'The missing pieces, please.'

Laura tried her best to answer her boss's questions. After about half an hour he paused.

'There is something else I think you should know. Earlier this year the English security services uncovered an unexploded bomb outside a mosque in Christian Street in London, just hours before it was to be detonated to coincide with Friday prayers. The culprits were from a cell of activists, students at a London technical college, who had been under surveillance for some months. By attacking one of their own mosques they hoped to engineer a Muslim backlash against the Christians. Also, it did not go unnoticed that Hussain Barzal's father, who was staunchly opposed to acts of violence, was one of the imams at that particular mosque. They were apprehended as a result of mobile phone conversations deciphered by the Cyber Centre at GCHQ. Information obtained after their arrest confirms links with another cell based in Norwich, whom the UK authorities have also been watching for some time – Hussain's cell. We suspect they were responsible for the explosion at the laboratory in Norwich, killing three scientists, but have no proof. One of them, Abu Nawaz, the laboratory assistant, we now believe to have been a "sleeper". He was unknown to the UK authorities, but we now believe he was a suicide bomber, ordered by persons unknown to destroy the laboratory and with it the parchment he had so unexpectedly come upon, and which he thought was still stored there. There is conflicting evidence, but it does appear that he had links with a Christian radical group as well as Muslim Fundamentalists; perhaps some kind of religious double agent. Both sides had motive; the radical Christians obviously, but also the Fundamentalists could have wanted to destroy the evidence in order to de-stabilise the Christian Church - especially should the authenticity of the parchments be subsequently discredited. It would seem that the arrival of the parchment in his laboratory was pure chance, an opportunity not to be missed. What we do know is that the Norwich cell is also implicated in a plot to destroy the Anglican Cathedral there. Their names are Malik, the ringleader, Abdul, Jarmal, and Hussain Barzal. They all learned their craft as aspiring Jihadists in Pakistan, with the implicit backing of Al-Qa'ida. They may also have links with The Muslim Brotherhood. They are all in custody, including your target, Paul Morgan, who has been associating with Hussain for years,' he added menacingly.

'Now, what did Paul Morgan tell you? Can you shed any light on this? Did this Abu Nawaz have links with Hussain's cell?'

Unable to reply, she thought of Paul and shivered. Surely he could not have been part of it? She could not believe that. She thought she knew him well, too well perhaps, but surely he would never get involved with something like that, betray his father, and attempt to destroy the beautiful Norman cathedral that had been so much a part of his childhood? And yet, he had been led astray in his teens, perhaps...? No, it was unthinkable. But so had been the destruction of Christchurch Cathedral, but that was described as an 'Act of God'. Or did Paul and his friends see that as an act of Allah? Maybe, based on some convoluted logic, they believed they were doing His bidding in Norwich.

'I notice you are wearing an engagement ring. It was not there when I gave you this assignment. You have got too close to the target, gone beyond your brief, (which she had). It was apparent from the manner of your parting at Christchurch Airport. You know the rules, to what extent you can mix business with pleasure in the course of your duties. It is supposed to be a means to an end, and you have arrived at the wrong end. You failed to find out anything much we didn't already know about Hussain, and you never engineered a meeting with him, not even when you were with Mr Morgan in Norwich. He successfully manipulated things so that you never met Hussain. You are a trained agent, yet you have clearly been outmanoeuvred by Morgan, failed to be objective, even over his trail right at the beginning, in Napier. Fortunately, Agent Neon was not so remiss, but even he succumbed to slumber on occasions, particularly on the journey to and from Queenstown; the paucity of information you extracted was pitiful. Your flat, your car, were both bugged, as you would have expected. The last straw for us was your habit of playing music to drown out our bugging devices. You have let us down, your colleagues, the Government, and your country.'

'But, sir, that's…' she stammered, interrupted before she could say anything further.

'There are no "buts" in this business. You will clear your office, hand over your identity badge and mobile phone, and be escorted off the premises. Your computer is being removed from your flat as we speak, as are any documents relating to your employment. You will be paid for three months in lieu of notice. I remind you that any breach of confidentiality is punishable by imprisonment.'

With that broadside ringing in her ears, she left Mike Tucker's office for the last time. When she returned to her flat the security officials were waiting for her. She was escorted round her living room and bedroom, accompanied by a female officer, as they concluded their search.

In a daze, she tidied up after them. She was devastated. She had no job, no computer, no mobile phone and, above all else, no Paul. She had misled him, betrayed him, and he would never speak to her again. She had instinctively wanted to warn him, but knew she couldn't; it would have been a suicide mission for her, at least professionally. Now it was anyway. She had never set out to take advantage of him, to fall in love; it had just happened, starting at the sheep farm. And, once again, she was deep in the mire.

Chapter 34

Laura spent the evening alone in her flat, which was destined never to be upgraded to an apartment, a bottle of wine her only company. She was simply not prepared to accept that Paul was a terrorist. It was alien to everything she had found out about him. He was too kind, too trusting, too naïve, and it was now too late to contact him; she had burnt her boats with him. He would no doubt have put two and two together and blamed her.

Next morning, her head clearing, but still very emotional, she began to consider her options. Being methodical by nature she eventually decided not to keep churning them around in her head, leading in all sorts of directions to nowhere. Grabbing a mug of strong coffee, she sat at her small, oak bureau which masqueraded as a desk, and made lists of anything that came to mind. She could prioritise them later.

1. Start job-hunting.

2. Buy a new laptop.

3. Buy a new mobile.

4. Contact her few friends on Facebook, see if they could help her.

She had lost touch with most of her fellow university students, as her job often took her away from Christchurch and its confidential nature meant she was restrained from joining in any of the usual kind of wine-bar gossip. The friends she made at work had perished in the earthquake. She thought of going to see her mother, but they had not spoken in months and she was not ready to receive any guidance from her. They were no longer close. Perhaps there would be a time, but not yet. Laura's mother had long been an alcoholic, causing untold grief to those around her, including her husband. It had all taken its toll, her father dying in his late fifties from a heart attack, and she had no doubt in her mind that it was caused by stress. It had taken some time to get over it, the shame and the feeling of guilt that had consumed her, that she should have done more to help and support her father. She had not trusted herself to confide all this to Paul until just before her return to New Zealand; it was all still too raw. She had left it until the last possible moment, unashamedly using her mother to deter him until she had time to untangle the noose she had tied herself in. Now she was home, the knot had tightened further; he would know of her deception. She was still too befuddled by the loss of her job to think straight; she did not immediately realise her sacking removed one obstacle – she was no longer a duplicitous agent. She was free to love him, wholly, unreservedly; but she had blown his trust - was it too late? Another thought was to contact Paul's uncle, but she soon ruled that out. He would be biased against her for what she had done to his nephew and, besides, the incident at the farm over her dress had not endeared her to Kiwita. In any case, she knew that getting close to Oliver would make matters worse should she ever see Paul's family again. She liked them despite all their various eccentricities; she could sense the warmth, the love that had been denied her as she grew up. She was loath to lose all her engagement had meant.

Shaking off her gloomy thoughts, she decided to go out and purchase the laptop and phone.

Returning home later that afternoon, armed with her purchases, she sat on the bus once again weighing up her options. It was a tedious journey now that the route went all the way round the outskirts of the city, weaving its way through the armies of traffic cones lining the streets, like toy soldiers on parade. Some seventy thousand homes had needed to be repaired and there remained thousands not yet done. There was plenty of time to think.

The job search would have to wait - there was only one thing to do. She still had the trust fund, and that had not been a deceit. She must go to England, find out for herself what had happened to him. Her belief in his innocence was so strong, and a woman's instinct was rarely wrong. She had to attempt to salvage her relationship with Paul. It was the only thing worth living for, or so it seemed at that moment. She loved him, and that must count for something. If the trip was futile, so be it. The worst he could do was to send her back home.

★★★

At around 6pm on the second day, Paul was told he was free to go. They had retained his passport, but returned his wallet, his watch and his anorak. Furious at his own naïvety, he headed straight for the *White Lion* pub. He tried to contact Hussain on his mobile. He had plenty he wanted to say to him, but there was no reply. They must still be holding him. There was only one thing to do - down some pints and get pissed. He had no idea how he got back to his flat that night.

Next day he went to see his anxious parents and told them what had happened to him, how he had protested his innocence, and the authorities had insufficient evidence to hold him and had let him go. His father had soon left them, having to officiate at one of the many christenings which were now again much in demand; a lot of catching up to do after the cancellations. Relieved to be alone with his mother, he took the opportunity to speak to her. She, always supportive, ever wise, told him of her female intuition - that Laura was right for him.

'Opticians, like women, can judge a great deal from the eye. They can spot signs of illness or disease not necessarily related to the eye condition itself. We women can tell a great deal about someone from the look in their eyes. As for your Laura, sincerity shines through like a beacon, although I do recall a hint of some anxiety; perhaps now we know what that was.'

As she spoke she remembered the early days, and nights, with Thomas but sadly, she reflected, he no longer did passion, and precious little romance. She knew he just found it embarrassing. There were no candlelit meals for two, no more early nights. She suspected Peter was very different, despite being from the same stable.

She told Paul that women see things that men cannot, that Laura's love was not fabricated, whatever circumstances had led to their being brought together. She also told him to ignore his father, who was telling him to get a job and move on, find someone else.

'Have faith, Paul; if it's meant to be, as I believe, the two of you will sort it out.'

'Not 'faith', Mother, please; you know how I feel about that word.'

'With faith comes hope, Paul; you will learn that one day.'

Reflecting on his mother's words, although still distraught at Laura's betrayal, he knew he had to find out if her love was true or false. They had been so right for each other, they had been soul mates, and he could not imagine anyone else in his life, or hers, for that matter. He thought of the moonlit night in Auckland Harbour, the dinner overlooking the Norfolk broad, their laughter, their shared interests, and much else besides. He reminded himself of their first night together, her warm and sumptuous bed, her smooth and silky golden hair brushing against his body, her skin like velvet, the first coming. He could not let go.

Encouraged by his mother, he decided he must return to Christchurch and put this whole thing to bed, including, he still hoped, Laura. There was one significant problem - no money. He knew his mother had no savings and that his father would not approve. Thomas was scathing about Laura, the harlot who had deceived young Paul. Paul knew what response he would get if he mentioned his mission to him. He could imagine his patronising words:

'Get a grip, boy, there's plenty of fish in the sea. Stay clear of that woman, get a job, find someone local, and settle down. And have two and a half children etc., etc.'

Paul was not in the mood for a sermon, or to risk another row with his father. There had been no mention of the spat they had before he left for New Zealand, but both men could feel that the tension between them had not evaporated. Perhaps it never would.

Paul considered Uncle Peter to be a possibility; he was never short of funds and had, it seemed, readily offered the reward money for Jane's return. But there was Carol, whom Paul regarded as a financial leech and borrowing from Peter would further antagonise his dad. He could not go to the bank for further credit as he still had his student loan to repay.

Back in his car, he decided there was only one course open to him - Aunt Jane. They had always been close. She was the one who had got him back on track as a teenager. She had told him straight that he was in danger of wasting his talent, falling into bad company, becoming inescapably hooked on drugs, alcohol and finally facing the scrap-heap, or worse. She had been right. Surely now, she would help him again? She had no husband, no children, at least that he knew of, and she must have saved a great deal of her salary.

★★★

'Jane, we need to talk. Paul came over this afternoon. Fortunately, Thomas was out so we were able to chat. He wants to go to New Zealand to face down Laura. He needs funds for the flight. More than likely he will pay you a visit. I can't see that he will be able to raise the money anywhere else. I think he has to follow this through otherwise he will never settle, and we don't want to go back to the problems of the past.' Jane knew full well to what Mary was alluding.

'I think we have to tell him, Jane, otherwise it may be too late. He has a right to know. It will also get him away from those friends of his. I've long had concerns about them.'

'We knew we would have to tell him one day. You're right - it's got to be now.'

Driving back to his flat, his mind on Aunt Jane, not for the first time he did not notice the blue Ford Focus following not far behind. As he opened his front door he received a call. It was Hussain, freed, but required to report daily to the local constabulary until such time as he was summoned to 'further assist the police with their enquiries'. Except it didn't sound like Hussain, Paul thought, as he ended the call. His voice sounded different, strained, his tone unusually abrupt, even a hint of anger. They were to meet up. It would have to be during the day - Hussain was under a police curfew after 6pm. The suggested venue seemed odd; Norwich Cathedral, next morning at midday, in St Luke's chapel.

'*Morgan and Barzal are to meet in the Cathedral. This might be a dry run. There is no mention of the others.*'

'*Keep close, watch every move and, above all, keep out of sight. Hopefully we can nail them.*'

The two targets had no idea their wristwatches contained state-of-the-art bugging devices. They did not record that Hussain was under orders to carry out Malik's instructions to the letter. Although there was no choice in such matters, he said he would relish the opportunity to oblige.

That afternoon, Paul went to see Aunt Jane. He felt pangs of apprehension, a knot in his stomach, nerves even, not emotions he normally experienced when visiting his aunt. But this was different. He did not like having to ask for money.

'Aunt, I need your help. You sorted me out all those years ago, and I am hugely grateful for that and the way it changed my life. I can't really believe my engagement was a sham. I need to go to New Zealand to find out for myself, but I haven't any funds. I won't get anything from the bank with my credit history and I still have a student loan round my neck. I don't want to speak to Dad, and Mum has no money of her own.'

She had been expecting Paul's visit. Her sister Mary could read the male mind like a book, and her instincts had been proved right, again - she had met Laura over Christmas and liked her. She seemed to be the girl for him and, at least as far she was aware, they were still technically engaged.

Jane, apprehensive, let him go on a bit, just to see how genuine he was, how much it really meant to him. Or was she playing for time, putting off the dreaded moment, for her, the one revelation that mattered? She too, was unusually nervous; more so than Paul, but he could not know the reason for that.

'Paul, there's something I need to tell you. Perhaps I have left this too long, I really don't know; it's been difficult...' She hesitated, clearly agitated. Paul sensed it immediately; he had never seen her like this before. Her face was drawn, haggard almost, and she was shaking, stammering even, words not coming easily. Had she been affected by the kidnap? Was there psychological damage? It would be understandable.

'Are you all right, Aunt Jane?'

'Not really. I'm sorry, I must explain.' She paused again. 'My sister, Mary, is not your real mother. She and

Thomas were unable to have children. They adopted you at birth.'

Paul stared at her open-mouthed, at first bewildered, and then shocked to his core, trembling with the enormity of what she had said. It was as if he were suddenly enveloped by a thick, dense fog swirling all round him, trapping him. His legs had turned to jelly. He could feel his whole body welling up; he felt he could be sick at any moment. As the extent of the deception overwhelmed him, a tidal wave of rage engulfed him; he tried to speak, but words would not come. Jane put up her hand to stop him.

'I'm your real mother. I'm so very sorry. I know that sounds pathetic, utterly inadequate, insulting. I don't know how else to put it. Please hear me out. I was a poor student; no money, no career, no prospects, or so I thought.'

'A bit like me, you mean,' intoned Paul, his voice acerbic, angry. Jane tried desperately to ignore the interruption.

'I knew I did not have the resources, nor, I thought, the temperament, to give you a proper and fulfilling upbringing. On the other hand Mary and Thomas wanted, but could not have, children of their own. 'Thomas, your uncle, always felt inadequate as a result, a guilt that has hardly diminished with time. That was the unseen, unknown source of some of his subsequent depressions, his insecurities. At the time they were married and settled. I know it was wrong but, in the climate of those times, illegitimate children were the ultimate disgrace for a family. Back then it seemed to be the best solution, right for everyone.'

'Except me,' Paul intervened, his tone aggressive, full of bitterness.

Again she hesitated. 'In hindsight, except you. I don't know what to say, other than perhaps something trite and crude, as in: the money's yours anyway, what's left of it. I set up a fund when I got my first salary cheque.'

'To alleviate your guilt, I suppose. I don't want your sordid money. I'll do things my own way, without your help. And my father, who is he? You haven't told me.'

'He's...' again a pause; 'He's the Bishop, Bishop Banham,' then adding: 'Even Mark has no idea you're his half-brother.' Paul just sat there bemused, his face a ghostly white. There was a prolonged and suffocating silence.

Eventually he simply exclaimed: 'You bitch; how could you deceive me for all these years? Deny me my proper childhood? Keep all these secrets? I trusted you, always have, and now it's all destroyed, obliterated.'

Neither spoke, Jane ashen and ashamed, with Paul dazed and bewildered, barely able to absorb the enormity of her revelations.

'Tell me about Uncle Oliver. I have a right to know what really happened. All that time I was staying on the farm he never spoke about why he emigrated. I want to know everything there is to know about our stupid family, here, now!' he demanded.

Hesitantly, Jane replied. 'He had an affair with a married woman, became something of a playboy, and then he just upped and left. Initially no one fully understood how he had become so rich in the first place, enough to drive a Porsche and have an apartment in sunny Spain near Malaga. There were suggestions of "insider dealing" on the stock market, but it was only later we found out exactly what went on.'

'And what was that? You have to tell me; and while you're at it, what did you mean about the money, when you said "what's left of it"? I want answers.'

'I deposited it with a financial adviser, someone I trusted implicitly. He defrauded his clients, stole the monies which he was investing on their behalf. It was Oliver. I naturally placed your fund with him. He promised high returns. I knew nothing about that world, and he was my brother.'

'You mean he stole my money.' Jane just looked down at the floor without replying. Again there was a stony silence; both could feel the tension, unseen but pervasive and intrusive. Once again Paul felt betrayed; all that time he had spent on the sheep farm, fleeced by his own uncle.

'No wonder Oliver clammed up so quickly over that beer,' he thought to himself.

'Uncle Peter has no offspring. Does it run in the family?' Paul eventually asked.

'Yes, but often skips a generation, if that's what's worrying you.'

For what seemed an age there was a void. Neither spoke. Then, suddenly, unexpectedly, Paul rose from his chair, crossed over to Jane, slapped her across the face and stormed out through the door, slamming it shut as he left. It was as if a knife had pierced her heart. She didn't normally do crying, but this time she could not hold back. Out into the street, neither could Paul.

I felt trapped, lost in swirling currents as my world spun around me, powerless to save myself. Such was my stress I was ready to die, as if on death row like the doomed swans. Such was the effect on me I feel compelled to relate the events which unfolded in my own words.

Chapter 35

Next morning I awoke, bereft, my mind in turmoil. I neither slept, nor wanted to. I had just lain on my bed, trying to make sense of it all. Sleep eventually came, but it was of no comfort. In my dream I was swimming in a rectangular pit in the gardens of an old monastery, a giant, rectangular whirlpool, surrounded by hysterical swans, frantically fighting the swirling currents pulling me down, down to the cavern below, then inevitably to drown. I awoke with a start, my body damp with sweat from the frenzy of my troubled sleep.

As reality slowly returned, I began to ponder what I should do. No way did I feel ready to contact Mary, no longer 'Mother Mary', now my aunt, nor my father by adoption, Thomas, who had betrayed me all these years, never telling me the truth. It was, I reflected, so appropriate that he should be named after St Thomas, to whom the sayings of the *Coptic Gospel of Thomas* were attributed - and whose name was widely thought to be Didymes *Judas* Thomas.

'How apt is that?' I grumbled. I then turned my ire on my biological father, the Bishop. I recalled the Bible-reading classes of my childhood.

'Our leader or Bishop must be above reproach, faithful to his one wife... a man of the highest principles. If a man does not know how to control his own family, how can he look after a congregation of God's people?'

As far as I was concerned, I now had no family.

I set out for my rendezvous with my long-term friend at the Cathedral. Right now I needed Hussain more than ever. I couldn't really believe him to be a terrorist, but now couldn't care if he was. I would take up Islam, start a new life; head for Mecca rather than Damascus. I couldn't wait to tell my friend about my 'conversion'.

Hussain had been freed from custody, just as I had, but under a re-vamped control order known as a 'Terrorism Prevention and Investigation Measure'. Had I known that Hussain had been released solely to enable the watching security services to incriminate him further, or to seek more evidence, I might not have gone to the Cathedral. It was the venue within the Cathedral that intrigued me. After all, we had met many times in the Refectory. I entered through the Visitor's Education Centre, pausing to admire the abstract paintings on display, depicting Jesus' final days, his betrayal by Judas, being nailed to the cross. In my mind I pictured Jesus in the centre and two of His followers, either side - my real father, the Bishop, and my erstwhile father, Thomas. No more than they deserved. I then headed to the Cathedral shop where Jane, then known as my aunt, had previously purchased the book entitled *Henry Despenser the Fighting Bishop*. I glanced at the leaflets on display, and picked up a guide book to check the location of St Luke's Chapel. I walked down towards the altar, under the organ loft with the Chapel of the Holy Innocents on my right. I had the feeling of being watched, of something not as it should be. Thinking of what the police had told me, surely Hussain was not actually going to do something crazy, and hardly with me in the vicinity? I certainly did not have my friend categorised as any kind of suicide bomber. Nevertheless, I felt a quiver of apprehension, even alarm, running through me. It was a strange, tingling sensation, one I could not recall experiencing before. My legs had also gone weak and wobbly, and I again felt my stomach churn, just as the previous day.

'Pull yourself together, man, you're letting your imagination run riot,' I said to myself. The inscription near the entrance to the chapel told me this was where prayers and intercessions were said for the victims of cruelty, persecution and intolerance. I went inside the chapel to see if anyone followed. No one did. On the wall was the famous 'Reredos', an ornamental screen, behind an altar, depicting the 'Innocents', young Jewish boys slaughtered by King Herod. The plaque suggested spending a few minutes reflecting on the human capacity for evil. I also read that prayers were said here 'for dialogue and reconciliation between various faiths'.

'Too late for that,' I reflected, 'At least as far as I am concerned.' On the altar I found a prayer discovered at a Nazi concentration camp. I started to read:

'*O Lord, remember not only the men and women of good will but also those of ill will.*'

Mindful of the time, and deciding the coast was clear, I walked on past the choir stalls where I had sung as a boy. I remembered once singing a choral piece from Handel's *Messiah* right there, in front of the Bishop, the man who now turned out to be my own father. '*He was despised; despised and rejected*'; that's what the solo was, and it was spot on. I recalled the nerves I had felt then. I was experiencing those same anxieties, whether I would hit the right note, get the timing spot on, all over again, but tenfold. Something did not feel right about this rendezvous.

'They're both inside. Morgan is heading towards the chapel. Barzal is lurking in St Saviour's Chapel, at the far end of the cathedral, adjacent to St Luke's Chapel. It appears to be a dry run. Neither is carrying a rucksack or anything which might contain explosives, although Barzal is wearing a long, grey cloak. We have cameras in there and listening devices. All systems go.'

On my right, further down, was St Luke's Chapel. I could not fathom why Hussain should want to meet there, of all places. I was drawn to a second 'Reredos', a celebrated piece of fine art said to be one of the finest paintings in Europe in its time. There were five panels of the flagellation of Jesus. As my birth mother, Jane, knew, it had been given to the Cathedral by none other than Bishop Henry Despenser, somewhere between 1380 and 1400.

I felt a presence behind me, a sudden chill. Turning, I saw Hussain staring at me, a look full of hatred, his eyes cold and hostile, and his face contorted with a malevolence I had not seen before, as if a violent rage had engulfed him. It was then that the penny finally dropped. Hussain stood motionless, his hands in the pockets of his long, grey cloak, not stretched out in greeting.

'Die infidel, you betraying bastard!' he shouted, his description more apt than he knew, lunging towards me. I saw a glint of silver reflected from the lights above. I instinctively leaped sideways, kicking out with my left leg as I jumped to the right. Hussain, in full flight, tripped over my outstretched foot, crashing downwards, his knife clattering on the stone floor, shattering the calm tranquillity of St Luke's Chapel. I kicked the knife to the far corner as I fled, sprinting down the aisle, past the font, a brightly-burnished copper vessel formerly used in the Norwich chocolate factory, then out of the side door through into the cloisters. I raced round two sides bordering the grassed central square, where Bishop Banham had addressed the concert-goers, with its central labyrinth fittingly reflecting the many twists and turns of life, or potentially death for me, as I pounded past. The clatter of footsteps echoed menacingly on the stone floor not far behind. I was then out of the cloisters, racing past groups of people with binoculars watching the peregrine falcons high above up in the Cathedral spire, and across to the lawns of the lower close. The chase was short-lived, but felt a lot longer. I knew I was fitter and stronger than Hussain, strength built up in those months working on the sheep farm and then playing rugby for my uncle's village team. Hussain was no longer the Smithfield runner of his youth and I was sure I could outrun him. My fear was the thud of a knife in my back, like many years before, and the sharp pain which would follow, then the collapse into darkness.

Leaving the grassy lawn behind, I was back on the tarmac road, down past the school playing fields to my left, and towards the river and Pull's Ferry. I realised there was no sound of racing feet behind. I glanced back. There was no sign of Hussain, but I could hear sirens and the screech of tyres, vehicles entering the Cathedral close from the main Ethelbert gate. I gingerly headed back, unsure about the alleyways and who might be lurking. I was right to be wary. Suddenly, from nowhere, two men were on me, wrestling me to the ground. It was with a sense of relief I felt the click of handcuffs round my wrists. I was frogmarched back to the lower close, through a gathering of gawping tourists, elderly residents at the gates of their fine houses, and smartly-dressed office workers eager to find out what it was all about. I was led back to the lawn area, where a man in a grey cloak was lying prostrate on the ground, three policemen holding him down. More police cars, then vans, came screaming in to the Cathedral close, blue lights flashing, headlights dazzling the curious onlookers, even in broad daylight. Then I could see Hussain being thrown into the back of one of the waiting vans. I was firmly and forcibly manhandled into the back of one of the waiting police cars. Within a few minutes I was once again being chauffeur-driven through the streets of Norwich, and back to Police Headquarters for another round of interviews.

It was fortunate that we had both been under observation. I only later discovered that I had been monitored for a considerable time by the security services. They were routinely monitoring me because of my association with Hussain, and that surveillance extended to my close family, including the woman they knew to be my mother – but I did not.

I later realised those officers had probably saved my life. The Dean of the Cathedral had co-operated fully with the security services in a well-planned operation to foil the anticipated bomb plot and apprehend the culprits, although they clearly had not anticipated the attack on me. That particular morning, plain-clothes police had mingled with worshippers, posing as priests, with shotguns in their cassocks, watching every move on closed-circuit cameras. There were listening devices planted in pews, between gargoyles, and in all manner of places. It was obvious to me that my long-time friend had assumed that I was an informer. I never saw Hussain again - he was arrested, along with Malik, Abdul and Jarmal, charged with attending a terrorist training camp and facilitating terrorism. Nevertheless, I still retain a nagging sense of anxiety that one day he will emerge to exact his revenge – as he will see it. I can only hope that time will heal his wounds but somehow, knowing him as I do, that seems unlikely.

Laura, knowing nothing of my release or my subsequent traumas, was on her way to England, arriving at a dark and dismal Heathrow Airport, the swirling fog and dank drizzle far removed from the summer she had left behind. She had not dared to contact me in case I refused to speak to her. She boarded the underground train, finding a corner seat amidst the sea of men and women in suits, all with laptops, smartphones and I-pads. Gradually the train filled up completely, commuters squashed together like sardines. She wondered how they could do this every day, already missing the wide open spaces and deep-blue skies of her own country.

It seemed like an age as the train wound its way through strange-sounding stations like 'South Ealing', 'Acton' and 'Hammersmith', destination 'Cockfosters'. She had not particularly noticed the names on her first journey with me before Christmas. She had that funny feeling of being watched, like she had experienced in Napier. Was it God or, more likely, her former employers, Agent Neon perhaps, or his UK counterpart? Even if it was, she no longer cared. Those days had gone.

She studied the station map above the seat opposite as best she could, through the crush of office-goers standing in front of her, hanging on to anything they could, including each other, just to stay upright. She decided to change trains at South Kensington, then on to the Circle Line and east to Liverpool Street. There she would have time to grab a baguette and a coffee, or perhaps a hot chocolate. She should arrive in Norwich with plenty of time to find a hotel. She would then decide how best to find me.

I had been held overnight, then released and told I was free to go, my passport returned. The experience had chastened me, especially discovering I was the unwitting Trojan Horse. I had told them all I knew. My new-found support for Hussain and his cause evaporated with the morning sun. I had not been converted after all. But I had lost faith in my family, in my friends and everything to do with the city of Norwich, the county of Norfolk, even England itself.

I returned to my flat to find an envelope posted through the letter-box. I instantly recognised the handwriting - it was from my new mother. Inside I found a cheque and an air ticket to New Zealand – for the following day. It took only moments to dismiss my scruples of the previous day and accept the money. It was my money, after all, and I had one overriding need for it - to help me find Laura.

Next day, I boarded the 9.30am train from Norwich to London, Liverpool Street. I slumped down on the seat, my mind still a jumbled mess. Now I knew why my bluish-grey eyes and large pupils so resembled those of my former aunt, now revealed as my mother, whereas Mary had brown eyes. I felt lost and alone, like the biblical lost sheep. I could not then imagine any joy in Heaven would await me, and certainly not the vestal virgins that Hussain had been dreaming of. I wondered how the disgraced Uncle Oliver had felt all those years before, leaving England never to return.

I was on autopilot, just knowing I had somehow to get to Heathrow Airport and to New Zealand. If Laura did not want me I didn't know what I would do, just that I would be another outcast. I had tried her mobile but the number was unobtainable, and I had no other means of contact. I would not have cared if they sent me to the slaughterhouse, along with Oliver's lambs, but before that I would find an opportunity to confront my uncle and exact revenge. Quite how I had not yet fathomed; that was for later. I did not know that a contrite Uncle Oliver had made a new will, giving Kiwita the farm for her lifetime or until she re-married, then absolute possession to me.

The train stopped at Ipswich to pick up yet more London commuters, and I was now surrounded, my carriage full. Pulling out of the station we went into a short tunnel, darkness briefly descending. As we emerged into daylight, I felt as if some symbolic chink of light was permeating my personal darkness. In some strange way I felt a sense of freedom, the escape from the shackles of the past, a new dawn. I was doing something positive, and leaving England behind seemed like a good idea, just like it must have done for Oliver all those years before. Some things did make more sense now I thought about it; like Thomas had always called me 'boy', never 'son'. Now, too, I realised why there had been that strange likeness with the Bishop's son, Mark, five years my junior and now revealed as my younger half-brother. I was right to get the hell out of it and, though it wasn't his fault, I couldn't face seeing, talking to, being with, young Mark. The thoughts churned round my head as the train headed south through the Suffolk countryside and into Essex.

The Bishop of Norwich, my father, would have known by now that the dirty and dishonest secret had been revealed to me, his son. I found it amazing that the Press had not picked it up. I might have found out in a newspaper. I was not to know that they had, but, leaned on by the Government, they had agreed not to publish, much to the intense embitterment of journalist Mike Burrows, now on bail and awaiting trial for his misdemeanours.

I wondered if my father had yet told his other, legitimate, son of his deceit? What a challenge that would be. He had put his church, his love of God or rather, more likely, love of himself, before his family. I thought that one day, perhaps, I could forgive, but not then and not for years probably, even perhaps decades, and then it may be too late. My father, the Bishop, would perhaps have had to confess his sins by visiting the 'listening post', in St Catherine's Chapel near the South door of the Cathedral. I recalled the advisory leaflet I had spotted in the Cathedral bookshop: '*Are you in need of a listening ear? Just drop in for a confidential conversation,*' it had read.

My thoughts turned to my new mother. I thought of all the things she had done for me; I had perhaps not been without her love - it had been there, but unseen, unidentified. Thomas and Mary had done their best for me. My feelings for them all began to mellow the further I travelled. I thought of Mary's last words to me; perhaps faith had a meaning after all. I thought it must be better than this empty void.

Arriving at Liverpool Street Station from Norwich, I fought my way through passengers thronging the concourse and headed for the Underground, then taking the Circle Line train to South Kensington, where I would change trains for the Piccadilly Line to Heathrow. Standing on the platform, I checked the monitor screen for the next train, due in one minute; next one three minutes. I happened to glance across the platform. For a split second I caught a glimpse of a girl with long, blonde hair and red jacket waiting to board a train heading east on the other line. I thought she was carrying a large, purple back-pack, but the moment was gone as other passengers blocked my view. Rooted to the spot, I did a double-take and froze. At much the same time my own train came thundering in and then came to a halt in front of me. It had looked so like her, but was it my imagination playing tricks? I screamed 'Laura! Laura!' inviting some strange looks from my fellow passengers now pushing past me and onto the waiting train. I had only seconds to make up my mind. Surely it must have been her? The hair and the coat, the purple back-pack, all so recognisable, and so familiar. The next train on the other platform was heading to Liverpool Street Station. I would still have time to get back there, have half an hour to comb the concourse to see if she was there, before retracing my steps towards Heathrow. My check-in time for the flight to New Zealand was still one and a half hours away. I should just make it.

Arriving back at Liverpool Street Station I bounded up the escalator, scattering the other passengers in my wake, jumped off the end, and came to an abrupt halt at the ticket barrier. I did not have a valid ticket. Luckily there was an attendant nearby. I pleaded with her to let me through, making up some story of leaving my wallet behind at one of the coffee-houses on the Liverpool Street Station concourse. After what seemed like an age, but really was only moments, I was through. I quickly pulled my back-pack firmly into position, not bothering with the bottom straps. I bounded towards gates nine and ten, from which the Norwich train normally departed, my back-pack swinging wildly from side to side as I ran, knocking into and almost felling more irritated bystanders as I went, pushing aside people gathering round numerous stalls of flower-sellers, who seemed to be attracting people like magnets. The next Norwich train was not yet in and there were no queues waiting. It was mid-morning and the crowds were now beginning to diminish. I ran back towards the shops inside the station, some up steps above, others at ground level, eyes roving like searchlights, this way then that, as I finally headed towards the taxi ranks and the road outside. Still there was no sign of a blonde in a red jacket. If, and it was now feeling like a big if, it had been her, I would have spotted her by now. It must have been her twin, probably not even travelling to Liverpool Street after all. Someone had once told me we all have one somewhere. Finally I came to a standstill, exhausted and covered in sweat from my exertion. I needed to rest for a few moments and compose myself. There was, I reckoned, time for a quick fix of caffeine.

On my way back towards the Underground was one of a chain of coffee-houses. It would do. I shuffled through the door, throwing off my back-pack which now seemed heavier than ever. My back was sore and bruised, protesting about the impact of the bag which had thumped me as I ran, continually, repeatedly, like a piston. Taking stock of my surroundings, out of the corner of my eye I caught a glimpse of a girl in a red jacket, carrying a drink and a baguette to a table. I blinked to get my focus. At the same time the girl looked up. Our eyes met, realising, recognising. I crashed through the empty tables and chairs barring my way, scattering them in all directions, landing locked in her arms, the tears streaming as we embraced, no words passing. Those at nearby tables looked up, startled by the commotion, but, as if such interruptions were commonplace, were soon reconnected to their laptops and phones. One man was not so lucky; his coffee was sent flying all over his keyboard and smartly-pressed suit trousers, but Neon could only fume and say nothing - we were clamped like limpets, oblivious to all around us.

We later realised at least one ancient prophecy had been fulfilled. With faith restored, and love triumphant, a new golden age really had begun. There was a lot of joy in one small corner of the earth that day, and it belonged to the two of us. It was also 14th February.

The Epilogue
Nine Years Later

'Thomas, they're coming here for Christmas – with Alice and Richard. And there's a special duty they want you to undertake for them.'

Laura and I had been married in Christchurch, New Zealand on 12th February 2016, Laura's birthday. There were three notable absentees from the wedding. Thomas had developed severe arthritis and could not travel. Bishop Marcus had too many engagements and thought it better to stay away; he knew my feelings towards him had not yet mellowed. My half-brother, Mark, came instead to represent my father. Uncle Oliver was not invited. For Mary it was the trip of a lifetime, her travel funded by Uncle Peter, who accompanied her, along with Jane – a rare opportunity to see her grandchildren. As she had recently retired, she looked forward to seeing more of them – her relationship with me had quickly been restored.

It was a bright and sunny morning in Norfolk on Sunday, 19th December 2021. The Morgan family and their entourage attended church at 11am. A beaming Thomas was officiating at the christening service for Alice and Richard. Bishop Marcus pitched up to give the blessing, seeing me for the first time since that momentous revelation and hoping the passage of time had lessened his son's pain.

Peter provided the vintage champagne at the celebratory lunch afterwards. Immediately after Jane proposed a toast to her grandchildren, I tapped the side of my glass to speak. My announcement was met with astonishment by a stunned audience, then loud applause. I spoke slowly, quietly, but clearly, first glancing down at Laura beside me for reassurance, then facing the assembled throng.

'Thanks to my wonderful wife and her faith, I have found my true self. I am taking up a new post in our home town of Christchurch – I am to take up the priesthood!'

Thomas whispered to Mary: 'God moves in mysterious ways, his wonders to perform!'

The next day Laura and I took the family to the beach, a chance to walk by the sea and see the seals with their young. Such was the occasion, the memories of my childhood, my thoughts for the future, that I did not take note of the date. Mindful of the numbers, not only those in her own life, but also those in her family tree, there was one person who did. She had been reminded by the darkness over the world some two weeks previously, on the morning of 4th December, when there had been a total eclipse of the sun. Sustained by her faith, Laura was able to accept it as an act of nature rather than a harbinger of doom - but what would tomorrow bring? At midnight, the new day that dawned would be 21st December 2021. I had forgotten, but had Mother Nature?